Look for . . .

The President's Henchman

It's inevitable, and probably not too far off, that the United States will elect its first female president. Which will make her husband ... what?

Well, if he's the ex-cop who solved the murder of the president's first husband and brought the killers to justice ... and if he's not the kind to stand on formality ... and if he doesn't want to be appointed head of the FBI ... and if he takes out a private license and becomes the first private eye to live in the White House ...

That would make him *The President's Henchman.*

Coming soon from Joseph Flynn

By Joseph Flynn

The Concrete Inquisition
Digger
The Next President
Hot Type

Praise for Joseph Flynn and his novels

Digger

"A mystery cloaked as cleverly as (and perhaps better than) any John Grisham work."
— *Denver Post*

"Engrossing ... non-stop action and original plot ... rapid-fire suspense."
— Phillip Margolin
New York Times Bestselling Author of *Wild Justice*

"A deftly mapped thriller. Page-turner of the week."
— *People Magazine*

"A straightforward, pulse-pounding novel ... a forceful hard-boned book."
— Carsten Stroud
New York Times Bestselling Author of *Deadly Force*

"Mix Dashiell Hammet's *Red Harvest* and *The X-Files* and you'll get some idea of how original this concept is. Recommended book."
— Thriller Editor, *amazon.com*

"An exciting, gritty, emotional page-turner."
— Robert K. Tanenbaum
New York Times Bestselling Author of *True Justice*

"Surefooted, suspenseful, and in its breathless final moments, unexpectedly heartbreaking."
— *Booklist*

The Next President

"Flynn [is] a master of high-octane plotting."
— *Chicago Tribune*

"Flynn keeps the pages turning in this well-done thriller."
— *Houston Chronicle*

"An original, suspenseful thriller that will keep you turning the pages."
— *amazon.com*

"A thriller that's fast enough to keep reading straight through (in) one sitting."
— *Rocky Mountain News* (Denver)

"(A) tough, stylish tale ... (Flynn) propels his plot with potent but flexible force, using just the right mix of pressure and release to maintain suspense deep into the story."
— *Publishers Weekly*

"Readers raved about this book ... cat and mouse suspense ... full of twists ... a well-written, timely thriller. Highest marks."
— *Barnes & Noble Guide to New Fiction*

"Flynn is an excellent storyteller with a well-tuned ear for dialogue and a gift for creating memorable characters placed in believable settings ... *The Next President* bears favorable comparison to such classics as *The Best Man*, *Advise and Consent*, and *The Manchurian Candidate*."
— *Booklist*

Hot Type

Joseph Flynn

Stray Dog Press, Inc.

SPRINGFIELD, IL

2005

Published by Stray Dog Press, Inc.
Springfield, IL 62704, U.S.A.

First Stray Dog Press, Inc. Printing, January 2005

Copyright © Stray Dog Press, Inc., 2005
All rights reserved

Visit the author's web site: www.josephflynn.com

Flynn, Joseph
Hot Type / Joseph Flynn.
382 p.
ISBN 0-9764170-2-2

Printed in the United States of America

PUBLISHER'S NOTE
This is a work of fiction. Names, characters, places, and incidents either are the product of the author's imagination or are used fictiontiously, any resemblance to actual persons, living or dead, events, or locales is entirely coincidental.

Book design by Aha! Designs
Typeface: ITC Caslon 224

For Catherine and Caitie.

Acknowledgments

The following people were kind enough to help me in this endeavor. Their information, I'm sure, is deadly accurate; my recounting of it may be somewhat less so.

Bill Hageman, author and scribe, *Chicago Tribune*; Kathy Woodruff and Michael Militello, kind and generous Buffalonians; Leslie Feazell Schill, former Canisius College scholar; Nic Howell and John Mundstock, Illinois Department of Corrections (Ret.)

My thanks to one and all.

Hot Type

CHAPTER 1

Ben Hecht wanted his typewriter back. Or so his lawyers said.

Dan Cameron took one look at the registered letter that arrived at his Evanston, Illinois home and replied, "Too fucking bad. It's mine now."

The typewriter in question was a mint-condition 1938 Remington Noiseless Portable in Glossy Black. Dan loved it. Loved it from the first second he saw the sleek little Art Deco machine. After he used it to write his bestselling first novel, *Indecision Kills*, he became even more attached to it. He wasn't giving it back.

Not without a helluva fight.

Not at all, before he got a second novel out of it.

Dan's wife, Erin, had given him the Remington for his fortieth birthday. She hoped it would get Dan out of his rut. That was, she wanted him to be more than the beat reporter for the *Chicago Tribune* he'd been for the past seventeen years. She'd wanted him to write the novel he'd been talking about ever since they'd met. Though he hadn't talked about it much lately.

Dan had once saved Erin's life, kept her from plunging into the cone of a Hawaiian volcano. But in the past few

1

years — three at least — Erin felt that some — *a lot* — of the magic had gone out of their marriage.

She thought if Dan finally became a novelist, got famous, and dedicated his undying love to her in every book he wrote, that might be a good start in getting things back on track.

Okay, he didn't have to dedicate every book to her. In fact, she'd be happy if he wrote only one novel. Just so long as he followed through on the ambition he'd talked about for years. Didn't simply settle into middle age on the treadmill of pension plans, retirement, and pre-paid cemetery plots.

Erin was having Dan's mid-life crisis for him.

She was five years younger than her husband and an admitted excitement junkie, in recovery for more than a decade. But now she felt the old pressures building. Pretty soon she and Dan would have to make some big changes in their lives — or she was going to need a fix. It'd be back to the bad old days: she might find herself on the crumbling lip of Mount Haleakala once again.

She didn't think that would help her marriage at all, so she had to give Dan a nudge — a shove — to finally write his novel.

She hadn't been looking for a typewriter that day she'd been browsing eBay. She'd been open to any literary icon that would turn the trick. The auction site had a surprising number of possibilities: a dressing gown worn by Oscar Wilde, a pipe smoked by Ernest Hemingway, even a Smith & Wesson .38 Police Special (*sans* firing-pin as eBay didn't trade in firearms) said to have belonged to Mickey Spillane.

It was the *said to* about Spillane's gun that gave Erin pause. How could she know if any of this stuff was genuine? Oscar Wilde's dressing gown? Hemingway's pipe?

"Gimme a break," Erin muttered at her computer.

Then she saw Ben Hecht's typewriter. The one Hecht had used in 1946 to write *Notorious,* supposedly. Erin remembered seeing the movie back in her college days. Hitchcock had directed. Cary Grant and Ingrid Bergman had starred. The story had spies, Nazis in Brazil, and one of the hottest kisses in cinematic history. *Whew.* Thinking about that kiss still got her going.

If that wasn't enough, the biographical note on Hecht mentioned that he'd received an Oscar nomination for his script, had once been the most famous newspaperman in Chicago, and had been the co-author, with Charles MacArthur, of *The Front Page.*

Jeez, could she find a better gift for Dan?

Had to be too good to be true.

But who cared? The machine looked so cool that even if it hadn't been used to write *Notorious,* it should have been. Erin snapped it up for $500. A bargain.

But what was really great was the way she gave it to Dan.

There'd been the obligatory party for family and friends with much kidding about Dan's advancing age. Was his dark hair showing some gray? Were those baby-blue peepers starting to squint a bit myopically? Was he still able to keep his beautiful blonde wife happy?

Respectively, the answers were: No gray hair yet. The eyes still worked fine except in dim restaurant light, and yes, he still kept Erin satisfied, if not with quite the same frequency.

Erin shooed everyone out by ten p.m., which only brought on more jests about old guys needing their rest. Dan rolled with it. He was by nature easy going, comfortable with who he was. He stood alongside his wife at the kitchen sink and dried the dishes she washed.

When the last one was done, he asked, "There a reason you wanted me to yourself so early?" He waggled his eyebrows at his wife. Tonight, he was interested.

Erin took his hands, gave him a big wet kiss, and said, "I thought we'd watch a movie. I got a classic from the video store this afternoon."

Not exactly what he'd expected, but snuggling on the couch with your honey could lead to other things, especially if ...

Hitchcock, Grant and Bergman grabbed you. Erin lay back against Dan's chest as they watched. He enfolded her in his arms. When the movie got to the kiss they both got excited. Who the heck needed porn when you had Hollywood legends getting you worked up? They barely made it to the end of the movie before they tore each other's clothes off.

They did it right there on the couch ... on the coffee table ... and on the floor. Then with the furniture askew and clothes flung to the four corners of the room, they lay looking at the ceiling, panting, holding hands.

"That was amazing," Erin murmured.

"Yeah ... and the sex wasn't bad either," Dan said. It was a joke, but Erin immediately got up and Dan thought he'd offended her. "Honey, I was just—"

She shushed him, but with a smile. "Wait, I'll be right back."

Erin returned, still naked, and by the light of the TV screen Dan saw she was holding this cool little old-timey typewriter between her breasts and her bush. Great presentation.

"Happy birthday, sweetheart," she said to Dan.

"For me?" She'd told him his surprise birthday present was back-ordered.

Erin nodded. She said, "This is the typewriter used to write the movie we just saw."

"You're kidding."

Erin shook her head.

Dan asked, "That scene where Grant and Bergman ..."
Erin nodded again. "It used to belong to Ben Hecht.
Now, it belongs to you. I thought you might like to use it to
write your novel."
She handed the typewriter to her husband. They both
laughed when Dan got a new erection the moment it was in
his grasp. This led to a running joke that every time Dan
touched the Remington he got hard; and every time he saw
Erin naked he felt compelled to write. But over the course
of the following year he was productive in both areas.
Erin got all the excitement she needed and Dan wrote
his novel.
And they bought their own copy of *Notorious*.

Dan's first novel, *Indecision Kills*, was a suspense story
inspired by a crime he'd covered for the *Trib*. Emeric Walls
had been a small-time burglar. He'd already had two strikes
against him when a cop interrupted him during yet another break-in. Knowing he'd be locked up for life as a career
criminal if he were caught, Walls had taken off with the cop
in hot pursuit. The chase led across three rooftops. But the
cop missed the second jump and fell to his death.
Committing a crime that leads to the death of a police
officer is a capital offense in Illinois. Given his propensity
for getting caught, Walls undoubtedly would have faced a
date with a lethal injection only he managed to get himself
shot to death by another cop first.
The interesting thing was that Walls had a gun in hand
when he was shot — he hadn't used a weapon in any of his
previous jobs — but he never fired at the cop who killed
him.
Several witnesses testified that the cop hadn't planted
the gun on Walls.
That was the platform from which Dan's novel sprang.
Emeric Walls became Esteban Paredes. The cop who'd

been chasing him across those rooftops hadn't completely missed the second jump. He'd caught the parapet of the third roof by his fingertips. He'd begged Paredes to help him, to save his life.

For Paredes that was the worst dilemma possible. If he saved the cop, he'd be busted and sent away for life. If he didn't help and the cop died, he'd likely be caught and given the death penalty. Paredes' choice wasn't just a matter of self-interest. It was a moral problem, too. Yeah, he was a degenerate gambler and a thief, but he wasn't a killer. But if he didn't let this man die, he could be throwing away the rest of his own life. Because just maybe this one time he wouldn't get caught.

While Paredes agonized over his decision, the cop lost his grip and fell to his death.

From that awful moment on, Paredes was seized by a terrible sense of fatalism. There'd be no escape for him. He'd been kidding himself about that. One way or another he was a dead man. With his luck, death probably wouldn't be that long in coming, either. All for a fucking break-in that hadn't even put a hundred bucks in his pocket. Not nearly enough to pay his gambling debt.

The certainty that he didn't have long to live changed Paredes' whole point of view. He'd always limited himself to being a small-timer in the vain hope that he wouldn't be caught. Now, it was time to go after a big score. He decided to hit the Outfit bookmaking operation that held his marker; he felt he had to leave something, some substantive legacy, to his ex-wife, Evelyn, and their young son, Eddy. To do that, he'd need a gun. Paredes got one and, much to his surprise, he pulled off his heist, got away with close to a quarter-million dollars.

Only now both the cops and the Outfit were after him, and both wanted him dead. He gave the money to Evelyn, and her circumstances were desperate enough that she took it. At Paredes' urging, she left town with Eddy.

Now, all Paredes had to do was stay free long enough for the only two people he loved to disappear. Well, no, he had to do more than that. He had to make sure he didn't talk when he was caught. Because even though Evelyn hadn't told him where she was going, he could make some good guesses. He certainly knew where her family lived in Texas. Not letting that slip would be tough if the Outfit found him first. Those bastards would tear him apart on general principles, and they'd certainly want to know where they could find their money.

After some narrow escapes from the guys with the bent noses, though, it was a cop who cornered him. Having lived with 'round-the-clock fear for over two weeks, Paredes was only mildly surprised to find his gun in his hand. In fact, he had his gun out while the cop was still reaching for his. He could shoot the cop and maybe get away again.

Yeah, but for how long? Two dead cops to his name. The Outfit still after him.

Besides he really wasn't a killer. The first cop, that was just fuckin' bad luck. Paredes didn't want anyone else's blood on his hands. He only wanted Evelyn and Eddy to get away with the money he'd given them. Hell, he just wanted it all to be over.

He barely heard the cop yell "— your last warning!"

The cop had his gun on Paredes now. But before the thief could make his next move, the cop shot him. The round knocked Paredes flat on his back and he knew he was dying.

The cop came hustling over and kicked the gun out of Paredes' hand, looked like he might put another round into him. Still, the only thing Paredes could think was he was glad he hadn't killed this guy. Didn't have somebody else on his conscience.

"Sorry," Paredes gasped. "Sorry 'bout the whole fuckin'

7

thing."

He hoped his remorse counted for something. If not here, then—

"Fuck," the cop said with a grimace, stepping away from the body.

He'd never killed anyone before.

And he knew this guy'd had the chance to kill him, could've shot first.

Maybe the guy really was sorry about what he'd done.

Or maybe he just couldn't make up his mind.

Erin thought the novel was brilliant. Every Friday night in bed, she read the twenty or so pages that Dan had written that week. He was usually drifting off beside her as she read, tired from doing his job at the paper and writing his book. But there wasn't a single Friday that he didn't rouse himself to talk to her when she asked, "What happens next?"

Learning what twists and turns the story would take, what dangers the doomed Paredes would face, how he'd barely escape, always got Erin excited. Not just in a literary sense. She made a point of sharing her excitement with Dan in any way that pleased him. Their love-life took on a new vibrancy. Or maybe it was restored to its old ardor.

Which got Erin thinking: Wouldn't this be a great time to have a child? She decided to hold off talking about it until Dan finished writing his novel.

When the Friday came that would bring the final installment of the novel for Erin to read, she was sad. It would be like leaving an old friend behind. But when she didn't find those last twenty pages on the nightstand next to her side of the bed, where Dan had always left them, she was puzzled. Even a little anxious. There was Dan, already in bed and from the sound of his breathing already asleep, too.

So where were the pages?

She knew how the story turned out. Dan had warned her that Paredes didn't make it; he'd told her so she wouldn't sock him one in outrage as he was drifting off to sleep. But, damnit, she wanted to see how he had written that sad ending. She searched the whole house, including the basement, for those final pages. Couldn't find the damn things anywhere. She stormed back upstairs ready to dump a glass of water on her sleeping husband. She'd make him tell her where those pages were, and what kind of joke he was pulling on her.

Except when she got back to their bedroom, the pages were resting on her pillow.

Dan was still lying there with his eyes closed. Pretending to be asleep. Like he hadn't gaslighted her. Well, she wasn't going to let him get away with—

She came close enough to read the top page. It wasn't part of the story; it was the dedication page. *For my wife Erin, the love of my life. Thanks for the typewriter, Toots.*

Erin slid into bed without a word, had to wipe tears from her eyes before she could read the final pages. When she finished, she put the pages aside and turned out the light. She didn't wake Dan, who really was sleeping by now. She cuddled up next to him and held him close until the morning came.

Then Erin flipped Dan onto his back and quickly climbed astride him. Neither of them wore pajamas, household nudity being a shared personality trait.

"That was a dirty trick you pulled with those pages last night, buddy!" she told him.

Dan shifted his wife's hips to better accommodate his changing anatomy.

He grinned up at her and said, "Made you eager to read those last pages, didn't it?"

She gave him a fierce look as if trying to decide which part of him to bite, but she changed the angle of her pelvis so they slid together neatly. Then she contracted her sphincter muscles to let him know he was still at her mercy.

"Oh, Mama!" Dan moaned. Then he added slyly, "You like the dedication?"

Erin fell forward against her husband and hugged him. "I loved it."

"The deal with the missing pages? That's how I'm going to submit the manuscript to those New York agents."

Friends at the newspaper had provided Dan with the names of three literary agents who had agreed to take a look at his novel.

Erin pushed herself up high enough to look Dan in the eye. "Really?"

"Yeah."

"Why?"

"I figure the one who's the most interested will call back first. You think it'll work?"

Erin grinned. "They'll go crazy wanting to know how the story ends."

"And I'll want the winning agent to do the same thing when he submits copies of the manuscript to publishers."

"You're diabolical. Where did all this deviousness come from?"

"Must be a by-product of all the kinky sex we novelists get."

"In that case," Erin said, her smile growing wider, "we better make sure you get all you can handle."

"Oh, Mama!"

The winning literary agent was Enzo (Hank) DeMitri; the publisher was Pendragon Press, which gave Dan a hardcover/mass-market deal with a $75,000 advance. Hank promised that Dan's next book would bring a six-figure advance, mid-six-figures if *Indecision Kills* sold as well as they expected.

Dan's novel got terrific reviews from the big newspapers — except for the *New York Times*, which didn't review it — and zoomed up to number 150 on the amazon.com sales chart.

There it stalled. Erin blamed the snub by the *Times*.

"You know what the *New York Times* is?" she asked angrily.

"The 800-pound gorilla of American journalism?" Dan suggested. He was a little ticked himself, but not nearly so much as his wife.

"*New York Times* is an anagram for Monkeys Write."

Dan laughed. He asked Erin where she got that, his wife not being known for her prowess at anagrams. She grinned and admitted she found it on the wordsmith.org site.

The moment of levity passed and Erin got indignant again. She told Dan, "I'm not going to let this rest. Your book needs more publicity, that's all. Not enough people know about it. Once they do, it'll be a bestseller for sure."

"Honey, Oprah's closed down her book club," Dan said, jokingly.

He left for work, his first advance not being sufficient to free him from his day job. He didn't mind. He'd just come across a story he thought he could use for his second novel.

Erin departed for work on foot five minutes later. She was the buyer for her family's store, Wilderness Adventures, retail outfitters to the recreationally daring. She'd come by her excitement jones honestly and from an early age. The brisk mile-and-a-half walk each way was part of her physical discipline.

She'd trod the path so often she could do it while re-reading Dan's book. She intended to find some kind of hook in the story she could use to launch a new publicity effort.

She'd be damned if she was going to let sales of *Indecision Kills* stall out short of the best-seller list. The novel had been so long in coming, and Dan had done such a good job with it that—

They were going to piggyback Dan's book to Ben Hecht. Erin hadn't had to read any farther than the dedication page.

... Thanks for the typewriter, Toots.

Dan had used Ben Hecht's typewriter to write his book. The same typewriter that had been used to write *Notorious*. The same typewriter that had once belonged to the guy who'd written *The Front Page*. Seemed like a pretty good hook to her.

Hell, it was great.

As for any remaining doubt that the little Remington had really belonged to Hecht ... she'd just rely on the little card authenticating its provenance that had come with the machine.

As soon as she got to work, Erin called a friend of Dan's who worked on the Tempo — features — section of the *Trib* and told him the story about the typewriter. He loved it, but he didn't want to make the paper look too self-serving — boosting one of its own writers — so he farmed it out to a friend who worked on the *Wall Street Journal*. Dan, his book, and his typewriter were the lead of a story on the increasing value of antique typewriters as collectibles. *People* magazine picked up on the story, placing the emphasis on Dan and *Indecision Kills*. After an appearance on the *Today* show, Dan's book entered the *New York Times* bestseller list at number eight, even though the *Times* had yet to review it.

Within a week, Hank DeMitri called to say that Pendragon was offering a million-dollar advance on Dan's next book, a story unknown to everyone except Dan himself at that point.

And then the registered letter arrived from the Hecht estate's lawyers —the writer having died in 1963. They laid to rest any doubt Erin might have had about the Remington's authenticity.

They said it was in fact Ben Hecht's machine. They said it was still the property of the Hecht estate. They claimed it had been stolen and illegally auctioned on eBay.

A fact of which they'd been unaware until the recent flood of publicity.

They wanted the typewriter back immediately.

"Too fucking bad," Dan Cameron replied. "It's mine now."

He contacted Hank DeMitri, who got in touch with Pendragon Press, which sent forth its own attorneys to do battle with the Hecht estate.

Meanwhile, Dan took an indefinite leave of absence from his job. He told Erin to pack everything they'd need for a prolonged absence from home. He was going to fuel up the SUV.

"Where are we going?" she asked.

"I don't know," Dan confessed. "Somewhere nobody will find us. Not until I get another novel out of my typewriter."

"Hot damn!" said Erin the excitement junkie.

She'd never loved her husband more than at that moment. Not even when he'd saved her life. She wondered if this would be a good time to talk about having a baby.

They wound up lighting out for western New York State. Erin's father had a friend there, the retired postmaster of the city of Buffalo, who owned a cabin in the woods of the Allegheny State Park. He wouldn't be using the cabin for the next eleven months. No one outside of their families would know where they were. It was perfect.

That was in September.

CHAPTER 2

The following June, Fetch Mcdonald sat in his dorm at Camp Alphonse, a minimum-security correctional facility just west of Bolivar, New York. Fetch was a bank robber. He'd gotten away clean with fourteen jobs. He'd been caught his fifteenth time out, knocking over a credit union.

His downfall had come when he'd stumbled off the lifts in his shoes while chasing a repo man who'd just made off with the car Fetch had stolen for his getaway.

Fetch seemed to be staring at a needlepoint limerick that hung on the wall next to his bed.

It read:

> *There once was a robber named Ruct,*
> *Who entered a bank through a duct,*
> *But that narrow crevasse,*
> *Was half as wide as his ass,*
> *And when it got wedged, he was fuct.*

The first time Fetch had seen the limerick it had been chalked on the wall of his cell at Collins Correctional, a medium-security prison. That had been a week after his incarceration. By then, the general population had learned the ignominious facts of Fetch's capture: tripping over his own feet, having his getaway car repossessed. The inmates and staff hadn't laughed so hard for a very long time.

Then some jailbird wit had chalked the limerick in his cell. Fetch left it there. Later, another con's mom had rendered it in needlepoint for him.

As a new guy — who was white and only five-eleven and one-sixty-five — there was nothing he could do about the ridicule. He had enough to do just staying safe. And he was bound and determined not to commit the tiniest infraction of the rules — each of which could add as much as a year to an inmate's sentence — that would extend his time behind bars.

Fetch consoled himself with the fact that he had $480,000, from his 14 successful jobs, stashed and waiting for him when he got out. None of the assholes laughing at him could match that, he'd bet. So he'd do his time — 14 years ironically — as quietly and peacefully as possible. That way he could cut the number of years he'd actually serve in half, as he moved on to ever more lenient and comfortable places of custody.

The thing about prisons was, everybody wanted to get out fast. Seemed obvious. But it wasn't only the inmates. The staff bugged out as soon as their shifts were over. Visitors got itchy to be going after just a few minutes. Vendors never hung out and shot the breeze with secretaries. Nobody'd ever admit it, but there was a real fear that confinement was contagious: stick around one minute too long and it'd be your ass they were locking up.

Maybe for a very long time.

So Fetch gave it his all not to offend anyone. He forged the necessary alliances among the inmate population to safeguard both his health and his chastity. With the staff, he was more self-effacing than a Buddhist nun. Had to be. There were a million rules to follow and a con could get screwed on any one of them. A correctional officer could write you up because he was pissed at his old lady for not coming across the night before.

Despite his meek demeanor, some of the bigger assholes among the COs threatened to write Fetch up a few times. He never uttered a peep of protest, never let them get a rise out him. Looked like he was offering up his suffering to Jesus. Fetch had made a point of attending services from the first Sunday he was locked up; most cons got religion only a year before their parole was due. None of the citations against Fetch ever went the distance because none of the shift captains ever believed Fetch would cause any sort of trouble.

Hell, Fetch was the guy with the limerick on the futility of crime on his cell wall.

Right in line with his plan, Fetch worked his way from Collins, medium security, to Buffalo Correctional, his hometown minimum-security facility, to Camp Alphonse. There was nothing devious about this. Model prisoners were routinely stepped down from medium security to minimum security. An inmate only had to keep his nose clean and meet the time-served requirements. His counselor reviewed his record every six months, and when the time was right submitted Fetch's name to the headquarters of the Department of Corrections. When a slot opened up in a minimum-security facility he was moved.

The benefits of minimum security were less danger, more programs, and more freedom of movement. Inmates at state correctional camps, like Camp Alphonse, even got to work outside of the facility occasionally, helping to clean up after wind storms or to sandbag flooding rivers. The correctional officers who watched over them on these trips carried only two-way radios.

If you had to do time at all, a camp was the way to go. And unlike any other penal facility, it was possible to just walk away from a work camp.

Knowing if you did, of course, you'd most likely be caught, prosecuted for escape, and sent to some maximum-security joint, which would not be nearly as nice.

Fetch was due to be paroled in three weeks. He'd served eight years of his sentence. He made 17¢ an hour working in the prison library, but his ill-gotten gains worked out to $60,000 per year. Net. Which was as good as his best year selling copiers for Xerox, before the recession hit, before Jap machines took over the market, before he got laid off and started robbing banks.

Normally, Fetch would have been out already, paroled after seven years, earning a day off for each day served. Only Fetch hadn't robbed banks with a gun ... he'd done it with fake explosives.

Fetch's *modus operandi* had been to present himself as a human bomb. He'd stroll into a bank he'd targeted wearing a disguise — he'd read a book about how the CIA altered its agents' appearances — and he'd put his attaché case on the counter in front of a window and show the teller a note.

Don't say a word. Don't press the alarm. Just fill the case. No dye packs. Or I blow up every-damn-body in the bank.

Then Fetch would open his coat with one hand to reveal what looked like a bandoleer of dynamite sticks strung across his chest. For good measure, he wore two bottles that had originally held Chanel No. 5 but now bore the labels Nitro. In his left hand, he held a small plastic box with a glowing red button.

The tellers hadn't been able to give him the money fast enough. He'd finish his inside work by flipping over his message card.

Anybody tries to stop me, we all go boom.

Once outside, he'd get in a car he'd stolen less than an hour earlier and drive off. Just as soon as he could, he'd tear off his disguise, ditch the car, and be on his way.

The CIA book told Fetch that the best disguise was the one that was the hardest to remember, that he should look as ordinary as possible. Just not like himself. To accomplish this goal, he wore different hairpieces, sometimes with a baseball cap, sometimes with a snap-brim hat. He wore different combinations of facial hair: mustaches, beards, sideburns. He wore glasses, colored contact lenses, sometimes both. He wore different clothes for every job.

There were only two constants: the fake explosives and the lifts in his shoes. The descriptions and drawings of the Everyman Bank Robber varied widely, but they all agreed that the criminal was six-two, at least. Clearly taller than Fetch's five-eleven.

Actually, there had been one giveaway, and if Fetch hadn't thought about it before going out on his last job, he'd have been sunk. They'd have had him for the whole string of robberies and he'd have spent the rest of his life behind bars — in maximum security.

For his first 14 jobs, Fetch had used the same black attaché case. Some smart cop looking at the tapes of all his jobs might have picked up on that. For his last job — which he'd intended to be his last job, having set a goal of $500,000 for himself — Fetch used a brown calfskin case.

That was what he was carrying when he fell off his lifts, broke his ankle, knocked himself senseless, and got caught.

By the time he came to, he was handcuffed to a hospital bed and had six cops and two FBI agents for company. They liked him for all 15 robberies, but Fetch would admit to only the one for which he'd been caught. The fact that he'd been carrying a different attaché case allowed his lawyer to claim that he'd been a copycat criminal, a particularly inept one doing his first job. Fetch obviously wasn't as competent as the slick-as-hell master thief who'd gotten away with all those other robberies.

Fetch agreed to plead guilty to the credit union job and serve 14 years in return for the other 14 charges being dropped.

That agreement had been reached during a period of relative calm in the Middle East. By the time Fetch was well into his sentence, however, Palestinian suicide-bombers started attacking Israel, blowing up civilians. Suddenly, Fetch's means of stealing made him cringe. He took a lot of shit from the inmates and the staff about it, too. Luckily, by then, he was living among mostly white-collar criminals.

Still, he wanted to shout, "My stuff was all fake, harmless! Nobody was ever in a bit of danger!" But thinking about it, he knew how lame that would sound. People were being blown to bits. He wasn't going to get any sympathy.

Then the attacks on New York City and Washington, D.C. came nine months before Fetch's first parole hearing. Officials of the criminal justice system were as outraged by the atrocities as any other Americans. Maybe more so as they had to deal every day with people who committed violent acts. The parole board was still plenty pissed when Fetch appeared before them.

Fetch pleaded his case with just two lines: "Please look at my record as an inmate." And, "I might be a felon, but I'm a loyal American."

The parole board decided to keep Fetch in custody an extra year just to make sure.

Fetch felt so badly about what had happened, and how stupid he'd been, that he wouldn't have blamed them if they made him serve his whole term. He kept on quietly doing his time. The only people who made him mad were all those assholes from the Middle East. A man who'd been relatively free of bigotry, Fetch came to loathe those jihadi motherfuckers.

And now the fact that his parole had been delayed was

driving him crazy.

Fetch's dad had just come to visit. Fetch had gotten the call in the library where he'd been reading *Investor's Daily* — there were lots of crooked businessmen at Camp Alphonse who needed to stay current. Fetch took his cue from them. He wanted to make his money grow when he got out. It surprised the hell out of him that his old man had come to visit.

Fetch and his father, Archer Mcdonald, were not close. His father had almost never been around when Fetch was growing up, and for good reason. Archer had been a bank robber himself. He'd pulled only two jobs, and had been caught for both of them. The old man had spent over 20 years in prison — maximum security.

Talk about a visitor who'd get itchy to be going. Before this, Archer had never visited Fetch while he was locked up. But then neither had anyone else.

"I was kinda surprised I didn't hear from you, son," Archer began.

The old ex-con was already looking around nervously.

Fetch didn't understand what his father was getting at. "What, I forgot your birthday?"

Archer grinned. Though there was a close resemblance between the two of them, Archer knew there was little love lost between him and his boy. Fetch blamed his father for his mother's premature death.

The old man asked, "You ain't read about it? Don't you get the newspaper here?"

Fetch knew Archer meant the *Buffalo News*. Camp Alphonse did get the Buffalo paper, but Fetch didn't read it. He wasn't going home — at least not for long — when he got out. He was going somewhere far away. Where people wouldn't know him, wouldn't think to ask where he got the $480,000 he intended to dig up. When Fetch wasn't honing his future investment strategies, he read the *New York*

Times. Like everybody else at Camp Alphonse.

"I musta missed it, Dad," Fetch said. "Whatever the hell you're talking about."

"This is what I'm talking about," the old man said.

He handed his son a newspaper clipping.

The two men were sitting in the camp visiting room. Visitors were patted down and their possessions were searched upon entering any penal facility. Inmates were strip-searched with body-cavity examinations both before and after they met with visitors. Made Fetch glad nobody'd come to see him up till now.

When he saw the clipping his heart just about stopped. The newspaper story showed Fetch a picture of his ex-wife, Verene. Looking as good as ever. Looking the way he imagined her every single night in his dreams — except in his dreams Verene wasn't wearing any clothes.

Verene was what — Fetch did the math — thirty-two now? But she didn't look a day older than when he'd first met her eleven years ago. Same thick russet hair and big brown eyes. Sharp little nose, pouty rosebud mouth, and pointy chin. All in all, it was a foxy face, not just in its beauty, but also in its sense of cunning.

The newspaper photo was a head-and-shoulders shot, but Fetch would bet her body looked as good as ever, too. Petite. Slender arms and legs, perky little rear end, but with a bust that seemed too big to be real, unless you had the privilege of diving into that bountiful bosom.

Fetch had met Verene when he'd gone on a sales call at the offices of a small chain of appliance stores. She'd been the receptionist for the guy he was supposed to see. Verene Digby her nameplate said. Fetch thought he'd met her somewhere before. Or had at least seen her.

As if she could read his mind, she said, "You think you know me, don't you?"

"Just wishful thinking," Fetch answered. He was sure he

21

would have remembered if he'd actually met her.

She liked his reply and gave him a grin. Then she got him going.

"Maybe you do know me," she said with a sparkle in her eyes. "Better than you think."

Fetch had to dial it back before he embarrassed himself. He said he was just there to see if he could sell a copier or two. Verene asked if he sold good copiers. The best, he assured her. Screw what the Japs had to say about their machines.

"Yeah?" Verene asked. "I always wondered. Any copiers out there good enough to make ... hundred dollar bills?"

For a crazed moment, Fetch gave the question serious consideration. Then he said, "No reason to commit a crime when you make enough honest money."

"You do okay, huh?"

Fetch just nodded. That was his peak earning year — prior to robbing banks. At the time, though, his quiet self-confidence was good enough for Verene. First she became his girlfriend and then his wife. As both, she spent every penny he ever made.

Not that Fetch gave a damn. Verene Digby was everything he wanted in a woman.

He couldn't wait to get home at the end of the day and hear her ask, "Hey, baby, how'd you like a little VD tonight?"

Keeping Verene pampered, after he'd lost his job, was the reason Fetch started robbing banks. While he'd stashed the overwhelming majority of his proceeds, he'd spent $9,856.27 from the Erie National Bank job on her. Had bought her a whole new wardrobe and a pair of sapphire earrings. Damn, she'd looked hot in that little red dress and those blue stones!

What galled Fetch was the amount of money he'd taken from the credit union would have put him over the top.

Gotten him the half-million he'd needed to keep Verene happy for a long, long time. He'd been so close that sometimes it made him want to cry.

For much of the time he'd been incarcerated — up till just about a year ago, when he should have been paroled — he was comforted by the way Verene had stuck by him. Not that he'd let her visit. He didn't want her to carry in her mind the picture of him as a jailbird. But she'd written regularly, and they'd talked on the phone at least once a week. Somehow her letters had carried her scent, not just her perfume but her skin, and when they talked he could hear in her voice how much she still loved him.

Then one day, she sent divorce papers. Not a damn word of warning. He'd almost hanged himself that day. He was suicidal for the better part of a month. What pulled him out of it, kept him going, was remembering two things.

Verene had been without his company for seven years by then. A woman like her, she needed a man. He couldn't fault her for that. Being true to him had to be tearing her up. It was like she was serving a sentence, too, when she hadn't done anything wrong.

The other thing was, he was sure Verene still loved the good life, enjoyed spending money like ... well, like she was xeroxing it down in the basement. Once she saw how much money Fetch had when he got out, how they could go away someplace warm, live nice, watch their investments grow, he was sure they'd be happily reunited.

Only now the newspaper clipping Fetch held in his hands, the one dear old dad had been kind enough to bring him, said his Verene was getting married — to some grinning wienie named Karl Hyacinth right there in the picture next to her — and the wedding was in two weeks.

Two weeks? The thought hit Fetch like a runaway truck. That'd make it Fetch and Verene's tenth anniversary. Exactly. And if Fetch sat tight, this fucker Hyacinth would be dicking Verene on their honeymoon by the time he got out! How could life be so unfair?

How could he let this happen?

Archer seemed to sense his son's pain.

"Sure is a shame, son. Your ma, God rest her soul, always waited for me."

Fetch glared. Fucking old man. His mother had died the second time the old bastard was locked up. Archer didn't miss his son's mood swing. He knew from experience it was never a good idea to find yourself too close to an angry con.

He stood up to leave, looking around to see if anybody would try to stop him.

"Well, I best be goin'. These old walls feel like they're closin' in."

Fetch tired of looking at the limerick. He'd adhered to its cautionary wisdom for eight years. But no more. Verene wasn't going to be anyone's wife but his.

He got up and went to make a phone call.

There was a bank of phones at one end of the recreation building. Plastic dividers separated the phones to afford the inmates some privacy from each other. But every call made from Camp Alphonse was recorded. However, due to heavy volume, not every call was monitored. In facilities with seriously dangerous criminals, the staff would monitor calls from, say, gang leaders. In theory, this would not permit them to run their gangs from prison. At Camp Alphonse, about the only inmates who got their calls monitored were wayward Wall Streeters; the staff was always on the lookout for hot stock tips.

Guys like Fetch, nobody paid much attention to them.

But all the inmates still had to pay for their calls, and when you made 17¢ an hour long-distance charges were a big consideration. You got right to the point and didn't tie up the line. Which was why Fetch didn't have to wait long for a phone. He tapped out the number from memory, even though it had been a year since he'd last called it.

The call was answered on the third ring. "Good to hear from you again," a male voice said. He had caller ID. Knew it was Fetch.

"I want you to pick me up," Fetch said.

"Sure, I was planning to. Three weeks, right?"

"Tomorrow," Fetch said.

There was a pause on the other end, but no argument.

"Yeah?"

"Four a.m. Half-mile down the road from the main gate."

The pause was shorter this time.

"Okay."

"What'll you be driving?"

"The only car that stops," came the reply.

That was it. They both hung up. The next inmate in line, who'd been politely waiting out of earshot — you couldn't beat white-collar criminals for good manners — took over from Fetch.

Fetch went back to his dorm. So far so good, he thought. When an inmate made an outgoing call, he had to punch in a personal identification number before he tapped out the phone number he wanted. He was also limited to making calls from a list of 20 family members and friends. That let the staff know who was calling whom and the time a call was made.

Only Fetch hadn't used his own ID number. He used one he'd bought for $20 bucks from a kid who'd been in for computer hacking. And the name of the person he'd called was an alias. And the number he'd called was a cloned cell phone.

It all seemed like a lot of secret-agent crap, but then Fetch had done pretty well with his CIA book until that last damn job. Fact was, though, he'd bought the bogus ID number as a joke. More because the kid hacker had made him laugh a lot than any thought he'd ever need it. But damn if it hadn't worked. Money well spent.

And the kid had been released six months ago, so he couldn't rat Fetch out. Things were going good. So why was he so scared? It was only natural, he told himself. Jailbreaks were hard on your nerves.

He went into the latrine to shave. Fetch had worn a beard for the past two years. Sometimes he thought that had been one of the reasons he'd been denied parole the first time. He'd looked like some kind of mullah-lover. But his beard was always neatly trimmed. And he sure as hell hadn't worn any turban.

As the whiskers came off, Fetch was surprised to see how he looked clean-shaven again. Took him a minute to remember his own face. Pretty big difference. Inmates were allowed to have any kind of facial hair they wanted; they were free to choose their hairstyles or shave their heads, too. But when they changed appearance, they had to have a new digital ID photo taken.

Fetch intended to be gone before that happened.

As for the guy picking him up, he'd have no problem recognizing Fetch.

They'd known each other all their lives.

CHAPTER 3

In the pre-dawn darkness, Erin Cameron sat in the kitchen of the luxury log cabin where she and Dan had lived for the past nine months. She sipped black coffee and thought about her husband's new novel, *Time Expires*. The author was still asleep upstairs.

Erin had read the last installment of the novel last night. Then after she and Dan had made love, she'd taken the manuscript downstairs and reread the whole thing in one sitting, both to see how well it held together and to proofread for typos.

The story was great, with a killer ending. Which, of course, would be withheld from Pendragon until Hank DeMitri decided the publisher had put into writing everything that had been agreed to verbally — and maybe a little more. Erin didn't foresee any problems. Dan's writing had grown stronger, sharper, and funnier.

It was a measure of Erin's flawed character that she wanted Dan to dedicate this book to her, too. Only she knew that this one belonged to Dan's family: his father, James, his sister, Madeleine, and especially to the memory of his mother, Mary Frances. If that wasn't bad enough, Dan had told her that if he wrote another novel, that one would be dedicated to her parents. She'd just have to wait her turn.

Word had been relayed from Illinois. Hank said that Pendragon's lawyers expected a decision over just who owned a certain Remington Noiseless Portable in Glossy Black within the next week or two. Dan had worked like a madman to complete the manuscript.

Erin had come to have some regrets about buying Ben Hecht's typewriter for Dan. Yes, it had prompted him to write two wonderful novels. Publicity from the machine's illustrious history had given *Indecision Kills* the readership to make it a bestseller. But, damnit, Dan's stories deserved to be bestsellers on their own merit. Dan was a wonderful writer who didn't have to depend on any particular machine to produce his work.

The magic was in him, not the typewriter.

Erin took the last chapter of *Time Expires* upstairs and slipped it into the drawer of the night table next to where Dan slumbered. They both liked the symbolism of keeping the last chapter separate. Erin blew a kiss to her sleeping husband and went back downstairs. She put the rest of the manuscript in the stationery box where Dan routinely kept it. The box occupied the space to the left of the Remington Noiseless Portable.

Dan liked to write in the living room at a trestle table in front of a window that looked out on the road that led to the cabin. On the far side of the road lay woods that might have kept Robert Frost up nights writing poetry. The view sure worked for Dan.

Erin patted the box that held *Time Expires* and said, "Ya done good, Danny-boy."

Far better than she had herself.

She opened the front door to the cabin and stepped outside. The air was pleasantly cool, and though a number of stars could still be seen, the first hint of the curtain going up on a new day was visible to the east. Erin sat on the front steps and began to cry silently.

She tried hard not to curse her body for betraying her. Last New Year's Eve, when Dan was well into his writing and Erin didn't think she would put him off his game, she had broached her idea. As the two of them sat in front of a crackling fire, sipping champagne and feeling very mellow, Erin asked, "You think we might top off the day with a little marital bliss?"

Dan grinned and held her close. "For you, anything."

"Really?"

"An-y-thing."

"I was thinking ... how about we make a baby?"

Dan put down his glass, hung his head, covered his face with his hands.

"What?" Erin demanded. "What?"

"I'm so ashamed," he said from behind his hands.

"Ashamed? Of what?"

He dropped his hands and was grinning like a madman. "That I didn't think of it first!"

With a roar of laughter, he leaped upon her. Erin flung her glass into the fireplace. They tumbled off the sofa and rolled halfway across the living room rug, stopping only when Dan plunked his elbows down, trapping his smiling wife beneath him.

"You know, of course, that more babies are conceived on New Year's Eve than any other night of the year. We might be creating a little cliché here."

Erin shook her head. "A couple of desperados like us? Unh-uh."

"You're right. Besides, all I care about is our tot looks like his — or her — mom."

From that moment on, they got off to what Erin had thought was a very fast start on the road to procreation. Only it didn't happen as quickly as she'd expected. In fact, it hadn't happened at all. Every month, right on time, she bled.

Dan had given her all the support she ever could have hoped for. He'd said they should drive up to Buffalo, get the both of them checked out by specialists. Do whatever they needed to do. But Erin said no. He had to get his novel finished. They'd see the doctors after that.

The truth was, she was scared to find out the problem was hers. Dan said it could be him, but she knew it wasn't. It was her.

"Fuck," Erin muttered.

"What, again?" Dan asked, stepping out of the cabin, startling her. He sat down beside her, a cup of coffee in his hands. "That all you think about? Sex, sex, sex."

"Yeah, I'm just insatiable."

He put his arm around her and she took the coffee cup from him.

"It will happen," Dan said. "Before you know it, you'll be as round as a beach ball. In the coming years, you'll be the mother of my many children, so domesticated that, famous writer that I'm certain to become, I'll need mistresses in exotic locales all over the world."

"Well, you've been a good sport humping me right and left these past six months, whenever you weren't writing. So if you've got anything left over, go for it."

Dan stood just as the sun crested the horizon.

"Come on," he said, extending a hand, "let's go for a walk in the woods. Maybe we'll do it up against a tree. Wouldn't that be something to tell junior?"

Dan helped Erin to her feet and pulled the cabin door closed.

But he didn't lock it.

What was there to worry about so deep in the woods at daybreak?

Erin put the coffee cup down on the porch rail. As they set off, birds chirping all around, she slipped her arm around Dan's waist.

"I hope our baby looks like you."

"Be careful what you wish for," Dan told her.

Fetch's ride was fifteen minutes late. When you were an inmate illegally outside the grounds of a prison, i.e. a fugitive, you got pretty damn jumpy waiting by the side of the road. The mission statement of the Department of Corrections was posted in each of its 70 facilities, and its very first objective was: Retain inmates in safe custody until released by law.

Wasn't a warden or a CO anywhere who didn't take that seriously.

First wake-up call at Camp Alphonse came over the loudspeaker system at six a.m., an hour and forty-five minutes away. But COs arriving for the shift change would start filtering in around five-thirty. And with the longest day of the year approaching, it'd start getting light by five. Fetch cursed softly but fervently.

Where the fuck was Lerome?

Fetch was torn over what he should do. Sneak back into the camp. Take off across country on foot. Or just keep on waiting.

His clothing didn't give him away as a fugitive. He was wearing gray sweats, black Converse high-tops and a navy stocking cap — prison recreation gear, but the same get-up a lot of early-morning runners would have on. Fetch'd rolled out of his bunk forty-five minutes ago. Most of the guys in the 20-man dorm had slept right through his departure. But there were always a couple of busybodies who made a point of watching everything. They could — and would — tell the warden what time he'd left the dorm.

Not that it was necessarily a big thing to step outside. More than a few inmates in the work camp got antsy and took night-time strolls when they were about to be released, especially if they'd been locked up a long time. They wondered, with good reason, if they'd be able to read-just to the outside world well enough that they wouldn't get yanked back inside before ... well, before a lot of things, but particularly before they had the chance to get laid again.

For Fetch, before he got a chance to see Verene again. Show her all the money he'd hidden for the two of them.

After leaving the cabin, Fetch started out jogging, like he was going to do laps of the rec yard that lay behind the gym and the administration building. The area was lighted all night long and a CO stationed in an upper-floor office of the admin building was assigned to keep watch over the area. But at four a.m., the guard was already six hours into his shift, probably reading a magazine to stay awake, or possibly taking a cat-nap.

In even a minimum-security facility, the perimeter was secured by two 12-foot high chain-link fences, separated by a distance of ten feet, and topped with razor wire. The space between the fences was festooned with coils of razor ribbon. A ninja, maybe, could make it out. Your average jailbird, no way.

The only things that confined inmates at a work camp were common sense and an absolute dread of what would happen to them when they were caught after an escape. You didn't get *Investor's Daily* in maximum security.

So Fetch was not surprised as he did his first lap of the rec yard that he didn't see anybody watching him from the admin building. As he rounded the far curve of the second lap, he made a hard left and kept going for a quarter-mile. Then he cut over to nearby state highway 417, jogged another quarter-mile down the blacktop and ... waited.

He couldn't believe Lerome was so late. He refused to believe that his cousin wasn't coming at all. All the tension started to step on his bladder, and he felt a sudden urge to pee. He yanked down his sweatpants to relieve himself.

His stream shot out like he was holding a fire hose. He felt like he might piss for hours — long enough that they'd catch him with his dick in his hand. Maybe some wiseass con would write a limerick about that. But still make it come out that in the end he was fuct.

By the time he finally drained himself, Fetch thought the sky had definitely brightened. He decided he had to go back to the camp. Something unavoidable must have delayed Lerome. The best thing to do would be to call him later today, find out what had happened, and set things up again for tomorrow morning.

Fetch liked that idea a whole lot better than trying to escape on foot and have cops with shotguns and bloodhounds chasing his ass.

Then just as he was pulling up his sweatpants, he heard it. A car was coming — a car with an engine missing on at least one cylinder and maybe two. He didn't see it immediately because its lights were out, but each passing second brought the sound of that misfiring engine closer.

Oh, please, God, Fetch thought, let it be anybody but ...

Lerome pulled to a stop opposite his cousin.

"Sorry, Fetch," he said of the car, or perhaps his tardiness. "First car I stole got a flat and the fucker didn't have a spare. This was all I could find on short notice."

The car was an old black Lincoln, the boxy kind with suicide doors for the rear seat. It looked good, but it sounded like someone had poured sand in the gas tank. That didn't seem to worry Lerome. With his dark hair combed back, his goatee, his sunglasses, dressed in black as always, Lerome looked cool sitting behind the wheel of the dying luxury car.

But Lerome always looked cool.

"You getting in, cuz?" he asked.

Fetch did.

Cursing his luck with getaway cars.

33

They made it as far as the Allegheny State Park, Fetch lying across the back seat listening for sirens, before the Lincoln's engine started smoking. Fetch smelled it before he saw it.

"Jesus Christ," he yelped, closing his eyes, "is this piece of shit on fire?"

"Not yet," his cousin responded evenly.

Lerome popped the hood release, an advanced feature on a car that old. The hood lifted a couple of inches until the safety catch grabbed it.

"Maybe a little breeze'll cool it down," Lerome suggested.

Fetch winced, then opened his eyes when he felt the car veer sharply off the road. He looked up and saw tall trees all around him. He thought Lerome was getting ready to dump the car. They were going to have to run for it after all, the two of them.

The road abruptly dropped away, leaving Fetch's stomach hanging up near the car's ceiling liner. At that point, Fetch heard Lerome cut the engine. He clambered to a sitting position.

"We'll coast from here," Lerome said.

"Fuck, why don't we just stop? Get out before—"

"We see where this road takes us? Where's the fun in that?"

Besides being cool, Lerome was also maybe a little nuts. But Fetch wasn't in the mood. Escaping from prison hadn't been physically hard, but it was proving to be an emotional ordeal.

"Fun? There's nothing fun about—"

"Look," Lerome said, pointing with his goatee, "a gingerbread house."

Fetch looked. Lerome still had the headlights off but now the sun was up high enough to shoot darts of light through the trees.

Lerome conceded, "Okay, it's not gingerbread, but it is a fancy log cabin, and, my oh my, if there isn't one of those yuppie SUVs parked right next to it."

He brought the Lincoln skidding to a stop alongside the silver Toyota Highlander.

Fetch shook his head balefully.

"If I had your luck, I'd never have served a day."

"Pays to keep a positive attitude," Lerome grinned. He glanced at the cabin's windows. "Looks like the three bears are not at home."

"Like I said," Fetch said.

CHAPTER 4

Warden R. Burt Parker started his workday at six a.m. along with the rest of the early shift at Camp Alphonse. He enjoyed having the latter part of his afternoon free. For some reason, that was when his missus got randy. Any other time of day, he'd have to coax, cajole, or downright plead. But along about three p.m., it was smooth sailing. Afterward, they'd catch forty winks, get up in time for dinner, and flip a coin to see who'd do the cooking. Might not seem exciting to a lot of people, but for the warden it was bliss.

Even better, it was dependable bliss. The warden's routine hadn't been interrupted for —

"Pardon me, sir."

Warden Parker frowned. It was 6:05. His butt hadn't hit his office chair yet, and here was his chief of security, Tanenbaum, the man in charge of the uniformed staff, giving him a worried look. Like there was anything to worry about at Camp Alphonse short of a fire or food poisoning.

The warden took his seat and spoke calmly. "Take a load off, chief."

Tanenbaum remained standing.

"We have a missing man, Warden."

Parker blinked. "Missing? Who?"

"Fetch Mcdonald."

There were 500 inmates at Camp Alphonse, but like a good elementary school principal, the warden knew all of those in his care by name, and he usually could summon up the crimes that had put them there, the time they had left on their sentences, and a few personal facts, too.

He had no trouble placing Mcdonald. Fetch was the guy in the library who routed the camp's copy of *Field & Stream* to his office the first thing each month. He was also only three weeks from discharge, and a model prisoner.

How could Fetch Mcdonald be missing? Him of all people.

"You're sure about this, Chief?" he asked, bothered that he heard a note of anxiety creeping into his voice.

"He wasn't in his dorm for the six a.m. nose count, sir."

"He's a short-timer. Maybe the separation jitters got him and he went out for a walk. Didn't realize the time. It's only..." the warden glanced at his watch, "...six-eleven."

"Yes, sir. He did go out for a walk — at three forty-five. Lochte and Gores saw him go."

Warden Parker's face fell. His gut began to churn in a way he hadn't felt since he'd left his last maximum-security assignment. Christ, he thought he'd put all that behind him for good.

"You're searching the whole facility? Just to make sure he didn't have an accident or something."

Please, God, the warden thought, let it be an accident. Even a fatal one.

"We're doing that right now, sir. Ought to be done in another thirty minutes."

"Let me know as soon as you are."

The chief nodded. He knew the dilemma the warden faced. The longer the warden waited to notify the state police and the Cattaraugus County sheriff, the farther the escapee could run. But if he picked up the phone now and put out the alert, only to find that Mcdonald was still on-site, he'd look like a horse's ass. Even so, the rules said that was the way he was supposed to go. Tanenbaum saluted and started for the door.

"Chief, I want a status report every two minutes."

"Yes, sir," he said, stopping at the door.

A look of genuine consternation crossed Warden Parker's face.

"A model prisoner with three weeks left to serve? He'd have to be insane to run."

"Crazy as a bedbug," Chief Tanenbaum agreed.

Then he went to look for Fetch Mcdonald.

The warden picked up the phone to call his brethren in law enforcement. He wasn't going to take any chance, get himself into any hot water. But he was sure he wouldn't be getting home today while the missus was still in the mood.

Fetch and Lerome stopped at the foot of the cabin's front steps when they saw the coffee cup on the railing. Was somebody home after all?

"Can you hotwire that SUV?" Fetch asked his cousin in a whisper.

"Probably not," Lerome said softly.

He explained that most late model cars, especially the rice-burners, had microchips in the ignition keys. No key, no go. At least for someone with his limited boosting knowledge.

Lerome quickly crept up the steps and touched the cup with the back of his hand.

"It's cool," he said, keeping his voice down. He peeked in a window. "Nobody."

Lerome depressed the front door latch with a knuckle and it swung open. He gestured Fetch to enter. Fetch scur-ried up the steps and slipped into the cabin. Lerome followed and bumped the door closed with a hip.

They looked around, listened hard.

Nice place, polished wood everywhere, exposed beams in the ceiling, big fireplace, comfortably furnished. But no sign that anyone was home.

Lerome raised his nose and quietly sniffed.

"Nobody's made breakfast yet," he said.

"Went out for a walk or something," Fetch surmised.

"Gathering nuts and berries maybe," Lerome added with a grin.

Fetch noticed the stairs leading to the second floor.

"Or they're just quiet sleepers."

Lerome closed his eyes, stood completely still and ...shook his head.

"We're alone."

Fetch spotted just what they needed on a pass-through counter to the kitchen. He scurried over and held up his prize. "Car keys," he exulted quietly.

"Who said you weren't lucky?" Lerome asked.

"Let's go." Fetch started toward the door.

Lerome held up a hand. "We take nothing but the car, the cops're bound to know it was you. We make it look like a random burglary, it'll confuse the issue."

"We get caught arguing here, there'll be no doubt at all."

A good point, but Lerome remained unswayed.

"Trust me, okay? Go upstairs. See if there's some clothes you can wear. I'll grab some things. We'll be ready to roll by the time you come down." When Fetch still hesitated, he added, "Hey, who found this place, anyway?"

Fetch muttered under his breath and went upstairs.

Lerome took a look out the front window just to be sure no one was coming home, and that's when he first noticed the cool little typewriter.

Remington Noiseless Portable. The name in gold leaf.

Remington. Like the shotguns and rifles. Only this one

was noiseless. Shiny and black.

Box of typing paper right there next to it, too.

He lifted his eyes to look out the window again. Nobody was coming down the road or through the woods. But Fetch was right. They really shouldn't spend too much time there. Lerome crossed the room and looked at what else lay on the kitchen counter. There was a wallet with ... Illinois driver's license in the name of Daniel Cameron. Guy about Fetch's size, similar appearance sorta, a few years older, though. Dan's wallet also had a picture of a nice looking blonde, three credit cards, and $289 in cash. Lerome stuck the wallet in his back pocket.

He went into the kitchen and snapped a paper towel off a roll hanging under a cabinet. Using the towel, he opened the fridge. He took lunch meat, beer, Coke, and a wedge of chocolate cake. He grabbed a loaf of Italian bread, a bottle of mustard, and a bag of natural potato chips from a cabinet. He put everything into a plastic shopping bag he found.

Who the hell stole food? Kids, that's who. More misinformation.

Returning to the living room, he spotted a really nice mini-component stereo system. Speakers weren't much bigger than decks of cards. He got another plastic bag and put the whole system into it.

Fetch came down the stairs dressed in new clothes: black plaid shirt, jeans, and boots. Looked like everything fit. He had his old stuff under his arm.

"I took these clothes from the back of the guy's closet," Fetch said. "Maybe he won't notice right away. Now can we go?"

Lerome nodded. He grabbed the two plastic bags and opened the front door using the paper towel. Then he stopped.

"What now?" Fetch demanded, eyes scanning the road for agents of doom closing in on them. Lerome handed the bags to his cousin.

"Get in the car. I'll be right out."

"Make it fast, Lerome. I really don't want to get caught."

Lerome nodded and quickly crossed to the table where the typewriter sat. Remington. Shiny and black. Noiseless. Just too cool to leave behind. And if you were going to steal a typewriter ... you might as well take some paper, too.

He grabbed both and hurried out the door.

Leaving it open, the way a kid would do.

They drove away from the cabin and were heading up state highway 219 to Buffalo five minutes before the sheriff's department blocked all roads into and out of the Allegheny State Park.

Dan and Erin did, in fact, do it up against a tree, Dan using his shirttail to cover his ass and Erin being careful not to bark her knees. The early morning air raised goose bumps on their exposed flesh, the clear light of dawn painted the woodland setting green and gold, and larks sang in the branches above them. All they needed was for Bambi to step into the frame and it'd look like Disney was doing a skin flick.

For Erin, the excitement junkie, there was also the thrill of possible discovery by other early-rising hikers. Dan thought of that, too, with less enthusiasm, but only until they got going. Then he wouldn't have noticed a brass band marching past.

After they finished, Dan whispered in Erin's ear, "Let's circle this day on our calendar. I think it's going to be meaningful."

Erin hugged him fiercely. How could a child conceived like this turn out to be anything but a world-beater? Once they were decently dressed again, they meandered through the woods until they came to a small glen next to a silver thread of a stream. There they lay down next to each other, looking at the sky, listening to the world come to life, and thinking good thoughts.

Dan felt the weight of the world had been lifted from his shoulders. He'd gotten his new novel done. *Time Expires* was ready to be photocopied and sent off to Hank DeMitri. Except for the last chapter, of course. That was tucked into the drawer of his night table. And if he had to give his Remington back soon ... shit, he still didn't know if he could write without it.

Then again, maybe two novels were all he was meant to write. Two were certainly twice as good as one. Maybe more so. Not only had his output doubled, he'd also shown that the first book wasn't a fluke. His success couldn't be totally dependent on his typewriter.

Add to that the significant fact that he and Erin had already made a pile of money from the royalties on *Indecision Kills* and would make another pile from *Time Expires*. He wouldn't have to go back to the newspaper, though he did miss the place more than he'd ever have suspected.

He wasn't sure what he'd do next, but he'd think of something — and if he didn't, the wood nymph lying beside him was bound to come up with an exciting idea or two.

Erin had her hand draped on Dan and could feel the pulse in his arm. She wondered if she'd be able to feel her baby's pulse as it grew in her. She pushed aside a sudden tremor of doubt. She would get pregnant. And that being the case, hell, she was probably getting pregnant right now. Dan's swift little swimmers were racing through her to see who'd be the first to her egg. It was the right time of the month for her to ovulate, and this time it was going to work.

Erin closed her eyes, clenched her jaw, and willed it to work.

She said a silent prayer, too.

Her prayers about Dan had already been answered. She didn't have a vocabulary big enough to express how much she loved him these days. She'd die for him. Gladly. Maybe even kill for him. And it had been a little less than two years ago that she'd wondered if their marriage had any future. What kind of spoiled brat had she been, anyway? But she knew her former discontent had been more than mere selfishness.

She did have a real need for excitement. It was probably pathological. But she understood now that she didn't have to do stuff that was completely crazy. Life threatening. Screwing in the forest had been a rush, had left her with a nice warm glow that would last until ... she could think of something else that was a kick but not suicidal.

It wasn't such a bad thing to be the way she was, now that she'd gotten a handle on it. In fact, it was good for Dan, too. If she hadn't lit a fire under him, if she hadn't bought him Ben Hecht's typewriter —

Damn, she hated the thought of losing that typewriter! There had to be something she could do about that.

But the larger point was, she and Dan were good for each other. They balanced one another. And if they had just one kid or ten, she was going to see to it that Danny-boy never needed any mistresses.

Erin pushed herself up on her elbows.

"You hungry?"

"Now that you mention it," Dan said.

"Lumberjack breakfast?"

Dan nodded.

They were back at the cabin in fifteen minutes.

Stopped cold when they saw their Toyota was gone — replaced by some old Lincoln — and the cabin door was hanging open.

CHAPTER 5

Dan's typewriter was gone. More important, so was *Time Expires.*

He'd sprinted no more than twenty-five yards, racing into the cabin ahead of Erin, but at that moment he couldn't seem to catch his breath. Then Erin arrived and saw what had happened. She started to say something when Dan was suddenly able to fill his lungs again.

And he roared!

He raced back outside wearing a look on his face the likes of which Erin had never seen before. It was rage. Murderous rage. Her gentle husband was looking for someone to kill.

For a moment, Erin felt pre-empted. She was the one who brought strong emotions to the party. Dan was always laid back. But not now. As she stepped back outside she saw Dan glaring down the road, clenching and unclenching his hands repeatedly. A strangler's gesture.

This staggering transformation in Dan left Erin awash in emotions. She was terrifically excited, but that was just her nature. What surprised the hell out of her was that she also felt ... well, submissive, and comfortable with it. Here was a man who would stand up for what was his. And, Gloria

Steinem be damned, that would include her.

And eventually, Erin thought with a warm glow, it would include their child.

Still, it wouldn't do to let him run amok.

When Dan turned to face her, she joined him on the road.

"You know who did this, don't you?" he asked grimly.

Erin had no idea and said so.

"It was the estate's lawyers. They came and got the typewriter. And they decided to take my novel. Maybe they'll claim it was the product of their property, entitling them to it. Or maybe they're just jerking me around because they think I've caused them a lot of trouble."

Now, Erin was worried. Outrage was fine. Lunacy was not.

She shook her head.

"Dan, stop and think." She nodded at where their Toyota had been parked. "When's the last time you heard of lawyers committing grand theft auto?"

Dan shoulders slumped.

"Well, shit," he said.

They went back inside and Dan called the cops. Then they looked around to see what else had been taken. Noticing that Dan's wallet was missing and the stereo was gone was easy. But it was only when they went to get some cold water to drink that they realized their fridge had been burgled, too.

"Who steals food?" Erin asked.

Dan had worked the police beat long enough to know. "Kids." But then he frowned. Sure, young punks would take food, and the stereo was a given. But a manuscript? And a typewriter? Kids didn't read and write. Not the ones who did break-ins.

Something wasn't right here ...

Like the response time of the cops. They got to the cabin — a remote place — almost comically fast. As if they'd been waiting just offstage. And they came in force. Four cars, including a canine unit. All that for a burglary? These cops were on edge, too. Dan could see that just as soon as he and Erin stepped onto the cabin's front porch. Eight uniforms, all with their eyes wide and their bodies stiff with tension. Each of them with a shotgun trained on Dan and Erin. Except for the two restraining snarling dogs.

Then another patrol unit pulled in, skidding to a stop. A tall cop with gray hair who looked like he'd gotten dressed in a hurry jumped out of the car. He took in the scene and in a voice of command said, "Stand easy."

The other cops were so keyed up he had to repeat himself before they obeyed.

The newcomer stepped over to Dan and Erin, buttoning his shirt as he walked. He glanced at Erin. Dan, he gave a long hard look and a frown.

"I'm Cattaraugas County Sheriff Timothy Finnegan," he said. "And you are?"

"Dan Cameron. My wife, Erin. I called 911 about the burglary." Dan looked out at all the other cops, the shotguns, the dogs. "Something going on, Sheriff?"

The sheriff answered with a question of his own. "You have some ID, Mr. Cameron?"

"My wallet was stolen," Dan replied.

Dan, Erin, the sheriff, and three of his people, minus their shotguns and dogs, went into the cabin. Erin had the helpful notion of showing Sheriff Finnegan the dustcover photo of Dan on a copy of *Indecision Kills*. Finnegan compared Dan to his picture, riffled through the first few pages of the book, and put it down.

"Sorry, haven't read it," he said.

The author shrugged.

The author's wife said, "You should."

"Be sorry?" Finnegan asked.

"Read it," Erin answered.

At that point, the sheriff asked two of his deputies, one of them female, to take Erin's statement in the kitchen. She frowned, but when Dan gave her a nod she went. After she stuck out her tongue. Dan and Finnegan each decided that the gesture was meant for the other.

The two of them talked in the living room, sitting opposite one another. Finnegan's third deputy remained on his feet and alert — just in case Dan proved to be a menace after all.

Dan told Finnegan what had happened.

"That Lincoln outside's not your car?" the sheriff asked.

"We drive a Toyota Highlander. Silver. It's gone."

"Then you don't know whose car that is?"

"Whoever robbed us, I guess," Dan answered. "Unless he stole that car, too"

Finnegan got the Toyota's license plate number from Dan. The sheriff turned to the deputy standing nearby. "Wambaugh, go out and radio the vehicle description and Illinois tag number to the state police."

Wambaugh gave Dan one last hard look and left.

"Had an uneasy moment there before you arrived," Dan said to Finnegan. "Your people looked like they were ready to go to war."

"We're a little on edge," the sheriff responded. "There's a state work camp not far from here. Early this morning, one of the inmates took off. Guy who robbed a bank, I'm told."

"A bankrobber stole my typewriter?" Dan asked.

Finnegan frowned. "That's what he took, besides your SUV?"

"That and the manuscript for my new book."

"And your wallet, you said."

"A couple hundred bucks and a few credit cards in my wallet. The manuscript's good for a million dollar advance — not that a thief could have known that."

Finnegan read between the lines. This guy was telling him he had money. He'd lost substantial belongings. Was someone who'd better get first-class service and not be fucked with. But he'd done it politely. Hadn't puffed himself up and yelled at the country cop how important he was. The sheriff appreciated that, but he still had to be honest with the man.

"You ever have any dealings with the police, Mr. Cameron?" Finnegan asked. "Of a friendly sort, I mean."

"I was a police beat reporter for the *Chicago Tribune* for six years."

The sheriff was glad to hear that.

"Then you know what our priorities have to be here."

Dan nodded. "First you catch the bad guy. Then — if I'm lucky — you get my things back."

"And you know how lucky you'll have to be, right?"

"Damn lucky," Dan said bleakly.

Except for a crime scene technician, who took the Camerons' fingerprints for elimination purposes and then started dusting the cabin for other prints, Dan and Erin were alone. Finnegan and the other cops had left to continue the hunt.

Dan and Erin washed the fingerprint ink off their hands in the kitchen and went upstairs to their bedroom. Erin called her father's friend, Lester Croart, the owner of the cabin, to let him know what had happened. On a hunch, Dan went to look in his closet. Erin was hanging up the phone when he turned to her.

"The SOB stole a shirt, the black plaid, a pair of jeans, and my old boots."

"Fetch Mcdonald."

"Who?"

"That's the name of the bankrobber who escaped. I decided to get over my pout, be nice to the cops who talked to me, and they told me the guy's name."

Dan nodded appreciatively. He said, "I'll be right back. I'm going to tell that crime scene guy about the missing clothes."

When Dan got back, Erin had more information for him.

"Mcdonald is about your size, a little smaller, lighter hair, brown eyes. But the cops don't have a picture of him yet, so—"

"I fit the general description. That's why Finnegan and the other cops were staring at me."

"Yeah."

"Okay, that explains that. But why would someone who's just broken out of prison steal my novel and my typewriter? That's what I can't figure out." Dan sighed. "Finnegan told me catching Mcdonald is the top of his to-do list. But if we expect him to get *Time Expires* and the Remington back, we'd better light a candle."

"Then we'll have to find them ourselves."

Erin made her declaration with a straight face, but Dan could see the light in her eyes.

He knew that crazy gleam all too well.

How cool would it be to chase down an escaped bank robber to get your stuff back?

Thing was, Dan was pissed enough to be a little crazy himself.

And there was one more consideration, a big one.

"You're right, we will," Dan said. "But do you know why?"

"Why?"

He sat down on the bed. Erin sat next to him and held his hand.

"Because we expect to get word of a certain court decision soon. And let's say the court rules against us." Dan looked Erin in the eye. "You think the Hecht estate will believe us if we tell them a fugitive bank robber broke into our cabin and made off with the Remington?"

Erin laughed.

"I know I wouldn't," she said. Then she added. "I know where the cops think Fetch Mcdonald is heading."

"Where?"

"His hometown. Buffalo."

CHAPTER 6

Fetch was home, back in Buffalo, cruising east on William Street past the main post office. Doing that gave him the creeps. For all he knew, his wanted poster could be up on a wall in there already. He slid lower in his seat and turned his face away from the window.

From behind the wheel, Lerome glanced at Fetch. "You want to be any more obvious, you could hold up a sign. 'Here I am, coppers. Come and get me.'"

"Very funny," Fetch grumbled. He straightened up but kept his head turned like he was checking his left shoulder for dandruff.

"You gotta take it easy, cuz. Cops're like dogs, they smell fear."

Lerome hung a left at Bailey Avenue. Fetch saw a large sign in a Tops supermarket window: *We've Got Octopus!* What the hell was that all about? Off to the right was the Lovejoy neighborhood. Which looked pretty much the way Fetch remembered it. Blue collar.

"You know," Lerome said, "this is the first time I could be on the hook for a crime."

At first, Fetch thought Lerome was bragging in a quiet way. "Look at me, I could get popped. You see me trying to get invisible?" Then Fetch realized what his cousin was getting at. He wanted to know why the fuck anyone who was going to be paroled in three weeks would bust out of prison.

The way Lerome had put it, though, Fetch didn't have to answer him. Not directly. He could just say, "Yeah, thanks," and pretend he'd missed Lerome's point.

Only that wasn't the way they were with each other. They were more like brothers than cousins. Brothers who'd go to the wall for each other. Or aid in a jailbreak.

Now, Fetch turned his face toward the window. So he wouldn't have to look at Lerome.

"It's Verene," he said.

Fetch wouldn't have blamed Lerome if he hit the brakes right there and booted his ass out into traffic. Or at least called him an end-stage dickhead.

All Lerome did was ask, "What about her?"

He turned right onto Hennepin and then made a left into the driveway of an old frame house across the street from the neighborhood park. The driveway was shaded by a large maple. The neighbors, mostly Poles and Germans in Lovejoy, were already off to work. The sidewalks were swept and empty. Fetch turned to look at his cousin.

"Verene's getting married."

"Yeah? She send you an invitation?"

"A week from Saturday."

Less than two weeks. Today was Monday.

"What's your point?" Lerome asked.

"I've got to stop her."

"Why? You're Romeo, she's Juliet? Only this time it'll all work out."

"Fuck," Fetch said. He knew how stupid it sounded. But he'd never told Lerome about all the money he had stashed. How he was sure he could get Verene back. Well, maybe he could get her back. Have a happy ending. If he got to her in time.

"Come on," Lerome said, getting out of the SUV. "I figured you'd need a place to hide."

The lady who owned the house was a lively old soul named Mathilde Severin. Born in Paris, she'd danced in a nightclub act, fought with the Resistance, been captured by the Gestapo, sent to the Ravensbrück concentration camp, escaped, met and married handsome displaced person Cyrek Dolinski, and emigrated to Buffalo.

Cy had died five years ago. Two years later, Mathilde lost her eyesight to diabetes. She didn't let it get her down; she'd survived worse. She met Lerome on the street one day when she heard someone speaking her native tongue and struck up a conversation. Lerome's family, the D'Arnoles, was originally from Canada. He'd learned French at home as a child.

Fetch's late mother, Dorothy, had also been a D'Arnole, but she'd been disowned by her father — for marrying Fetch's dad — and had never taught her son the ancestral language.

Now Lerome told Fetch he had to pretend he couldn't speak at all.

"Mathilde's blind. I told her you're mute. She can't see you, and if you keep quiet, she won't hear you. She won't know she has a fugitive in her house."

"How long is this supposed to last?"

Lerome shrugged. "Till you get outta Dodge ... or go see Verene."

They got Fetch tucked away in an upstairs bedroom. Mathilde stayed on the first floor; stairs were tough for her these days. But she'd cooked a meal for Fetch, roast pork and sauerkraut. With a cold beer to wash it down. Cy's favorite meal. Even for brunch. She said she'd leave food for him in the oven or the fridge. Just come and get something when he was hungry.

Mathilde called Fetch Mr. Connelly, the name Lerome had given her.

In his new digs, Fetch devoured the meal off a TV tray. After eight years of institutional fare, he'd forgotten how good food could taste, and he hadn't had a beer since he got locked up.

"Sit tight," Lerome told him. "I have to do something, then I'll be back."

Fetch nodded, said thanks, and told Lerome he was going to take a nap.

"Good," Lerome said. Then he asked, "How did you find out Verene is getting married, anyway?"

"Archer came to see me."

"Your dad, huh?"

"First time he ever visited."

"First time," Lerome repeated. "How about that?"

Lerome decided to keep the Toyota Highlander. He'd never given a thought to owning an SUV before. Wasn't him. He had a black '69 Mercury Cougar, the kind with the sequential turn signals. It was sitting in his garage right now.

He owned it legally. A guy had signed over the title to clear a debt.

But now ... now he could feel things changing. He'd just sold his business for one thing, returning to town the very day Fetch had called him from prison, after a trip to Texas and New Orleans. Then there was Ants. Anthea Lowney. He felt things were getting serious with her. The Cougar, it wasn't a serious car. It was a flashy little thing good for running around town, but after having it out on the road for a month he thought he needed something more substantial.

The Highlander felt good to him, had more style than he ever would have imagined in an SUV and, in his mind, it went with the Remington Noiseless Portable. They both had the same quiet cool that ... well, that he did.

Not that he could just go on driving the SUV. The owner of that fancy log cabin came home, the first thing he probably did was call the cops and report his car missing. Cops probably had the vehicle description and tags on their hot sheet already. Lerome wondered if they had a description of the Remington, too. How much was the owner missing that?

He pulled into the driveway of a corrugated metal building on a street just off the huge South Buffalo Redevelopment Site. He hit the horn twice. A surveillance camera was pointed at his vehicle and its red light came on. He gave a friendly wave.

The overhead door rolled up and Lerome drove into the chop shop.

During regular business hours, Baby's Auto Body was a legit business, a body shop that was a favorite of local claims adjusters for its first-rate work and its reasonable prices. Nobody cared that all of the people who bent sheet metal at Baby's were female ... lesbian ... and not particularly outgoing to the clientele.

As it should be, quality and value were all that mattered.

That same sensibility had made Baby's owner, Jessi Jaymes, a client, and later a friend, of Lerome's. After Ants had referred Jessi to him. Ants and Jessi having been cellmates once.

Crimes and the people who committed them, active and retired, had always been a part of Lerome's life.

His family, the D'Arnoles, had been in the smuggling business for well over a century. They'd smuggled runaway slaves into Canada prior to Emancipation; they'd smuggled Canadian whiskey into the U.S. during Prohibition; they'd smuggled American cigarettes into Canada to avoid

Ottawa's heavy tobacco taxes. All of this took place under the cover of legitimate front companies, first drayage and then trucking.

It was only after the family had moved its base of operations to Buffalo and the federal government had passed the RICO act, under which the government could seize all of the belongings of anyone found to be operating a continuing criminal enterprise, that Lerome's — and Fetch's — grandfather, Jules D'Arnole, decided that the family should go straight.

That didn't mean, of course, that Grandpere Jules couldn't regale Lerome with secret stories of his ancestors many adventures outwitting lawmen on both sides of the border.

Lerome couldn't get enough of story-time with Grandpa. But, from the beginning, Jules had told his grandson that the D'Arnoles were no longer involved in such daring exploits because the stakes had been raised to an unacceptable height.

Which made it a challenge for Lerome to find something he could do that would be worthy of a D'Arnole without threatening either his freedom or property. What he hit on at the age of 17 was the idea of getting into traffic reporting.

Not with a helicopter. Not telling commuters where traffic was jammed.

Rather, he would recruit a large number of long-haul truckers, guys who drove the interstates all hours of the night and have them note where and when they saw cops. They'd call Lerome with the information. He'd mail them cash — usually in care of their girlfriends or favorite bars — and compile reports for resale.

There was a ready market for such data. The D'Arnoles were almost unique in retiring in the face of the RICO laws. Plenty of people still moved goods they didn't want the cops to find. Knowing the times and places the cops were not likely to be watching was valuable information.

Not that Lerome would ever know the uses to which his clients would put his services. He never directly asked anyone what their business was, and he only took on clients who came with references. Even then he sometimes turned people down. After all, there were assholes who trafficked in human cargo. Grandpa Jules had told him about those creeps, too.

So there he'd been, a young man with vision. And Fetch had lent him $5,000 to get started. Fetch had also refused to take more than 10K in repayment rather than the 50% stake Lerome had offered, a terrible mistake financially, but one that further endeared him to Lerome.

Of course, they'd been tight right from the start.

Fetch had saved Lerome's life when they were kids. Fetch'd been eight, Lerome five. They'd gone out walking along a stretch of Norfolk Southern tracks one day— when they should have been playing in Lerome's back yard — and Lerome had tried to kick a stone that lay on a tie.

He'd misjudged his kick and firmly wedged his foot in the space between the main rail line and that of a siding. He also pitched forward and split his head open on a rail. He didn't cry even though he was gushing blood. He was probably too dazed to be scared; he couldn't even help Fetch dislodge his foot. Despite everything, Lerome figured it'd all work out okay. They'd go home, get cleaned up, eat some ice cream.

Then Fetch's eyes went wide and he started to cry.

"Lerome," Fetch shrieked, "I feel a train!"

Fetch was kneeling on a rail, trying to free Lerome's foot.

"You'll get me out, Fetch," Lerome said dreamily.

When you were five and you believed in someone, your faith was absolute.

The only thing Fetch could think of was maybe

Lerome's foot would come free if he peed on it. And the only reason he thought of that was because he was about to wet his pants anyway. But it worked. Fetch peed, pulled, and they both got off the tracks.

Lerome thought it was hilarious, Fetch peeing on his foot.

A few seconds later, just time enough for Fetch to tuck back in, a train came around the bend in the tracks. The driver never would have seen them in time. As it was, they were standing off to the side and the driver waved and tooted his horn for them. The guy's face fell when Fetch gave him the finger in return.

It never occurred to Lerome at the time but he often thought later that Fetch could have saved his own life by just leaving his dumb little cousin to get killed. But he hadn't. So when Fetch asked for his help in escaping from prison, Lerome was there for him.

No matter how fucking stupid Fetch's reason was.

Lerome had never liked Verene Digby.

She'd come on to him both before and after she'd married Fetch.

He was probably the first guy who hadn't wanted a little V.D.

The only exception to Lerome's ability to deny that he was facilitating illegal acts was Baby's Auto Body. Because of the referral from Ants, Lerome knew that Jessi's shop moved hot cars and auto parts. But Jessi wouldn't rat on anyone. Not if you turned one of her oxy-acetylene torches on her. She came over to Lerome and gave the Highlander a glance.

"Nice wheels, but I never pictured you in a yup-mobile. You here to sell?"

"Let's talk in your office," he said.

They went into Jessi's office and seated themselves on

opposite sides of her desk. There was a cheesecake calendar on the wall. The model was long and whipcord lean. She had cropped ginger hair and blue eyes. Looked a whole lot like Jessi herself.

Lerome told her he'd sold his business. He gave her the name and phone number of the new owner. She could call and see if she wanted to do business with him.

"A guy," Jessi stated.

"Young guy. Knows computers. Very smart."

"Straight?"

"I didn't ask."

"So you want to sell your Toyota?"

"I want to keep it."

Jessi looked at Lerome, sizing things up.

"But you need a paint job and maximum detailing."

No trace of the former owner to be left behind.

"A records adjustment, too," Lerome told her.

"Middleman cutout."

Lerome nodded.

"You got a head-start for me?"

He flipped Daniel Cameron's Illinois driver's license onto her desk.

Lerome had taken it from the wallet he had grabbed.

Jessi knew computers, too, and Cameron's license would be all the head-start she'd need. She'd hack into the state vehicle registration database, in Illinois that fell under the Secretary of State's office, and change the name of the registered owner of the Toyota Highlander from Daniel Cameron to some good ethnic name. That straw man, in turn, would sell the vehicle to Lerome. Lerome would have a freshly printed title to prove it. In the unlikely event that something went wrong, Lerome could claim he was a victim, taken in by the ethnic guy. Who'd be very hard to find.

Auto theft had entered the digital age.

"Black, right?"

Meaning the color Lerome wanted his SUV painted.

"Yeah."

"This new guy, the one you sold your business to, he can be trusted?"

Lerome said, "He's selling the same thing I used to, legal information. You buy it, where's the crime?"

"Just don't tell him why I want it."

"I wouldn't," Lerome agreed.

"I'd like it better if I knew him. I'd like it better if he was gay."

"Maybe he is. Give him a call. Ask him."

Jessi flipped Lerome a set of car keys.

"You can take mine. Yours will be ready tomorrow."

They walked back out into the shop. Lerome took the typewriter off the back seat of the Highlander. Jessi's eyes widened when she saw it.

"Cool. You want to sell that?"

Lerome shook his head.

"I think I'm going to give it to Ants."

"Well, she doesn't want it, I'll buy it."

"I'll keep that in mind."

But if Ants didn't want it, Lerome was going to keep it for himself.

"Hey," Jessi said, "there's a box on the back seat there. Don't forget that."

The typing paper.

"Yeah, thanks," Lerome said.

He grabbed the box. A minute later he was gone.

CHAPTER 7

Dan and Erin packed their remaining belongings and were waiting on the front porch of the cabin when Lester Croart, old friend of Erin's dad, retired postmaster of Buffalo, and their host the past nine months, brought his gunmetal gray Buick Roadmaster to a dust-raising stop in front of them. He popped out of his car, red-faced, white-haired, and blue-eyed, and bounded up the steps.

He waved to the Camerons as he went past, saying, "Erin, Dan," but didn't stop. He opened the door to his cabin and charged inside.

Looking through a window, Dan and Erin saw Les peer into all sorts of nooks and crannies, occasionally stopping to sniff the air.

Erin asked, "What's he smelling?"

Dan thought he knew, but wanted to wait to be sure. Les ran upstairs and the Camerons sat on the front steps until he returned. Les locked the door as he exited the cabin. No more taking chances now.

"Well, at least he didn't shit the place," Les said.

"*What?*" Erin asked as she and Dan stood up.

Dan had guessed right, his police beat experience coming through once again.

He told Erin, "Burglars sometimes crap in the houses they break into. It's a sign of contempt for their victims. Sometimes they do it in the most conspicuous places, say, on the dining room table. Other times they like to make people look for their droppings."

"That's disgusting," Erin said, wrinkling her face.

"For the homeowner, sure. But these days, the cops are glad to have a DNA sample."

They loaded their luggage into the Buick and took off. Les looked in the rearview mirror and shook his head. "Damn shame when you can't be safe even out here."

Both Camerons agreed glumly.

"Didn't see the thief took any of my stuff, only yours."

"Yeah," Dan said unhappily from the back seat.

Les glanced at Erin, sitting beside him.

"Knowing you, sweetie, I bet you're taking this personally."

Erin nodded. "That's why we're sticking around."

"Anything you want me to tell your parents? I called them, you know."

"I'll get in touch, tell them not to worry."

"Okay. Anything I can do, you just let me know."

"Were you able to get us a hotel room?" Erin asked.

"I got you a suite. That's what you said, right? 'The best money can buy.'"

"That's what I said, all right."

Erin's tone was defiant, but she didn't turn to look at her husband. She knew Dan would have gone for value over comfort; his spending habits hadn't caught up with his bank balance. But luxury was a big part of Erin's new plan.

"Good," Les responded, "because you'll be staying at the Chateau on Delaware."

"Sounds perfect."

Dan wasn't going to argue money now. He had other things to think about.

He said, "Les, your cabin ever been burgled before?"

"The place you stayed in is only three years old," Les answered. "The cabin it replaced, though, I think that one was built by Dan'l Boone on his way west. Both of 'em together, never got broken into once. This is the first damn time."

"I don't think it's a coincidence then," Dan said. "Fetch Mcdonald is our man." Then he added, "You know any cops in Buffalo, Les?"

The Chateau on Delaware was a four-story red brick confection with a mansard roof and a mere twenty-eight luxury accommodations. Everyone on the hotel staff was delighted to have the Camerons staying with them, a famous author and his lovely wife. Thing was, they weren't just blowing smoke — or if they were, they were masters — the assistant manager/concierge had a copy of *Indecision Kills* and asked Dan to inscribe it for him.

He assured the Camerons their suite was the best in the house.

Which was easy to believe. The suite was spacious and designed by someone with a gift for understated elegance. That and a lot of money to spend. There were fresh flowers in the salon and room for a work station with high-speed Internet access. The bedroom was an invitation to both sweet dreams and mad passion. The bathroom offered a whirlpool bath and a shower stall with multiple jets. Butler service and a licensed massage therapist were but a phone call away. The bellman's tour of the rooms and spiel of complimentary amenities ran on for five minutes. When he finished, Dan tipped him and he bowed his way out.

Dan laughed, "If the scribes at the *Trib* could see me now."

"You like it, don't you?"

"Yeah, sure. You think that guy downstairs has really

read my book? Or did Les tell him about me and he had someone run out and buy a copy?"

Erin knew about newsies. "If your mother tells you she loves you, check it out."

"Right."

"I'll bet you a hundred bucks you could quiz Rudy," Erin said, remembering the assistant manager's name, "ask him ten questions about your book, and he'd get 'em all right."

"A guy like that, he's probably a speed reader."

Dan sat down on a wonderfully comfortable white silk sofa, hoping his jeans were clean, and gestured to Erin to join him. She didn't have to worry about smudging the upholstery. She sat on Dan's lap and watched as his attention drifted away.

"Thinking about the bad guys?" she asked. Guys, plural.

"So you think our friend Fetch had some help, too."

"Unless he stole the warden's old Lincoln, somebody picked him up."

"Exactly. But who the hell steals a Lincoln as a getaway car?"

"Too flashy?" Erin asked.

Dan rolled his eyes.

"Well," Erin said, "maybe these guys are stupid. You used to tell me dumb criminal stories, ones that never got printed in the paper. Some of them were uproariously inept. The criminals, I mean."

Dan sighed. "We should be so lucky, because if these guys are that dumb, the cops will catch them fast." Then he shook his head. "But I'm feeling anything but lucky. And morons stealing my novel and typewriter makes no more sense than kids taking them."

"Who then?"

"Someone ... strange. What I think happened was ..." Dan paused as if checking his reasoning. "Okay, if you know better than to steal a big easily noticed car, but you take it anyway, it must be because ..."

"You had to," Erin answered.

"Right. You're helping somebody escape from prison, you can't be late. If we say the accomplice isn't stupid, he probably didn't oversleep. So some other reason created a sense of urgency, made him grab the first car that came to hand, even if it was a Lincoln."

"What?"

Dan laughed harshly. "How about this? The first car you steal, something inconspicuous, breaks down. That'd be ironic."

"Why ironic?"

"Well, why do you think that Lincoln turned off the highway and came down the road to Les' cabin?"

Erin made the leap. "It broke down, too. Wow, this guy Mcdonald and his buddy must have really bad luck. That has to be good for us."

"Yeah," Dan said grimly, "except their luck seemed to turn when they found us."

The cops came calling on Archer Mcdonald.

Unlike most former bank robbers, he had his own house. Owned it free and clear. It'd belonged to his late wife, Dorothy, bought for her by her brothers. When Dorothy had died intestate, Archer was her legal heir: her husband. Dorothy had meant to divorce him, but she was chronically depressed by the time she reached that decision and never got around to acting on it. That omission had galled Fetch, who'd grown up in the house and thought of it as his own.

The D'Arnole brothers would have bought their sister any house she wanted, especially since Archer was locked up at the time and wouldn't be around to enjoy it. But Dorothy had been proud. If she had to accept any charity at all, it would only be to provide shelter for her son, and even then she would only go so far.

She'd live humbly, even meanly, to spite the father who'd disowned her.

She also wanted to punish herself. Marrying Archer had been the dumbest thing she'd ever done. All because the SOB had terrific hair, a great smile, and danced like a dream. Okay, the dance floor wasn't the only place he had rhythm. But as far as everything else went — except for giving her Fetch — he was a dead loss.

A fact made worse by her unforgiving father having been right about him.

The place she'd let her brothers buy her was humble to begin with, an old frame house with just four rooms. Now, in the years since her death, it was badly in need of paint, the front porch sagged, and the roof leaked. The house sat on a tiny lot on Prospect Road on the lower west side. Most of the neighbors were Puerto Rican.

That didn't bother Archer. All his years in prison had exposed him to more kinds of people than he knew existed when he was growing up. Of course, every ethnic group had its own prison gang, but that was just a matter of survival. Archer never took any real hate for people into his heart. At least in terms of skin color or the language they spoke.

As individuals, he'd met plenty of cons he'd have liked to shank.

Which was pretty much the way he felt about the cops hammering on his door right now. He wished to hell he could have shouted at them to get the fuck off his property.

He didn't, though. He opened his front door. Even put a smile on his face.

"Morning, gents," he said to the four uniformed coppers who stood on his porch with their guns drawn, "You haven't come to shoot me, have ya?"

Dan sat at the suite's workstation, Erin's Powerbook

plugged into the cable modem connection, the Web site for the *Buffalo News* up on the laptop's monitor. Erin looked over her husband's shoulder as he entered Fetch Mcdonald into the search engine of the paper's archives.

Dan looked up at Erin. "You think Fetch is this guy's real name? What the hell kind of name is that?"

"Something you'd give a dog." She grinned. "Something to turn a good man bad."

Dan didn't see the humor. The sonofabitch had his novel and typewriter.

Having no other name to work with, Dan went with Fetch Mcdonald.

While the computer whirred and chirped its way through his request, Dan asked Erin, "You think you could call your good friend Rudy? Have him send up half-a-dozen lined notepads and a box of my favorite pens."

Dan's writing tools. The stuff he worked with before he sat down at a keyboard.

Erin gave him a look.

"What?" he asked.

"Nothing. Sure, I'll give Rudy a call."

But as Erin walked away she wondered if Dan had read her mind. Did he have the same idea she'd had? Or was it something else?

When Dan looked back at the computer, he saw his search had produced two stories on Fetch Mcdonald — that apparently was his real name — and one on an Archer Mcdonald. He started with the most recent story.

Accompanied by a photo of a man chained to a hospital bed, it recounted a failed attempt to rob a credit union. The guy had fallen off the lifts in his shoes. While chasing his getaway car. Which was being repossessed.

Damn! Maybe this guy was so unlucky they didn't have to worry.

"If you put that in a story, nobody'd ever believe it."

Erin was back, reading over his shoulder again. "Rudy says five minutes for the notepads and pens. Hey, look, they think he might have done a bunch of other robberies."

Dan resumed reading. The story went on to mention that the authorities suspected Fetch Mcdonald might be the Everyman Bank Robber who'd gotten away with 14 other bank robberies, but they had no evidence to connect him with those crimes, which remained unsolved with close to half-a-million dollars still missing.

Dan started scribbling the facts on hotel stationery; he'd transfer the information to a notepad later. Erin watched him work, understanding now that he had a different plan in mind. Not the one she was thinking of. Dan clicked on the earlier Fetch Mcdonald story.

It was a wedding announcement. With a photo of the betrothed.

Fetch Mcdonald, a sales rep for Xerox, was going to marry Verene Digby, an administrative assistant with the Baxter Brothers appliance stores.

"Did we look that young when we got married?" Erin asked. "Seems impossible."

"You still look that young," Dan said.

His wife smiled at him.

"On your better days."

She smacked him on the back of his head.

He laughed and wrote down the name Verene Digby.

"Was I a prettier bride?"

"Of course."

"No punchline?"

"Especially with your clothes off."

Erin kissed the spot she'd whacked. Dan clicked on the Archer Mcdonald story.

There was another picture. Fetch was a kid this time, standing with his mother, Dorothy, in a courtroom as — in the foreground — his father, Archer Mcdonald, was led off to prison.

"Jeez," Erin said, reading ahead, "this guy's a bankrobber and the son of a bankrobber."

Dan took down the information, without the Jeez. Then he exited the Web site and turned to his wife. You may have noticed I'm working on something here."

"I did. I've got an idea for you, too."

Dan stood up, slipped an arm around Erin's waist and led her over to the sofa, not worrying about soiling it this time. He was already feeling proprietary about their new digs. He thought Erin might sit on his lap again, but she sat beside him.

"I think there may be a book here," Dan said.

"Where?" Erin asked.

"Getting robbed by this Mcdonald guy and whoever's helping him."

"Yeah? True crime?"

Dan nodded. He could see Erin was already jazzed.

"Call it *Kidnapping Ben Hecht,*"Dan said.

"That's terrific. But you know how it'd have to work, don't you?"

"How?" inquired the man who'd had the idea.

"We'd have to be the ones to solve the case. I mean, if you're looking for a killer hook."

"Interesting context for the word killer. Fugitive bank robber and all. We'll investigate ... as long as we don't expose ourselves to any actual danger."

"Maybe a little?" Erin held her thumb and index finger an inch apart. "It'd add some spice to the narrative."

Dan laughed. His wife was incorrigible, and likely a bit loony.

"Okay, a little. But we leave the heavy lifting to the cops. That's why I asked Les if he knew somebody I could call."

Les'd had a name. But hadn't known if the guy was still around.

Erin took Dan's hands in hers. "My turn. I've brought you to this wonderful place to put you in the mood — and no, not for that."

"What then?" Dan asked.

"I want you to tell me a story."

"Any story in particular?" he asked warily.

Erin felt Dan's discomfort and held on tight. Looked him right in the eye.

"I want you to tell me *Time Expires*. We've got all your notes, your outline, your bios, even your last chapter. You won't have to do any actual writing. Just tell it to me. I'll transcribe it on my Powerbook."

Erin released her husband. The decision was in Dan's hands now.

"You think I can remember 412 pages verbatim?" he asked.

"No. But I bet you remember a lot more than you'd think, and if you change a word here or there, so what? You're worried about finding your novel, right? Well, we already know where one copy is: right inside your noggin. Are you willing to give it a try?"

Dan knew better than to just say no. But he wanted to pout. Or shout. He'd just spent nine months — busting his ass — to write that novel. He shouldn't have to do it all over again.

But Erin didn't relent.

"This Fetch Mcdonald character may have come back to his hometown, but unless he is really dumb, he isn't going to stay here. Your publisher might start screaming for the manuscript long before we catch him."

Dan grunted. Both in agreement and displeasure.

"Let me think about it, okay?"

"Not too long."

Could he do it, he wondered. Could he even reproduce a novel without his Remington?

"Not too long," he agreed.

In the meantime, though, he suggested they check the Buffalo phone book and see if there were any Mcdonalds in it.

Before they could do that, though, there was a discreet knock at the door.

Rudy with the notepads and pens.

The cop got right to the point with Archer Mcdonald. "Where the hell is he old man?" Meaning Fetch.

The speaker was the oldest of the four cops on Archer's porch, maybe all of thirty years old. Another one was peeking in the living room window. The peeper shook his head at the other cops. The one who'd done the talking gave a nod and two of the cops went around back.

Archer felt flattered that they thought it'd take the remaining two to keep an eye on him.

"Who?" he asked innocently.

The cop pointed his gun at the bridge of Archer's nose, looked like he might shoot him dead right there. Being an ex-con, he knew that was more of a possibility than if he'd been John Q. Public. No longer flattered, Archer felt his bowels knot, and hated the cop for terrorizing him.

"Where the hell is your son, Fetch? You went to see him yesterday at Camp Alphonse."

"That's right where I left him, too." Archer let his eyes go wide. "You tellin' me Fetch broke out? That's crazy. He's gettin' out on parole in three weeks."

"Not anymore, he's not," the cop snarled.

"Well, I hope to God you don't think I got him."

Archer kept a close watch on the cop's trigger finger.

"You don't," the cop said, "you'll let us take a look inside your place."

Archer ached to tell the bastard to go fuck himself if he didn't have a search warrant. Instead he kicked the door open and extended an arm in mock welcome. "Look all you want. Place is so small it won't take long."

The cop lowered his gun and brushed past the old bank robber. The other one kept an eye, if not his weapon, on Archer. Which Archer felt was a great improvement. As predicted, all the cops were soon out front again. Letting Archer know he wasn't out of the woods yet.

"Here's the deal, old man," said the cop who'd pointed the gun at him. He was in Archer's face again, so close Archer could smell chicken-salad on his breath. Heavy on the onion. "You hear from your son, you call us. You take him in, you get word to us. You don't, we'll get you for obstruction, harboring a fugitive. You want to go back to the joint at your age?"

"Wait right here, okay?" Archer asked.

Thinking Archer might be about to cooperate, the cop nodded. Archer went inside. Five minutes later, the four cops saw him tape a hand-lettered sign to the inside of his living room window and their faces tightened with anger. Archer walked back outside with a battered suitcase in his hand. He locked his front door behind him.

"You're a wiseass, aren't you, old man?" the cop sneered.

Archer's sign read: *The cops run me outta my own house with threats of jail. Gone into hiding. A.M.*

For the first time, Archer let his anger show. "I can't help my boy if he don't know where the hell to find me, now can I?"

Not waiting for an answer, the old bank robber walked to a 20-year-old Pontiac parked at the curb and drove off. He tried to look fearless, but stayed well within the speed limit and checked his rearview mirror every other heartbeat. He'd gotten away clean, though.

The cops weren't following him.

***

Dan and Erin were.

Rudy had gotten them a white Chevy Impala rental almost as quickly as he'd arranged for the notepads and pens. Then they'd all looked at the listings for Mcdonalds in the Buffalo phone book; there were no Archer Mcdonalds, but there were four A. Mcdonalds.

Dan had asked, "If one of these people was a former bank robber, where would he live?"

Rudy had pointed to the address on Prospect Road.

And showed them on a map how to find it.

Dan and Erin had arrived in time to see the whole drama with Archer and the cops.

They followed him as he drove off.

"What do you think of Rudy now?" Erin asked.

"He just earned an acknowledgment in my new book," Dan told her.

CHAPTER 8

Gamble Murtree turned sixty that Monday, and he wasn't at all sure he liked it. He hadn't minded any of his other birthdays that ended in a zero, not even the last one. Hell, at fifty he'd considered himself to be in his prime, an FBI special agent in charge of the bank robbery detail for the Buffalo field office. He'd had a record replete with commendations, and with Bill Clinton just getting started in the Oval Office — as Gamble had turned 50 — a black man could hope that no position in the bureau would be beyond his reach.

Except for the top one, of course. At least for him. Skin color aside, Gamble knew he just didn't have the right appearance. At five-eight and one-ninety-five, he was a fireplug. Not that he was fat, not a bit. But with the arms, shoulders, and chest he had on him, well, people were more likely to figure him for a steelworker than a federal agent.

Only steel workers didn't dress in pinstriped suits and two-hundred-dollar wingtips. Didn't graduate *summa cum laude* from Morehouse College. Didn't get a law degree from Emory University. Didn't take down two armed bank robbers after being shot in the leg.

Didn't ... hell, didn't fail to make the one big case that could have meant a bump to a special-agent-in-charge slot and then some pie-in-the-sky day a deputy director's job.

Now, at sixty, a lifelong bachelor, and wearing casual clothes, he was retired two years and wondering what in God's name he was going to do with the rest of his life. Which could be a very long time, as his daddy was still farming down in Georgia at 92.

He left his condo on South Elmwood, walking distance from the Dulski Federal Building where he used to work, and went out for a coffee and a bran muf— No! No damn muffin today. A man turned sixty, he deserved a cinnamon roll. Maybe two. He'd already begun to indulge himself, sleeping in and loafing around almost to lunchtime.

He picked up a copy of the *News* from the vending machine outside of Teddy's, the diner he'd favored ever since he'd hit town thirteen years ago. Thirteen years. He could hardly believe it. Paper said the Sabres just made the Stanley Cup finals. That was hard to believe, too.

The hockey team was going places, though.

He was just hanging around, and for what? Actually, he knew for what. He just didn't know if he'd ever get it.

Doubt had been creeping in since he retired.

Gamble pushed open Teddy's front door. The diner was mostly empty as the midday rush had yet to start. He took his preferred stool at the counter, the one all the way across the room from where the TV was on — and it was on every minute the place was open.

The owners, a Greek family named Mylonas, had used that TV, an old black-and-white Zenith that never seemed to break down, to teach English to three generations of relatives from the Old Country. Adara, the grandniece of the owner, who was new and didn't have many hours of TV under her belt, nodded and smiled at Gamble as he sat down. She then nudged her Uncle Nicky who was watching a soap opera. He glanced at Gamble and told her in their native tongue what the former fed would order.

The young woman quickly brought Gamble a cup of coffee and a bran muffin. She smiled at him, hoping she'd done well, and said, "Dollar ninety-sex."

Gamble replied gently, "I think you mean a dollar ninety-six."

The girl furrowed her brow. "Six no sex?"

Gamble nodded. "Six." He still wanted a cinnamon roll. "You know cinnamon?"

"You add tip if you like me," Adara replied, hoping that covered the question.

Gamble followed with a non-sequitur of his own. "It's my birthday."

Birthday, Adara knew. She beamed, leaned forward, and kissed Gamble's cheeks.

"Birthday presents, yes?"

"Very nice presents," Gamble said, heat rising in his face. He couldn't remember the last time he'd been kissed, even on his cheeks.

Adara turned and called to Uncle Nicky in Greek, telling him of the occasion. Her timing was good as Nicky's soap opera had just ended and gone to commercial. He came rushing down the counter to shake Gamble's hand.

"How many years do you have, my friend?"

"Sixty," Gamble said neutrally.

Adara said brightly, "Sixty no sexty."

Nicky gave her a puzzled look for a moment, then turned his attention back to Gamble and whipped out a menu for him.

"Anything you want, my friend. On our house. If not on menu, I make special."

Adara pointed out her favorite entree. Nicky countered with his opinion. The two of them immediately fell into a passionate debate that was Greek to Gamble. All he wanted, really, was a cinnamon roll. Maybe two.

He was about to make his point when a face appeared on the TV screen across the diner that stopped him cold. Fetch Mcdonald.

Gamble recognized him immediately — even with the beard. He hurried across the room, straining to tune out the arguing Greeks and hear the narration of the news bulletin. He missed a word here and there but he got the gist of it.

Fetch Mcdonald had escaped from Camp Alphonse.

Three weeks before he was due to be paroled.

He was thought to have broken into a cabin being used by author Daniel Cameron.

The picture from Dan's book jacket momentarily replaced Fetch Mcdonald's prison ID photo. Then a blonde anchorwoman came on.

"Mcdonald was at one time suspected of being the Everyman Bank Robber, but the authorities could never make that case. Even though he used no actual weapons in the robbery of a credit union for which he was imprisoned, police officials say that any inmate who escapes confinement has to be considered dangerous, and it's thought that Fetch Mcdonald was headed for home — right here in Buffalo — when he broke out this morning."

Fetch Mcdonald, Gamble thought again.

The reason he'd stayed in Buffalo so long.

The man who'd dead-ended his career.

The man he'd been unable to prove was the Everyman Bank Robber.

Until it was too late.

Fetch was finally going for all that cash he'd hidden almost eight years ago. And retired or not, Gamble Murtree was going to catch him.

Nicky and Adara tracked down the birthday boy, still looking to give him a free feed.

"What I want," he told them, "is a coffee and two cinnamon rolls. To go."

Fetch woke from his nap uncertain for a moment of where he was. The softness of the bed on which he lay was the first thing to remind him that he was no longer in any penal institution. Then he noticed there were curtains on the windows not bars or wire mesh. The feather pillow beneath his head and the light cotton blanket covering him were as soothing as a lover's embrace.

Lover. Verene. Jesus!

He had to get up. He had work to do. He had to dig up all his money and find his wife before she married ... no his wife could not get married. That'd make her a bigamist. Verene was his *ex*-wife — that was the first time he ever thought of her that way — and it left a bitter taste in his mouth.

Any-fucking-way, he had to get his money and find Verene. Before she could marry that fucking Karl ... whatever the hell his last name was.

He rolled out of bed and came to an abrupt halt. Looked around. Saw no one. Listened. It was a damn hard thing for a man fresh out of the joint to accept he was actually alone.

Fetch thought he heard the old blind lady downstairs, singing along with a record or the radio in French. For a dizzying moment that took him right back to his childhood. About the only time he could remember his mother smiling was when she'd danced with him and hummed along to old records. As often as not, blues records.

In particular, Billie Holliday's rendition of *God Bless the Child*. Which Lerome had given to her after a trip to New Orleans.

His mother had started dancing with Fetch when he was a baby. He'd seen black-and- white snapshots his Uncle Rene, Lerome's dad, had taken of him in his mother's arms, the two of them looking impossibly happy as they moved to the music. As he'd grown older, Mama had shown him real dance steps, everything from the waltz to the tango, the jitterbug to the polka. The quiet lady who had punched a cash register at the Tops supermarket eight hours a day had one joy in her life and she'd shared it with her son.

She'd taught Lerome to dance, too; he'd loved his Aunt Dottie. Had called her *mon autre mère*. My other mother. But as cool as Lerome was, the dance floor was the one place where Fetch was cooler. He was a natural. His steps were so sure and light, his movements so fluid, it was like he had music flowing through his veins instead of blood.

When Fetch was fifteen, he and his mother went to a party in honor of Lerome's Confirmation, his mother accepting the invitation only after she'd heard her estranged father was too sick to attend. As they danced, his mother told Fetch, "Any girl who dances with you will feel beautiful for as long as the music plays and you hold her in your arms."

That compliment made Fetch's heart soar for all of three seconds. Until he heard his Uncle Louis say, "That little sonofagun's just as smooth out there as his no-good old man ever was. Better warn all the good families with girls quick."

The fat fucker hadn't even tried to keep his voice down.

Fetch stood paralyzed as he tried to think of something he could do that would be both vicious and acceptable within the context of a family gathering. His mother beat him to the punch. She threw a glass of wine — not just the wine, the glass, too — at her eldest brother and chipped both his front teeth.

As Uncle Louis sat there sputtering and turning as red as the wine that stained his shirt, he grabbed a dessert fork. Nobody doubted that he intended to implant it somewhere in his sister. Now, Fetch was on the move, but again he was anticipated. Uncle Rene, the host of the party, yanked his older brother out of his chair and hurried him to the door, jamming his hat on his head and shoving his coat against his chest. Uncle Rene didn't try to keep his voice down, either.

"You provoked Dorothy, Louie. You insulted our nephew and my godson, Fetch, who has never done anything to offend you, me, or anyone else. And you've ruined Lerome's Confirmation party. Now, get out and don't talk to me again until you're ready to apologize."

Lerome didn't think his party was ruined. He thought his dad had made it great. Uncle Louis differed. He never spoke to his youngest brother again.

And Fetch wished, not for the first time, that Uncle Rene was his dad, too.

The music downstairs stopped playing, the old blind lady stopped singing, and Fetch snapped out of his reverie. He looked around again.

It was going to take some getting used to not having somebody — cons or correctional officers — watching his every move. Assuming he stayed free long enough to get used to privacy again.

He walked quietly down the hall to use the bathroom. After he peed and washed his hands, he looked inside the medicine cabinet. It was there, he looked, that simple. The concept of private property that wasn't enforced by threat of death would also have to be reacquired.

There wasn't much of interest. Box of band-aids and a few ancient cosmetic items. Eyebrow pencil, pancake make-up and ... a bottle of hair dye. Black. Fetch grabbed it and closed the mirrored door.

The old blind lady had white hair. But maybe before she lost her sight and was still able to give a damn about appearances she'd colored her hair. Fetch looked at his reflection.

Getting rid of his beard had been a good first step in altering his appearance, but there were still people who remembered what he'd looked like without it. Changing his hair to a color it had never been, that would be good. Maybe he'd change his eye color, too, like he'd done with the contact lenses. Have Lerome pick up some for him.

He wondered, though, could he trust a bottle of dye that said best used by AUG 99? Hell, wasn't like he hadn't taken enough chances already.

Fetch started the water running in the sink. He began thinking about the order in which he'd retrieve his stashes of cash. Imagining the smile on Verene's face when she saw him with all his money.

Remembering how much she'd liked his dancing.

Karl Hyacinth had his hand up Verene Digby's skirt. Not that it had far to go. Verene wore her skirts short. And when she sat on Karl's lap in his office at his insurance agency, it pretty much rode up around her waist like a hula-hoop.

But when Karl tried to edge aside the filmy fabric of Verene's panties and go straight for the Promised Land, he felt her hand land on his crotch. Grabbing hold just hard enough to imply there would be serious pain if he tried to explore any farther.

"Not yet, baby," Verene whispered, her breath hot in Karl's ear. "We're gonna wait until our honeymoon, remember?"

Verene had always told him she was an old-fashioned girl at heart. When he'd come to accept that there would be no intercourse until they were married, he'd tried to negotiate some oral gratification from his beloved — saying that nobody from the guy in the Oval Office on down to kids in middle school considered that was real sex anymore.

Verene had replied, "Honey, if giving head wasn't sex, hookers couldn't charge for it."

The businessman in Karl couldn't argue with that.

Now, he was mollified as Verene undid her blouse and let him nuzzle her cleavage.

He was deeply engaged when Verene's cell phone rang. He paid no attention when she answered and began a conversation. He never saw the wicked smile that lit the face of his betrothed. He was too busy listening to his pounding pulse and ...

His hand darted between her thighs like a heat-seeking missile. This time — hallelujah! — she didn't try to restrain him physically.

All she did was whisper in his ear once more.

"Baby, I just got some news."

Karl was not interested. His target was in sight.

"Remember I told you about my ex-husband, the bank robber?"

Karl's fingers started to twitch.

"Seems he broke out of prison this morning."

Karl's hand went into full carpal-tunnel lock up. He pulled it away from Verene and held it against his chest with his other hand.

Verene stood up and rolled down her skirt; she always wore wrinkle-resistant fabric. She buttoned her blouse and slipped into her fuck-me pumps. With a fluff of her hair, she was ready to go out in public. An old-fashioned girl once more.

By now, Karl had recovered sufficiently to ask, "You think he'll be caught soon? Your ex-husband."

"He fell off the lifts in his shoes trying to make his getaway."

"That's right," Karl said, grinning. "I remember you telling me that."

"He'll be locked up tight for a long, long time before our wedding day." Verene bent over and gave Karl a kiss with plenty of tongue. Then with a hand on each of his shoulders, she added, "But until the cops catch him, we have to be careful, okay?"

"Absolutely," he agreed.

To make sure Karl stayed in the right frame of mind, Verene let him give her boobs one last squeeze before she left.

Dan and Erin followed Archer to a house on Norwood Avenue south of Bryant. The area was neatly middle class with well-maintained single and two-family homes. The Camerons saw the old bank robber swing his aged Pontiac into the driveway of a rehabbed Victorian with lots of gingerbread ornamentation and leaded glass eyebrows over the front windows and doorway. Dan pulled the rental Chevy to the curb up the street as the beater disappeared around the back of the house — where it couldn't be seen from the street.

Stifling a yawn, Erin wrote down the house's address.

"Sonofagun's moving up in the world, isn't he?" she asked.

Dan stared at the house. It looked too pretty for a fugitive's hideout, he thought.

"I don't think he's got Fetch in there, do you?" he asked Erin.

When he didn't get an answer, he looked over at his wife. She was nodding off, her eyes just about shut.

"Erin, you okay?" He gently rocked her shoulder. Her eyelids opened grudgingly, one millimeter at a time.

"Didn't sleep last night," she mumbled. "Guess it's caught up with me."

Truer words ... her eyes closed once more.

Dan saw Archer Mcdonald appear in a front window of the gingerbread Victorian. He'd apparently entered the house through a rear door, but he wasn't trying to be furtive about his presence. He opened the window and stuck his head out, looking up and down the street as if he was expecting to see someone.

Not exactly the behavior of a burglar, Dan knew. Archer belonged in the house.

The old bank robber looked directly at the white Chevy, and then right past it. The car blended into the neighborhood perfectly. As for the couple sitting inside, they fit, too. The woman seemed to be napping, the man was writing something down. Jotting a reminder before he took off.

Something like that.

Watching surreptitiously over the notes he was making for his new book, Dan saw the old robber's expression change. His eyes widened and a grin lit his face. He ducked back inside and lowered the window. A moment later, an electric blue Corvette Stingray — a '67, Dan thought — rumbled past the parked rental car.

Dan got just a glimpse of the driver, but he thought that vulpine face surrounded by all that russet hair reminded him a whole lot of the photo he'd seen of Verene Digby. Fetch Mcdonald's fiancée of some years back. The Corvette turned into the driveway of the Victorian.

Dan made a note. Fetch's father and his ex-wife together. He still didn't think Fetch was in there with them.

Nah, he wasn't. The old man wouldn't have been sticking his head out the window. He'd have been drawing the curtains, shutting out the world. And Verene — Dan was now sure that was who he'd seen — hadn't even looked around as she drove past. Not a sign she was looking for anyone following her or staking out the house.

Fetch wasn't in the Victorian. There was nothing for Dan to bring to the cops. Not yet, anyway.

He would've liked to ask Erin what she thought was going on, but by now her head was resting against the passenger-side window. He'd let her sleep. Maybe get Rudy to carry her up to their suite. But before he did that there was one thing he could do.

Go back to Archer's old dive and look at the sign he'd put in his window.

They'd been parked too far away to read it before.

Maybe it was nothing, but a good reporter never overlooked details.

Dan started the Chevy and drove off, trying to make it a smooth ride so he wouldn't disturb his sleeping wife.

CHAPTER 9

Lerome pulled into the parking lot of the Delaware Park branch of the Buffalo Public Library in Jessi Jaymes' Porsche 911 Turbo. Cool car, Lerome thought. Midnight blue. The color got Lerome thinking. A blue that deep had pretty much all the weight of black but it also had a little element of surprise. Like a grin or a wink you weren't expecting. He might have to expand his palette a bit.

Then he looked at the Remington. Black was exactly right for some things. So if he was going to experiment, he'd have to be careful.

He grabbed the typewriter, got out of the car, activated its electronic security system and walked into the one-story red brick building through the rear entrance. He'd left the box of stationery behind. Ants, being a librarian, had all the paper she'd ever need.

She sat on her chair behind the circulation desk as he approached. This time of day, Lerome knew, the other two librarians would be at lunch. Mondays, they liked to go out for Mexican. Have a margarita if they were feeling daring. With school out, there could be a kid or two around working as summer help. Ants could send them out, too, if she wanted.

As for the reading public, Lerome saw one elderly couple just heading out the front door, their week's supply of books being carried off in two canvas bags. And that was it. Lerome had always liked the feel of a quiet library. This was despite the fact that he was a slow reader. At school, they'd thought at first maybe he was dyslexic like his dad. It wasn't quite like that. It just took him longer than usual to process visual symbols.

People, on the other hand, he could read at a glance.

Like now. Ants wasn't looking at him, had her head down reading a magazine that lay on the counter in front of her. But she knew he was approaching. He could see the tension increasing in her upper body: head, shoulders, and arms all getting ready to lift and deal with whoever might be coming at her.

So he stopped.

Looked at her. Ants had dark brown hair. Almost black. Behind the clear-lens glasses that she wore only for effect were dark brown eyes. She had a strong nose, generous mouth, and chiseled jaw line. She was five-nine and, Lerome guessed, about one-forty. The right size for someone like him at six-three.

"You playing games?" she asked, still not looking up.

She knew who she was talking to. Lerome stepped up to the desk.

"Brought you something."

Ants looked up and grinned. Lerome knew right then he was in love with her.

He didn't give it a second thought that she'd done eight years in prison — same as Fetch — for manslaughter. When Ants had gotten tired of slugging it out with her husband, a year after her son had been born, she'd gotten into her car with the baby to leave. Her husband stood at the end of the driveway with his arms spread, as if to block her departure.

Ants ran him flat over. Spent her time on the manslaughter rap earning degrees in library and computer sciences. Lost custody of her son to her late husband's parents, who'd since disappeared with the boy. She'd spent the two years she'd been out looking for Jimmy via cyberspace.

She told Lerome, "Other girls get flowers, candy, maybe a necklace if they're lucky. I get a typewriter."

"With a brand new ribbon," Lerome pointed out.

She laughed, leaned over the counter and kissed him.

"Everything go all right this morning?" she asked.

Lerome had told her about going to get Fetch.

"Pretty much."

"Did I have it right, why he broke out?"

"Unh-huh."

Ants had told Lerome it had to be a woman. Jessi had almost attempted the same thing, until Ants had talked her out of it.

"What's he going to do now?"

"Remains to be seen. I've got to get back to him. I just wanted to drop by and give you your gift."

Ants kissed him again. "It's great. A cool little machine."

Knowing people the way he did, Lerome asked, "But?"

"Well ... I got one just like it in the store room."

She showed him. Turned out she had two just like it. Almost. The first was another Remington Noiseless Portable. Black. Dusty not glossy. But a dead ringer once it was cleaned and polished. The other machine looked just the same only its brand name was Underwood.

"I think they were both made by the same company," Ants said. "I'll check and see."

Acting on instinct, Lerome said, "Can you put these two aside for me?"

"They're the library's, but disposable property. I can sell them to you."

"Yeah, whatever you want for them."

"I'm going to keep the one from you."

"Sure, who else'd give you a typewriter?"

Ants laughed and embraced Lerome. For a long time she'd thought she'd never find another man to love. Or had even wanted to. She'd given women a good long try, but her heart just wasn't in it.

"You going to want a receipt?" she asked Lerome. "For the typewriters."

"No," he answered.

"Okay, cash then. As far as the library's concerned, Joe Blow bought them."

"Better make it ... Lorenz Altbusser," Lerome suggested.

"Middleman cutout, huh? Bet you've been talking to Jessi."

Lerome deactivated the security system on Jessi's Porsche and entered the car. The box of stationery sat right where he left it on the shelf behind the seats. He should have given it to Ants, even if she didn't need it. What else was he going to do with it?

Not throw it away; Lerome hated waste.

He decided to take a look at the paper inside the box. See if there was anything special about it. Maybe that'd suggest a place he could donate it, if he didn't want to go back and bother Ants with it. He grabbed the box and pulled the top off.

Saw right away what was special.

The paper was written on ... by the Remington?

Yeah. Had to be. The box'd been right there with the typewriter when he'd taken it.

Time Expires. By Daniel Cameron.

The good thing about being a slow reader, Lerome thought, it gave you time to sort out what the words were telling you. He knew what he had before he even riffled through the thick stack of paper. He had Daniel Cameron's story here. Three hundred and ninety-two pages of it.

Man must've put a lot of work into that, Lerome decided.

Meant he had to be looking for it. Hard.

Pulling out of the library lot, Lerome wondered if he had any stories that'd be worth taking that many pages to tell. Accelerating past the Albright-Knox Art Gallery, where he and Ants went to the free jazz concerts on Sunday nights, he thought, yeah, he did have some stories.

At least a couple.

The dye worked.

Fetch found a hand mirror in the bathroom vanity and checked out the back of his head. The hair back there was evenly covered, too. He hadn't missed any spots. As for the color, well, it was a little intense. But not so bad it'd stop people on the street.

He was still young enough at thirty-six, it could be real.

Even if it wasn't perfect, it went a long way toward changing his appearance.

With Lerome still gone, Fetch was at a loss for something to do. There was a phone in the bedroom; he was tempted to call Verene just to hear her voice again. But he wasn't sure how she'd react. They hadn't talked since he'd gotten the divorce papers from her at Camp Alphonse.

He'd called immediately that day.

Verene had told him, "I'm sorry, Fetch. I won't ask for alimony."

Big concession to a guy making 17¢ an hour. Fetch'd tried to play it like a joke.

"Great sense of humor, Verene."

But she didn't have anything more to say and hung up on him. When he tried again the next day the number was no longer in service. So if he wanted to call her now, he'd have to get Verene's new number from 411, if it was listed.

If she'd talk to him.

If she wasn't actually in love with this prick Karl.

For all his doubt and dread, Fetch couldn't help himself. He had to talk with Verene. He had to know if he stood a chance with her. He picked up the phone — and heard the old blind lady yakking at someone in French. What a dipshit he was. Of course, this phone was an extension. And the old lady paused in her frog-talk as if she'd heard him pick up.

Him, Mr. Connelly, who was supposed to be mute.

He eased the phone silently back into its cradle. If the old woman wondered what had happened, so what? He hadn't said anything.

Cut off from his desperation call, Fetch realized he'd been lucky. His escape had to be TV news by now. If Verene knew about it, if she got a call from him, if she didn't love him anymore — that fucking Karl — she might actually call the cops. Then where would he be?

In deep doo-doo was where.

Besides, he didn't want to just hear Verene's voice. He wanted to see her, hold her, smell her, taste her. Hell, he wanted to *absorb* her. After eight years, that was only natural.

So the thing to do was ... show her the money!

Fetch had seen the video of *Jerry McGuire* at Camp Alphonse. Greed, sex, and sports were perennial favorites among the inmate population. The staff, too.

He was sure that Verene was still as mercenary as any pro athlete who'd ever lived.

If she didn't love him, she'd love his money. And then learn to love him again.

Lerome had left that Cameron guy's wallet with Fetch. It had a nice chunk of cash in it. He'd need the money to buy a knapsack, a collapsible entrenching tool, and an NFTA bus ride or two. He stuffed the wad of bills in his pocket. He was about to drop the wallet back on the dresser where it had lain when he noticed a photo ID.

Daniel Cameron. *Chicago Tribune.*

Now that Fetch's hair was black, he had to admit ... there was some resemblance.

But he shoved that thought aside. He had business to attend to.

He found a pad of paper and an old ballpoint in the room's nightstand.

He left a note for Lerome printed in block letters: *Back by five.*

He hoped.

Fetch made it with time to spare. Got back by four-thirty and found Lerome lying on his bed reading a sheet of paper. Lerome had a stack of fifteen, maybe twenty pages to his right, and a box of paper — the one from the cabin that morning? — on his left. There was a big plastic bag from Target sitting on the overstuffed chair in the near corner of the room.

Lerome looked up at Fetch and smiled. "Your hair looks good."

Then he added, "Otherwise, something's bothering you."

Fetch picked up the Target bag and glanced inside. Pants, shirts, underwear, socks. A Nike shoebox. None of the clothes was black, so Fetch knew they were for him. He dropped the bag on the floor and flopped into the chair.

"The money's gone, Lerome," Fetch said in a ragged whisper.

Lerome wasn't supposed to know about the money, but he did.

"Sorry to hear that."

"You knew?" Fetch wasn't really surprised.

"I suspected."

"I never said a word," Fetch mumbled. "Not to anyone."

"That was good. Knowing would make someone an accomplice."

"But you knew." This time it wasn't a question.

"Figured it out. You had a heckuva streak going. Until that last job."

"Fucking repo man stealing my stolen car," Fetch muttered bitterly.

"Or you could blame the guy who'd missed his payments," Lerome suggested.

Through eight years of confinement, Fetch had never looked at it that way. Now he nodded his head. "Him, too, the fucker."

"I thought for a while maybe I'd go get the money and hold it for you," Lerome told him.

"How'd you know?" Fetch moaned. "How'd anybody know."

"Come on, man." Lerome sat up, gathered the pages he'd read and stacked them neatly sideways across the ones in the box. "Everybody suspected you were the Everyman Bank Robber. Cops couldn't prove it was all."

"Damn right, they couldn't. But what I meant was, how'd you, or anybody, know where I hid the money?"

Lerome moved to the end of the bed, put his feet on the floor, and rested his forearms across his legs. He looked right at Fetch.

"Just anybody couldn't know. But take me for example. I know you're the neatest, best organized guy I ever met."

Lerome had always thought this was Fetch's way of compensating for his family life being so fucked up. Not that he'd ever said so.

"That was the giveaway?" Fetch demanded, incredulous.

"Back when you were selling copiers, making some nice money, what was the first thing you did when you got your paycheck?"

"Put it in the bank."

"And the second thing?"

"Enter the deposit in my check book."

"All those things you were buying Verene back then, you paid by check as I recall."

"Yeah, who the hell needs credit card debt?"

Fetch still didn't see what Lerome was getting at, and he was losing patience.

"You ever forget to enter any of those deposits or purchases in your check register?"

"Hell, no. You get out of balance, you tear your hair out trying to straighten out the numbers, maybe bounce a check, have the bank slap you with an NSF charge."

"So, all your deposits and all the checks you wrote were very orderly?"

"Yes, goddamnit! Now, stop screwin' with me and—"

"Fetch, I guessed a long time ago how you decided to hide your take. You pulled a job and right away you needed a safe place to put your money. Just like you always took your paycheck straight to the bank. Now, I didn't think you kept anything in writing, where you hid the loot."

"Glad you don't think I'm that damn dumb," Fetch grumbled.

Lerome continued, "But I knew you'd have an easy — orderly — way of remembering where you stashed the take from each job. I also assumed you hid the money right here in town. Me, I'd have taken it up to Canada."

"I don't like Canada as much as you do."

Fetch never visited any of the D'Arnoles up there the way Lerome did.

Lerome grinned. "That's why I knew the money was right here in Buffalo. What else were you going to do, drive to Cleveland and hide it? Unh-uh. So the money's here and, you being you, it's buried in some neat sequence just like deposits noted in a check register."

Lerome sighed. He wasn't trying to show off. Didn't want to make it seem like Fetch's ingenious plan was about as tough to grasp as tic-tac-toe.

"It makes you feel any better, I had to look at a map before I worked it out."

"But then you saw it right away."

"Yeah. The map had zip codes printed right on it, and that's what you used, Buffalo zip codes. Made them your check register. You took the swag from your first job and buried it somewhere in the 14201 zip code. Some park or other place where nobody'd ever build a Starbucks on top of your money. Somewhere nobody'd be looking when you hid your loot. Or when you dug it up."

Lerome had nailed Fetch. He felt bad about it but played it out.

"The money from your second job you buried somewhere in 14202. You kept on right through 14214. I thought maybe you even took things a step farther. Like in 01 you'd buried the money near an apple tree."

"Alder," Fetch said, stricken.

"Okay. Then birch, cherry, dogwood, elm. Like that."

Fetch looked like he was about to cry. Eight years in the joint, and for what?

Lerome knew he didn't have to say it, but he did anyway.

"It wasn't me, Fetch."

Fetch shook his head, then found his voice.

"Never thought it was."

"But you know who it has to be, right? Someone who knows you."

Fetch managed to choke out the name. "Verene."

"Your dad, too," Lerome added. "He was the one brought you the news about Verene getting married."

Fetch nodded disconsolately.

"Fucking old man," he said.

95

"They set you up. Got you to break jail so you'd get caught, get sent back, have your sentence extended a long time. Then no sweat. They enjoy your money and you can't bother them."

Fetch understood things now. At least some of them. When had Verene decided to divorce him? The day she'd dug up the last of his money. Her and his rotten old man. If he'd had the two of them in front of him, no question he'd kill them both.

As it was, he decided to take advantage of a cooler head. "What do I do now, Lerome?"

Lerome told his cousin — his brother — that he'd sold his business recently and he was perfectly willing to give Fetch the same half-share of the proceeds he'd offered way back when. Lerome didn't know exactly how much money Fetch had gotten away with, but he'd bet what he was offering was even more. Fetch could take the money with Lerome's thanks, go to Costa Rica maybe, forget the past, and have a nice life.

Fetch shook his head sadly. "Thanks, but I can't do that. Just can't."

Lerome knew why. Ever the poor relation, Fetch simply couldn't accept charity. Not even from him. Maybe especially not from him. Lerome understood how Fetch felt. The guy had robbed his banks fair and square. His acts had been criminal but he'd earned every dollar.

"Okay," Lerome said. "Here are a couple other things to think about."

"What?"

"If Verene's really getting married a week from Saturday, she must be around. Nearby, anyway. Why would she do that? Take a chance you'd find out about the money being gone and grab her?"

Fetch hadn't thought about that. Lerome had.

"What I think, this guy she's got lined up must have

some money."

Now Fetch saw. "She's gonna strip him bare."

"Unless we get him first," Lerome said.

Fetch finally smiled. Fucking Karl, they'd fix his ass. Verene's, too.

Then he remembered what Lerome had just said.

"What else? You said there were a couple things."

Lerome pulled the stationery box forward, picked up the top pages.

"When I took that typewriter this morning, I didn't know it but I grabbed a story, too. The man must've used the typewriter to write it."

Fetch didn't get it. "So?"

"Well, I'm just getting into it but already I can see ..." Lerome grinned. "...the man has some interesting ideas about how to commit crimes."

CHAPTER 10

Erin made it up to their suite without any help from Rudy, but she fell asleep leaning against Dan as he opened the door. He had to carry her across the threshold. Made him feel like they were honeymooners again, carrying the sweet weight of his wife in his arms. He kicked the door shut behind him. They weren't newlyweds anymore, but they still did pretty well for themselves. Making love up against a tree.

As Dan gently deposited Erin on their creampuff hotel bed, he wanted her again.

But he didn't have the heart to wake her.

He kissed her brow lightly and stared down at her. Looking better than ever, he thought. It scared him when he thought how close he might've come to losing her. He knew they'd been emotionally flat a couple years back. Erin had been repressing the hell out of her natural instinct to bungee jump off the Golden Gate ... while he'd been comfortable in his job and was prone to coasting. Probably never would have written his novel without Erin.

Without her giving him the Remington.

That was why there was no way he could turn down her request to try to recreate *Time Expires*, even though it infuriated him every time he thought about losing his manuscript. He'd have to get over that. Work with Erin full out. Because if she hadn't actually saved their marriage, she'd at least made it a hell of a lot of fun again. He'd have to honor her wish and ... God, he hoped Erin got pregnant, and their daughter would look exactly like her.

Dan left the bedroom and closed the door just as the phone rang. He grabbed it before it could ring again. Rudy was calling.

"A gentleman formerly with the FBI would like to see you, Mr. Cameron."

FBI? Formerly? What the heck?

Whatever the reason this guy had for wanting to see him, it might be good material for *Kidnapping Ben Hecht*.

"Send him right up."

The former FBI man, Dan saw, was short, husky, and black. He had closely cropped gray hair and wore the kind of blue suit the *Trib's* senior management people favored. He was escorted by one of the Chateau's bellmen. The bellman gave Dan a nod and a smile and departed. Delivering a visitor was not a tippable service at the Chateau.

Dan invited the fed into the suite and closed the door behind him. He noticed he'd left a scuff mark on it from when he'd carried Erin in. Left it for later to decide whether he should clean it himself.

He extended his hand, "Dan Cameron."

"Gamble Murtree, FBI special agent, retired." Gamble shook Dan's hand.

Dan gestured Gamble to the white silk sofa. His blue suit would contrast nicely.

"You like something to drink, Mr. Murtree, or you want to get right to it? The reason for your visit."

"Let's talk, Mr. Cameron."

Dan said fine and sat in an easy chair opposite the sofa.

"You were robbed this morning," Gamble said.

It stung Dan more than ever to hear somebody else voice those words.

He nodded curtly. "My novel, my typewriter, my wallet, my stereo, and my SUV. Pardon me for asking, Mr. Murtree, but what's your interest? You being retired and all. I mean, I haven't even heard from the police who are working the case."

"The police are busy looking for Fetch Mcdonald."

"And whoever helped him, I hope."

Gamble nodded approvingly. "I see you've figured that out. My guess is you also understand if you want to recover your property you might well have to ... take the initiative."

"And you're here to help me out? You do private investigations now?"

Didn't seem like it to Dan, not wearing a suit like that.

Gamble shook his head. "I was the agent in charge of the bank robbery detail for the Buffalo field office. It was my job to catch the Everyman Bank Robber. You know about him?"

Dan nodded. "I did an Internet search on Fetch Mcdonald." Dan held up a hand. "Hold on a minute, will you?"

He got up and went to the salon's work station, grabbed a pad and a pen. Returning to his chair, he made notes catching up on the conversation. Gamble gave him a look.

Dan said, "A story ran in the *Buffalo News* that the authorities liked Mcdonald for the Everyman robberies, but couldn't make the case. That how you feel, too?"

Gamble frowned as he watched Dan write.

"You're going to take down everything I say?"

"I'm writing a new book. About my novel and typewriter getting stolen. And what's being done to recover them."

"I see. Then you won't mind ..."

Gamble took out a mini-recorder, set it on the coffee table, and turned it on.

Now Dan gave Gamble a look. Reporters never liked having the tables turned on them. But then he shrugged, and Gamble continued.

"Mr. Cameron, I'd like to suggest we have a convergence of interests."

"Let me guess. Our reasons may be different, but we're looking for the same man. Or men. And we're both on the outside of the official investigation looking in. Your old pals at the bureau politely declined your offer of help?"

"I didn't consult them on the matter," Gamble said evenly. "To answer your earlier question, yes, I think Mcdonald is the Everyman Bank Robber and ..." Gamble paused to consider his words. "And I learned your missing Remington typewriter is currently the subject of litigation. You might need to move fast, Mr. Cameron."

Dan smiled mirthlessly. This guy was good. Not only did he do his research, he also switched gears pretty smoothly. He'd been about to tell Dan something but had decided it was too soon to trust him. At least if what he had to say was going to wind up in print.

Dan laid his notepad and his pen down. Didn't say they were going off the record. If the former fed wanted to take it that way it'd be his mistake. Others had fallen for the ruse.

But Gamble didn't turn off his recorder.

He went on, "Besides the points you've articulated, we both bring a certain expertise to the arena. Me from my law enforcement background and you from your experience as a journalist who has worked with the police."

Dan thought maybe this guy in the blue suit was showing off, letting him know how thoroughly he'd checked him out. Which wasn't all bad. Dan wanted to leave the dirty work to professionals, but —

"How do we decide we can trust one another, Mr. Murtree?"

Now, Gamble leaned forward and turned off the recorder.

"You mean, how do we insure an equitable exchange of information?"

"Yeah. The FBI isn't known for playing well with others. You guys don't like to share."

Dan had heard that complaint from a thousand Chicago cops.

"True enough, Mr. Cameron. But I'm retired. I'm —"

Whatever the former special agent intended to say was lost when the bedroom door opened and Erin appeared in her underwear rubbing the sleep from her eyes.

"Did I hear you talking out here?" she asked Dan. "Oh ...we have a guest."

Erin was never burdened by modesty, false or otherwise. The day she'd introduced herself to Dan she'd been topless on a Spanish beach. Leaning over him as he lay on the sand. Now, wearing a bra and panties, white cotton yet, what was the big deal?

"Aren't you going to introduce me?" Erin asked Dan.

Dan said equably, "The underdressed lady is my wife, Erin." Turning to Gamble, he saw the gray-haired former fed was blushing, his face noticeably darker than a moment ago. "The well-dressed gentleman is Gamble Murtree, one-time special agent of the FBI."

Erin beamed. "Have you come to help us?"

Gamble was speechless, cat firmly in possession of his tongue.

That was when Dan knew they could work together. The former fed might lie, bluff, or stonewall him. But Gamble Murtree's weakness was a pretty woman. He'd be putty in Erin's hands.

Gamble excused himself to use the bathroom, presumably to splash cold water onto his overheated face. Erin, sensitive that not everyone was the semi-nudist soul she was, slipped on a pair of khaki walking shorts and a coral pink T-shirt. She still looked delectable and those long legs and slender feet of hers remained bare.

There was something about a woman's bare feet and legs: a man couldn't help but wonder where they ended. Especially if he'd already seen the woman in her drawers.

Gamble Murtree didn't stand a chance.

When he returned, though, he did a manly job of maintaining his composure. It helped that the Camerons were now sitting on the sofa, Erin's feet tucked under Dan's leg, and Gamble got to take the easy chair.

Erin smiled at the ex-fed. "So we're all going to work together? I think that's great."

"Yes, well," Gamble began, trying to find his balance with Erin, "there are still a few issues to discuss."

Dan said, "You know what? I think I can trust you. You're no longer bound by institutional imperatives. I think you'll play things straight."

Gamble regarded Dan coolly, wishing he only had him to deal with.

"That's kind of you to say, Mr. Cameron ... but I still have a point or two to consider."

"What's that, Gamble?" Erin asked, breezily permitting herself a first-name familiarity. "Cool name, by the way. Gamble."

"Thank you," he said, trying to rein in another blush. He cleared his throat and went on. "I'm concerned that anything we discuss not appear in the newspaper, at least not until we've achieved our goals."

"What? You mean, Dan?" Erin asked, patting her husband's leg. "He don't need no stinkin' newspaper." Her attempt at a Mexican bandito accent was atrocious.

"In point of fact," Gamble rebutted, "he's still employed

by the *Chicago Tribune.*"

Dan had been sitting back enjoying the show. Now it was time to join in.

"Mr. Murtree's checked me out, honey."

"Gamble," Erin chided in a naughty-child tone. "You didn't investigate me, too?"

This time the former fed couldn't stop the blush. Dan interceded on his behalf.

"It's true that I'm still technically with the *Trib*. And I suppose if I sent my old editor something newsworthy it would run in the paper. But that's not what I'm doing these days. As I said, I'm writing a new book."

"*Kidnapping Ben Hecht*," Erin told Gamble. "How's that for a title?"

"Very nice," Gamble said in a husky voice. He was trying not to look at Erin's feet, which she'd just pulled out from under her husband's leg.

"You don't have to worry about the book," Erin assured Gamble. "It'll take months to write and a year to publish after that."

Dan said, "Perhaps Mr. Murtree is concerned how he might look whenever his actions find their way into print."

"Why would he worry about that?" Erin asked innocently. Then it hit her. "Oh, no, no, no, Gamble! Dan always plays fair. You don't think I'd marry some sleazy, slandering tabloid type, do you?"

Gamble knew safety lay not in answering Erin's question directly but in turning her point back on Dan.

"Is that right, Mr. Cameron, you always play fair?"

"Tell him, Dan," Erin said.

"Always," Dan confirmed. "With everyone who plays fair with me."

There, he thought, now I've got two holds over you.

Gamble knew it, too. He stood up, anxious to go, and said, "Well, why don't we all take the night to think things over?"

Then as the Camerons showed him to the door, he added, "By the way, I don't think Fetch Mcdonald is the Everyman Bank Robber, I know it."

Showing them he had the goods and would share.

"And I know where Archer Mcdonald is hiding out," Dan replied.

That's where they left it, not going into details. When the door was closed, Erin put her arms around Dan and looked at him with a mischievous grin.

"This is fun," she said. "You think I handled poor Gamble okay?"

As Karl Hyacinth said goodbye to Judy — no, she wanted to be called Judith these days — he couldn't tell if his office manager wanted him or was trying to repress laughter. Her eyes sparkled and a smile played at the corners of her mouth. He hadn't hired Ju ... dith for her looks. Not that she was at all uncomely. He just wasn't that sort of employer. Not that kind of guy.

He'd hired Judith — there, it was getting easier — for her broad range of business skills and her years of experience. He knew that as he took a month off to prepare for his wedding and go on his honeymoon, his insurance brokerage — Hyacinth Insurance, Incorporated: We insure every blooming thing under the sun — would be in the best of hands.

That knowledge was reassuring but ever since Verene had masterminded Karl's new image he'd been getting a lot more looks from a lot more women. Which was why he wondered if Judith — whom he was coming to realize was something of a sultry brunette — was interested in him. If they didn't work together, raising the red flags of a sexual harassment lawsuit and the possibility of losing a valuable employee, he might have asked her if she was interested in a brief, torrid fling before he got hitched.

Karl was still heated up from Verene's lunchtime visit. He also looked hot. Verene had told him so. His former Opie Taylor orange hair had been transformed into butterscotch blonde with platinum highlights. Retouched and candle-trimmed weekly for only a hundred bucks. His watery green eyes were now Tahiti blue thanks to his new soft contact lenses. His acrylically bonded teeth were so white he sometimes thought he could read by their light. His PermaTan skin was so brown he finally looked good in Hawaiian shirts. And his fingernails were enameled black just like Billy Idol's lead guitarist.

Then there was the heart-shaped ring inscribed with his true love's name piercing his left nipple. Of course, Judith couldn't see that, but she must have noticed the effects of all the bench-presses he'd been doing — now up to 110 pounds — to pump up his pecs.

Karl favored his office manager with his new dazzling smile.

She turned away. To hide her blush, no doubt.

"I leave everything in your capable hands ... Judith."

He'd almost whispered her name.

She opened a file drawer and said, "Thanks, Mr. H. See ya a week from Saturday."

"Sooner if you need me."

Maybe they'd cross the Peace Bridge, go to a Canadian casino, play baccarat in evening wear, and —

"I'll be just dandy," Judith said. "You keep your lady friend happy."

It disturbed Karl that now he did hear Judith laugh. Not loud, not long, but it was there.

"Yes, I'll do that," Karl answered stiffly, the mood shattered.

He slammed the door as he left.

Fucking Judy.

***

"You know where this place is?" Fetch asked Lerome, meaning Karl Hyacinth's house, which they currently occupied.

"Cleveland Avenue, between Delaware and Elmwood," Lerome answered. "Nice house, nice neighborhood."

"I could throw a baseball from here to where I buried my take in 14209."

Fetch never had the arm to make that throw, Lerome knew. But he also understood hyperbole thanks to hanging out with Ants.

Fetch had more to say, but Lerome touched his arm, warning him. Their pigeon was about to roost. Footsteps climbed the front stairs. A key hit the lock Lerome had opened with lock picks an hour earlier. Then the front door swung open and in stepped —

"This fucking peroxide pansy," Fetch said with a sneer. "This is the guy who's gonna take my Verene from me?"

"Guess so," Lerome answered.

A slack-jawed Karl took one look at the two men who were uninvited guests in his home and turned to run. But Fetch tackled him and Lerome closed the door. Double-locked it.

"You 'n' me, pal," Fetch whispered in Karl's ear, "we're gonna have a little talk."

In her rehabbed Victorian — less than a mile from where her ex-husband had brought down her fiancé — Verene Digby enjoyed a post-coital moment with her ex-husband's father. At the foot of the bed where she and Archer lay was an upholstered bench. On it rested stacks of cash, $470,000, the twice-stolen money that had once been entrusted to various banks and S&Ls in the greater Buffalo area.

Screwing with so much loot so close was a big turn-on

for both of them.

Archer looked at the money and shook his head in wonder. "Never thought Fetch'd do so well in the family business."

Verene smiled. "I gave him lots of incentive."

"You sure you don't want to just take off with all that cash?"

"I keep telling you, honey, Karl could be worth twice that."

Archer didn't say anything, but he knew why Verene was promising him a cut of Karl's money: she might need him to kill the man she intended to marry. The way he saw it, though, he'd have a hard time living long enough to spend the money right there in front of them.

The pain in his gut which had started about a year ago was getting more frequent. But it wasn't so bad right now he wasn't interested when she climbed on top of him.

"I know you're a stud for an old man," Verene said, "but you ready to go again?"

He pulled her close and showed her how ready he was.

Before they got started, Archer asked, "You're gonna keep your promise, right? I tell you the time has come, you'll fuck me to death."

"I'd do it right now if I didn't need you," Verene replied.

They both laughed, the two of them meant for each other.

Lerome pulled Fetch off Karl before any serious damage could be done. More likely to Fetch than Karl. The dandified insurance man had rolled himself up into a ball and Fetch was raining punches off Karl's shins and elbows. Fetch kept up he'd probably break a bone or two in his hands. He'd never been much of a fighter, a good thing for all concerned.

Liberated from Fetch's assault, Karl dared to peek out

from between the arms covering his face. When he saw Lerome, a far bigger foe than the one whose attack he'd just survived, he went back into hiding.

Lerome told him, "Come on, get up. We're going downstairs."

Karl didn't like the sound of that one bit. He kept his posture circular.

Lerome added, "I let Fetch get going again, he'll start biting. A lot harder than he punches."

A picture of Mike Tyson munching on Evander Holyfield's ear popped into Karl's mind. He bounced to his feet like he had a spring up his ass.

"Wasn't so hard," Lerome told him. "Come on, let's go."

Both Fetch and Lerome started for the stairs that led to the basement. They'd checked out Karl's house top to bottom before he arrived. Neither of them, though, was between Karl and the front door. Fetch disappeared down the basement stairs without a backward glance.

Karl would have to undo the chain-lock, the deadbolt, and yank the door open before he could escape. Lerome was looking at him from the doorway to the basement. He wasn't smiling, but seemed amused nevertheless. Genuinely interested in what Karl's next move would be. Big guy dressed all in black, swept back hair, goatee. He reminded Karl of a panther.

Which'd make Karl ... whatever the hell it was panthers ate.

With a sudden pang of regret, Karl wished Verene had redone his image to look more like the guy he now feared would kill him. Yielding to an inevitable sense of doom, he walked toward Lerome, and descended the stairs to meet whatever horrible fate awaited him.

Lerome closed the basement door behind them.

"I oughta kill him, Lerome." Fetch had a hard time not

wincing, his hands were hurting so bad from hitting Karl.

"Who knows how long he's been boning my Verene?"

Lerome thought that could be Verene's song: *Who's Boning Her Now?*

Karl sat on the sofa in his home office closely observing his two captors. The comfortably furnished room was in a corner of his large basement. He used it just often enough to legitimately take a home-office tax deduction. He'd noticed immediately a change in his decor. Somebody had covered the ground-level windows with aluminum foil. He'd nearly hersheyed himself when he saw that.

But just now the smaller thug — clearly Verene's fugitive bank robber ex-husband — had said something that gave him hope. And every sales course he'd ever taken had taught him: React to opportunity fast.

"I never fucked your wife!" Karl blurted.

Fetch turned to look at Karl.

"What'd you say?" he asked in a deadly whisper.

Lerome looked on in amused silence once more.

Karl realized it would be a good idea to rephrase his statement.

"I ... I've never had sexual relations with that woman." Hearing a strangely familiar echo to those words, he quickly added, "Not even oral sex."

Karl was now immensely glad that Verene had turned him down. He fervently hoped this maniac could see the truth.

"How long have you two been engaged?" Fetch demanded.

"Six months."

Lerome was curious. "How long did you know her before that? How long did you date before you got engaged?"

"I've been acquainted with Verene a little over a year. We dated about three months before we got engaged."

Fetch looked incredulous. "In all that time, you never once—"

Karl shook his head. To his dismay, though, he saw the truth wasn't going over. So he told the whole truth. "I tried, all right. God how I tried! But she never let me."

"Said you had to wait till you're married?" Lerome inquired knowingly.

Karl nodded, a study in dejection. Then he remembered his line of defense.

"That's what matters, right?" he asked anxiously. "We never had sex!"

Fetch flopped down on the sofa next to Karl. He believed the poor sap. Verene had been stringing Karl along the whole time. The same Verene who'd come across the first time she'd gone out with Fetch. Verene who ... God, the thought just about killed him.

If she hadn't been fucking Karl, and no way she'd been waiting for him, and if Archer had helped her find Fetch's money and had provoked him into breaking jail ...

Damnit, his wife was fucking his father!

Fetch put his face in his hands and sobbed.

Karl looked at Fetch. He certainly hadn't been expecting this. He turned to Lerome. "Why's he crying?"

Lerome chose to focus on another aspect of the situation. "Karl, we need to find a *modus vivendi* here." Lerome had also picked up a smattering of Latin from Ants.

"A working arrangement?" Karl asked. "What do we have to work out?" His continued existence, he hoped, but he didn't dare bring that up.

"Let's give Fetch a minute," Lerome told him. "Then we'll figure out what we do next."

CHAPTER 11

Tuesday morning, while Erin was in the shower, Dan put in a call to the Buffalo Police Department and asked for the cop whose name Lester Croart had given to him.

"Detective Hillerman, please." Dan said.

The voice on the other end of the call laughed.

"You're about two years late, buddy. Hillerman retired, moved to Florida, or Arizona, or California. Forget which, but someplace with sun and palm trees ... or cactus."

Well, Les had warned Dan that his contact might not be around.

"Can you tell me who's taken his place, please? I'm looking for whoever's heading the Fetch Mcdonald escape investigation."

Dan sensed official interest take a big jump.

"You know something, buddy, you can tell me."

Sure, Dan thought, I know right where Mcdonald's hiding, and I'd love to make your career.

He said, "My name's Daniel Cameron. The cabin I was using in Cattaraugus County was burgled yesterday and my SUV was stolen. By Mcdonald. I was wondering if the sheriff's department down there had relayed that information to the Buffalo PD. Specifically, I'm interested in recovering the manuscript for my new novel and a valuable antique typewriter."

The anonymous copper's disappointment was palpable.

"Oh, yeah, sure. Let me see." It sounded to Dan as if the cop was deliberately rustling papers next to the phone. "Yeah, got the sheriff's report right here. And don't you worry, finding hot manuscripts and typewriters, that's our specialty."

Cops liked to think they were funny.

"May I have your name, detective?"

"Dick Tracey," he answered and hung up.

Dan made notes summarizing the conversation. More material for the new book.

Be funny if the guy's name really was Dick Tracy.

Erin was setting out the breakfast room service had delivered while Dan called his agent, Hank DeMitri. Dan was hoping for good news. Like the Hecht estate had lost the battle for the Remington. No such luck.

"Judge hasn't decided yet," Hank told him, "but the lawyers for our side think a decision will come soon."

"They have any feeling how it might go?"

"They're hopeful."

"Yeah?" Dan knew hedging when he heard it.

"They think it looks like a win for the estate."

"Shit," Dan said.

"I feel the same way."

There was a pause, then Hank asked the inevitable question.

"You finish the new book yet?"

Agents always wanted to know that. Just like writers always wanted good news. The only good thing about the cops giving his problems short shrift, the media hadn't heard about his novel and the Remington being stolen. He still had a little time in hand.

Very little, most likely.

"I'm close," Dan told his agent.

Erin let Dan finish his breakfast before she said, "Hank wanted to know about *Time Expires,* didn't he?"

Dan nodded, and added, "The lawyers don't think it looks good for our side."

He expected his wife to curse at the news; after all, she was the one who'd bought the Remington. Instead, she nodded, as if accepting the inevitable instead of raging against it.

Not at all like Erin.

She asked, "Well, have you decided about reconstructing the story?"

Dan tossed his napkin on the table.

"Guess, I better. My publisher's blowing a pile of money on legal fees, I ought to give them something in return."

"But we'll keep working both sides of the street, right? You dictate the story to me and we keep looking for the bad guys."

"Sure. Like you said, that's what makes *Kidnapping Ben Hecht* go."

"It's okay to admit you're pissed off," Erin told Dan.

"I'm pissed off." He was even if he didn't sound like it.

"I'm gonna have Rudy send up a speed-bag. We can both beat on it."

Dan smiled. "Put Fetch Mcdonald's picture on it, I'll give it a whack or two."

Erin took her husband's hand and gave it a squeeze.

"What do you want to do first?" she asked.

"Let's go take another look at that Victorian on Norwood Avenue."

"Catch the bad guys red-handed, maybe. Wrestle them to the ground."

"If they're not too big. Or too many. Otherwise, we'll call

the cops."

Erin considered. "You go. I had an idea when I was waking up this morning. I want to think about it some more. See if it holds up."

"You want to talk about it?"

Erin chose to keep her own counsel for the moment. So Dan went out on his own.

Nobody answered the doorbell — a four-toned chime — at the Victorian house on Norwood Avenue. Dan had parked the rental Chevy opposite the house and spent five minutes looking at the place before he ventured across the street. It still seemed too ... precious, he guessed, to be a hideout for a fugitive.

Of course, that would be a big advantage if Fetch Mcdonald was really in there.

If he was, though, and he had his accomplice with him, things could get risky for Dan if he confronted them directly. He wanted *Kidnapping Ben Hecht* to be a good story, but he wasn't willing to die for it.

Still, it wasn't like reporters never tried to con people. Maybe he'd pretend to be a Jehovah's Witness come to spread the good word. Unless he was really unlucky, they wouldn't ask him for a copy of *The Watchtower*. He crossed the street. But after listening to the chime do its thing three times he thought he'd wasted a trip. Nobody was home. Then he heard an engine turn over out back. A big powerful one. He remembered the Corvette Stingray he'd seen Verene Digby drive up in yesterday.

He scampered down the stairs and was standing next to the driveway as she nosed the sports car out, stopping at the sidewalk to check for traffic. She saw Dan and gave him a long, frank look. Like she was trying to guess how much money he might have in his pocket.

She watched him cross in front of her car and wasn't

scared when he stepped up to the driver's side door. In fact, she lowered the window.

"Looking for something, honey?" Her voice was both soft and challenging.

Her dress was the same electric blue as the car and showed all the cleavage the law allowed. A whole lot of leg, too. She was so cocksure of her sexuality Dan felt compelled to see if he could shake her up.

He lowered himself into a crouch and said, "Looking for someone. Fetch Mcdonald."

She didn't flinch but hearing Fetch's name raised goosebumps across the hills and dales of exposed flesh. She was looking for something to say when Dan spoke again.

"You being his wife, I thought maybe you might know where he is."

Now she had a reply and it was tart.

"*Ex*-wife, and I don't know where Fetch is."

The response had the ring of truth to it, and a heartbeat later she was back on her game, playing Dan once more. She turned in her seat to give him a new perspective on her chest.

"If I should happen to see him, anything you want me to tell him?"

Dan took out a business card and wrote the Chateau's phone number on the back. He passed it to her and she glanced at it. He half-thought she'd stick it between her boobs, but she slipped it into a slot in her sun visor.

"Reporter. Didn't think you were a cop." She studied Dan again, this time more thoughtfully. Saw his wedding band, didn't appear put off by it. "You want more than an interview with the big bad bankrobber, don't you?"

Dan stood up, took a step back.

"He took a couple of things that belong to me. I want them back."

Dan could practically hear the calculator in her head

whirring.

She smiled and said, "Well, I've got your number — and you know where I live."

"You and Fetch's dad," Dan replied.

That shook her up.

She put the Vette in gear and roared off.

Fetch and Karl had gotten drunk the previous night and exchanged Verene stories. Fetch wept some more and Karl joined in. They both passed out. Lerome who never had more than one drink of alcohol in any 24-hour period — something Ants loved about him — could only shake his head at human folly.

Goddamn Verene just wasn't worth all the heartache.

Not that these two would ever listen.

For a fleeting moment, Lerome had considered the possibility of holding Karl hostage. Demanding Fetch's money back if Verene wanted to get her clutches on the sucker she was planning to marry and eat alive. But he had to admit that wouldn't work. Verene was the type who never gave money back. It'd be easier for her to find a new sucker.

There were always plenty of guys who liked big tits.

So he'd had to think of another role for Karl.

Another way to get Fetch some getaway money

Lerome came up with a plan for both Fetch and Karl. While the two of them had been crying in Karl's imported beer, Lerome had tuned out and read some more of *Time Expires*. That sonofagun Cameron could really write. Wasn't only what he had to say — which was cool — but the way he said it.

Made Lerome wonder if he could play with words like that. Well, he was looking for something new to do. He had the money to let him take his time with it. He could work out his own style. Hell, Cameron had to be writing plenty long to get that good. Lerome grinned.

Maybe Cameron had left some of his magic in the Remington.

He'd have to ask Ants to look up Daniel Cameron on her computer. See what else he'd done. And when Fetch and Karl woke up, Lerome'd tell them what Cameron had written for them. He ate a quick breakfast, raiding Karl's fridge and pantry, and then called Jessi.

She told him it'd been a slow night, so his new car was ready.

Lerome drove out to Baby's Auto Body and swapped Jessi's Porsche for his new black Highlander. It was so clean, so shiny, so black, it just about took his breath away. Maybe it was only Porsches he liked in midnight blue.

He gave Jessi cash for her work, of course. Five K extra he was so pleased.

"That guy you sold your business to?" Jessi said.

"Yeah."

"He's not gay."

Lerome shrugged.

"He's bi."

"That good enough?"

"Yeah," Jessi said. "I think it'll work out."

"That's great."

Jessi extended her hand and Lerome shook it. First time he'd ever touched her. One of the things she'd always liked about him, he respected her space.

"I think about you and Ants sometimes."

Lerome knew Jessi'd been Ants' lover in the joint. Two women so strong, he wondered how they ever worked things out. Who played which role. Maybe they took turns.

"Yeah?" he asked.

"Yeah. I think if she needs a real live dick, I'm glad it's yours."

"Me, too," Lerome said.

***

Before returning to Karl's house, Lerome decided to stop by Fetch's old home, see if Uncle Archer was in residence. He wasn't, not by the note in his window.

The cops run me outta my own house with threats of jail. Gone into hiding. A.M.

Cute, Lerome thought. Like it was the cop's fault he was hiding. No way he was in cahoots with Verene, hadn't had a hand in stealing all of Fetch's money. He turned to go, but he saw four cops, weapons drawn, coming his way.

Lerome stopped and watched them, not bothered.

He had no criminal record to worry about.

And he had absolute faith in the new registration papers on his stolen SUV.

"Who's that?" Erin asked, looking at a picture of a darkly handsome man.

"Lerome D'Arnole, Fetch Mcdonald's cousin," Gamble Murtree told her. "Their relationship's closer than that, though. They're more like brothers."

Gamble had dropped by the Chateau to tell Dan he thought they could work together. He was reluctant to stay when he learned Dan wasn't there. Truth was, he was out the door until Erin grabbed him and pulled him back, making a simple but compelling argument.

"If you want to work with Dan, you'll have to work with me, too. Don't worry, no more lingerie shows."

Gamble was relieved to hear that, and when Erin ordered coffee and cinnamon rolls for him from room service, he was won over. As he ate, the two of them looked over the background material Gamble had brought as a sign of good faith. Lerome's picture was the first thing he'd pulled from his attaché case.

"Guy could be a movie star," Erin said. She looked at the photo this way and that. "But it'd be hard to tell if he was the hero or the villain."

Gamble rolled his eyes. He had no trouble deciding.

"What kind of name is Lerome anyway? Erin asked.

"Story is, his father was going for Jerome, but being dyslexic he mistook the L for a J. A Filipina nurse saw what he wrote down, didn't know any better, entered it in the birth registry."

"Somebody had to catch it later."

"Sure. Only Lerome's mother got such a kick out of it, she decided to keep it."

"Wonder if he had the same sense of humor about it."

Gamble took a sip of coffee. One look at him and Erin knew.

"You've got a story about that, don't you?"

Gamble told her. "Lerome's rep is he's easy going. Cannot ruffle the man."

Erin took another look at Lerome's picture. She could see that.

"He's also big, about six-three, good shoulders on him. One night he's in a bar over on Chippewa Street. Upscale place, well-dressed clientele. Not the kind of scene where guys brawl. Only that night some kid the Bills were thinking of drafting as a defensive back is there and overhears someone use Lerome's name. Kid thinks it's a scream. Especially after Lerome takes the trouble to explain how he got it."

"And there was a big fight," Erin said.

"No. Lerome just says he thinks a dyslexic getting five out of six letters right is pretty good. Sticking up for his dad, you know. Then he pays for his drink and leaves."

"That's it?"

"Not quite. That night was the last time anybody ever saw the funnyman again. He never showed up for his workout with the Bills."

"Wow," Erin said softly.

"Yeah. Thing was, how could the cops pin it on Lerome?

He took the guy's crap in stride. Walked away without so much as a harsh word. And never finding the body, that always makes everything harder."

"But you think he did it, Lerome?"

"Don't you?"

Erin nodded. Even the wife of a police beat reporter hated coincidences.

Gamble smiled and shook his head, evincing mixed emotions.

"Never heard of anyone making fun of Lerome's name again."

"And this is the guy you think helped Fetch escape from prison?" she asked.

"Can't imagine anyone else."

"Come on," Erin said, standing up. "I'll show you where Dan went this morning." She didn't want anybody dying over *Kidnapping Ben Hecht* either.

As they drove in Gamble's car, Erin told him her idea for finding Fetch Mcdonald.

"The United States Postal Service?" Gamble asked as they stopped for a red light.

He sounded like he couldn't quite believe his ears.

"Think about it," Erin replied. "What other organization makes house calls at every address in the city? Six days a week."

Having been one of the first black special agents in the FBI had taught Gamble that a closed mind is an ugly thing. He gave Erin's idea fair consideration. The more he thought about it, the more he liked it. The light turned green and he hit the gas.

"How you gonna get them to cooperate? That seems like the biggest hurdle to me."

"My dad's best friend is the retired postmaster for Buffalo. He's my unofficial uncle."

Gamble grinned. "Connections will lower those hurdles every time."

"Yeah. Anyway, we'll just make it an informal deal. A private reward funded by Dan and me. Any letter carrier spots Fetch—"

"Or Lerome."

"Okay. They see where either of them is staying, call us, get ... how much money should we offer?"

"Five K. That's enough to be appreciated. Not so much you get people makin' things up." For people staying at the Chateau, Gamble thought that money should be doable.

He was right.

"Five thousand it is," Erin said.

Gamble turned onto Norwood Avenue and Erin pointed out the Victorian.

"I don't see our rental car," she told Gamble.

He pulled over to the curb, short of the house, studied it. He was trying to get a sense of things. Were the bad guys there? Had they grabbed Dan Cameron? Were they slicing 'n' dicing his ass right now? Gamble didn't think so. House looked too peaceful, empty even. The curtains were open and the lights were off.

Still, he wasn't too proud to admit he'd been wrong before.

"Why don't you call your hotel?" he asked Erin. "See if he's gone back there."

Erin used her cell phone. Got an answer on the first ring. She talked with her husband a minute and told him to stay there. They'd join him.

"Everything fine?" Gamble asked.

"Dan said he spoke with Verene Digby. Shook her up when he told her he knew Fetch Mcdonald's father is staying with her."

Gamble's eyes widened.

"Archer Mcdonald's in that house, too?"

"He was yesterday." Erin thought a moment. "You going to call the cops?"

Gamble was going to ask did she think they should. Instead, he said, "How'd that work out for your husband's new book?"

"Probably kill all the excitement," she admitted.

"Then we'll just keep things to ourselves a little longer."

The two of them shared a small laugh, becoming fast friends.

Both of them enjoying the hunt.

CHAPTER 12

Fetch and Karl woke up while Lerome was out. Both of them wished they hadn't. Karl threw up in the toilet. Fetch heaved in the laundry sink. Neither of them wanted to climb the stairs to get the aspirin their pounding heads cried out for. So they turned to the next best thing. Karl grabbed a couple more beers — St. Pauli Girl — from the downstairs fridge.

Relief was immediate The looks on both their faces said they'd never tasted anything better in their lives. A couple more pulls and their headaches were in full retreat, the cotton was washed from their mouths. Within seconds the bottles were dead soldiers.

Neither of them thought to get up for another.

Both of them were staring at the buxom blonde beer-maiden on the label.

"She's fucking with you, you know that, don't you?" Fetch asked Karl.

Karl knew Fetch meant Verene. He'd heard a lot of stories about Verene last night. Some of the things Fetch'd told him about his fiancée got him so worked up he wanted to race out and find her, rip her clothes off and have his way with her. Which he certainly would have done if he wasn't afraid Lerome might kill him if he made one wrong move. His ardor was further dampened by some of the other things Fetch had gone on to tell him, things that really made him cringe.

Even now, he was hoping he hadn't really heard Fetch say that Verene was sleeping with Fetch's father. Another bank robber. An old one. Karl desperately wanted that to be a nightmare. The kind that was killed by the dawn's early light.

"Point is," Karl said glumly, "she's not fucking with me."

He wanted Fetch to remember that.

"How much you make a year?" Fetch asked out of the blue.

Karl preferred not to say.

Fetch told him, "I pulled in $75,000, before taxes, my best year with Xerox. Pretty damn good back then for a guy in his twenties. Made Verene happy. Every last cent of it."

Karl absorbed that tidbit silently.

Fetch went off down another path. "Those black fingernails your idea?"

Not wanting to discuss his makeover, Karl responded, "I gross about 200K a year ... and I've got some family money."

"Your parents rich?"

"They owned a hardware store, didn't spend a lot. Me either. I ... I started spending after I met Verene. Clothes. Jewelry. A Corvette Stingray, just like her mom had."

"Her mom?" Fetch grinned. "Damn, I haven't thought about Sabina in ... did I tell you about Sabina last night?"

Karl couldn't remember.

"Listen," Fetch said, "for all the money you're spending on Verene, what you ought to do is send some Sabina's way. At least she'd come across for you."

Fetch laughed at the look of disgust on Karl's face.

"Sabina looks just like Verene, only her hair's redder,

and she can't be more than sixteen years older. Bet she still keeps up her looks, too."

Fetch told Karl how when he was a kid and Archer was between prison sentences, the old man had given Fetch a deck of cards with pictures of naked ladies on the back. Sabina was one of them. Years later, when he'd first met Verene, he'd thought she looked familiar.

"What she said was, 'You think you know me, don't you?'" Fetch told Karl.

Thing was, he'd been remembering the playing cards his father had given him. Later, Verene had told him Sabina had also done some cheesecake calendars, a skin magazine or two, and maybe a porn video, but Verene wasn't sure about that.

"You, uh, still have those cards?" Karl asked quietly.

Fetch shook his head. Told him you lost track of a lot of stuff when you got sent to prison. Like the $480,000 you buried, he thought grimly.

Which started to bring his headache back.

"I could probably find those cards on the Internet," Karl told him.

Fetch went with that, fought off the pounding in his temples.

"Probably could. But my point is, Verene doesn't come across for you, tell her you're going to see her mother. See what kind of reaction that gets."

Karl's reaction was to be hopeful. Fetch was talking like he still had a future. One that would still include Verene ... or her mother. Sex with *someone*.

Then Lerome came back.

"Nice to see you two up and around," he said, taking a seat on the sofa next to Karl.

"Where've you been?" Fetch wanted to know.

"Talking to the cops."

Karl didn't know how to take that; Fetch knew Lerome

would never rat him out, but he was curious, too. "Yeah?" he asked.

"They don't have a clue where you are."

That news made Fetch feel better than the beer had.

Lerome continued, "So, now, since you won't take any of my money—"

"You need money?" Karl asked. "I can let you have some How much you need?"

Fetch and Lerome both looked at him.

They knew what Karl was trying to do — pay his own ransom.

"Twenty thousand do it? Fifty?"

Lerome looked at Fetch. He was curious how Fetch would respond to Karl's offer.

Fetch looked back at his cousin. "What do you have in mind?"

"How'd you like to rob a hair salon?" Lerome asked.

"There money in that these days?"

Karl got agitated, being present at a criminal conspiracy. "You don't have to do that. I'll give you the money. Really."

Fetch turned such a cold gaze on Karl he was no longer sure he had a future.

"I *work* for a living," Fetch told him in a flat voice.

Lerome nodded his approval, and said, "You, too, Karl."

"Me, too, what?" Karl asked, voice quavering.

"You're going to help Fetch."

"W-why?"

Fetch was still ticked at the guy.

"Don't you get it, Karl?" he asked. "You just became Patty Hearst."

When they got back to the Chateau, Erin introduced Gamble to Rudy.

"This is Special Agent Gamble Murtree of the FBI," she

told Rudy. "He'll be helping Dan and me with Dan's new book. Will you let the staff know he can come to our suite anytime he needs to see us?"

"Yes, ma'am. *Former* Special Agent Murtree and I have met. Do you mean he should be allowed up anytime at all?"

Erin felt she and Rudy were friends but now he was in a bit of a snit. Rudy thought Gamble was replacing him in her affections, platonic though they might be. Erin had been through this kind of thing before. To reassure him, she put one of her hands over one of his.

"Let's say anytime between eight a.m. and ten p.m. I'm sure Gamble is far too much of a gentleman to stop by in the middle of the night."

Gamble nodded. Erin gave Rudy's hand a squeeze. All was well.

After they got upstairs and Erin was opening the door, Gamble asked, "Every man you meet fall in love with you, Mrs. Cameron?"

"A lot of 'em," Erin admitted. "Dan's the only one I love back."

Lucky SOB, Gamble thought.

"The day Fetch Mcdonald got caught I was down in Georgia burying my mother," Gamble told Dan and Erin.

The Camerons expressed their sympathy.

Dan said, "I lost my mother, too. An aneurysm. When I was thirty."

Each man recognized the sorrow in the other's eyes.

"Then you can understand how rushing back up here wasn't the first thing on my mind. I wanted to be with my father. I figured I had time to help tie Mcdonald in to all the other crimes. But by the time I got back, the plea deal was in place. One lousy count for the credit union job. The guy skates on fourteen other bank robberies. I about went nuts when I found out."

Now, Erin squeezed Gamble's hand.

The former fed warmed at her touch. *Back at ya, Rudy.* He didn't even mind that his tale of woe would be going into Dan Cameron's book.

"Mcdonald thought he was smart changing his attaché case for his last job."

"That's what got him off on the others, wasn't it?" Dan asked. "So it was smart."

Gamble bit his lip a minute, then reached into his own case. He pulled out a plastic bag that held a scrap of soiled white card stock. Looked like an unlined index card. On it were words written in block letters. Only the ink had run, rounding off a lot of the corners.

Gamble extended it to Dan. "Leave it in the bag."

Erin leaned in so she could read the message, too.

Dan read aloud, slowly deciphering the smeared letters. *"Don't say a word. Don't ..."*

"Press, I think," Erin said.

"Yeah. *Don't press the alarm. Just fill the case. No ..."*

"Dye packs," Gamble supplied.

"No dye packs." Dan looked up. *"Or I blow up every-damn-body in the bank."*

"Read the other side," Gamble told them.

Dan turned the bag around. The writing on this side of the card was more legible.

"Anybody tries to stop me, we all go boom."

"That's what Mcdonald showed the teller after he had the money in hand."

"The Everyman Bank Robber never said a word," Erin guessed correctly.

Dan did a quick memory scan of what he'd read about the crimes.

This written message was never mentioned in any of the press accounts. The cops held it back. So anybody who had this card had to be the guy who pulled the other jobs — if you got the same wording from some of the tellers he robbed.

"Six of them remembered it verbatim. Others came very close."

"Then how come—" Erin began. In the next second, she answered her own question. "The cops didn't find this, you did. Too late."

"After it had been rained on," Dan added. "No DNA evidence?"

Gamble shook his head. He took the plastic bag back.

He said, "Fetch Mcdonald changed his attaché case, but not his gimme-the-money note. His attaché case popped open when he fell doing that last job. The bank guards and the cops were so happy to recover all the cash they must not have noticed this card blow off. After I got back, I found it in a pile of trash two blocks away." The retired G-man sighed. "After the plea deal had been struck."

"So Fetch was luckier than he was smart," Dan said.

Gamble nodded. He told Dan and Erin they'd have to excuse him. He had an angle he wanted to work on. He'd let them know if it worked out. They walked him to the door and said goodbye.

Dan was suspicious. Gamble had given them information, all right. Some of it was even personal. But cynical newsman that he was, he wanted to know the one thing Gamble hadn't shared with them. What was this new angle he was working on?

Erin, though, was feeling sympathetic.

"You can see why the poor guy wants to catch Fetch Mcdonald."

Dan nodded absently.

"Hey," Erin continued, "let me tell you about my idea how to find him."

She did and Dan concurred that Erin should contact Uncle Les and see what could be done. He was agreeable to offering a $5,000 reward. But privately he wondered how much a letter carrier observed about the people on his route. Probably not a lot.

Or maybe he was wrong. Delivering mail to the same places every day might make you nosy. You wanted to know who your people were ... every last little detail of their lives.

Dan sat down and made notes about the new information.

Then Erin told him about Lerome and the guy who disappeared.

Damn, he thought, *Kidnapping Ben Hecht* was getting off to a good start.

Have to be careful about this Lerome, though.

"So what'd she look like?" Erin asked.

"Who?"

"Verene Digby. Sitting there in her Stingray." Dan had given her the basics of the encounter over the phone. "I mean, from that newspaper photo she struck me as a low-rent Madonna. But what's she like in person?"

Dan pushed his notepad aside. "She looks like trouble."

That answer seemed to satisfy Erin.

"How about we start on *Time Expires?*" she asked.

"This evening," Dan said. "Right after I take you somewhere nice for dinner."

"Okay. But no hanky-panky for dessert."

"Not even after we do some work?"

"Well ... five pages might get you a little of this." Erin flashed him. "Ten pages might get you some of that. But only if I like your work."

"You sound just like my editor," Dan told her.

Lerome decided to wait until Fetch and Karl were past their hangovers and had showered and shaved before he gave them his whole plan. Once everyone was clean and composed, they went upstairs and pulled the curtains. Karl grilled salmon filets for dinner. They moved to the living room for the reading. Fetch and Karl sat on opposite ends of the sofa, each with a cup of coffee in front of him,

They were as mellow as a hostage and hostage-takers could be. Even if Karl was still worried enough about his circumstances to have offered Fetch a full partnership in his business.

Lerome sat facing them in a leather wing chair. He had the manuscript for *Time Expires* on his lap. While his silent-reading speed was slower than most, the way he read aloud was very pleasing, each word clearly articulated. He also brought his intuitive understanding of human nature to voicing each character's dialogue.

Erin Cameron had been right; Lerome could've been an actor. He crossed his legs comfortably. Setting the mood. He wanted Fetch and Karl to sit back and relax. Get into the story the way he had.

"Everybody ready? Okay, here we go ..."

... Terry Phelan got pissed when the two kids stealing his BMW couldn't manage to do more in their first five minutes of work than set off the alarm.

Dan smiled. He remembered the opening sentence of his new novel word for word, and Erin effortlessly keyed them into her Powerbook. Looking at the outline for chapter one sitting on his lap, he began to feel confident.

Maybe this would work after all.

Terry'd been ...

... watching the young black male and Hispanic female through the eyebrow window above the front door of the two-story red brick building he'd closed on the week before. He was up a step-ladder patching a hole in the ceiling of the entryway. His old man had taught him how

to feather in layers of plaster, spread it so smooth you wouldn't even need to sand it. Just prime it and paint. Nobody'd ever know the previous owner had put a hole in the ceiling with a shotgun — after receiving a fatal wound from a drug dealer who'd come by to argue an overdue bill.

It was still that kind of neighborhood, but Terry was betting it would be less than a year before lawyers and commodity traders pushed the dealers and the junkies out. Strivers mainlined real estate the way dopers shot up drugs, and they had a lot more money to indulge their habits.

The trick was to get the jump on the next land rush, and have the balls to stick it out before the soon-to-arrive gentry pulled increased police protection along with them. Terry's dad had taught him to box, too, and his three older brothers had made daily practice a necessity. Coping with a mugger or two would seem like old home week to him.

Lerome glanced at Fetch and Karl, happy to see they were listening closely.

Terry also learned to concentrate at home. Which wasn't easy, five guys in a house, Mom gone since Terry was two. Reading was how he shut out all those other guys. The ability to read through his brothers' fistfights — the ones that didn't involve him — had helped him make it through college and grad school. He'd earned a B.S. in Psych and an MBA, both from DePaul, graduating at the top of his class both times. But right now he couldn't focus on a skill he'd mastered when he was twelve. He'd just put a big ragged gouge in the wet plaster.

He didn't mind losing the car. It was insured and he was ready for something new. But that goddamn alarm was driving him nuts.

At her keyboard, Erin's head bobbed as if keeping time with a familiar melody.

Those fucking kids out there, they still hadn't jimmied the car door. Christ, you'd think they'd just break a window. Terry jumped down from the ladder and —

Fetch and Karl had to wait till Lerome got to the next page.

— threw open the door.

"Hey!" he shouted. "If you can't steal a car any better than that, give it the fuck up. Go find some damn crime you're suited for."

Fetch laughed and even Karl grinned.

Lerome loved Terry's point of view.

Terry turned the alarm off with the transmitter on his key chain and while the two kids gaped at him he slammed the door, going back up the ladder to fix the plaster before it dried. But before he could pick up his trowel someone was hammering at his door.

Karl said, "This oughta be good."

Fetch shushed him.

Erin smiled, knowing what was coming.

"You got a gun out there? Terry asked, standing off to one side of the door.

"Fuckin' right I do, you white motherfucker."

"Prove it," Terry said.

"Ah'll cap yo ass right now."

"Go ahead."

The door wouldn't have stopped anything bigger than a .22. Terry thought it might be a good idea to replace it with a steel model. But no shots were fired. The only thing that came through the door were voices. Arguing. The girl wanted to go. The boy wanted satisfaction.

Terry just wanted to plaster in peace.

He yanked the door open, caught the two kids flat-footed. He grabbed one in each hand and pulled them inside.

Lerome loved that line, too. The man just wanted to plaster in peace.

Terry kicked the door shut and dragged the two of them into his living room, furnished at that point with only an old leather sofa and a 19-inch TV sitting on a cardboard box. The black kid might've been a bit taller than Terry's six feet, but he didn't weigh an ounce over 150; the girl was similarly tall and thin. Terry, with a fistful of each of their shirts, shoved them down side by side on the sofa.

A quick look told him the boy didn't have a gun.

Another glance told him he'd have to start his repair job all over again.

"Shit," he said heatedly. "You two idiots are costing me time. You know how much money I charge for my time?"

The black kid's upper lip started to curl. A smartass response was on its way but Terry cut it off, pointing a finger at the kid.

"That was a rhetorical question, if you know what that means."

Terry could see that they didn't. So he started with something basic.

"What're your names?"

The boy just sneered. The girl said, "Alita. Everybody calls me Allie."

"Don't be tellin' him nothin'," the boy ordered her.

"Don't you be tellin' me what to do!" Allie barked back. "You listened to me, we wouldn't be here!"

"You wanted to steal that car, too!" the boy shouted.

Allie pushed her face right up to the boy's, just begging him to belt her.

"That's when I thought you knew how."

Might as well have told him his dick was too small.

135

"Women," said Fetch.

"Men," Erin said. "Why's it always about their dicks?"
Dan wondered if there'd be a problem with dictation after all.

The black kid looked at Terry, trying to see how this white cocksucker might react if he smacked Allie one. Terry shook his head. Guys beating on each other was a part of his upbringing. Hitting a woman was something he couldn't relate to.

Terry was having regrets he ever brought these two into his house. All he wanted now was to get back to work and not have anyone disturb him. He wouldn't put it past these dummies to give his car another shot if he just threw them out. So he decided a little education was in order.

"You two know how long the police response time is on this block? I mean, once somebody calls the cops."

The black kid laughed. "Nobody calls the cops 'round here."

Terry ignored the remark, answered his own question. "It's twelve minutes."

"How you know that?" Allie asked.

"It's my job."

"He bullshittin'. He don't know. Response time. You ever hear a that?"

Terry said, "You were outside working on my car over five minutes. We've been in here getting acquainted a little longer than that. So ..."

Terry turned his head toward the living room windows. There were iron bars on the outside but no curtains on the inside. The black kid and Allie turned to look ...

Just as a CPD beat car pulled up opposite Terry's BMW.

Lerome excused himself to get a glass of water. His throat was getting dry. When he got back, Fetch and Karl were right where he left them. Clearly wanting to know what would happen now that the cops had arrived.

"Does Terry turn the thieves over to the cops?" Karl wanted to know.

"Of course not," Fetch responded.

"How do you know?"

"Jesus, Karl, look how many more pages there are. What's the story gonna be if Allie and the black guy get busted now. You think the rest of it's Terry fixing up his place?"

Lerome had understood that. But it surprised him a bit that Fetch did.

"Besides," Fetch continued, "how'd Terry prove anything? It's his word against theirs."

"Yeah, okay," Karl conceded, having been educated on both story structure and the law. "So what happens next?"

"Yeah, what?" Fetch asked Lerome.

There was now at least one person on the block who called the police, and her presence was the reason Terry Phelan had bought into the neighborhood. The cops might've seen some scratches on his Beemer but nothing bad enough to interest them in getting out of their car.

When Terry looked back, the black kid was crouching in the corner of the sofa, like he was trying to hide behind Allie, so the cops couldn't look through the windows and see him. Allie, on the other hand, was beaming. Like she'd just seen a real-life demonstration of a cool new video game. One she had to have.

Terry saw when she smiled she was really very pretty. He could understand now how she could get the black kid to steal a car or do pretty much anything else she wanted.

"Hey, you did know!" Allie said. "Me 'n' BooBoo—"

"Hey, shit!" The boy came alive, upset at having his name revealed.

"Shut up!" Allie ordered. "I call him BooBoo. He calls

himself Abu Ali Baba, or somethin', but his real name's Richard Millberry. His mama calls him Dickie."

If Terry hadn't been there, he was sure there would have been a punchout. But he was no longer certain who'd win. As it was, Allie went right on. "Me 'n' BooBoo, the cops woulda caught us for sure."

A point he might have considered earlier, Terry thought. Be rid of these two by now. He looked at BooBoo. The black kid wasn't about to concede that Terry had done them a favor.

"Hey," Allie said, "I got an idea."

"Yeah?" Terry asked. He could see the sparkle in her eyes.

"You said we oughta commit a crime we're suited for. You got any idea what it'd be?"

Terry thought this girl was crazy.

Then again, maybe he was, too.

Because he did have an idea for her.

Fetch picked up on it immediately.

"Terry's sending Allie and BooBoo out to rob a hair salon. That's what you were talking about before."

"Is that right?" Karl asked.

Lerome nodded.

"The cops are the CPD," Karl said, showing a good memory for detail. "Where is this, Cleveland?"

Fetch shook his head. "Chicago. The guy who wrote the story works for the *Tribune*."

He could remember a thing or two himself.

"Chicago," Lerome confirmed for Karl.

"Okay," Fetch said, "he's sending them out to do a job, but why a hair salon?"

"Why's he sending them out at all?" Karl asked.

"Because he's fucking with them," Fetch answered. "They screwed up the job he's doing, he's paying them back."

That was a little twisted, but Karl could see it.

"Yeah, all right, but there's still your question. Why a salon?"

They looked to Lerome for an answer. He waited them out.

Surprisingly, this time Karl got it.

"There's someone at the salon Terry wants to fuck with, too."

Lerome laughed. "You boys are pretty good at this."

"But who the hell robs a hair salon?" Fetch wanted to know. "How much money could there be in that?"

Lerome helped out this time.

"Would it be very interesting if it was just nickels and dimes?"

Fetch and Karl shook their heads in unison.

"Terry must have an idea how to up the action," Fetch said.

"And he's gotta know the police response time for the job, right?" Karl asked.

Lerome nodded.

"And," Fetch added, "Allie and BooBoo have to get away or you got the same problem as before, the story ends too soon."

Karl was so excited about this voyage of literary discover-er he was grinning and rubbing his hands together. He'd completely forgotten about his own precarious position.

"Come on, Lerome," he said, "let's hear what happens next."

"Sure, Karl. But the next question is, after you boys hear it, will you be ready to do it?"

That was the question, all right. Fetch and Karl turned and looked at each other.

Verene looked over at Archer. The old bank robber lay

sleeping quietly. One of his saving graces was, he didn't snore. She slipped out of bed and pulled on an oversized pink T-shirt that said *Bitch Kitty*. Just putting weight on her feet made her feel how sore her crotch was.

"For a sick old man, you got some pecker on you," she whispered.

She liked a rough ride, but there'd been a moment when her skull hit the headboard she'd seen stars. Only thing that saved her was all her thick hair.

It wouldn't do at all to have Archer fuck her to death.

Maybe next time they'd have to put all the money they'd stolen from Fetch somewhere beside the foot of the bed, if the damn old man was going to get that worked up.

She went to pee and when she came back to bed she picked up the TV remote from the night stand and turned on the set in time for the beginning of the late news. People all over the world were shooting the asses off one another, but there was no mention of Fetch being captured and sent back to prison.

That worried Verene.

She and Archer had been sure Fetch would be caught fast. Probably on the road within a few miles of Camp Alphonse. But if the cops had caught him there or anywhere else it'd be news, a story that'd be on before the weather forecast. Once Verene saw that tomorrow would be a nice day, sunny in the 70s, she turned off the TV.

She looked at the money stacked at the foot of the bed.

They'd been good about not spending too much. Only ten grand. With Archer, sex, food, and liquor were all he needed. Well, he'd bought a CD or two of dance music. Him and Fetch, the two of them could move like those guys in the old Hollywood musicals. There were moments when Verene was in their arms, one or the other, she thought she actually loved them.

Then the music stopped, she wasn't Ginger Rogers anymore, and she remembered the way the world really was. It was like mama said: *love don't pay the rent.*

Mama knew. The Victorian house was hers and she was renting it to Verene at market rate. Only concession, Verene didn't have to pay a security deposit.

She glanced at Archer again. Babies didn't sleep any better. She could pack up all that money right there, be gone, and Archer wouldn't know it until he woke up in the morning.

Probably wouldn't try that hard to find her, either.

Just go back to that shacky little place where Fetch grew up, and collect his disability checks. Die before too long. Leave her free and clear.

Except she wasn't about to give up Karl.

Certainly, Fetch would get caught before her wedding day. Wouldn't he?

A chilling thought occurred to Verene. She shook Archer hard enough to rouse him momentarily.

"What?" he mumbled. "What the fuck's goin' on?"

"Lerome's not back, is he?" Verene asked, peering down at Archer.

"He's been gone a long time. Nobody knows when ..."

Archer fell asleep once more.

Verene hated Lerome. He was the only man she knew who'd never liked her wiggle 'n' jiggle. Wasn't like he was queer, either. He went out with women. He just didn't like her.

If there got to be many more like him ...

Like that Daniel Cameron guy today. Verene hopped out of bed and got his card off the dresser. Looking at it again, she remembered how much Cameron had scared her. It was bad enough he'd found out where she lived, but to know Archer was there with her —

Archer hadn't given a fuck. Said it was only natural family got together in times of crisis. Hell, they could be saying the rosary together for all any goddamn reporter knew.

Verene knew better than that.

What the hell had Fetch taken from Cameron anyway? When did he have the time?

And how could she make some money out of the situation?

There was too much Verene didn't know.

But one thing for sure, she wasn't going to let men start scaring her.

She looked at the business card again, and the phone number on the back.

Verene said, "Time I got to know you better, sweetie."

CHAPTER 13

Dan and Erin had breakfast in their room that Wednesday morning, Erin finishing her coffee as she ran a spell-check on last night's work. Her typing was fast, but she was only a C+ speller. Then there were times Dan deliberately misspelled dialogue for effect. She had to ask him about that. Later, it'd be his fight with the copy editor to preserve intentional errors.

Dan would look up from reading the *Buffalo News* whenever Erin had a question about the manuscript. Otherwise, he was following the story of the continuing hunt for Fetch Mcdonald. It was still front-page news. But there had been no mention of the jailbreak in the *USA Today* either yesterday or today. It was strictly a local story.

Even the *News* had nothing to say about the break-in at Lester Croart's cabin. They were still flying under the media radar about the loss of the Remington.

Erin finished her chore, saved the file, and backed it up to disk. Before they went out, she'd put the disk and Dan's supporting materials in the suite's safe. She sat next to Dan on the sofa and put a hand on his leg.

"The dictation went very well last night," she said "I

think you covered everything and might even have improved on the previous draft."

Dan put his newspaper down. "Except for your observation about men and their dicks," he said. A writer could turn on even his most well-meaning critic.

"Well, yeah, but you're a man — and after what followed the writing last night I might even have more sympathy for the male point of view."

She kissed her husband and gave his crotch a friendly squeeze. "So what'd the Buffalo paper have to say?" Erin had seen the headline about Fetch Mcdonald but hadn't read the story yet.

"They mention that the cops still suspect him of being the Everyman Bank Robber."

"After what Gamble showed us yesterday, there's no doubt, is there?"

Dan decided to play devil's advocate, reporters being natural skeptics. "What was it we saw? A piece of card stock with a smeared block-letter note."

"A note only the bank robber knew," Erin reminded him.

Dan shook his head. "Some tellers remembered it, too. Verbatim, Gamble said. And then Gamble himself knew the messages. You think maybe—"

"Gamble wrote that note, faked it?"

Erin's initial reaction was to be indignant, but she wasn't naive, she knew people could do almost anything that was in their self-interest. The man she'd been engaged to before she'd met Dan had once tried to outrace her on cross-country skis so a pissed-off grizzly bear would eat her instead of him. He'd failed. After that, she'd taken a more suspicious view of human nature.

Even so, she shook her head now.

"I think Gamble's playing it straight. I think Fetch Mcdonald wrote that note, and it was only his dumb luck it wasn't found at the right time."

Dan valued Erin's judgment even when it contradicted his own. He also accepted that fate liked to stick it to certain people. Him, for example. Getting Ben Hecht's typewriter only — maybe — to lose it. Along with the sole copy of the manuscript of his new novel.

"Okay," Dan said. "Fetch robbed all those other banks, and since the money wasn't found, let's assume he had it waiting for him."

"Yeah."

"What good reason would he have had to escape three weeks before he's paroled?"

"Yeah, what?" Erin thought Fetch's breakout sounded crazier than ever.

"Remember I said Verene Digby looked like nothing but trouble? And she's got Fetch's dad staying with her. Who would know Fetch better than the two of them?"

"Lerome," Erin answered. "Gamble said they're like brothers."

That threw Dan but only for a second.

"True, but Gamble also said he thinks Lerome's the one who helped Fetch escape."

"So?"

So if Gamble's right, Fetch obviously trusts Lerome, and likely for good reason," said Dan. "But what if Verene and Archer figured out where Fetch hid his money?"

"What if they did? How would Fetch know that?"

"He wouldn't. They wouldn't want him to know."

"Then we're back to the original problem. Why would Fetch break out with only three weeks left on his sentence?"

Dan grinned. "Before you woke up this morning, I Googled Verene Digby."

Erin hung her head. "The wife is always the last to know." Then she looked up and laughed. "What'd you find?"

"Verene is getting married again."

Erin's eyes went wide. "No."

"Yes. There was an announcement in the *Buffalo News*. And unless you're a celebrity, you have to pay a newspaper to print the details of your wedding. The date is set for the Saturday before Fetch's previously scheduled release."

"Jeez, that's not just bad, it's wicked." Then Erin frowned. "But Fetch would still have to read about it. Do prisons get newspapers?"

The very idea that *any* American, incarcerated or not, didn't have access to a newspaper was an affront to Dan. But he said, "We'll have to check, but the evidence — Fetch's escape — suggests that Camp Alphonse does."

"Let me put this all together and see if I've got it right," Erin said. "Fetch breaks out of jail — with Lerome's help, Gamble says — because he learns his ex-wife is getting remarried. He has to want her back or he'd serve out what little time he has left."

Dan nodded.

Erin continued, "Since we know from Gamble that Fetch was the Everyman Bank Robber, we assume he's hidden the loot from all the other bank jobs. That means he can return to Verene a monied man. Win her back before she marries this other guy. What's his name, anyway?"

Dan got up and consulted his notes. "Karl Hyacinth."

"But Fetch doesn't know it's all a trap. His ex-wife and his father want him to get caught and sent back to prison for a long time so they can share Fetch's money and not worry about him taking his money back or wreaking his vengeance on them."

Dan and Erin both fell silent looking for holes in their reasoning.

"I think it works," Dan said, sitting down next to his wife once more.

"Yeah, but one thing. If Fetch is hell bent to get Verene back, I can see him stealing our car — he needed it — but what about the point you made? Why take your typewriter and novel? A guy in a hurry's gonna do that?"

That was when it hit Dan. "Who does Gamble say helped Fetch?"

Erin got it, too "Lerome! He took your stuff."

"We better learn everything we can about him," Dan said.

"Wait. One more thing."

"What?"

"If Verene has Fetch's money ... she must hold the whip-hand over Archer, right?"

The pussy-whip hand, Dan thought, but he just nodded.

"Then why's she still around?" Erin asked. "Why not get the hell outta town? Why take a chance Fetch will find her?"

All good questions, Dan thought. Ones that would have to be answered for his new book. But all he could say was, "I don't think she's normal. You've got to see her."

"Yeah, I think I should," Erin replied. "Let's go."

Dan and Erin had just driven off in their rental car when the taxi carrying Verene pulled up in front of the Chateau. The doorman helped Verene out of the cab and she handed him a twenty-dollar bill to pay the fare, which was only eight dollars.

"Take care of the meter," Verene told him. "You two can work out the tips."

Verene didn't look back, but she knew she'd caused no small amount of mischief, leaving two guys who lived for tips to decide who got what.

She knew what kind of place the Chateau was and by her standards her attire was conservative. Her maroon dress was buttoned primly to her throat and the hemline reached almost to her knees. But the dress was molded to her figure — a thong eliminating visible panty lines — and she wore three-inch spike heels.

Verene just couldn't go a day without inspiring a few male fantasies. There were two guys in blue suits staring at her right now. The older one with a fringe of white hair said something to his middle-aged friend and left. The one who'd stayed behind walked right over to her. For a knee-knocking second, Verene thought he was the house dick.

Then her critical eye told her his suit was too good for any kind of flatfoot. And what was getting into her anyway? A man scaring her again. She wasn't a whore. She had money. She was nicely dressed.

"May I help you, madam?" Rudy asked.

"I'm looking for—"

"A room? I'm so sorry," he said. "We're completely booked."

His expression was full of regret; Verene didn't buy it for a minute.

"I'm looking for a man," she said, iron in her voice, "this man."

She showed Dan's card to Rudy.

He managed to keep the frown off his face. He realized this creature might actually have business with one of the hotel's guests. Worse, reading the card, he saw the guest was the husband of the lovely ... Rudy couldn't help himself. He gave Verene the once-over, mentally comparing her to Erin and—

"You having a good time?" Verene asked, her tone contemptuous, but secretly pleased.

Rudy did his best to keep his face from going red.

"I'm sorry but Mr. Cameron left not five minutes ago," he said.

"He checked out?"

Rudy wanted to lie and say yes, but if Dan Cameron had

actually invited ...

"No," he said, "but he did go out. With his wife."

When he saw the woman frown he knew he'd done the right thing mentioning Erin. Just as it would be proper — should he see Erin before her husband — to mention this woman to her.

"Is there anything I might do for you, madam?"

"Not on your salary," Verene said and slipped him a ten.

Rudy looked at the money in his hand as Verene walked off. The creature had tipped him. The general manager had just spoken with Rudy about the advisability of accepting members of the arts community as guests, e.g. Dan Cameron, object of the creature's interest and friend of former federal coppers. Rudy was beginning to see his point.

He passed the ten on to his favorite bellman, reassuring himself he was quite well-paid, thank you.

Verene hit the sidewalk. She had the final fitting for her wedding gown in twenty-five minutes. Okay, she thought, Cameron hadn't been in and he had his wife with him. Made things a little harder but not impossible. She'd taken a lot of guys away from a lot of wives, and she was a patient hunter. But not always the most discerning of predators.

She'd noticed the stocky black man walking up Delaware Avenue toward the Chateau. Figured him for one of the hotel's guests. His suit was every bit as good as the one on that gasbag inside; of course, that could make him another member of the hotel's snooty staff.

In any case, she turned her back on him and went about her business.

Gamble Murtree, who had been on his way to visit Dan and Erin, knew Fetch Mcdonald's ex-wife when he saw her. He decided on a new plan for his morning. He'd follow Verene Digby. See what she might be up to today.

***

Karl did his best not to cry as Fetch shaved his head. All that beautifully colored blonde hair falling on his lap and down his collar. It was so downy soft from his jicamilla root conditioner it didn't even itch. He consoled himself that he could always grow it back. If he survived.

Fetch brought a hand-mirror over and said, "Take a look."

Karl didn't want to. He was sure his face didn't have the character to carry off the clean-shaved look like, say, Yul Brynner. Or Telly Savalas Or even G. Gordon Liddy.

"Come on," Fetch urged. "You got a nice smooth dome. No bumps or lumps, and I didn't put a nick on you."

"It is kinda cool, Karl," Lerome said from where he sat on the lip of Karl's clawfooted bathtub. "You might have the beginning of a look there."

Well, if Lerome thought it was cool ... Karl raised his eyes. At least his ears didn't stick out. And he did have a nice strong brow, a broad forehead, and a really round head. Planes and curves. Very geometric, but ...

"My scalp's a lot whiter than my face," Karl whined.

Chalk to basketball orange, but Fetch assured him, "We'll get you some makeup or something."

"I have my own tanning bed," Karl told him.

"There you go," Lerome put in with a smile.

"But .... I just don't know if Verene is going to like this," he said.

"You know who Verene's favorite president is?" Fetch asked.

"Who?" Karl played along.

"Ben Franklin."

"Franklin wasn't a president."

"Yeah, I told her that. She told me he's on hundred dollar bills so he had to be a president. Ben was an old and bald guy but he's serious money and Verene loves him. You get what I'm saying?"

Karl did and it depressed him.

"Here, try these," Lerome told him.

He took off his sunglasses and extended them to Karl. Karl noticed two things. Lerome looked cool even without his sunglasses, and his eyes weren't black. Karl had expected they'd be as dark as his shades. But Lerome's eyes were such a light shade of brown they were almost khaki. Karl wondered if he could get contact lenses that color. For now, though, he said thanks and slipped on Lerome's sunglasses.

Karl looked in the mirror and the first thing that caught his attention was his mouth. He'd never appreciated it before but he had cruel lips. Kinda like Elvis when he sneered. He did his best to imitate the King.

Fetch and Lerome looked at each other.

Last night, Fetch had raised the possibility of hiding out until a week from Saturday, when Karl and Verene were supposed to get married, then take everybody in the church hostage until Verene gave him his money back.

Lerome had said, "And maybe Verene'll have a change of heart and run off with you?"

Fetch had nodded sullenly.

"All right," Lerome continued, "let's think of your idea like a story. You're sitting down at Dan Cameron's Remington going to write it out. Fetch seizes control of the church and then what?"

"Who's going to help him?" Karl wanted to know. "It's a big church."

"Lot of doors?" Lerome asked.

Karl counted in his head. "At least eight."

"And how many guests?"

"Two hundred and forty-six."

"Fetch couldn't very well ask you to help take hostages at your own wedding, Karl. Some things a man just won't do."

Karl agreed.

"So, Fetch, here's the scene: one guy tries to keep two hundred and forty-six people hostage in a church with eight doors. How're you going to write that one?"

With the cops shooting him down like a dog, Fetch thought. After every last person except Verene has escaped. And he doesn't have the heart to shoot Verene because he still wants her to tell him she loves him. Only she doesn't. She laughs at him as he dies.

That was when Fetch agreed to do the hair salon job.

For which Karl, to be fair to him, would have to change his appearance. And with his head shaved and wearing Lerome's sunglasses it was unlikely anyone would recognize Karl for who he really was.

They didn't know if the Buffalo PD was faster on its feet than the cops in Chicago, so to be safe they decided that Fetch and Karl would have seven minutes to do the job and get away, unlike the nine minutes Allie and BooBoo had in the story.

After that ... time expired.

Karl was still working up a repertoire of menacing expressions in front of the mirror when Lerome told Fetch, "Remember to have him take off the nail polish."

Fetch nodded. Black nail polish on a robber was something that'd be noticed at a beauty salon robbery.

"You'll get the guns for me?" No more phony explosives for Fetch.

Yeah. Be back later," Lerome told his cousin.

On his way out, he grabbed Dan Cameron's manuscript. He wanted to show it to Ants.

"You forget your keys, baby?" Archer Mcdonald called out as he unlocked the front door of the Victorian house on Norwood Avenue. He threw open the door wearing only soiled tightie-whities with a noticeable bulge at the crotch.

He blinked when he saw Dan and Erin. No reflection on Erin, but his erection withered.

"Who the hell're you?" he demanded.

Neither of the Camerons answered.

Both of them looked past the old robber's bony bare shoulders to where the door to a bedroom stood open not fifteen feet away. Archer finally realized he was revealing more than his scrawny anatomy.

He scuttled over to the bedroom and pulled the door shut. Then he returned to the front door and repeated his question. He got a response this time but it was not on point.

Erin told him, "That looked like a whole lot of money in there."

"About $480,000 is my guess," Dan added.

Dan and Erin looked at each other, then back at Archer. He seemed to be having a hard time controlling his bowels. And he decided at that point he didn't really need to know who his visitors were. He slammed the door in their faces.

Verene stood on a pedestal at The Bride Wore White. She figured a girl was entitled to wear white if it was the first time she got married — to any given man. Besides, once anybody saw her dress they'd know she wasn't trying to pretend she was a virgin.

The neckline V'ed so deeply that the only thing that would keep the ceremony PG-13 was the elaborate diamond necklace she'd had Karl buy her. All those sparklers covered a lot of flesh. Offered guys a great excuse to give their dates for staring at her.

"Her tits? No, dear, I was just admiring that beautiful necklace."

If the women were smart they'd say, "Great, I'll get one just like it."

"You have such a stunning figure," the shop owner told Verene. "I think the dress is perfect the way it is."

The wedding gown was slit up the sides to mid-thigh. Verene thought maybe go all the way to the hips, but deferred to the expert's judgment that that would be a little over the top. After all, this was Buffalo not Vegas.

The shop owner brought out a Polaroid camera to photograph Verene.

A memento of perfection, she said. In fact, it was protection in case the bride changed her mind. Wanted a free alteration. She snapped one for Verene and one for herself. But frowned as the prints developed.

Verene saw the owner's critical expression from the pedestal where she'd remained. She loved being up there. Thought maybe she'd have Karl buy one for her.

"What's wrong?" she asked. "Is it me or the dress? The dress, right?"

The owner shook her head.

"Me?" Verene's voice was a squeak.

"Neither you nor the dress, my dear. She looked past Verene at the front window of the shop and sighed. "Let me get another couple of shots."

Verene stepped down from the pedestal.

"No, let me see what you have."

The owner reluctantly showed her, saying, "I didn't notice when I took the pictures, but apparently there was a peeper staring through the window at you."

Verene looked at the prints. In each one, wearing a startled expression, was the black man she'd seen out in front of the Chateau. What kind of creep would—

She recognized him. Having the borders of the photograph around his face jarred her memory. She'd seen his picture in the paper. He was with the FBI.

What the hell was his name again? Had something to do with money.

Gamble, that was it! She couldn't remember if Gamble was his first name or last. But he was definitely a fed, the one who'd been after Fetch. In fact, this was the guy who'd gone on and on about how Fetch had to be the Everyman Bank Robber. Which was what had started her thinking.

After Fetch had been arrested, she'd learned that he'd lost his job six months earlier and had never told her. So where had the money come from for them to live on? How had Fetch bought her that new wardrobe and those sapphire earrings?

Wasn't long before Verene decided this FBI guy was right. Her husband had been the Everyman Bank Robber. She'd been thrilled. Not that Fetch had been a daring and elusive criminal, but that he must've left a pile of money around for her to find.

Only thing was she hadn't been able to find it by herself. But once she and Archer put their heads, and other things, together they'd succeeded. Found every last dollar Fetch stole. Okay, it took them almost seven years ... Jesus, seven years! They'd *earned* that money.

They'd had to be careful not to spend it all, too. They started spending big, what were they going to say if someone with a badge was keeping an eye on them and asked where all the money came from? Besides, she and Archer had both enjoyed seeing the pile of cash grow bigger and bigger. In the meantime, Archer had his welfare check, and she had —

A chill ran through Verene.

The money. It was sitting right there in her bedroom. That reporter had already found out where she lived. What if this FBI guy did, too? What if he got a search warrant?

Not only would she lose the money, she'd probably go to jail as Fetch's accomplice.

Verene had a hard time not running out of the store in her bridal gown. She had the shop owner call a cab for her while she changed. She certainly didn't bother about another photo.

But she took the one with Gamble in it.

Jennifer, a summer intern, was sitting behind the circulation desk of the Delaware Park Branch Library when Lerome came in. There were five older people he could see browsing the new-books shelves or reading at the long wooden tables. A pair of boys who looked about sixteen were at a computer in a far corner giggling and casting furtive looks for any sign of an approaching librarian: either downloading porn or hacking into somebody else's computer. They froze when Lerome headed their way. Then the one at the keyboard started typing very fast.

Lerome stopped short of where he could see the computer monitor.

"Having a good time?" he asked.

"Schoolwork," said the one at the keyboard.

"World history," added the one standing at his buddy's shoulder.

"Summer school do-over, ya know?"

"Went to summer school myself," Lerome said. Not because he had to. He'd figured it'd be a good way to finish high school in three years. But the statement established rapport.

"Sucks, don't it?" asked the standing kid.

"Has its advantages if you can figure them out."

Lerome saw they couldn't, not today anyway.

He continued, "Listen, my friend's the librarian here."

"Her?" The sitting kid nodded at Jennifer who was looking their way. Smiling.

Jennifer was eighteen, and if either of these guys could spend time with her they wouldn't bother with computers. Or each other.

"No," Lerome answered, "but if you like girls like that —

real ones, I mean — think about what you have to offer them. Then see if you can add a little to the package. Meanwhile, don't mess with my friend's computers, okay?"

Both boys nodded. They got up and left the library whispering to each other. Forgetting their schoolbooks. The name scrawled on one book was Axel; the other said Petey.

When Lerome got to the circulation desk, Jennifer asked, "Any more like you at home?"

"Not unless Mom and Dad have been keeping secrets," he told her.

She giggled and said, "I'll get Ms. Lowney."

Jennifer walked to the librarian's office, giving her hips a little extra sway.

Ants came out a moment later, smiled, and stepped over to Lerome.

"Come on," she said, "I want to show you something."

She looked at the box Lerome was carrying; he observed the sheaf of papers she had.

They headed for the storage room while Jennifer held down the fort.

"Still knocking the summer help dead," Ants told him.

"Rousting underage peepers, too," he said.

Ants opened the door to the storage room and flipped on the lights. Lerome saw immediately that Ants had staged a show for his benefit. On a table directly in front of him she'd placed three Remington Noiseless Portables. Not a one was dusty. All of them had mirror finishes and each had a fresh ribbon.

"Did a heckuva job restoring them," Lerome observed.

"Jessi did that."

"Sure, right up her alley."

"One of them is the one you gave me. One of them is the one I had back here. One them used to be the Underwood."

Lerome nodded.

"Which one's yours?" Ants asked.

He grinned at her, liking the way she was playing with him.

"You mean yours, don't you? I gave it to you."

"Yeah, but we both know who wants to use it."

Lerome had never seriously considered marriage until just that moment; now he was thinking Ants was the one.

"What've you got there?" he asked, nodding at the papers in her hand.

"Well, being a librarian I read a lot. I seemed to remember a story or two about a typewriter just like the one you gave me. I checked." She waved the sheets of paper. "A guy by the name of Daniel Cameron got one from his wife. Used to belong to Ben Hecht."

Lerome didn't recognize the name Hecht but he knew Ants would fill in the details. Like: "Interesting thing is, Cameron used the Hecht typewriter to write a best-selling novel."

"Yeah? You got a copy here?"

"Two, in fact. I put one aside. Now, what's that you've got?"

Lerome tucked the cardboard box under his arm and patted it. "Dan Cameron's new novel, I guess. Only copy as far as I know."

Ants nodded. "Let's do some reading tonight. My place."

"Sounds good," Lerome said. He looked over at the three Remingtons again. Tried to see which one he'd taken from his new favorite author. "You know which one I gave you?"

Ants smiled. "Yeah, but do you?" Before he could answer, she added, "One other thing."

"What?"

"I might have a lead on finding Jimmy." Her son.

Lerome said, "I have a new SUV. Take us anywhere we want to go."

"Looks like we have plenty to talk about."

CHAPTER 14

Lerome stopped by Karl's house. He brought two guns.
A Beretta for Fetch, a Ruger for Karl. Karl's gun was loaded
— to give him the feel of a serious weapon — but it didn't
have a firing pin. Fetch's semi-auto was a working model.
Fetch told his cousin, "A prop would've been good for
me, too. It's not like I'm going to shoot anyone."
Lerome reminded him, "You might have to shoot Karl if
he tries to leave the team."
"Karl won't give me up," Fetch responded. "He knows
he'd have to deal with you."
Karl looked at Lerome, who was wearing a new pair of
sunglasses. The insurance broker thought nobody'd under-
write a life policy for anyone who messed with Lerome.
"I-I'll be good," he said.
"We know you will, Karl," Fetch told him.
In fact, it had been Karl who'd picked their target, a
place called The Permanent Fave. It was on a high-end
retail block on the Elmwood Strip between downtown and
Buffalo State. The college or its neighbor the psychiatric
center, take your pick. Karl said lots of professional women
had their hair done there. Wives of politicians, too. From
what he'd heard and read, it was as fancy a women's hair

place as Buffalo had to offer.

Lerome thought Karl's knowledge sounded more personal than anecdotal.

"You ever do business with this place, Karl?"

Karl confessed he'd bid on fire and liability insurance for the salon a couple of years ago, but the owner had gone with someone else. Even though Karl's price had been lower.

"The owner told me she didn't like my haircut," Karl said in a quiet voice.

Fetch and Lerome looked at each other, thinking the same thing. Payback. Just like in *Time Expires*. Both of them felt better that Karl would actually hold up his end, knowing he had an axe to grind.

But Fetch asked, "This broad didn't like your blonde 'do?"

"This was before I met Verene. My hair was kinda ... orange."

"Well, nobody'll recognize you now," Lerome told him.

Fetch called the salon, asked how late they were open and could he get an appointment. The place was open till ten, extended hours because of a gala at the Albright-Knox Art Gallery tomorrow. But they didn't do men's hair.

Sexist, Fetch thought. But he asked, "Busy, huh?"

"Crazy!" Click.

Lerome gave Fetch new license plates to put on Karl's car. They hadn't been stolen; Jessi had made them. They purported to be Canadian, from Quebec. *Je me souviens.* If some eagle-eye spotted the plates and told the cops, they would be traced to a Monsieur Arnaud Dutetre of Trois Rivieres. M. Dutetre better have an alibi that put him north of the border when The Permanent Fave was robbed because no way he'd ever guess an American auto thief had hacked into the provincial automobile registration database and filched his number. Used it to make plates for someone else who also drove a 2001 white Ford Focus. When the job was done, Jessi'd get the plates back, melt them down, and start all over again. Identity theft on wheels. Another of Lerome's ideas.

He told Fetch, "Good luck." Added, "You, too, Karl." Then he was gone.

Fetch looked at his partner in crime. "You ready?"

Karl nodded, his throat too dry to speak.

"Good. One last thing then." Fetch had to be sure. "Your car running right?"

When Fetch and Karl arrived at the Permanent Fave at 9:30 p.m. a valet came to park their getaway car. The joint was jumping, but the rest of the block was quiet. Most Buffalonians sensibly chose to get their rest on a work night. Fetch — now wearing sunglasses; Karl wearing Lerome's shades — stuck his gun under the valet's nose, left the car double-parked, and prayed to God it wouldn't be towed in the seven minutes they had to do the job. He walked his captive toward the shop. When he got to the front door, he looked back and saw Karl was still in the car.

He gave his accomplice a short, sharp whistle. *Come on, fuckhead. Showtime.*

Karl got out of the car. A shudder passed through him. Looked almost like a *grand mal* seizure to Fetch. He hoped to Christ his new partner in crime wasn't epileptic. But Karl straightened up. Even moved toward the salon with a surprising sense of purpose.

Fetch opened the shop's door and pushed the valet into a maelstrom of women whose hair was undergoing cosmetic alchemy, changing from lead to gold. The first thing any of them noticed, the valet went down on his knees and clasped his hands together like an altar boy.

"Please," the kid sobbed, "please don't."

The valet obviously thought his number was up.

Probably everyone else's, too. Massacre city. Made Fetch feel like a real creep.

"Shut the hell up!" Fetch ordered. "Ladies, we're here to do business and that's all."

Every woman in the shop looked at him blankly. Even with the gun in his hand. The problem with robbing a place where nobody expected it, the victims couldn't believe it was for real. Then a voice sounded behind Fetch that raised the hair on his neck.

"This's a fuckin' robbery! Everybody into the nose-candy room!"

Fetch swiveled his head. Karl was supposed to be watching the door. Making sure none of these broads slipped outside and started screaming. Instead, he had a skinny brunette by her shirt collar and had his non-functional gun stuck in her ear.

Fetch'd bet she was the one who picked the wrong insurance broker.

Karl's scalp, which he might have overdone in the tanning bed trying to even things out with his face, was glowing bright red. A vein throbbed in his crimson dome.

If that's what the kid on the floor had been looking at, Fetch didn't blame him for being scared. And where the hell had Karl gotten that voice: James Earl Jones with 'roid rage.

But it got everyone on their feet, running and bleating toward the ladies room at the back of the place. As Karl had visited the premises in his earlier life as a mild-mannered businessman, he knew the layout. Fetch had agreed that the ladies room was the place to confine everyone while they made off with the money.

Karl had confided it was an open secret that more than a few of the salon's customers elevated their moods in the lavishly appointed lavatory. Which was probably another reason he hadn't gotten the account, he'd said. He wasn't a part of the drug scene.

But he had just betrayed knowledge of what went on in the ladies loo. Everybody was too panicked to pick up on that now, but somebody'd remember later. Fetch would have to point out that little misstep — if Karl ever regained his sanity.

Right now, the woman Karl had grabbed was about to liquify. Karl wasn't saying a word to her. Just hyperventilating in her ear. The one that didn't have a gun in it. Poor thing was too terrified to do more than whimper.

Karl obviously didn't take rejection well, but Fetch didn't want anybody dying of a heart attack. He stepped up behind Karl and stuck his gun against Karl's right kidney where no one else could see it.

"Let her go," Fetch whispered.

Karl turned to look at him, like he didn't want to. So Fetch pushed harder with his gun until the message sank in. The woman would have fallen if Fetch hadn't caught her arm. He led her to the bathroom where the others waited.

One older woman with curlers in her hair and a little more fiber in her diet had her cell phone out.

"911?" Fetch asked. He shook his head. "That's a no-no. You want Psycho to come in and explain to you?"

The phone fell from the woman's hand, shattered on the marble floor.

Fetch told them, "Just relax, give it half-an-hour, you'll all be fine. Do something silly, I let Psycho off his leash."

He closed the door to the ladies room.

As Fetch turned around, he was pleased to see Karl already had the straps of 15-20 purses looped over his arms. "You get the register, too?" he asked.

Karl nodded.

"Great Let's go."

They were out of there in six minutes and forty-five seconds, Fetch driving away without a cop in sight. That was when Karl decided to have a breakdown, started blubbering like a baby.

Fetch backhanded him a good one.

"No time for that," he said. "Separate the cash, write down the names, account numbers, and expiration dates from the credit cards."

Jarred back to his senses, Karl took a pen and a pad of paper out from under his seat. He got to work with the methodical speed of a true paper shuffler. After he'd established a rhythm, and without looking up, he asked Fetch, "Did I do okay? I tried to channel my fear into my performance."

That'd explain Karl's seizure, Fetch thought.

He grinned and said, "You were maybe a little over the top, Karl. But I think if we refine your act a bit, you might be on to something."

Karl asked, "You mean we're going to do this again?"

Fetch wasn't sure at first if Karl was fearful or excited. Then, out of the corner of his eye, he saw Psycho was smiling as he wrote down the credit card information. Fetch knew he was going to be pleasantly surprised by how much money they'd net. More than he'd ever expected from a hair salon robbery. But it wouldn't enough for him to start a new life.

He told Karl, "Well, we have to keep up with Allie 'n' BooBoo, don't we?"

Karl nodded happily. Never breaking pace on the task at hand.

They dumped all of the stolen purses at the Buffalo Crushed Stone Quarry in Cheektowaga. The credit cards were left in the purses to give the impression that the robbers were low-tech loons — drug crazies no doubt — who couldn't handle anything more complicated than cash. In fact, Karl had compiled the data from more than a hundred separate credit card accounts, for which Lerome said he could get them fifty bucks a pop.

Not that they'd thought of that scam. Not even Lerome had. It'd come from Terry Phelan in *Time Expires*. Which meant it was really Dan Cameron's idea. Who knew a writer could plan a crime so well? Fetch wondered how Cameron would feel when he heard what happened.

Probably have mixed feelings. Pissed somebody'd stolen his idea. Proud it'd worked so well in real life. It'd give his work more credibility. Let any snot-nosed reviewer try to criticize him now.

The cash haul was $5,400. Add the sale of credit card data, the grand total was over 10K.

Once they got back to Karl's place, Fetch and Karl toasted each other with a St. Pauli Girl. But they didn't get drunk. They sat in Karl's finished basement and replayed the robbery in their heads. Fetch was surprised how much he'd enjoyed it.

Eight years in confinement, all he ever thought about was getting his hands on the money he'd stolen — and on Verene — so he could sit back and enjoy life. Never considered that he'd want to commit another crime for the thrill of it. Hell, he thought he was rehabilitated.

Now he had to wonder. If Verene had waited for him, if he had both her and the money ... would that have been enough? Or would he have gotten bored? Needed to find an outlet for whatever madness ran through his veins.

Archer had told him once that his branch of the Mcdonald family was a bad lot. From the time they'd arrived in the New World to the dawn of the 20th century wasn't a one of them who hadn't been hanged for one crime or another. And since then, all of the men had done at least some time behind bars. Maybe it was just some kind of genetic curse. Fetch seemed to remember reading something about a biological predisposition to committing crimes in the *Wall Street Journal.*

But what about Karl He'd been a straight arrow. Forced into committing his first crime. But once he'd channeled his fear, he was a real rip-snorter. Had Fetch ready to piss his pants So had Fetch and Lerome created a monster?

Fetch told Karl, "Half the take's yours, buddy."

"No, I don't need it. You keep it," Karl replied.

Hadn't even looked at Fetch. Still too busy reliving everything.

"You have to take it or I'll have to kill you."

Now Karl looked at Fetch. Not in fear but with a smile.

"Okay, I'll take it then."

Didn't exactly have to twist his arm, Fetch thought.

"Admit it, Karl," Fetch said, "you had fun tonight."

Karl didn't admit it, but he said, "You know, my whole working life, I've always had to sell people things. Usually things they didn't want."

Fetch said, "I used to sell, too. Copiers. I told you that, remember?"

"Yeah, you did So you understand then. It's so much easier just to *take* what you want. A lot more satisfying, too."

Uh-huh, Fetch thought. Until you got caught and they sent your ass to prison. But Fetch didn't want to burden Karl with that reality. Not while they still had more jobs to pull.

The two of them retreated to their thoughts and sipped their beers.

More alike than either would ever have imagined. Or admitted.

None of the women in the ladies room at the Permanent Fave wanted anything more to do with that red-skulled crazyman so they did as they were told and waited thirty minutes before another woman took out her cell phone and called 911.

While they waited, some of their number asked Nicole, the owner, if she minded if they soothed themselves with some non-prescription medication. But Nicole was still too traumatized to offer her consent. Then it was suggested that since they had summoned the police perhaps it would be better if they all stayed clean and sober.

That settled, it was decided they should all look their best for what was sure to become a media circus. The stylists used such combs, brushes, and scissors as they'd carried with them to work on their clients' tresses. For laboring under such adverse conditions, everyone was quite pleased with the results. They congratulated themselves for being a plucky bunch.

Except for one sourpuss. Teresa Runcy. Who still had curlers in her hair. Who was pissed that her $400 Nokia phone, a gift from her daughter, was broken into tiny pieces. Who was furious that she'd been scared silly and robbed by two thugs.

Who was also the wife of Buffalo mayor Ted Runcy. She was the first one to talk to the cops when they came. Her presence guaranteed that a strange little armed robbery became page-one news.

Verene hadn't moved for hours. Hadn't even closed her front door after she'd raced into her house. Her mother's house. Which she wouldn't be able to afford much longer if she didn't do something quick, because ...

That shit-eating bastard Archer Mcdonald had stolen her money!

Okay, okay. Technically, it was their money. They were partners in taking it from Fetch, but they'd both understood that Archer wasn't going to live forever — or even very much longer — and whatever was left would be Verene's.

Even before Archer died — once Fetch got caught and sent back to prison — the old man was supposed to move back to his shacky old place. He'd been okay with that. Verene had promised to come by at least three times a week to give Archer a quickie or a hummer. Make sure he had whatever he needed. Groceries, booze, a dance or two. Be his own visiting nurse.

Archer had to move out because Karl would be moving in. Karl's own house was every bit as nice as the Victorian and even bigger, but Verene wanted all of Karl's assets to be liquid as soon as they were man and wife. She could make a pile of Karl's money disappear no problem, but you couldn't put a house into a numbered account in the Cayman Islands.

Goddamnit, that was the plan!

It was good for both Archer and Verene.

But when she'd come home to warn Archer that they had to hide the money Fetch stole, before the FBI caught them and sent both of them to prison, Archer wasn't there. More important, neither was the money.

Four hundred and seventy thousand dollars and change, at last count.

She'd had a hard time catching her breath when she saw the money was gone. Thought she might faint dead away. Might die from the shock. She barely got to the living room sofa before her legs gave way.

After some time, her hope began to build. Maybe the FBI man, Gamble, had come by the house before he started following her. Maybe Archer had realized the danger and gone to hide the money on his own. Sure, a former bankrobber, he'd be smart enough to do that. After that was taken care of, he'd come back and get her.

She knew how much the old man wanted her. Her body, anyway. Couldn't get enough of that good stuff. He'd be back. But hours passed and a hateful realization took shape. With all that money even an old goat like Archer Mcdonald could buy all the sex he wanted. With women younger and prettier than her. She felt like such a fool. She felt like ... Fetch.

He'd been out of jail long enough by now to go after his money. And to see that it was gone. Figure out he'd been suckered. Used.

But nobody was going to use Verene Digby like that.

Anger finally got Verene off the sofa. Even if she had lost all of Fetch's money to Archer — and no way was she conceding that yet — she still had Karl. But the way things had changed, it might be a good idea to give the sap a little nookie. Make sure she locked him up tight.

She sure as hell couldn't afford to lose Karl. Not now. She went into the bathroom, fixed herself up. She got the Polaroid of herself in her wedding gown, cropped it judiciously — no more FBI Peeping Tom — and headed out.

Fetch'd just uncapped a couple more St. Pauli Girls, only the second bottles for him and Karl in the past two hours, when the doorbell rang. Fetch grabbed his gun and looked at Karl.

Karl looked at the stolen money sitting in front of them.

"You expecting anyone?" Fetch whispered.

Karl shook his head.

"Maybe we better hide the money," he suggested.

"Yeah," Fetch agreed. "But where?"

The doorbell rang again. Then someone pounded on the door.

Karl stood up quickly, removed the sofa cushion on which he'd been sitting, unzipped the fabric liner from the base of the sofa — and there was a safe. Fetch'd never seen a safe hidden in a sofa before, but now that he thought about it, Karl always made sure he sat right there. On top of his money. Which Fetch saw, as Karl opened the safe, was easily three or four times what they'd stolen that night. The two of them threw the hot cash into the safe. Karl locked it, rezipped the liner, and replaced the cushion. By now, the hammering on the door was relentless.

"Jesus, that's gotta be the cops," Fetch muttered.

"Do we shoot it out?" Karl asked.

Fetch looked at him, saw that Psycho was warming up for an encore.

Then the assault on the front door ceased. Still, Fetch thought it prudent to inform his protégé," You don't ever shoot it out with the cops. Don't ever get that crazy on me, okay?"

Before Karl could answer, they heard a familiar voice yell, "Shit!"

"Verene," they said in unison.

Fetch asked, "You never gave her a key?"

"Yeah, sure. But she always forgets it. Should we go see if she has to pee or something?"

Hard as it had been for him, Fetch had come to accept Lerome's explanation of things. Verene and Archer had stolen his money, set him up to break out of prison, and hoped he'd get caught and sent back for a long time. If Verene learned he was at Karl's, she would undoubtedly turn him in. Even so, he'd dreamed of her every night for eight years, and now she was nearby.

"We'll go take a peek," Fetch said. He added slyly, "I don't know if she's ready to see the new you."

Karl's hands went to his shaved and sunburned scalp. He'd forgotten about that. Still, he agreed it wouldn't hurt to take a look. The two of them crept upstairs and pulled a curtain back an inch, but Verene was gone.

They still got to see her, though.

She'd slipped a Polaroid under the door.

Verene in her wedding dress.

CHAPTER 15

The Camerons were sitting on the white silk sofa at the Chateau when Gamble Murtree called. Erin picked up the phone.

"Hey, stranger," Erin said cheerily. She enjoyed teasing the former fed. "Surprised we didn't see you today."

She silently mouthed Gamble's name to Dan. He picked up his writing pad and pen. Then he put his head next to Erin's so he could hear Gamble, too.

"I followed Verene Digby today," Gamble said.

Dan started taking notes but stayed silent.

"Yeah, what'd she do?" Erin asked.

"Went to try on her wedding dress." Gamble didn't mention that he let himself get photographed.

"What did it look like?" Erin asked, interested.

"Like something to make the best man run off with the bride."

Erin laughed. Dan put Gamble's description in quotes and underlined it.

"After that, she spent a lot of time at home."

Gamble also neglected to pass along that Verene had left the bridal shop in a big hurry, ran up the stairs at her house, and didn't even bother to close the door. He'd wondered about that. First, he thought she'd run right back out. Then he wondered if maybe she wasn't doing something desperate to herself. But he just couldn't picture her as the type to slash her wrists. So he'd waited her out.

"Little while ago, she came out driving a blue Corvette Stingray. Very nice old car. She drove over to her fiancé's house, a guy name of—"

"Karl Hyacinth," Erin provided.

"Right. Nobody answered the door. Which seemed to tick her off a lot. Then she got back in her car and went back home. And that's it. What'd you and your husband do today?"

Erin looked at Dan. He held his right thumb and index finger an inch apart. Give a little but not all. Erin knew what to hold back.

"We went over to Verene's house, too."

"Yeah?"

"Must've been there and gone before you arrived."

"You see Verene, talk to her?"

"No, just Archer Mcdonald."

Gamble thought about that a bit. "I didn't see him around at all."

"No? Well, he didn't have much to say to us, either. Slammed the door in our faces."

The Camerons didn't mention all the money they saw. Which they were more sure than ever had been the proceeds from Fetch Mcdonald's string of bank robberies.

"I wonder if Verene and Archer had a falling out," Gamble mused aloud.

"Gone their own ways?" Erin asked.

If so, who's got the money? Dan wrote.

"Well, we'll have to see if that means anything," Gamble said. Then he added, "Erin?"

"Yes, Gamble?"

"Tell Dan not to get so close to the phone. I can hear

him breathing."

Lerome and Ants sat up resting against the headboard of her bed. They'd gone out to dinner. Went to Ants' apartment on West Ferry Street and made love. Afterward, Ants put on a T-shirt that said: *Librarians do it by the book.* Lerome had his sunglasses off.

Ants told him he had dreamy eyes whenever they were in bed.

After they'd shared their bodies, they always shared their thoughts. Which was usually almost as much fun. Now, Ants told Lerome her lead on finding her son, Jimmy.

"I found this guy at the IRS. I might contribute to his early retirement."

Lerome looked at her but said nothing. He doubted his eyes still looked dreamy.

"I know, I know," Ants said. "It could be big trouble if it goes wrong."

"You want me to talk with this guy? See what kind of feeling I get?"

He made the offer; that was all he could do. Ants had survived eight years in the joint. Came out with two college degrees. Got herself a responsible job as a rehabilitated person. Of course, it didn't hurt that most women, including those in charge of the public library system, didn't think it was necessarily a bad thing to run over a wife-beater.

Still, he had to respect her rights as an independent person. Just like he couldn't make Fetch take the money he'd offered him, he had to let Ants choose her own road. It was harder in this case, though.

Ants knew how much discomfort she was causing Lerome. She couldn't see it — he held his feelings close — but she could feel it. She rested her head against his shoulder.

"I'll handle this myself," she said. "It's be okay. I'll know if he's trying to set me up. But if he isn't, well, Jerry's parents aren't tax outlaws." Jerry was her late, unlamented ex. "They'll be filing returns somewhere and then I'll know where to find Jimmy."

Ants had told Lerome once that she had her former in-law's Social Security numbers because Jerry used to do their taxes.

Lerome said, "Okay. Let me know if there's anything I can do."

If nothing else, Lerome would take care of the IRS guy if he busted Ants.

But for now he changed the subject. On the night table on Ants' side of the bed lay a copy of *Indecision Kills*. He nodded at it and asked, "How much does a writer get for a book?"

Ants shrugged. "As an advance, a few thousand to a few million. After that, it depends on how many copies it sells."

"How about Dan Cameron's book there?"

"Well, it was a first novel. But it's from a solid publisher, and he was a reporter for a big newspaper, so that might've given it a bit of a bump. Say mid-five to low-six figures for the advance. But a whole lot more later because it became a top-ten bestseller."

Ants looked at the cardboard box with *Time Expires* in it on the night table next to Lerome. "Now that one, that's going to be big money front end and back. The author's got a name now. Book buyers will be looking for him."

"So it's a valuable commodity," Lerome said.

"Yeah. That and the magic typewriter you stole for me. You stung Cameron good." Ants felt somewhat sorry for the writer. But the way she saw it, she'd had her son and eight years of her life stolen from her. You toughed it out and did whatever you could to make things right. She asked Lerome, "You thinking of ransoming Cameron's stuff back to him?"

"Not the typewriter," Lerome said, "that was a gift to you."

"But maybe one that looks just like it?"

Lerome grinned. "Let's read the first chapter together. We'll catch up with what I read to Fetch and his new friend, Karl, yesterday. Then we'll call the boys and read a little more."

"On the phone?"

"Yeah, Karl's got a speakerphone at his place. Something I noticed."

Dan sat at the desk in the suite at the Chateau and hummed to himself as he finished writing his notes of Erin's conversation with Gamble: *Got caught breathing too loudly. Embarrassing.*

Not that he was worried about it. As a mistake, it made for nice comic relief. Readers would enjoy it.

"You're having a good time, aren't you?" Erin asked.

Dan nodded, smiling.

"I think *Kidnapping Ben Hecht* is going to be good."

"Every dark cloud ..." Erin said. "But remember what you always tell me."

"What?" Dan asked. He put his pen down, finished for now.

"A book's only as good as its ending." Erin gave him the thumb, telling him to get up and let her sit down. She slid onto the chair and booted up her PowerBook.

"That's true. But the way this story is developing ..." Dan nodded to himself. "I think we're going to have a ... I was going to say a killer ending. But I don't want anyone to die."

"Not in the true-crime book," Erin agreed. "Now, in your novel ..." She handed Dan his outline and notes and said, "Let's go, maestro."

***

175

Ants looked at Lerome, "Wait a minute. You're having Fetch and this Karl guy commit the crime we just read about? Rob a hair salon?"

Lerome glanced at the clock on the night table. "They should have done it by now."

"Why? Why would they do it?"

"Fetch needs the money and is too proud to take it from me even though I offered."

Ants understood the subtext but said nothing.

"Karl has to incriminate himself so he won't rat on Fetch."

"He's the guy who's going to marry Verene?"

"That's another thing. A prison term'd be better for Karl than Verene."

"So now you want me to call Fetch and Karl and read them chapter two?"

"If you don't mind."

"I don't mind. I read to kids at the library all the time."

"Then you know what I better go get you."

"A glass of water," said Ants. "Reading aloud is thirsty work."

Lerome got out of bed to go for the water but Ants stopped him.

"What if it didn't work out like in the book? What if Fetch and Karl got caught? What if I call and a cop answers the phone?"

"Hang up," Lerome said.

Karl answered the phone when it rang. Fetch leaned in close to hear. Both of them expected the call to be from Verene.

"Hello," Karl said.

He had to remind himself not to say Sweetheart.

"Hello." A woman, but not Verene. "Is this Karl?"

"Yes."

"That Fetch I hear breathing next to you?"

Fetch took the phone from Karl. "Who is this?"

"Anthea Lowney of the Buffalo Public Library."

"What?"

Lerome came on the line, chuckling. "Ants is my very good friend."

"You bastard!"

"Who is it?" Karl demanded.

"Guess everything went okay," Lerome said.

Fetch couldn't help but smile. To Karl he said, "It's Lerome and a friend of his. He wants to know did everything go okay."

"Fucking great!" Karl exclaimed.

Lerome heard. "You can give me the details later. Right now, you guys want to hear chapter two of *Time Expires*, Ants'll read it to you."

"Karl," Fetch said, "turn on the speaker-phone."

Erin stretched her fingers over the PowerBook keyboard and gave Dan a nod.

He looked at his notes and began to dictate:

Terry Phelan picked up the rake that lay against Fayre Sanderson's front stoop and started pulling dead leaves, cigarette butts, malt liquor bottles, and other crap out of the small lawn in front of the two-flat graystone. He stopped to look at the building and compared it to the one he'd just purchased up the block.

This one was nicer, he thought Probably came at a cheaper price, too. But when you were the very first person to buy into a neighborhood you thought would gentrify, you got the pick of the litter. Which was only right. You had the smarts — the guts — to take the biggest risk, you deserved the biggest return.

Only Fayre Sanderson seemed to have an angle on taking a lot of the risk out of the proposition. She'd led the charge twice before, moving into neighborhoods that were marginal at best, war-zones at worst. Both times, though, the neighborhoods had come roaring back — not long after Fayre had moved in and started rehabbing her new places.

If the old neighbors had known her arrival meant they would soon be priced out of their homes, they would have burned her out the first night. But they didn't have a clue.

Terry Phelan did, and he'd decided to hitch his wagon to Fayre Sanderson's star. He went back to raking and a moment later heard a woman's voice behind him.

"You just being neighborly?"

He turned and saw her. Medium height, slender figure, bushy brunette hair, and green eyes. Wearing a blue chambray shirt, jeans, scuffed sneakers, and no makeup. She held a big brown yard waste bag in her hands.

Didn't look tough, but anybody who took the chances she did ...

Terry nodded. "Sure, neighborly. The way you were when you saw those kids messing with my car. That was you, wasn't it?"

When he'd first read her name, Fayre, in Crain's Chicago Business *— the story about her previous success in picking coming neighborhoods — he'd seen the way it was pronounced. Fair. But when he'd looked up Fayre's meaning in a naming dictionary, it said: beautiful.*

He'd put her about halfway between the two.

"Terry's getting a girlfriend," Karl said, as he and Fetch sat sipping St. Pauli Girls and listening to Ants' voice coming over the speaker phone.

"Story's gotta have a love interest," Fetch observed sagely. "Rounds out the characters."

"Lets you have sex scenes, too," Karl added.

"That, too," Fetch agreed.

Ants broke in to ask, "Hey, am I interrupting your conversation here?"

"Sorry," Fetch and Karl responded.

Lerome had his own observation. "Terry's checked her out. He's got plans for her."

Ants said, "Yeah, but you know he's going to fall for her."

"Sure, but if Cameron's any kind of writer, he'll have a good twist on that."

"Hey," Fetch said, "who's yakking now?"

Ants got back to the story.

"Did everything work out okay?" Fayre asked. "With your car, I mean?"

Terry shrugged. "Would have been okay with me if it was stolen."

The unexpected answer made Fayre look at him closely. Terry'd been stared at before. Unlike most of those times, he didn't think she was going to take a swing at him. Even if she did, he'd learned a long time ago not to flinch. Just roll with whatever punch got thrown your way.

Then hit back.

"So I shouldn't bother next time?" she asked.

"No, I'd appreciate it if you did. Keeps the cops on their toes. That's always important."

She stared at him some more, looking to see who the hell he was. Somebody to know or somebody to avoid. While she was sorting him out, Terry looked over her shoulder and saw Allie and BooBoo coming up the sidewalk on the opposite side of the street, both of them smiling, almost skipping like a couple of happy four-year-olds.

Terry was surprised they weren't both in jail — if they'd actually followed through on the plan to rob the hair salon. But if they hadn't done the job — and pulled it off — why would they be in such high spirits? Shit. They'd done it.

They stopped in front of Terry's house and that was when BooBoo spotted Terry watching him. He nudged Allie and pointed. She looked and saw Terry looking back at her. She smiled and waved, started walking his way until she realized he wasn't smiling back. And he was standing close to another woman.

Allie stopped dead and frowned.

"Did you hear me?" Fayre asked Terry.

He looked at her. It hit him then that she had been talking, but he hadn't caught a word she'd said. He said, "I'm sorry, what was that again?"

"I said, 'Do you want to hold the bag open or dump in that crap you raked?'"

He saw that she already had the bag open.

"I'll dump," Terry said.

He wasn't wearing yard gloves, but he didn't hesitate. Just grabbed a pile of dead vegetation, litter, and dirt and dropped it in the bag. She seemed to think about that, too. He grinned at her. She smiled back, watchfully.

"You're not the first, you know," Fayre said.

"What do you mean?"

"I mean there was a man who followed me the second time I went pioneering."

Now Terry laughed. He liked that. Pioneering.

"That's what you call it?"

Fayre nodded.

"How'd he do?" Terry asked. "The other guy."

He grabbed another pile to dump in the bag.

"Not as well as he'd hoped. Sold out too soon."

"Well, I—"

That was when Terry saw BooBoo hold up a ring of keys as big around as a tambourine. He even gave it a jingle and grinned at Terry. Fayre must've heard the sound,

Terry thought, but she was still busy focusing on him.

He saw Allie grab BooBoo's arm and start up the steps to Terry's front door. BooBoo might've been a bust with cars, but he seemed to know keys. First one he tried, he turned Terry's deadbolt lock.

"Something wrong?" Fayre asked. "The look that just crossed your face."

She turned to glance behind her, but Allie and BooBoo were already inside Terry's house. The only other person on the street was an old woman pulling a grocery cart. She had a load of junk in it, but no groceries. Terry wondered where she'd go when the neighborhood went upscale.

Fayre turned back to look at him.

"Suddenly remember something you had to do?" she asked.

Terry shook his head.

"Let's finish up here. I'm free for the rest of the day."

Ants paused to take a drink of water.

Dan had to hit the john.

Erin took the opportunity to stretch her legs. When she did she thought she might've gone too far. She felt a tug in her abdomen. She'd pulled a muscle there once when she'd gone rock-climbing But when she probed the area with her fingertips she couldn't find any sore spot.

Something she ate? A gas bubble or ...

Dan came back before she could explore her most recent thought.

"You ready?" he asked.

"Yeah," she said absently.

Could it really be?

"Erin, you okay?"

She gave herself a shake, locked onto the task at hand.

"Yeah, I'm fine. Let's go."

***

Terry continued to help Fayre with her scut work until shortly before dinnertime. He felt sure she was going to offer him food. It'd be something she'd either fix in her kitchen or they'd get carryout and bring it back. She wouldn't ask him out to a restaurant. That'd be too much like a date. All she had in mind was fair value for favors rendered.

But Terry didn't want her to even the account. Not yet. Not like that.

He'd also left Allie and BooBoo stewing long enough. Wondering why the hell he hadn't come racing after them once he saw them break into his house. Well, his house was also insured, not that he had enough in it yet to meet his deductible.

"Guy's a businessman," Karl said approvingly.

Nobody paid him any attention and Ants kept on reading.

"Now, I've got to go," Terry told Fayre.

He could see in her eyes she knew she owed him. Wasn't happy about that or the way he'd outmaneuvered her. But he also saw she'd enjoyed his company. Had appreciated an extra pair of hands to help with the grunt work. Wouldn't have minded talking with him some more. Figure out what his game was.

She left it at saying thanks, shaking his hand, telling him she'd see him around. That much was easy to figure out. Five minutes later he was back in his own place.

Allie and BooBoo were sitting on his sofa watching Nickelodeon. SpongeBob. Allie saw him first but BooBoo was the one who jumped up.

"Where the hell you been, man? We coulda—" BooBoo looked around and had to laugh at himself. "Was gonna say strip the place clean."

Today, BooBoo was the gregarious one. He told Terry he and Allie had made off with eight grand from the hair salon, including what they got for the credit card numbers they sold.

Having beaten the fictional couple from a bigger town by better than two grand, Fetch and Karl gave each other a high-five.

"Never had so much money our whole lives, right baby?" BooBoo asked Allie.
"Fuckin' millionaires, one a those hundred lotto tickets I bought hits."
She gave her man a tight grin, but the look she had for Terry was pure venom. He understood. Thought it was crazy but he knew what she was feeling. Jealous.
Of Fayre Sanderson. BooBoo had no idea.
BooBoo had invested part of his take in the ring of keys. He was trying to decide whether to get into the B&E business himself or resell the suckers at a profit.
Before he made up his mind, he wanted to know did Terry have any other place he and Allie might hit. Since the first job went so smooth.
In fact, Terry had a few more places in mind.
Should Allie and BooBoo last that long.

CHAPTER 16

"We're going to hit a coffee house?" Fetch asked in disbelief.

"It's not like some old-timey beatnik place, if that's what you're thinking," Karl told him. "We're gonna hit a Java Joe's."

Karl was perfectly rational about it, not a hint of Pyscho anywhere to be found.

Fetch squinted at him nonetheless. "I think your scalp's beginning to peel."

Karl put a hand to his sunburned cranium, started feeling for dead skin.

"No, leave it," Fetch said, "could be a nice effect. Really creep people out."

The conference call with Lerome and Ants had ended a few minutes ago when everyone had learned where Terry was sending Allie and BooBoo on their next robbery. They'd also learned that the two young criminals had shown some initiative and scouted the hair salon before they struck, and intended to case their coffee shop as well. Wanting to be both as careful as their counterparts and as true to Dan Cameron's book as possible, Lerome promised to check out a Java Joe's for them.

"I know what Java Joe's is," Fetch told Karl. He'd read about the high-end 24-hour coffee shop chain in *Money* magazine. Bunch of techies in Cambridge, Mass started it after they couldn't find a place that served a decent cup of joe at three a.m. When they were working on all their best ideas. So they started the place as a goof. Now they had 1,600 stores across the country.

Fetch knew all that, but it was hard to accept on a gut level. He was still working off the old Willie Sutton idea that you robbed banks because that's where the money was. Of course, it was also where the guards, silent alarms, and security cameras were. With the FBI waiting to jump on your ass if you hit a federally chartered place.

What Dan Cameron was showing — and Fetch really liked his story — was that today money was everywhere, and with a little imagination you could find places that were ripe for the picking and much easier scores than banks.

"So you're okay with it then? We'll do the job?" Karl asked.

Now, Fetch could see Pyscho peeking out. Karl's eyes were just a little brighter than normal. His heart must've been beating faster, too, because his body looked pumped up. Harder. Ready to take what he wanted.

Fetch wondered if Karl had ever seen a shrink before he and Lerome had met him. Whatever. Fetch still needed more money so, of course, they'd do another job.

"Yeah, Karl, we'll do it. Thing is ... I don't know. I guess I'm not used to the way the world is now. I was inside for eight years. The way things change so fast, that's a long time."

Karl nodded sympathetically.

Fetch thought aloud, "Maybe what I need to get right is some sex."

Apprehension spread across Karl's face like an oil spill.

"Jesus Christ, Karl. With a *woman.*"

"Now you want to start playing, too?" Ants asked Lerome.

"I'm just a guy going to buy a cup of coffee," he said. Then he grinned and owned up. "Didn't you ever wonder? I mean, could anyone really pull off that slick stuff they do in the movies and books? This is a good chance to find out."

For just a flash Ants got to see what Lerome had been like as a boy. Before puberty imposed all the weight of becoming a man and relating to women. When enthusiasm still held the upper hand over being cool. She didn't doubt for a minute that she was the only one Lerome would let see this side of him.

Ants had intended never to get married again. You ended your first try by running over the sonofabitch you'd promised to love forever, it made you cynical. You didn't want to even think about doing it again. But now, with Lerome, she thought, yeah, if he asks, I'll say yes.

Maybe even ask him.

She nodded at the dresser across the room. Sitting on top were two Remington Noiseless Portables. She still wanted to see if Lerome could guess the right one.

"That's what you really want to try, isn't it?" she asked. "What Dan Cameron does."

"I think I've got the stories," he said earnestly, "but can I do the writing?"

"Why not?" Ants asked. "You've got style."

Erin looked at Dan sleeping next to her. After finishing the dictation of chapter two, they'd gone to bed and made love. Not hard. Not here's something we never tried before. But slow and holding on tight. Barely moving. Making it last and last and last.

Dan fell asleep before he could even say goodnight. But he was happy, she could tell. He looked as boneless as a newborn. His breathing was inaudible. A well-deserved rest for her guy. Working on two books at the same time. Trying to track down a couple of thieves. Living with her, which was often fun but always demanding. And likely to get more so.

While Dan had been showering and brushing his teeth, Erin had checked her personal calendar on the PowerBook. Early on, when they'd first gotten to Uncle Les' cabin, Erin had tracked her fertility cycle like a hawk. She'd made sure they'd had sex every time she should have been ovulating, but two weeks later, jabbing her hopes like a stick in the eye, she'd always menstruated.

No pregnancy this month, lady.

The last couple of months she'd barely kept tabs. Couldn't stand inflicting the pain on herself any longer. So, tonight, she had ice in her heart when she pulled up the date of the last time she'd bled. Was she kidding herself? Setting herself up for yet another fall.

Maybe. But it wasn't her nature to retreat from anything for long. And she found she was two weeks overdue for her period. Her wonderfully punctual period. So precise it might have been Swiss made.

She wasn't ready to tell Dan. Not yet. Not before she was sure. Tomorrow she'd sneak out and buy a pregnancy test.

Or have Rudy send one up in a plain brown wrapper.

The Buffalo P.D.'s chief of detectives brought the story of the armed robbery at the Permanent Fave over to Dick Tracey and his junior partner, Mickey Gruber.

"You think Mcdonald coulda hit this hair place?" the chief asked Tracey. "Looking to score some loot for his get-away."

Tracey shook his head. "Guy I want hits banks."

"We got him for a credit union," Gruber pointed out.

"Financial institutions, okay?" Tracey said. Gruber had an eye for detail but sometimes he could drive you crazy. "And Mcdonald worked alone. Ask me, it was probably a couple of envious hairdressers from another salon. They're the doers in your case, chief."

"Your case," the chief corrected Tracey. "As of now, I'm assigning all detectives to finding out who ripped off the mayor's old lady."

"And the cases we were working?" Gruber asked politely.

"They come after. Like Mcdonald. If he didn't do this job, he's gone. You think he's dumb enough to just hang around town? Forget him. It's Tracey's hairdressers we want now."

After a few more beers, Fetch taped the Polaroid of Verene to a lamp shade. He and Karl stared at it. They hoped the light would let them see through Verene's wedding dress.

No such luck.

Archer Mcdonald was still spry enough to clamber over the wall of St. Norbert's Cemetery just north of Broadway in East Buffalo. But he landed hard and jarred something in his gut that hurt like hell. He rolled onto his left side and drew his knees up to his chest. It was all he could do not to cry out in pain.

It was the sight of the laundry bag and the spade he'd brought with him that kept him quiet. All of the money that he and Verene had stolen from Fetch was in the bag. The spade was for burying the loot. If he started caterwauling now, all that money might go right back to the banks Fetch stole it from. That happened, he might as well dig his own grave with the spade.

Helluva thing getting so old and sick at 58.

He got to his feet and started looking around. Place was dark, but not that bad. Shopping center off to one side, big street on another, light found its way in. He tried to remember where the grave he wanted was. He'd only visited it once, more years ago than he could remember. On top of that, he'd spent the last few hours drinking in his car, waiting for everything to get quiet.

He wandered for a while looking at names on tombstones, people he'd never known. Didn't matter. In the end, graveyard duty was the one roll call everybody answered.

Then he found the marker he was looking for: Dorothy D'Arnole Mcdonald. His late wife. Fetch's mother. Gone to her rest at 37. Sweet Jesus. How he had loved Dottie.

He whispered, "I always said I'd shower you with money, sweetheart. Sorry it wasn't sooner." He carefully buried all but ten grand of the money Fetch stole.

What he kept ought to be enough to drink and whore himself to death. Of course, if Verene caught up with him, she might think of some other way for him to die.

CHAPTER 17

Dan slept in, but Erin got up early. She didn't involve Rudy in the purchase of the pregnancy test. If it came up negative, she wasn't going to say a word to Dan. So she didn't want anyone else to know either. She slipped out to a drug store just up Delaware Avenue and was back to her suite in fifteen minutes.

She brought the newspapers in with her. *USA Today* and the *Buffalo News.* She dropped the papers on the coffee table and went into the bathroom. She was in the middle of peeing into the cup when Dan knocked on the door.

"Not now!" she ordered. Far more harshly than she'd intended.

He mumbled sor-ree and went away.

She felt like such a bitch, but pushed self-criticism aside to finish the job. When she came out of the bathroom, Erin found Dan sitting on the white sofa with the Buffalo paper in his hands and his mouth hanging open. Wide enough for dental work.

"What's wrong?" she asked.

It took Dan a moment to remember how to talk.

"You brought the papers in. Didn't you see the headline?"

Erin shook her head. "Just hauled them in."

"Well, look at this." Dan handed her the Buffalo paper. She sat next to him and took in the headline. *Mayor's wife, eighteen others, robbed at beauty salon.* There was a photo of cops and victims. Erin's eyes went wide. She looked over at Dan.

"Read," he told her. "Read."

Erin did. Now her jaw went slack. When she finished she looked back at her husband. "You really think they're crazy enough to—"

"Sure as hell seems like it."

Erin took Dan's hand.

He said, "It's not bad enough they stole my manuscript and my typewriter. Now they're stealing my storyline, acting it out." A disconcerting thought struck him. "Jesus! You think I have any liability here?"

"No. Not if you call the cops and let them know. I don't think so anyway."

Erin's reassurance calmed Dan somewhat, but he thought her words were pretty weak tea. Not Erin-like at all. Rotgut and profanity would have been more in character. *They can't do that, those lousy bastards. This is plagiarism. Copyright infringement. Something. We'll not only throw those fuckers in jail, we'll sue their asses off, too.* Words to that effect.

Which led Dan to suspect that his wife was preoccupied. "You have anything you want to tell me?" he asked.

Erin added her other hand to Dan's and started to cry.

"What?" Dan asked, alarmed. "What is it?"

"Dan," she said, smiling through her tears, "I'm pregnant."

Lerome stood in front of the dresser and looked at the two Remington Noiseless Portables. It was like one of those picture-puzzles: How many differences can you spot between these two objects? Lerome — showered, shaved, and dressed — had been examining the two typewriters for twenty minutes and he hadn't been able to spot a single one.

Ants, who was now using the bathroom, assured him that one of the machines was Dan Cameron's typewriter — Ben Hecht's before that. She'd even made things easier by having Jessi take away the third typewriter, the former Underwood.

For a second, he thought she might be messing with his mind, but he decided, no, Ants wouldn't do that to him. She'd have more fun playing it straight. But he was stumped. Even the serial numbers stamped into the frames of the machines were the same. So how was he ... then he smiled.

He had it. He looked at the two typewriters one more time and he knew which one he'd given to Ants. Even better, he had a piece of constructive criticism to offer.

"You figure it out yet?"

Lerome turned to look at Ants. She was dressed for a day at the library. Hair up, glasses on, hemline at mid-calf. Little Miss Innocent. If people only knew. Teen-age boys wouldn't bother with computers; they'd stare at her.

"Yeah, I did," Lerome said nonchalantly.

Ants gave him a skeptical look.

"Serial numbers gave it away. Jessi copied the real number, just like she makes fake license plates. Don't know how she did the metal work. It looks flawless, don't see any sign of joins. But there was one tiny mistake."

"Damn," Ants said, "I really thought we had you."

"You want to know?"

"Yeah." Her voice was heavy with disappointment.

"The serial number Jessi did, the numbers are cut fresh. Crisp, clean, new. Cameron's typewriter, the number imprints are softened. Rounded by age. That's how I knew."

"That's it, huh?" Now Ants was grinning wickedly.

"What?" Lerome asked.

Ants laughed and kissed him.

"We thought about that, the old numbers. Jessi switched those pieces. Cameron's numbers are on the other machine; the new numbers are on Cameron's machine."

Now Lerome laughed. He couldn't remember the last time he'd been tricked.

"You ever consider getting married again?" he asked.

"Yeah. In fact, I've been giving it some thought."

They discussed the notion further as Lerome drove Ants to work. When they pulled into the library's parking lot, Lerome changed the subject.

"How could we go about finding Dan Cameron?"

"Well ..." Ants started to think. Wasn't long before she had an idea. "I noticed in the acknowledgements for *Indecision Kills* he thanks his agent. Man's name is Hank DeMitri, I think. He should know how to reach Cameron. The question is, will he tell you?"

Lerome smiled. "Yeah, I think he will — but I'd like you to make the call."

Dan and Erin were in bed when the phone rang, Dan being very careful because he'd never made love to a pregnant woman before. Erin, by contrast, was feeling hugely empowered. They both looked at the phone and by silent consent agreed to ignore it.

Erin kidded Dan, "You don't have to be that gentle. Not yet anyway."

After they'd finished and showered together, Erin retrieved the phone message from the Chateau's voice-mail system.

"It was Uncle Les," she told Dan. "He said it's all unofficial, but the word has gone out to all Buffalo letter carriers. Five grand for the whereabouts of Fetch and Lerome."

"That's great."

"You going to call the cops?"

What with Erin's good news, he'd forgotten.

"Oh, yeah. Guess I'd better."

Mickey Gruber took the call from a man identifying himself as Daniel Cameron.

"Yes, sir, how may I help you?" Gruber believed in good manners and proper grammar. His goal in life was first to become a legendary police detective and then the creator of a TV show based on his exploits. He wanted to come across as understated. Suave once he could afford nicer clothes.

"You know that I'm the guy who called before about Fetch Mcdonald stealing my typewriter, right?"

"I didn't know that, sir." But Gruber made a note. He thought it was interesting that someone would think a fugitive credit union robber would take his typewriter. Also, Gruber loved to take notes. Future grist for his mill.

"Don't you people talk to each other?"

"In fact, we do. Do you remember the name of the detective you spoke to earlier?" Patience was another of Gruber's virtues.

"Some wiseass. Said his name is Dick Tracy."

"That is, in fact, his name. He spells it T-r-a-c-e-y, though. He's also my boss." Gruber noted that Tracey had already heard about this man's theft complaint.

"Yeah? Sorry about that. But the important thing is, I can tell you how to find Fetch Mcdonald."

"You can?"

"Well, maybe. I think I know what his next move will be."

"You do?"

Gruber was also very good at keeping skepticism out of his voice. Most people never would have doubted his sincerity. But Dan was a long-time reporter.

"You don't believe a word I'm saying, do you?"

"I have no reason to doubt you, sir, but I'm the junior detective here. Detective Tracey decides which leads get followed, which cases are pursued."

"Well, then have Dick give me a call at the Chateau on Delaware, will you? He doesn't, I guarantee you there will be some very embarrassed cops in the Buffalo PD."

That had the ring of truth to Gruber's ear. Somebody with the money to stay at the Chateau probably could cause trouble. He wrote down: *Daniel Cameron. Chateau on Delaware. Call re Fetch Mcdonald.*

"I'll give Detective Tracey your message, Mr. Cameron. I'm sure he'll call you." And if Tracey didn't, nobody would be able blame Mickey Gruber.

"But I shouldn't hold my breath waiting, right?" Cameron asked.

"I'm not qualified to offer medical advice, sir."

Gruber liked that. Wrote it down.

"Any luck?" Erin asked.

"Yeah, I learned how to spell Dick Tracey's name."

Dan added that bit of wisdom to the growing body of facts and observations that would become *Kidnapping Ben Hecht.*

"The cops aren't interested?"

Dan made a note to that very effect. Then he asked his wife, "You have Gamble Murtree's phone number?"

"Sure. He gave it to me. I put it in the *Book of All Knowledge.*"

Which was the file in Erin's PowerBook that contained all the information she and Dan needed to organize their personal lives.

"Let's talk to him."

"We're going to have to do this ourselves?"

Normally, the prospect of catching a couple of bad guys who had ripped them off yet again would fill Erin with glee. This was hands-on *America's Most Wanted*. What more could an excitement junkie want? It'd been exactly what she wanted after the typewriter and manuscript had been stolen.

But now Erin was carrying new life inside of her. That seemed to be having an immediate effect on her appetite for risk-taking. Which was a relief to Dan ... except he hoped she didn't take this domesticity thing too far. He decided to test her.

"Well, you can stay here. Gamble and I will go out looking." That notion drew a mighty scowl from Erin. Which softened into a look of introspection.

Ending with, "No, I think I'll be all right for now. I still feel fine. But if I start getting morning sickness or waddling ..." Such sobering prospects didn't allow Erin to finish her thought.

Dan did it for her. "I'll leave you home with the other womenfolk."

This time, he was happy to see, her scowl didn't fade.

Dan and Erin met Gamble at Teddy's diner, sat at a corner table. The dregs of the breakfast rush had just left. Uncle Nicky was busy watching a sitcom rerun. Comely young Adara brought three cups of coffee, a cinnamon roll, a croissant, and a doughnut to the table.

Adara asked Gamble in her immigrant English if he knew Whoopsy Goldberg. She pointed at the television to make sure he understood.

Gamble said he didn't.

"Is very funny lady," Adara informed him. "You write ..."

She couldn't find the words and yelled to Uncle Nicky in Greek. He yelled back, "Fan letter."

"Yes, you write fan letter and maybe — " Adara waggled

her eyebrows. She left Gamble with a wink and a grin.

"Girl likes you," Erin said.

"Age difference isn't a big thing to Europeans," Dan commented.

"You two through?" Gamble asked.

In case they weren't, he busied himself stirring cream and sugar into his coffee. There were no more cracks, but Dan slid the front page of the *Buffalo News* in front of him. Mayor's wife and a bunch of other gilded lilies got ripped off. Big deal. Wasn't a federal case.

He wasn't a fed anymore, either.

But when Dan said, "Fetch Mcdonald pulled that job," he slopped some coffee right out of his cup. As Gamble blotted up the spill, he looked at Dan.

Dan told him about calling the cops and their distinct lack of enthusiasm.

"Who took your call?" Gamble wanted to know.

"Young guy named Gruber. Before that I talked to some guy named Dick—"

"Tracey," Gambled finished. "His real name. Used to be a good cop."

"And now?"

Gamble shrugged. "Just a guess. One day he woke up, realized he'd never be chief, decided to mark time until he maxes out his pension."

Dan made a note on the pad he'd brought with him.

"I said that was a guess."

"Just what I wrote down. An expert guess."

Gamble looked at Erin.

She said, "He can't help it. He was a reporter too long."

Dan told Gamble how they knew it was Fetch who did the hair salon job.

"They're using the plot of your book? The one they stole?" Gamble seemed skeptical.

"The FBI doesn't run into that much?" Erin asked.

"Not a lot of felons have library cards."

Dan laid a ten-dollar bill on the table. "Okay, you're not interested. Have another sweet roll on us. Come on, Erin."

Erin got up when Dan did. "So long, Gamble."

Only thing that would have been crazier than what he'd just heard, Gamble thought, was if he ignored it and found out he'd been wrong. Fetch Mcdonald'd get away from him again.

"Wait," the former fed said. "If you're right, then what?"

"If they follow the manuscript," Dan told Gamble, "we know what's coming next."

"What?"

Dan and Erin sat down again.

Dan told him, "They're going to hit a coffee shop."

"Like Teddy's here?" Gamble rolled his eyes.

Erin said, "Unh-uh. A Java Joe's."

"Lots of yuppies carrying lots of cash," Dan explained.

"High-limit credit cards," Erin added.

"No security to speak of," Dan finished.

Gamble looked at Dan and Erin suspiciously. Sounded like they were planning a stick-up. Selling him on what a bright idea they'd had.

"You two ever—"

"Only on paper," Dan assured him.

"The only way to make crime pay," Erin offered.

Gamble took a sip of his coffee, decided they were telling the truth.

"So what do you think, Gamble?" Erin asked. "You up to nabbing the bad guys?"

Gamble thought maybe all three of them were crazy.

But he said, "How'll we know which Java Joe's?"

A couple minutes later, Dan and Gamble stood outside Teddy's waiting while Erin used the ladies room.

"You know what occurs to me?" Gamble asked.

"What?"

"A smart guy like you, a reporter with police-beat experience, you'd know how to get a rise out of the cops. Just tell them you know who ripped off the mayor's wife. They'd fall all over themselves getting to you."

"Wouldn't have known how hard they're looking for Fetch Mcdonald that way. Him or my typewriter and manuscript."

Gamble smiled. "Nice details for that new book you're working on."

Dan replied, "I warned them they'd be embarrassed."

"Another point you can write about."

"Only if Dick Tracey doesn't follow up."

CHAPTER 18

Fetch woke up with an idea in mind.

Since Verene — and Fetch's no-good old man — stole all his money, and confronting her in the church at her wedding would be suicidal, why not have Karl invite her over to his house? Take her hostage right there. Make her tell him where his money was.

Of course, that'd require Karl's cooperation.

Fetch looked over at his partner in crime.

Karl was sacked out in a sleeping bag, had it pulled up to his chin even though the basement wasn't cold. Not in June. Karl was still worried, despite Fetch's disclaimer, that Fetch might take his sex where he could find it. And since a woman wasn't available, Karl was going to zip himself up tight. Wasn't going to have Fetch sidling up to him in the night.

Poor sap, Fetch thought. Look at that red noggin, peeling like crazy now.

Still, he couldn't forget that Pyscho lurked within that innocent shell. If Fetch started making Verene too unhappy about giving him the money back, he might have a real fight on his hands if Psycho didn't like it.

Add in how hard Verene might fight, it might not look

good for him.

Hell, maybe he should just take Karl up on his offer. Take all that cash Karl had hidden in his sofa-safe and get out of town. For that matter, he could take the money Lerome had offered. Get out of town in style. Life was a lot more complicated outside of prison, all the choices you had. But he still didn't like the ones that were available to him.

Maybe the thing to do was get Karl to turn against Verene first and then grab her. Seemed to Fetch that the way to do that was to get Karl laid soon, too. Get his mind thinking about some other tight body in a tiny dress ... lipstick ... eye-shadow.

Before Fetch got too excited, Lerome showed up.

With cups of coffee from Java Joe's.

And the morning paper headlining the job they'd pulled last night.

Hank DeMitri — Dan Cameron's literary agent — was at his desk in his office on Broadway in lower Manhattan when the phone rang. On the third ring, he yelled to his secretary to answer the friggin' phone. No response, and the phone kept ringing.

Damnit!

Tina had great skills but her bladder was smaller than a thimble. And she was drinking a lot of water as part of some new health kick. Water in, water out. Might as well move her desk into the ladies room. The SOB on the other end of the line wasn't giving up either.

Hank answered on the sixth ring. "Hank DeMitri."

He tried to slot the call into one of the usual categories — complaining client, wannabe writer, editor who loves something but just didn't have a spot for it on his/her list — but it wasn't any of those things. Hank took his mind off autopilot and actually started to listen.

"Yes, I represent Daniel Cameron. Are you calling on behalf of the Hecht estate? Because .... Well, who the hell are you then?"

The agent's mouth fell open as he heard the response. And he thought: *Nothing good can come of answering your own fucking phone.*

Dan and Erin sat in a Java Joe's in Allentown, south of the Delaware district. There was another one on Chippewa Street downtown, a third on Elmwood, and a fourth at the airport. By consensus, they agreed that the one at the airport was the least likely target, airport security being what it was these days. That left three possibilities. Which divided neatly among three people.

Except Dan wasn't going to let Erin work alone, a surprising paternal instinct coming to the fore, and Erin in a momentary passive prospective-mommy mode didn't argue about it. Gamble decided he'd cover the shop on Elmwood. That left Allentown and Chippewa Avenue for the Camerons to choose between. They decided to look at each shop first, see if they got a stronger vibe from either location. See if one location had a bigger restroom for holding the victims.

Dan made notes about the shop's layout as Erin sipped her latté.

"Maybe I shouldn't be drinking this stuff anymore," she said. "I'll have to get a book about pre-natal do's and don'ts."

Dan didn't respond, had a faraway look on his face.

"What?" Erin asked. "What're you thinking?"

Dan looked at his wife. "Just wondering if we should have grabbed that money from Archer Mcdonald."

"Are you kidding?"

"Well, we've decided it was the money Fetch stole, right?"

"Yeah."

"And Archer looked pretty pathetic. I could've taken him."

"Dan."

"Think about it. We take the money. We find some way to let Fetch know that the only way he gets it back is to return my manuscript and typewriter. We set up a swap and we have the cops waiting in the wings. We get what we want, we're heroes, and we have a terrific ending for *Kidnapping Ben Hecht.*"

Erin was nodding her head but she was thinking maybe what they ought to do was just go home and have their baby. They had their health, plenty of money, what did they need this craziness for?

It was then that Erin realized they'd switched roles: she was being sensible, Dan was acting crazy. She wondered briefly if this was psychological or hormonal on her part. The half of her that remained the Old Erin didn't like it; the incipient Mama Erin said tough.

What she said to Dan was, "Well, let's see. You'd have had to enter that house without permission. That's a crime. You'd have had to knock old Archer down, no matter how pathetic he is. That's a bigger crime. You'd have to steal a lot of money that's already been stolen twice. That's a real big crime. Maybe you'd be finishing your new book from a prison cell."

"Well, if you're going to nitpick," Dan replied. Then he asked, "You still up for tonight?"

Meaning lying in wait for the armed robbers to strike.

Old Erin beat Mama Erin on that one — in a photo finish.

"Yeah ... sure. You just worried me, talking crazy like that."

Dan grinned. "Wait until you have to save me from falling into a volcano."

***

Rudy collared Dan and Erin as soon as they got back to the Chateau. He handed Dan half-a-dozen phone-message slips, saying, "Mr. Cameron, your agent, Mr. DeMitri, has been calling all morning. He made me swear that I'd have you call him back as soon as I saw you."

Dan took the message slips, but all they said was please call immediately.

But then Rudy had one more tidbit to impart.

"I'm sorry I forgot to tell you." He flicked a glance at Erin. "A woman came by to see you yesterday while you and Mrs. Cameron were out. She had one of your business cards."

"Did she leave a message?" Erin asked.

"What'd she look like?" Dan wanted to know.

No message, Rudy said, but his description, though tactful, sounded familiar to Dan. After they left Rudy and went upstairs to their suite, Dan said, "That had to be Verene."

"What do you think she wanted?" Erin asked.

Dan could only shrug. But they were both certain they knew what Hank wanted. To deliver bad news. The court had ruled against them. Dan gritted his teeth and made the call. Hank answered the phone himself. On the first ring.

"You know who called me?" he asked once he heard Dan's voice.

"The Hecht estate."

"We should be so lucky. A woman called. She offered to sell Ben Hecht's typewriter to you. Why should she offer to sell you something you already have?"

"I don't have it."

Dan heard Hank moan.

"She said she'd throw in the manuscript for *Time Expires,* no extra charge."

Hank's question was implicit.

"I don't have that, either," Dan told him.

Hank moaned again, louder. Then he got mad.

"And you didn't think I should know all this?"

"I'm planning to get everything back."

"Well, you can. The woman wants $100,000 within a week. Or she'll see how much the Hecht estate is willing to pay." Another potential migraine hit the agent. "Your manuscript. You wrote it on the typewriter. Tell me you made a xerox. A carbon. Something."

"I didn't." Before his agent began to cry, Dan added, "I'm redoing the book, dictating the story to Erin from my outline and notes. It's going pretty well."

Hank didn't say anything, but he stopped moaning.

Dan knew what would perk him up. "Hank."

"Yeah?"

"This whole thing, crazy as it is, there's a new book in it."

Like giving Popeye a can of spinach.

"There is? Tell me about it. Now."

After Dan recounted Hank's message to Erin, she had a very pertinent question.

"Who's this woman who called Hank ... Verene?"

That didn't sound right to Dan. Verene contacting a literary agent? Knowing about their legal battle with the Hecht estate? Nah.

"Then who is she?" Erin wanted to know.

"Another accomplice," Dan answered. "Someone who reads, apparently."

Erin made an intuitive leap. "Remember we decided that Fetch broke out of jail to get Verene back? Stop her from marrying that other guy."

"Karl," Dan said with a nod.

"So if Fetch is hot for his ex, it doesn't make sense that he'd have some girlfriend around who'd call Hank for him, right?"

"Right."

"But who helped Fetch escape, according to Gamble?"

"Lerome." Dan saw where she was going now and smiled. "Lerome has a wife or a girlfriend who made the call for him."

Erin bobbed her head. "Lerome who doesn't leave any footprints behind."

"Cracking good, Watson," Dan said.

"My pleasure, Holmes," Erin responded.

Dan sat down and started making notes.

"Dan?"

"What?" He looked up from his notepad.

"Are we going to pay the ransom? Get your stuff back?"

Dan gave it a moment's thought.

"We'll see. We've got a week. That's what Hank said."

Karl was looking at his face in a hand mirror he'd taken from the downstairs bathroom. He was picking at the peeling skin on his scalp. Fetch kept interrupting his conversation with Lerome to tell Karl to let his skin be. Then Karl got both Fetch and Lerome to turn their heads.

"You think I should draw a little swastika between my eyebrows?" he asked.

Lerome spared a glance at Fetch. Then he told Karl, "Too Charlie Manson."

"How about a little dollar sign?" Fetch suggested.

Karl liked that. He went to work with a fine-tip marker but didn't allow for the reflection. Drew the symbol backwards. Not a problem, Fetch thought. Made him look crazier than ever.

"Tension getting to Karl?" Lerome asked Fetch quietly.

"Just finding out who he really is."

"This going to work out okay?"

Karl turned to show them his effort. "Look like a real jailhouse tattoo, Fetch?"

"Just like one, Karl." Pleased with the compliment, Karl

returned his attention to the mirror, admiring his handiwork.

"A swastika," Fetch muttered. "We get caught, we'll be sent somewhere there are plenty of Aryan Brotherhood types."

"I'm working on something," Lerome told his cousin. Then he explained the plan to ransom Dan Cameron's typewriter and manuscript.

Fetch complained, "Hey, I want to hear how that story comes out!"

"Ants copied it. Point is, maybe we can get you a hundred grand and you can take off."

"Oh."

"You wouldn't have any problem taking that money, would you?"

"No ... I guess not."

Lerome heard the hesitation. "You're not getting as crazy as Karl, are you?"

"I hate to say it, but I'm having fun."

Lerome confessed: "So am I."

Fetch brightened. "Yeah?"

"Yeah, but it's your ass on the line here. So let's go over how tonight is going to work again. Gotta be at least as careful as Allie and BooBoo."

But before they got back to the Java Joe's job, Fetch told Lerome, "After we're done with the stickup? I'm going to get Karl and me laid."

He asked Lerome if an East Buffalo bordello was still where he remembered it. He'd had to haul Archer out of there once.

Lerome nodded. "That's a good idea," he said. "You guys need something to take the edge off."

Verene peeked out her living room window and saw that damn black guy, Gamble whatever the hell his name was,

was sitting in his car across the street again. What the hell could you do about that? Call the cops and tell them the FBI was stalking you?

She let the curtain drop back into place, but that didn't change things. She was stuck. Couldn't figure out how to find that old fuck Archer. Of course, she wouldn't give a damn about him if she just knew where the money was. Slipperiest damn money she'd ever heard of. First the banks lose it. Then Fetch. Then her.

It worried her greatly that Archer's hands would be the last ones ever to hold it. If that thieving piece of shit had any sense, he was already on his way somewhere warm. Like he'd always talked about. He'd find some little monthly motel place. Have booze and hookers sent in. Whatever it was eating his guts would finally kill him and that would be it.

He'd have the money hidden somewhere, and either rats would eat it or it'd just stay lost forever and ever. It was enough to make Verene weep.

Except she never wept, goddammit.

What she had to do was concentrate on Karl. Karl who wasn't at work according to that snotty bitch Judy who worked for him. Karl who didn't answer his phone at home. Karl the sonofabitch who used to call her ten times a day. Minimum. But now ... nothing.

Verene didn't like that silence one little bit. She couldn't stand losing Karl's money, too. It was time to put the wimp back on a short leash. Pussy-whip him good.

Bridal shops weren't the only ones who had Polaroid cameras. Verene got hers out. The tripod. The self-timer. The lights. The works.

She knew cheesecake photography cold. Sabina had taught Verene from the time she was little. Good old mom. Verene shot a dozen exposures. In the bedroom. The kitchen. The bathtub. Wearing nothing but pearls, spike heels, and a come-get-me smile.

She put the collection of photos in an envelope with a note to Karl: *Can't wait to have you any longer.*

She called a neighbor kid on the phone, the teenage twerp whose bedroom was across from hers. Kid spent all night trying to get a peek at her undressing for bed. He came over like a shot. She gave him twenty bucks to deliver the envelope to Karl's house.

"Listen," she told him, "what's inside is strictly for my friend. I'm going to ask him if the envelope was sealed when he got it."

She knew this would only inflame the dweeb's imagination, so she added, "It's supposed to be warm tonight. I might leave my bedroom curtains open — if you're good."

Kid disappeared like Houdini. Probably sell tickets to his friends tonight. As long as Karl got the pictures, she didn't care. She peeked out the front window again. Damn FBI guy was still there.

She thought he might follow the kid but he didn't. She was still stuck. Feeling unlucky now, too. If anything went wrong with Karl. she'd have to take another run at that writer.

CHAPTER 19

Dan and Erin went back to the Java Joe's in Allentown. As agreed, Gamble covered the franchise on Elmwood. But Fetch and Karl targeted the store on Chippewa Street because that was the one Lerome had cased that morning. Psycho thought it'd be cool to hit all three Java Joe's in town. Maybe do the one at the airport, too, for good measure.

Fetch hit him upside his head. "Don't get crazy until I tell you to."

Instead of Karl's car, they took the motorcycle that Verene had made Karl buy, a Honda VTX 1300cc. Candy red with retro package. They dimmed the finish with dirt and smeared the license plate and the manufacturer's badges with mud. Since Fetch didn't know how to drive a motorcycle, he had to entrust Karl with this responsibility.

Which made Fetch uneasy. Damn machine looked monstrously big to him.

"You actually know how to drive this thing?" he asked.

"Absolutely," Karl said. "Verene likes to go fast."

Fetch didn't doubt that.

"She said once we get married, some night when the

moon's full, we'll go out riding naked. Get the cops to chase
us. After we lose them, we'll—"
Fetch didn't need to hear more.
"Let's go," he said. "I've got a car to steal."
Karl got on the cycle with an air of familiarity.
Something to be grateful for, Fetch supposed. But when he
got on behind Karl, felt the vibration of the engine, his nuts
shriveled so bad he almost called the whole thing off. It was
only stubbornness that kept him on the machine.
Karl opened the throttle, let in the clutch, and took off
so fast Fetch's heart leaped into his throat. Psycho paying
him back for that head-slap.
He'd really have to watch this nutcase close.

Axel Dengler — Verene's teenage neighbor — got to
Karl's house two minutes after Fetch and Karl took off. Had
he followed Verene's instructions, he would have made his
delivery much earlier. But he was as enthusiastic an entre-
preneur as he was a voyeur.
The first thing he'd done was check the 9x12 manila
envelope Verene had given him. Nothing special. Security
was limited to a gummed flap. Pathetic. Axel went to a
Staples, bought a package of five envelopes just like it, and
hot-footed it over to his boy Petey's house.
In Petey's bedroom, they opened the envelope, salivated
over what they saw, took a few of their favorites into the
bathroom and jacked off. Then they got down to business.
They scanned all twelve Polaroids into Petey's computer
and posted three of them to an Internet site featuring older
babes with big knockers.
That was just the come on. Verene had been right about
Axel selling tickets. But she'd thought small: live audience.
Axel and Petey thought global: live Webcast. They'd taken
in six grand from subscribers around the world by the time
Axel dropped off the Polaroids.

Like any good entertainment programmers, they intended to do reruns. Use the remaining Polaroids to promote the shows. Build their audience. Axel had even put a note in the new envelope for Karl. *Check out this Web site, dude.* He put in the time and a complimentary password so Karl wouldn't have to pay.

Guy shouldn't have to pay to see his own hottie.

Fetch went looking for a car with a key left in the ignition in the parking structure of Buffalo General Hospital. He figured some guy bringing in a pregnant wife or a banged-up kid, he'd have more on his mind than taking his keys with him. He was right. In fact, he found two cars right next to each other, the keys still in them. A late model Honda Civic and a Ford Mustang, looked like something he remembered from the '80s.

He took the Japanese car. Dependability when it mattered most. When your ass was on the line.

He drove to the alley behind the Java Joe's on Chippewa and parked right up against the rear fire exit. Nobody'd be getting out that way. He hurried away from the stolen car. He had to get out front and get this show on the road.

They'd given themselves five minutes to pull this job.

Chippewa Street was lined with bars, many of them offering live music. The Sheas Center for the Performing Arts was just up Main Street and a host of other cultural venues were a short stroll away. It was a happening part of town, especially on a warm night in early summer.

The Java Joe's people had been smart enough to see that a significant number of people would tire of guzzling booze after a few hours and be in the mood for designer coffee. As Fetch approached the target on foot, he scanned the block for any sign of cops and found none.

Then he saw Karl. He had his bike idling perpendicular to the curb on the opposite side of the street in a no-parking zone. That was the only spot available. Everything else was parked in; a double-parked car down here would have somebody calling for a tow-truck fast. Which was why they'd taken the motorcycle.

As Fetch got to the entrance of the Java Joe's a couple of yuppies — younger babe, older guy — were leaving. He held the door for them. The woman thanked him, the guy nodded. Neither said anything about the fact that Fetch was wearing sunglasses at night — as was Karl.

The moment the yuppies were out of the way, Fetch gave Karl a nod. Karl waited for a lull in traffic, shot across the street on the cycle, and rode right through the door Fetch held open for him. Which served nicely to get everyone's attention.

Fetch entered, closed the door behind him, and said his piece. "Ladies and gentlemen, this is a hold-up."

He took out his gun to let them know he was serious. Must've been thirty-five customers there. A prosperous looking crowd, the expressions on their faces seemed to reflect they knew this was no joke. But a boy — too damn young to drink coffee or be out that late — was staring at Fetch. A woman who was probably his mother pulled him back. But the kid kept staring. Getting on Fetch's nerves.

Fetch gave the kid his full attention and said, "What?"

The kid replied, "I think you forgot to take the safety off your gun."

The little shit. Of course, Fetch had left the safety on. He didn't want to shoot anyone. But now he had to take the safety off, and he jacked a round into the chamber for effect.

Karl, with perfect timing, revved his 1300cc engine, making a roar in the enclosed space that sounded like a moon launch. Then Psycho swiveled his peeling red head around and grimaced at everyone.

Snotty kid wet his pants.

Fetch was happy to see that. He got everyone herded to the back of the store, relieved them of their wallets and purses, hit the register, and ran for the back of the getaway cycle. They'd been fast, but they were bumping up against their time limit. If anyone had seen Karl drive into the store or looked in while the robbery was in progress, the cops could be closing in.

"Go!" Fetch yelled as soon as his butt hit the saddle.

Psycho did. Popped a wheelie. Shot right through the glass door. Fetch had overlooked that he should have held the door open again. He screamed as the glass exploded around him.

In all the commotion, neither Fetch nor Karl had noticed the young woman with the sketch pad, a court-room artist who worked at WGRZ-TV which was practically right around the corner. She'd had to work quickly and surreptitiously but she thought she'd gotten two good like-nesses down on paper. She was adding shading as the rob-bers made their dramatic exit.

Fetch got a grip, both on the cycle and himself. Continuing to scream would only draw attention. As it was, Psycho was darting in and out of traffic and running red lights and laughing like a banshee. Lunatic thought he was on a ride at Disney World. As for Fetch, he was silently cursing Henry Ford or whoever the hell it was had invent-ed the internal combustion engine.

Karl got them out of downtown, though. Once again they didn't see a single cop, and soon they were into the quiet residential streets of Front Park, running without lights. Minutes later, the bike was back in Karl's garage. Karl copied down credit card information like a madman while Fetch harvested the cash. They threw the wallets and purses — complete with their credit cards— into the trunk of Karl's Ford. The cash they took into the Karl's house and locked it in the safe.

Before they went back out, Fetch asked, "You have a hat, Karl?"

"What for?" Dementia still danced in Karl's eyes. He couldn't comprehend the question.

"For your head, Karl. That dome of yours is getting famous. It'd be a good idea to cover it, don't you think?"

"You're always thinking, Fetch. Hope I'm as good as you one day."

"Yeah, Karl, me too," Fetch said deadpan.

Karl had only one hat in the house, a navy blue beret. But Fetch was not going to play fashion critic. Not now. Psycho was still wound too tight.

This time they dumped the wallets and purses in Fireman's Park, near the Children's Psychiatric Center. Let the cops think they'd been troubled kids who'd grown up. Which Fetch knew for a fact fit his background, and was becoming increasingly sure it applied to Karl, too.

Psycho giggled after they'd dumped the physical evidence. "Well, we did it again," he said gleefully.

"And now we're going to do something else, Karl."

"We are?"

"Relax," Fetch said, looking for a certain East Buffalo street as he drove. "What we're going to do is get you and me laid."

Karl got so quiet Fetch had to look over make sure he was still there.

"What?" he asked. "You don't want to?"

Karl looked at him. Karl not Psycho.

"I'm supposed to get married soon."

"I know," Fetch sighed.

"Maybe I shouldn't. But you ... you go ahead."

Fetch fully intended to; he wasn't going to argue either. Karl could check out the girls, do what he wanted. Play pinochle if it made him happy.

**

The black FBI man left his stakeout around dusk, Verene saw. But she was still trapped because she was waiting to hear from Karl. He should've received the Polaroids hours ago. By now, he should've broken down her door in his lust to get at her. Or at least phoned, damn him. But nothing. *Nothing.* Was she losing it? Had she suddenly become so unattractive that she couldn't even ensnare the Karl Hyacinths of the world anymore? If that was the case, she—

She remembered the boudoir performance she'd promised her pimply teenage neighbor. She'd intended to keep her word. Perfunctorily. Flash maybe one breast. Give a glimpse of backside. That was all the kid had earned.

But now Verene needed to prove to herself that she still appealed to *some* male. She went upstairs. Put on her sexiest lingerie. Lit her bedroom with a combination of candles and soft incandescent light. Let her silhouette preview what was coming.

Then she opened the curtains and put on quite a show.

The bordello was right where Fetch remembered it, a big old rambling three-story pile of bricks that had once been a grand manse. There were eight girls — none much younger than he was, Fetch thought — in the parlor with the madam. A model of equal opportunity, four girls were white, and four were black. The madam, an Inuit Indian, said they had a couple Asian girls, too, but they were booked for the night.

Fetch got the impression the Orientals were the only hookers working, and if he and Karl had arrived a week later they'd have found the place had gone out of business. Or at least moved to a new location.

"So what's your pleasure?" the madam asked.

Fetch looked at the girls and asked, "Who can dance?"

The madam snorted, "Oh, they can all dance real good,

honey."

"Dance on your feet," Fetch added, ignoring the crack.

"You mean they'll dance with us?" Karl asked. "I didn't know we could dance."

"Anything you pay for," the madam said with shrug.

"I like dancing," Karl said.

Fetch looked at him curiously. "You do?"

"Sure. I took two years of lessons at Arthur Murray. How about you?"

"My mom taught me," he said, daring anyone to laugh. Nobody did, but a slim girl with mocha skin stood up. "My mama taught me, too. Waltz, swing, boogie, anything you want."

"Her," Fetch told the madam.

"Anybody else?" Karl asked eagerly.

A stocky brunette got lightly to her feet. "My daddy showed me how. Danced with me right up to the day his army helicopter fell outta the sky. After that, mom wouldn't have any music in the house. Just a lotta drunk boyfriends."

"Her," Karl said, compassionately.

Fetch paid the madam for both girls and they all went upstairs to the second floor. There were four doors on one side of the hallway, three on the other. Karl and his girl took the room at the top of the stairs on the left. Fetch's girl walked him past the middle of the three doors.

"That one's busy," she said.

"Yeah, I can hear." Somebody torturing old bedsprings.

The girl opened the far door for Fetch. Wasn't the cleanest room he'd ever seen, but it wasn't the dirtiest, either. More important, it had a hardwood floor with enough room to dance. Fetch stepped inside and the girl closed the door behind them.

"You wanna dance clothes on or naked?" she asked.

"Clothes. For a while."

217

He hadn't seen a nude woman in over eight years. He didn't want to rush things.

She nodded. "Ain't got no music."

"That's all right, I can hum."

She smiled. "Me, too."

For a second, he wondered if she'd conned him, saying she could dance. But then she came into his arms. He felt the small bones of her right hand in his left and the lean strength of the small of her back in his right. She seemed to be weightless. Just floating there waiting for him to lead her wherever he cared to go. She knew how to dance all right. She seemed to be able to read Fetch's mind, too.

"Anybody special you want me to be, you just say the name."

It took Fetch a moment to clear his throat and ask, "What's your name?"

Now she looked at him in silence. Then she said, "Birdie."

"That's as special as I need," Fetch told her.

He began to hum *Moon River,* and led her in a gentle swaying two-step. They moved as if they'd been dancing together for years. A smile lit Birdie's face that she took care not to let Fetch see. Genuine emotion was something to be protected. But then she cocked an ear and pulled back her head. She looked at Fetch, letting him see her smile now.

"Well, listen to that. Somebody's got the same idea you do."

A full orchestral rendition of Henry Mancini's most famous song filtered softly through the wall from the room next door. Fetch didn't seem to notice. Just kept on humming.

And Birdie returned to pretending she was dancing with her mama again.

CHAPTER 20

Rudy called Dan and Erin's suite to let them know that Gamble Murtree was on his way up. Dan took the call and thought he heard a tremor in the assistant manager's voice.

"You okay, Rudy?" he asked.

"Yes, of course. Just a little ... well, honestly, I'm more than a little shaken up."

"Sorry. I shouldn't be so nosy."

But now Rudy wanted to talk.

"You've read about the ... um, excitement last night?"

A prominent member of the local hospitality industry, Rudy was loath to admit that Buffalo was anything less than Camelot. With maybe a bit more snow.

"You mean the Java Joe's robbery?" Dan responded.

"Yes. Well, last night I took a lady friend to see the Goo-Goo Dolls." A hometown rock band of renown. "After the show, we went to Java Joe's."

"You got robbed?"

"No. We walked out just before it happened. In fact, one of the robbers held the door open for us as we left. I ...I shudder to think what could have happened if we'd lingered just a moment longer."

"Yeah, really. Scary."

Erin came over as Dan hung up. "What's scary?"

"You and Gamble and I went to the wrong Java Joe's shops; Rudy went to the right one."

"Really?"

"One of the robbers — maybe Fetch — held the door open for Rudy and his girl."

"Oh, wow."

"We chose the other Java Joe's, that could have been us."

"You mean almost getting robbed?" asked Mama Erin.

"No, I mean close enough to wrap my hands around Fetch Mcdonald's throat."

Dan sat down to make notes for *Kidnapping Ben Hecht* while Erin answered the knock at the door.

Lerome stepped into a lower west side storefront called Queen City Pawn Brokerage. Looked like it hadn't been cleaned since McKinley got shot. But the guy with the three-day beard behind the counter was current with that morning's tip sheet for the harness races out at Buffalo Raceway. He also had a small-caliber revolver sticking out of the waistband of his pants. Shouldn't take him more than a minute or two to reach around his gut and grab it, Lerome thought. He put a Remington Noiseless Portable on the counter in front of the guy.

The one he'd taken from Dan Cameron. It gleamed like a dark star, but the pawnbroker barely gave it a glance and said dismissively, "Ten bucks, take it or leave it."

"I'll take it," Lerome said.

The guy sighed, disappointed he hadn't driven Lerome away with his lowball offer. He put the Remington on a shelf behind the counter, wrote up a ticket, gave Lerome his half and a ten-dollar bill. Without a word, he went back to his tip sheet.

Lerome didn't move.

After a minute, the guy looked up. "What?"

"Don't sell that typewriter to anyone who doesn't have this ticket. Not even if you're offered *eleven* dollars."

The guy laughed. It brought up something brown from his lungs. Lerome could see the color because he spat it into a corner.

"I don't get much call for typewriters," he said. "Don't worry."

Lerome didn't move. Didn't say a word.

"You gonna stand there all day?" The pawnbroker tried to decide if he should get mad or worried. This big guy in black with the sunglasses staring at him. His right hand started to creep toward his gun.

Lerome shook his head. The hand stopped.

"Not necessary. I'm going. But if you sell that typewriter to anyone who doesn't have this ticket ..." He held it up to make an impression. "It'd be a real shame."

The pawnbroker understood what kind of shame. His store could burn down. With him in it. Gun or no gun.

"Yeah, yeah," he grumped. "Nobody gets it without the ticket." He went back to his tip sheet, harder to read now that his hands shook.

Lerome left and drove to Karl's house. Where he found a manila envelope resting against the front door. A collection of Verene nudies inside.

He also found Karl's copy of the morning paper. Lerome pulled it out of its wrapper and read the lead story: the Java Joe's robbery. He looked at the artist's rendering of the robbers. Bad luck robbing someone who could draw your picture. But nothing he could do about it now. There was, however, one other detail he could clean up.

He took out his cell phone and made a call.

"Jessi? Lerome. Like to ask you a favor."

He looked around. None of Karl's neighbors was out eyeballing him, but no sense discussing this matter in public. He let himself into the house. Karl had given him a key.

* * *

Dan, Erin, and Gamble all agreed that they didn't want to be responsible for anyone getting killed or hurt by bad guys imitating the crimes in Dan's novel. Fetch Mcdonald, once upon a time, might have been a non-violent bank robber, might even have politely held open the door for Rudy and his date last night, but now he seemed to be working with an accomplice who showed a real potential for violence.

Erin looked at the artist's drawings on the front page of the newspaper. "That bald guy is creepy. But who is he? Not Lerome."

Everyone agreed on that.

"Maybe your friends at the FBI would know, Gamble," Dan said. "Since the cops aren't interested in our story, maybe you could see if the feds are."

Gamble knew that Dan knew retail holdups weren't federal crimes. Not the FBI's responsibility. The author just wanted another tidbit to put in his new book. But maybe the bureau would know who this bald guy was. Maybe a nudge from the FBI would get Dick Tracey on the right track. Yeah, sure. The way cops loved feds.

Gamble decided to give it a try anyway. Otherwise he'd have Dan writing about him not doing what he should. So he went down to the Dulski Federal Building to talk to his old boss. Only Gamble learned that SAC Harris Thomas now headed the field office in Dallas.

The new special agent in charge of Buffalo was Adriano Trinidad. Gamble's old nemesis. Trini had been the other minority up-and-comer in the Buffalo field office back in Gamble's heyday. Trini was not only Hispanic — Cuban — he was also black and bi-lingual. An affirmative action triple-threat. Some of the white guys had joked if Trini had tits, he'd be a deputy director by thirty-five.

As it was, he had to settle for being wealthy. His immigrant father who'd come over on a homemade raft now owned three yacht dealerships: Miami, Palm Beach and Sarasota. The Trinidad family's politics were right for the bureau, too: conservative Republican.

Or seemed to be.

One time back in '88 Trini gave a party at his house on Chapin Parkway. Huge place. Had a backyard big enough for the Bills to use as a practice field. The Seoul Olympics were going on at the time and Trini had TVs set up all over the house Every agent who wasn't on duty was invited.

Being a sports-themed event, there was a lot of cigar smoking, drinking, and yelling. Most of the female agents left early. Gamble had as good a time as anyone else. Except when he needed a bathroom and couldn't find one that was unoccupied. Damn house must've had six johns and he couldn't find a place to piss.

He wound up climbing the stairs to what he thought was the attic. If he could find one of Trini's old hats up there, he was going to piss in that. But the space had been remodeled into a servant's quarters or somesuch and it had its own bathroom.

After Gamble had blissfully drained himself, he was about to go back downstairs when he heard a voice speaking softly but excitedly in Spanish. He followed the sound to a room at the front of the top floor. He edged the door open and saw Trini sitting on a sofa watching a boxing match all by himself.

The sound had been turned down but a graphic showed it was a match between an American boxer and a Cuban. Trini was into it, rattling off his torrent of Spanish, throwing lefts and rights with his own fists. Then Gamble understood something that almost knocked him over.

Trini was rooting against the American. For the Cuban! In Spanish. All by himself. Keeping his voice low. Finally, Trini sensed he wasn't alone. He looked over his shoulder with an expression of alarm. But when he saw it was Gamble his look turned into a sneer. He slammed the door in Gamble's face. Ever since Gamble had wondered if Adriano Trinidad was a Communist mole.

He couldn't say anything. Without proof, it'd look like he was trying to knife the other most prominent minority special agent in the Buffalo field office. It was sure to backfire. Gamble would be the one who got screwed.

Maybe he'd made way too much of what he'd seen. It was just a boxing match after all. But Trini never invited Gamble to his house again. And a relationship that had been civil if competitive became distant and cold.

Whether Gamble was imagining bogeymen or not, one thing was sure. He wasn't about to do anything that would help Trini catch Fetch Mcdonald and claim credit for it.

But if Dan Cameron wanted to assume he'd passed the information along ...

Let the writer blast Trini if anything went wrong.

Dick Tracey sat at his desk looking at the drawings of the creeps who'd robbed Java Joe's. WGRZ-TV had faxed over copies of the originals. Police equipment being what it was, the resolution of the drawings on the front page of the *News* was better. Didn't matter, though. Either way, you had two guys in sunglasses, one bald, one black-haired. They took off their shades, the bald one let his hair grow — if he could — the other one dyed his hair — or let his natural color grow out — you'd never know who the hell they were.

Gruber came into the squad room with a well-dressed woman. In her late thirties, Tracey'd say. With the woman was a kid, maybe ten, talking to Gruber like they were old pals. They all stopped next to Tracey's desk and he got up to be polite as his partner made the introductions.

"Mrs. Sundquist, Elroy, this is Detective Tracey. He's

leading the investigation into the Java Joe's robbery."

"And the Permanent Fave, too?" the kid asked.

"Yeah, that too," Tracey said. "These people got something for us, Mickey?"

"Elroy does. He and his mom were at Java Joe's last night."

Tracey gestured the kid into his visitor's chair. Gruber pulled up another for Mrs. Sundquist. The senior detective leaned forward. "Whattya got, Elroy?"

"The robber's gun? It was a Beretta. Nine millimeter, semi-auto."

Tracey gave Gruber a look. The younger detective held up a finger: patience.

"He didn't have the safety off until I mentioned it to him."

"Something we had a long talk about," Mrs. Sundquist assured the detectives.

"Yeah," the kid admitted shamefaced. "I shoulda been smarter than that. I was just thinking, 'What kinda robber leaves the safety on when he's robbing a place?' Didn't make any sense to me."

"Me, either," Trace admitted. "You got anything else, Elroy?"

The boy smiled. "The motorcycle. The one the robbers used? It was a Honda VTX. That's V-Twin Extreme. Thirteen hundred cc's. With retro package. Candy red."

Tracey looked at Mrs. Sundquist.

She told him, "He reads all the time. Far more widely than I ever suspected." Mom put a hand on her son's shoulder. "But when it comes to details, believe every word he says."

Elroy beamed at his mother.

Tracey asked blandly, "You get the plate number, Elroy?"

The kid's smile disappeared and he shook his head.

225

"They were smart enough to cover it with mud ... but I did see it was a New York tag."

Kid was sharp, almost enough to make Tracey have hope for the future. He got up and thanked the Sundquists for their help. Gruber gave the kid one of his cards in case he thought of something else and walked them out.

When he came back he had another nugget.

"I re-interviewed all the vics from the first robbery, the beauty salon. One of them remembered the bald robber ordering everybody into 'the nose-candy room.'"

"Oh, yeah?" Interest creased Tracey's face.

"Yeah. Seems some of the patrons there like a snort in the ladies john. Not the woman who told me, of course. Certainly not the mayor's wife."

"Perish the thought," Tracey said deadpan. "But at least one of our robbers knew what went on there. That and the motorcycle with a New York tag. The field's narrowing."

"Yeah." Gruber looked thoughtful.

"What?" the older cop asked.

"These guys aren't done," Gruber said. "They're building up a head of steam."

Tracey nodded, thinking. "Question is, lunatics who rob hair salons and coffee shops, what the hell are they going to hit next?"

Gruber noticed something in Tracey's waste basket. The message slip he'd left for him from that writer Dan Cameron. Guy who lost his typewriter. Gruber couldn't get too worked up about that now.

"What're they going to do next?" the younger detective asked. "Who the hell knows?"

CHAPTER 21

All the cracks were plastered, the plumbing and wiring brought up to code, the chimney swept, the floors sanded and sealed, the walls and ceilings painted, and the furniture moved in.

Terry Phelan also had steel doors hung front and back, and the windows were wired to an armed response company.

He and Fayre Sanderson sat on his new leather sofa from Restoration Hardware and sipped after-dinner drinks, looking at the logs burning in his fireplace, listening to them pop and crackle, content in their own silence. Terry was two-thirds dozing when he felt Fayre nudge him.

"Hey," she said. "Gazing at a fire together is romantic. Listening to you snore ..." She shook her head, but she was smiling.

"Sorry." Terry sat up straighter. "Between work and making something of this place, I've been putting in a lot of hours."

"Should I thank you for a lovely evening and go home? Let you get your rest."

He shook his head. "Stay."

"All right. I'll cover you up if you nod off."

Fayre kept wondering when Terry was going to make his move. He'd not only been busy with his own life, but for the past two months he'd helped her with her new building. Anytime she asked, he came right over. Sometimes she needed the help. Other times she was testing him, seeing how far she could go Lately, though, it was because she enjoyed being with him.

She knew that if Terry had been smart enough to bird-dog her latest pioneering move, he'd also learned her net worth was approaching eight figures. Every last cent of it earned by her own smarts, hard work, and grit. Willingness to risk her money and her ass.

Her looks, she knew, were just passable, but when you added in her money, most guys'd breeze right past the beauty queens to talk to her. Terry Phelan, though ...

He was falling asleep again.

Gamble Murtree sat silently in a corner, watching Dan and Erin work. Dan had let him read the earlier chapters to catch up with the story. He'd enjoyed that, even though he didn't read much fiction. But once Dan started talking ...

It was like an old-time radio drama. He closed his eyes and he was a young boy again. He settled deeper into his easy chair, eager to hear what happened next.

Fetch and Karl listened to Ants read over the speakerphone.

"You almost dropped your cognac," Fayre said, taking the glass out of his hand.

She set it on an end table with her own glass.

Terry sighed, "Maybe I am too tired to be any kind of company. Let me get your jacket, I'll walk you home."

Always the gentleman, Fayre thought. Not always what she wanted.

Fayre didn't get up. She said, "Tell me about yourself, Terry. Most people can't wait to share their life stories. What I know about you could fit on a matchbook."

He shrugged, cleared his throat, turned so he was braced against an arm of the sofa. Fayre scooted around to face him, sitting tailor-fashion on the cushions.

"My family's blue-collar Chicago. My dad was in building trades. My older brothers still are. I aimed a little higher. Went to college. Grad school."

Fayre looked over at the mantle above the fireplace. Two framed pictures rested there. Terry with a group of young people, two men and two women besides himself. Terry in the middle. Everybody smiling like they had the world by the tail. The other photo was of a young woman, but it'd been taken long ago. The color looked hand-tinted.

"That your mom?" Fayre asked.

Terry nodded. "She died when I was little."

That got to Fetch. He knew from before that Terry lost his mom. But that was the writer telling you. This time it was Terry himself. Fetch backhanded a tear from the corner of an eye.

Karl pretended not to notice.

Ants' voice continued with the story.

Lerome knew that one had to hurt Fetch. Made him admire Dan Cameron even more, though. Man could make you laugh, maybe break your heart, too. He felt Ants take his hand, her narration never faltering.

"How about the group shot?" Fayre asked.

"The Chicago Psychos."

"What?"

"That was what we called ourselves   We worked together at Chicago Psychographics. Started at the same time. Biggest class of recruits the CP ever had."

"I don't know the company," Fayre said.

229

"No reason you should. We're consultants to big buyers and sellers of advertising. We tell companies if the reasoning behind their ad campaigns is sound; we tell ad agencies if their business pitches to prospective clients will hit the mark."

The security company for Terry's house had been one of his clients. They'd wanted to know if it would be smart to find out what police response times were around the city and do an ad campaign that showed that private security could ride to the rescue faster.

Terry'd looked into it. The security company was faster, but not by a lot. The sales angle he figured out was to do a series of TV spots that showed what could happen to you in even the 30 seconds — the length of your average commercial — that the cops lagged the security company. Business went up 500%.

Terry got his house wired into the armed response grid free. He could tell you the CPD response time anywhere in the city, too.

Fayre said, "So you're professional know-it-alls, huh?"

"Exactly."

They looked at each other straight-faced and then cracked up laughing.

"Man, we can throw numbers at people till our arms fall off," Terry said, still grinning, "but what it really gets down to is, 'Hey, buddy, our guess is better than yours.'"

"And people pay for this?"

"They pay a lot," he told her.

"No wonder you and your friends look so happy."

Terry's smile disappeared abruptly.

"You're not happy?" Fayre asked cautiously.

"The others ... they're all doing their own things now. Have their own businesses. We all said that if we could figure things out for other people we could do it for ourselves, too. Be our own bosses. Make ourselves rich."

"You see your friends much anymore?"

Terry shook his head, and Fayre got right to the point.

"You looking to get rich off me, Terry?"

"No. I just wanted to find a nice place to live where the price hadn't gone over the moon yet."

"But soon would?"

"That'd be okay ... but that was the only way I ever intended to take advantage of you. In fact, I've been trying to make it up to you ever since."

Which explained his unfaltering willingness to help her, Fayre thought.

"But you don't find me personally attractive."

"Sure, I do," Terry said with a smile.

"You just have a great sense of restraint."

"No, I haven't figured out a way to get close to you that wouldn't look like I was trying to get close to your money. Don't know if there is one."

"So?"

"So I can be your friend. I can lend a hand when you need it."

She looked at him a long time.

"And if I want more?"

"Well ... then you'll have to trust me."

"Trust a man. There's a novel idea," Erin told Dan with a grin.

"I am a novelist," he responded.

Gamble opened his eyes, annoyed, and said, "Hey, don't stop now."

Ants had to pee, leaving a moment for discussion.

"Terry's having Allie and BooBoo rip off his old friends," Fetch said.

Karl nodded. "Yeah. But not because they're successful."

"Unh-uh. Because they left him behind."

Lerome's voice came over the speakerphone. "There's more to it than that."

Karl asked, "Like what?"

"Don't know yet. That's where the fun is, finding out."

They all agreed on that. That and Terry and Fayre were going to get laid in the next scene.

"Yeah, but should Fayre trust Terry?" Fetch wanted to know. "Is he going to fuck her now and screw her later?"

Karl said no. Lerome said maybe. Fetch said whatever happened, they weren't going to live happily ever after.

"You want the light on or off?" Terry asked.

They'd gone upstairs to his bedroom, kissing deeply as they climbed the stairs, their hands beginning to stroke, grasp, explore. Terry'd flipped the light on as they entered the room, then he thought maybe that wasn't what Fayre wanted.

But she said, "Leave it on. Keep you from falling asleep again."

He laughed.

Fayre added, "I want to see how close I was."

"Close to what?"

"Imagining what you look like."

He grinned. "You do that, too, huh?"

With the light on, they began to undress each other, kissing once more.

Erin glanced over at Gamble. His eyes were closed, but his face was as flushed as when he'd seen her in her underwear. She was too polite to laugh.

Didn't want to put Dan off his game either.

Allie watched from across the street. Saw the whole thing. The beginning anyway. Like it was a live sex show. Exactly what it was. Then maybe the rich bitch said something or Terry thought of it himself.

Hey, close the damn curtains.

Allie'd found out about the rich bitch right after she'd first seen Terry with her. She'd heard some neighborhood activists complain about her. They were going to protest or something. Put up a fight so rich people wouldn't push them right outta their homes.

Terry walked right up to the window naked. And hard. He saw her, too, standing out in the street looking up at him. She'd have liked that to shock the shit out of him. Have his dick drop like somebody had tied a Buick to it. But it didn't. Stayed right where it was.

Terry didn't even look pissed. Looked like he was thinking. Maybe he'd have to do something about that crazy bitch down there.

Then he closed the curtains and it was all Allie could do not to scream, "I'm the one's gonna do something. Do it to you!"

She'd done her best the past couple of months to put Terry Phelan right out of her mind. There were days she'd done it, too. One of her lotto tickets had been a winner. Not the big forever-rich prize, but 25K. Add that to the 15 she and BooBoo had left from the two stickups they'd pulled, they'd felt like they had all the money in the world. Gotten themselves a nice crib, put ten down on this sweet five-year-old Firebird. Bought new clothes. Ate all their favorite foods. Drank real French champagne. Partied all the time.

Now, they were almost broke again.

Another week, they'd lose the car, get kicked out of their place. Fuckin' BooBoo had even let some asshole steal his ring of keys. That was the thing Allie had the biggest problem with. You invited people into your house and one of the fuckers rips you off. Jesus, if you were gonna steal, do it to people you didn't know.

The other thing about losing the keys was they had no

way to make some fast money. Not that BooBoo saw any problem. Dummy wouldn't know they were in trouble until their last dollar was gone. Then he'd piss and moan.

Man, it was hard for Allie to believe she ever loved that sucker. But when they were rolling in it, that's just what she'd thought. Made her want to kick her own ass. BooBoo was just one of those fools who'd let everything he'd ever have slip through his hands.

What she needed was somebody who knew how to make money. She thought maybe she'd drop in on Terry, say hello, see how he was getting on. See if maybe he'd like to get it on with her. Only what'd she see?

Him with his dick pointing at the moon and Miss Rich Bitch about to go for a ride.

It hadn't bothered her much about the neighborhood getting fancy when she'd had her own money, but now it pissed her off. That was when it hit Allie. Miss Rich Bitch was the one she'd have to do something about.

Get rid of her, things could be different with Terry.

"Ask me, Allie might be in for a big surprise," Ants told Lerome.

"Doesn't pay to underestimate people," he agreed.

Fayre was gone the next morning when Terry woke up. It was Saturday, meant he could sleep late. If you could call 6:45 a.m. late. But it was far enough into the day for Fayre to be up and gone. Made him feel like a slacker. Like he'd never amount to anything.

Then he found her note: Tonight, my place. Sorry to leave early. I'm meeting some neighborhood people for breakfast this morning. Trying to ease their fears about the neighborhood changing. Not sure that's possible.

Better you than me, Terry thought. Knowing Fayre wasn't out making her money grow, he felt it was all right to go back to sleep. The phone ringing at 7:30 woke him again. His boss. Asking him to come in ASAP. Which worried him.

Chicago Psychos didn't work weekends.

Dan finished the night's work with Allie still planning evil for Fayre, and with Terry setting up her and BooBoo with their next job.

"That's where we think Fetch and Baldy will hit next," Erin told Gamble.

"Yeah, yeah," the former fed said, "but what's going to happen to Fayre? And Allie's not buying that Terry really likes her again just because he's giving her and BooBoo this new job, is she? And will BooBoo ever wise up?"

Dan told him, "Stay tuned."

"A cigar bar?" Fetch asked. "What the hell is that, some kind of dive?"

A lifelong non-smoker, he had somehow missed reading of this particular social phenomenon during his time in the clink.

Karl tried to keep the grin off his face but wasn't successful.

"Now would Terry send Allie and BooBoo to a dive?" Karl wanted to know. "Would there be a big score in that?"

Fetch realized Karl was mocking him and thought he might have to smack him again. Camaraderie was all well and good, but Karl had to remember the pecking order here. Thing was, Karl seemed to be toughening up. Psycho was never far from the surface lately and ...

Fetch peered at Karl. What the hell was going on with his scalp now? Karl saw Fetch staring at him, his face all twisted.

"What?" Karl asked. "What is it?"

"Well ... your head. It's blistering or something. All these little bubbles."

Looked like Karl's head, faded now to a dusty rose, was covered with pebbles all of a sudden. Karl felt his head with both hands, a look of horror growing on his face.

"Don't break them," Fetch told him. "I think they scar if you do that."

He had no idea if they'd scar, but as a frightening visual effect this was even better than the peeling skin — and, uncharitably, the more attention Karl's head attracted the less would be paid to him.

"Well, shit," Karl said. "Damn."

"Don't worry about it. There's just you and me here."

"Yeah, now. But last night, when we were with the girls ..."

They hadn't swapped stories about their experiences, yet.

"Yeah?" Fetch asked.

"Well, well ... we got naked, you know?"

Fetch remembered Birdie undressing for him.

"That's what you wanted, wasn't it?" Fetch asked.

"Sure, it was. Only ... damn! There I was, naked as the day I was born, and I can't bring myself to take my beret off."

Picturing the sight, Fetch laughed. And stopped abruptly as he saw Psycho appear in Karl's eyes. He said, "You still had fun, didn't you?"

Psycho retreated as a broad, mischievous grin lit Karl's face. "Rhonda couldn't get enough of me, and I couldn't believe how much I had to give."

Fetch didn't need the details.

"Did you dance naked with your girl?" Karl asked, giggling.

"I don't kiss and tell," Fetch replied deadpan.

He had. You never knew when a memory might have to last you the rest of your life.

Karl sighed happily. "You know, I haven't had this much

fun since ... ever."

"That's swell, Karl. Now, tell me about these cigar bars."

Karl snapped out of his reverie, became businesslike.

"Right. Our next job. Cigar bars are for yuppie studs. Places they can show everybody else that their cigars, wallets, and dicks are bigger than the next guy's."

"Fag places?" Fetch asked aghast.

"The dick part was just a figure of speech," Karl said blandly.

The notion still shook Fetch. He'd spent too much time in places where guys *wanted* to show you their dicks. Up close and personal. Made him wish that Dan Cameron would pay the ransom for his typewriter. Today. He could just take that hundred grand and split.

Forget about his life of crime — until the next time he went crazy. But he knew better than to count on getting lucky. That wasn't how his life worked.

Karl interrupted his dark musing.

"Fetch, I'd kinda like to go see Rhonda again."

Verene's losing her grip on the sap, Fetch thought. Which didn't please him as much as he thought it would. Maybe being with Birdie had loosened her grip on him, too.

"No reason why you shouldn't," Fetch said.

"What I was thinking, though. Maybe I could get a wig to wear. They look dumb, I know. But it's better than a beret."

"Sure, Karl. Whatever you want."

CHAPTER 22

Lerome was sitting at Ants' kitchen table thinking. He'd gone out for coffee and rolls for their breakfast. Starbucks today. No sense showing his face at a Java Joe's again when he didn't have to. Ants came in and sat down across the table from him.

He didn't wear his sunglasses in her place. Made it a lot easier for her to read his mood. Though she was getting pretty good in any case.

"I won't say something's actually bothering you," she told him. "But your cool's being ruffled."

Lerome grinned. "I get bothered."

"Maybe if your beard was on fire."

"Definitely then."

"So what is it?"

"I've been thinking about Dan Cameron. How much of Terry Phelan is really him."

"Terry's just a character in a book. Fictional."

Lerome gave a small shake of his head. Took a sip of coffee. "How far can a character be from the writer?"

"Well, he writes female characters, too. Fayre, for example."

"Bet she's like women he's been close to, is close to."

Ants took a pull of her coffee.

"Literary analysis isn't what's on your mind."

"That's part of it," Lerome told her. "But I'm wondering what Dan Cameron is doing right now. Where is he? We all know Terry's devious, using Allie and BooBoo for his own ends. But what about the guy who created Terry?"

"What do you mean?"

"Well, when you called Cameron's agent, did you get the feeling he knew about Cameron losing his typewriter?"

Ants shook her head. "Wouldn't've been surprised if he wet his pants when I told him."

"Which tells us Cameron didn't run to NYC to share the bad news. You think he just shrugged off getting his book, typewriter, and SUV stolen and flew home to ... where is it?"

"Evanston, Illinois," Ants said, remembering that information from the dustcover of *Indecision Kills*. "Putting it like that, no, I don't think he did."

"So where is he?" Lerome asked.

"Right here in town would be my guess," Ants answered.

He nodded. "Have to think a former reporter reads the newspaper every day."

"So he knows Fetch and Karl are acting out his book."

"He knows about Fetch. Probably did some snooping, found the family connection, and guessed I'm involved. No way he could know about Karl. At least, I don't think so."

Ants laughed.

"What?" Lerome asked.

"I was just thinking. What we're doing here. The copy-cat crimes. Holding his stuff hostage. That would make a good book for him."

"If he thought about it." It took Lerome only a second to conclude, "Yeah, he has. Right up to the ending. Which is what I've had on my mind. The one guy who knows for sure where Fetch and Karl will hit next is Dan Cameron. He could have the cops waiting at the cigar bar. I've got to talk to Fetch."

Lerome examined his reasoning a moment longer.

"One thing you could do," he told Ants.

"What?"

"Read ahead. Maybe the thing to do is skip the cigar bar and hit whatever's next."

Ants took both of Lerome's hands in hers and smiled at him. "Two things you should know."

"What?"

"You can think like this, you're going to be a terrific storyteller."

"Yeah?" Lerome asked, smiling too.

"Yeah. The other thing is maybe Dan Cameron won't have the cops waiting even though he knows the cigar bar is next."

"Why not?"

"If he's writing a book about all this, you think he's going to cut it short?"

Lerome called Jessi before he left Ants' place and asked if she had the time that morning to meet him at Karl's house, and bring one of her crew along. Cool Jennie Kreuze. Jennie was able to pull off stunts on a motorcycle that'd make Evel Knievel whimper. Today, though, she'd only have to drive the bike away. Yesterday when he'd called about the favor, Jennie was tied up. Now, it was doable.

Lerome, Jessi, and Cool Jennie met in front of Karl's house and walked back to the insurance broker's garage. Lerome didn't have a key to the garage, but Jessi made short work of the lock. Lerome pointed to Karl's Honda VTX, the getaway vehicle on the Java Joe's job.

"All yours," Lerome told the women.

Jessi said, "Nice bike. You don't want a cut of the profits?"

"A gift," Lerome told her.

"Ants told me we faked you out with the typewriters."

"You're an artist," Lerome said with a grin.

"Damn right." Jessi grinned, too.

Cool Jennie, never one for small talk, started the VTX, not needing to bother about a key. Lerome opened the garage's pedestrian door wide for her and she was gone in a blur. Jessi said thanks and left in her Porsche.

Lerome went into Karl's house, not planning to mention to Karl that he'd just given away his $10,000 motorcycle .

But Karl got upset when Lerome woke up him and Fetch and told them there was a change in plans.

"I want to hit a cigar bar. I know just the place."

Fetch got disgusted. Karl kept forgetting who he was here. The guy with a gun to his head. Someone who's illegal acts were supposed to be coerced.

"Jesus, Karl, you're not even a real criminal."

"Maybe not ... but I'm getting there."

Psycho again. Lerome gave Fetch a quick glance, then raised a serious question. "This place you're thinking of, Karl. You don't have a prior business relationship there?"

You left too many clues, Lerome knew, even the cops couldn't keep missing them.

"No," Karl said. "Just a place I went. One time. Thought it was cool. Except for all the cigar smoke."

Fetch rolled his eyes.

Pscyho glared.

Lerome introduced a new dynamic to the situation. He took a collection of Polaroid photos out of his pocket.

"I almost forgot," he said. "I found these the other day. On your doorstep, Karl. So I guess they're for you. But Fetch might be interested, too."

He handed Karl the pictures and the note from Verene — *Can't wait to have you any longer* — but he kept the tidbit about checking out the Verene-featured Web site to himself.

Fetch looked on over Karl's shoulder. Verene's note was a knife to his already broken heart. He just had to get over her. The thing that surprised both Fetch and Lerome was Karl's reaction to the nudies. He looked ... let down.

"Everything okay?" Fetch asked.

Psycho was gone. Karl shook his head.

"It's just, you know, I never actually saw Verene naked before. It was always fantasy. I guess I must've over-idealized her. I think I actually like her better with her clothes on."

"Something for a man to consider," Lerome offered.

The phone rang. Welcoming the distraction, Karl handed the Polaroids to Fetch. Karl said hello. When he heard it was Ants, he put her on the speakerphone.

"There's another crime you can do," she told them. "I think you'll like it."

Dan was working on his notes for *Kidnapping Ben Hecht* when Erin came over to the workstation and said, "You think it's too early to start knitting booties?"

He looked up at her, wondering how you could be married to someone for 15 years and still have her take you by surprise.

"You don't know how to knit," he said. "Climb a mountain, set a broken bone, yeah. Knit, no."

"I can learn," she said. She walked over to the sofa and sat down. Dan followed, sat next to her.

He asked, "How'll you know which color to make them? It's too soon to tell, isn't it?"

"I'll do yellow. All babies look cute in yellow."

"You're serious about this?"

"I'm discovering new things about myself. I think you are, too."

He thought about that. He'd been pissed when he'd discovered his novel and his typewriter had been stolen. More angry than he could ever remember Even more upset than when his sister, Maddie, shot an arrow through his cheek when they were kids. What he felt now, though, was something beyond that.

Ever since Erin had told him about the baby, he'd felt protective of what was his. He'd never had to worry about that before. God knew, Erin could always take care of herself. Nobody'd ever messed with him. Not physically. Maybe it was nothing more than dumb luck but he'd never felt threatened in his person, his marriage, or his possessions.

All of that had changed suddenly. With Erin now pregnant and focused on the baby, she seemed — and seemed to be feeling — more vulnerable. Losing his two most important material possessions — *Time Expires* and the Remington — he felt aggrieved as he'd never had. Learning that Fetch Mcdonald et. al. were now stealing his ideas to commit a string of crimes, he felt intellectually violated. Most of all he felt determined to protect what was his: Erin, their child, and his work.

Which, he realized, was making him more aggressive. Just as Erin was, of necessity, becoming more passive. They'd have to adapt to their respective changes, no doubt both of them grinding their teeth at times.

"I was thinking," Erin said, interrupting his thoughts.

He was sure she'd say something about the baby, but she fooled him.

"Lerome, the guy who's never been arrested much less done time, he's got to be the one making all the smart moves. Planning the copycat crimes. Trying to ransom your stuff."

Dan nodded. "Yeah, so?"

"Well, if he's really smart, you know what he'll do?"

Dan knew intuitively. "He'll have Fetch and baldy skip a crime."

Erin smiled, loving the way they could think the same thoughts.

"Right. He'll figure out we know what's going on and wonder if we'll have a trap waiting for Fetch. So they'll skip the cigar bar and go straight to—"

"The wine tasting." Dan rubbed his chin. "Maybe."

"Maybe?"

"Don't forget, there are other players here: Verene and Archer Mcdonald." For a second, a thought popped into Dan's head, something about the bald robber, but he couldn't hold it. He'd make a note about it later. "They might do something that turns things around."

"Okay, yeah. So how about this? We divide our resources. Have Gamble work the cigar bar angle. We go see about wine tastings."

Dan nodded. He liked the idea.

"One thing we know for sure," Erin said.

What?"

"They can't skip all the way to the last crime."

"No they can't," Dan agreed with a glow of satisfaction. "I wonder if they know that yet. They stole everything but the final chapter of the book."

"If they don't, they will soon enough. Bet they'll be as anxious as anybody else to know how everything turns out."

Dan and Erin enjoyed a laugh, the best kind. One that comes at the expense of somebody who'd messed with you.

Archer Mcdonald went out for a drink. See if he could find his lawyer, too. Specifically, he was looking for I.B. Humphrey, the former public defender who'd represented him on both of his bank robbery falls. Archer didn't resent the fact that I.B. was 0-2 in his advocacy. It wasn't for the plea deals I.B. had worked out, Archer'd still be locked up. The lawyer had retired on a disability pension, suffering a nervous breakdown after he'd walked a wife-murderer on an illegal search technicality, only to have the asshole go straight to his former in-laws' house, set the place ablaze, hold off the fire department with a handgun, and be responsible for five more deaths. The sole survivor of the arson, the asshole had demanded he get the same attorney who'd represented him the last time.

I.B. tried to hang himself in the hospital where he was having his breakdown. That resulted in a two-year involuntary commitment. Upon his release, I.B. remained as determined as ever to end his miserable existence. Only this time he'd do it in a socially acceptable manner: one drink at a time.

Physically, I.B. was on his way. Mentally, he remained as functional and haunted as ever. Part of his curse he'd told Archer when they had bumped into each other a year ago.

Well, we all got our troubles, Archer thought. He, himself, was dying from whatever monster it was devouring his guts, and he certainly hadn't asked for that. Given a choice, he'd be healthy enough to take Fetch's money and drink, dance, and screw for many a year.

Thinking about sex turned his mind to Verene. She was certainly a hotter number than an old jailbird like him had any right to expect. They'd been partners for seven years in trying to find all that bank-money Fetch stole. The two of them busting their heads against the problem of where his son had hidden the swag.

What they'd agreed was, they'd split whatever they found right down the middle. And if one of them should die, the other got the remainder.

They'd both laughed about that, the thought that one of them might kill the other in his or her sleep. It kept you on your toes, added spice to every little kiss and pinch.

Then the excitement of finding the first hidden bundle of Fetch's money was just like a big hand shoving them into bed. Maybe it would have been only a short-time fling if Fetch had buried all of his money in one spot, but having to look for it one sack of cash at a time, year after year, the sex continued all the way through the treasure hunt, getting hotter and hotter.

In fact, it was the longest relationship either of them had ever had. But once they finally had all the money, it was coming up on time for Fetch to get out of prison. Having worked at least as hard as Fetch had to get the loot, neither of them was willing to give it up. So they hatched their plan. It'd be a shame to see Fetch get sent back to prison for another long jolt, but not as big a shame as losing the money.

Only the way things had worked out, Archer wasn't going to live long enough to spend more than a little bit of it. Life was like that, dangling something all shiny and bright in front of him, even letting him get his hands on it. But once he did, the bottom always fell out.

Well, fuck it. This time Archer Mcdonald was going to have the last laugh. He'd be generous, noble even, in his final act. Dying — and not being able to spend the money on himself — had given him that freedom.

What he'd do was take whatever cash he didn't spend and divide it evenly between Verene and Fetch. Fetch to receive his share when he got out of prison again.

Archer walked into a dive called T.K.'s on South Park Avenue, the kind of place no beer company would bother to hang a sign outside, but just the spot a man who'd recognized both the gravity of his crimes and the folly of his existence would go to drown himself in a glass.

As such, it was where I.B. Humphrey spent most of his time. Archer hoped his lawyer would help him draw up his last will and testament. Work out a way to get Verene and

Fetch their money. But I.B. Humphrey was not occupying his customary place at the bar just then.

Even so, the establishment was more than happy to sell Archer a drink.

Verene found the phone number of the pimply kid next door. Punk had his own phone listed in the book, right under his parents' number. Axel Dengler. What a geek name. Punching in the numbers, she intended to fry Axel's ear right off his head.

The show she'd put on for him, and he hadn't delivered her Polaroids. He was probably up there in his bedroom jacking off on them right now. It had to be something like that. Because if it wasn't, if Karl had gotten them ...

Where the hell was he?

She heard the phone pick up, but before she could get the first word out, a recorded message started to play.

"A&P Productions. We're out planning future projects. Leave a message."

What the hell? Verene certainly wasn't about to leave a tape recording of what she had to say. She slammed the phone down.

She looked around trying to decide what she could do now. Couldn't think of one damn thing. So she did what any normal person would do. She turned on the television.

Let her mind veg out until it was ready to start thinking again. The local news was on. Fine. Crime and suffering was their stock-in-trade. She'd let somebody else's misery make hers seem trivial by comparison. Cheer herself right up.

And she did get a lift. Only not the way she expected. The news anchors were talking in serious tones about a pair of armed robbers.

"These are the men who robbed the Java Joe's on Chippewa Street last night," the bottle-blonde female said.

A drawing of the two robbers filled the screen. And they were ... Fetch and Karl!

She knew them both immediately, even though Fetch's hair was darker than she'd ever seen it. And, Jesus, Karl had shaved his head and was wearing wraparound shades. But she'd know that weak chin of his anywhere.

But that was the only thing in the drawing that seemed weak about Karl. Otherwise, my God, he looked like more of a stud than she'd ever have thought possible.

Fetch looked good, too. That dark hair — had to be dyed — worked for him.

The drawing was reduced to an inset shot as the male anchor came on. His chin was the size of a steam-shovel. "These men are also suspected of robbing The Permanent Fave hair styling salon earlier in the week."

Verene could see Fetch pulling stickups. He had the history. But Karl? Karl had to be forced into it somehow. A stick of dynamite up his ass that Fetch threatened to explode.

That thought filled Verene with joy. Karl hadn't come to see her not because he didn't want to, but because he couldn't. Fetch'd found Karl and kidnapped him or something.

The TV picture cut to a two-shot of the news anchors. Ticked Verene off. She wanted to keep on looking at Fetch and Karl. She couldn't believe it but they were getting her hot. She wanted both of them — at the same time.

Then the bottle-blonde got her even more excited.

"The owners of The Permanent Fave and Java Joe's have pooled their resources and are offering $25,000 for information leading to the arrest and conviction of these men."

Verene jumped to her feet, bounced around like a kid on Christmas morning.

"I know, I know who they are!" she exulted.

"If you know who they are," square-jaw told her, "call

the police at this number." The drawing of Fetch and Karl filled the screen again with a phone number beneath it.

In voice-over the bottle-blonde said, "With good reason, the police are calling this pair the No-Place-Is-Safe Bandits."

The director cut back to the two-shot of his on-air personalities. "Please help local law enforcement catch these men," square-jaw finished.

Verene snapped the set off and had her hand on the phone to call in and claim the reward when her mind went back to work.

Karl was still waiting to be plucked. She couldn't do that if he was in jail. Fetch might possibly be able to give her a lead on finding Archer.

Twenty-five grand was nice money, but not compared to what else was out there. No, she had that wrong. She had to figure out a way to have it all. Karl's money. The money Fetch — and Archer — stole. *And the reward.*

She wanted every last cent ... and that threesome with Fetch and Karl, too.

After a lengthy discussion with Lerome, Fetch and Karl had agreed to put off the cigar bar job for at least a night. They'd sleep on things and decide in the morning what they wanted to do, stick with the sequence in *Time Expires* or skip ahead to the wine tasting.

As it was, the two of them were tasting some more St. Pauli Girl in Karl's basement.

"Beer's about gone," Karl said.

"We'll get more tomorrow," Fetch told him. He was shuffling through the stack of Verene's Polaroids.

Karl was twirling on his finger a wig Lerome had gone out and got him. Brown. About as subtle as a rug could be. Karl'd put it on for a minute to check the fit, then taken it off. Said it was hot. Now, here he was playing with it.

Fetch wished he'd put it back on. The stubble of Karl's real hair, in its natural shade of Sunkist orange, was growing in amidst all the pebbly blisters on his scalp. Made him look like a fuzzy basketball with ears. All he needed was *Spalding* tattooed on the back of his skull.

Karl asked, "You think women get off on that stuff?"

Fetch knew what he meant. "What, making us hot?" He laid the photos out on the coffee table in front of him, where Karl could see, too.

"Yeah."

"Depends. If they like men, it must give them a feeling of power."

"Everybody likes power," Karl said.

Fetch nodded. They lapsed into silence, the two of them in a funk.

Karl sighed. "I've been thinking about Verene's breasts. They're big all right, but not particularly sexy."

Fetch had come to the same conclusion. Which was funny. He sure as hell used to think they were sexy. So, what'd changed, him or them? Maybe everything had changed.

He picked up one picture. "She's getting a touch hippy, too, and her can's drooping a little." Fetch shook his head. "I had to be honest-to-God nuts to escape. What I ought to do is turn myself in."

"Yeah, it was crazy all right, only three weeks left to go." Then Karl grinned. Only it wasn't Karl. Psycho was back. "Thing is, you try to surrender now, I'll have to kill you."

Psycho laughed. Deep and loud No doubt about it, Karl was going around the bend — and Fetch would have felt a lot better if he'd had Lerome there to back him up.

"I mean," Psycho continued, "you've put me in deep shit. No way I want to go to prison."

Fetch considered. "No, you wouldn't do well there."

Unless you were Psycho all the time, he thought. Then

you'd fit right in. Unnerving himself with that thought, Fetch decided he didn't want to be alone with Karl and his evil twin any longer. It was time to go out.

He stood up and said, "Come on, I know a place where the girls like to dance."

Psycho was delighted with the idea. He grabbed his wig and out they went.

Leaving the Polaroids of Verene spread out on the coffee table.

When Lerome arrived at Ants' place, she greeted him with a frown not a smile.

"What's wrong?" he asked.

"This guy Cameron's a real joker."

"Yeah. I thought we'd figured that out already."

But apparently not everything, Lerome guessed.

Ants picked up the manuscript of *Time Expires*.

"I kept on reading, right to the last page — but the end of the story wasn't there. We don't know how it turns out."

Lerome's face got tight. He said, "Sonofabitch!"

Surprised himself. Most times, you'd hear more swearing in a convent.

"And look at this." Ants sat down in front of her computer. She had a page of text on the monitor. Lerome looked on over her shoulder. "This is a story from *Editor & Publisher,* a trade magazine. I found it after I saw the end of the manuscript was missing."

Ants tapped the screen with a fingernail.

"This tells how Cameron and his agent sold his first book, *Indecision Kills.* They sent out copies of the manuscript with the last chapter missing. They got all these readers on the edge of their seats, then made them bid to buy the book. To be the first one to know the ending."

Lerome sat down on the corner of the desk, facing Ants. He was impressed.

"This guy's good."

"You think we ought to be scared?"

"Maybe." Lerome couldn't remember the last time he'd been scared, but he took off his shades, looked Ants in the eye and said once more, "Maybe."

CHAPTER 23

On Monday morning, Dan didn't feel like such a threat. He was up before Erin, shaving, when the phone rang. He finished his right cheek so he wouldn't get foam on the receiver and then picked up. There was a phone in the bathroom.

His agent, Hank DeMitri, was on the other end.

Dan's face turned grim. He said, "Yeah, I understand. You'll get it soon ... yeah, won't be long on that, either."

Erin walked into the bathroom, wearing only a T-shirt, rubbing sleep from her eyes. Tired or not, she was able to pick up on Dan's vibe as he put the phone down.

"The Remington?" she asked.

He nodded.

"The court decision came down a few minutes ago. We lost. My publisher's attorneys won't appeal. They say it's hopeless. We have to give the typewriter back."

"That was Hank?"

"Yeah."

"And you told him you'd send the Remington soon?"

Dan nodded again.

"So we're going to pay the ransom?"

"No ... not yet anyway."

Erin looked bemused. "Well, Canada's right around the corner."

A thought popped into Dan's head, the one that had eluded him the other night, and it was a beauty. "Verene Digby's wedding is right around the corner, too. What's the name of that guy I told you she's marrying?"

Erin searched her memory. "Karl ... Hyacinth."

"We haven't looked into Karl, have we?"

"Unh-uh."

"You think Fetch might want to take a look at the man who's going to marry his ex?"

Erin — Mama Erin — looked apprehensive.

"My God. If he did, you think the poor guy's still alive?"

Dan finished shaving and said, "Yeah, I think he is."

"How can you be sure?"

"Who's the one player in this game we haven't been able to identify."

"The bald robber," Erin said. Then she got it. "Karl?"

"Stockholm Syndrome. Maybe Fetch and Lerome grabbed Karl. Don't know what they might have had in mind for him, but who's to say Karl hasn't thrown in with his captors?"

"You better write all this down," Erin told Dan.

"Yeah, I will." Dan smiled. "Let's see if we can locate this guy. Ask him if he's seen a fugitive bank robber and a typewriter thief."

Fetch woke up in the whorehouse that morning with Birdie gone and a folded piece of paper sticking out of his clenched left hand. He had no idea what it was till he opened it. He saw the handwriting was feminine and the spelling was atrocious. The note was neither addressed to him nor was it signed. But the message was so clear Fetch could hear the author's voice in his head.

Hope yu had a good time last nite. I shur did. That

was my musik yu herd playin. Moon Rivver an the uther Manseenee stuff, I meen. Aftur yu past out, I borrode yer gurl fer a threeway. Pade for yur time with hur, too. So Darleen downstares got some munny waitin fer yu. Glad to do it. Yu must shurly no by now somebuddy took all yer hard urned munny. It was just too temptin to let sit. I was yu, I'd git across the border. Don't lettem put yu back in stur. Woodint waist time lookin to git even with me eether. I figger I got maybe a munth or too at most afore my time is up fer good. All I ask is yu see I'm burreed next to yer muther. See to that personably an yu wont reegret it.

The note was from his goddamn old man! Fetch bellowed in anger. Which just about took off the top of his hungover head.

He lay back on the stained pillows, his mind reeling, cursing his fate. He and Archer — that fucking thief — had been whoring in the same dump last night. Right next door to one another. Both of them dancing to the music of Henry Mancini, no doubt. But had he made the connection? Hell, no. He was too busy falling in love with a hooker and making up for all the time his love-life had been limited to his right hand.

If he hadn't had his head so far up his ass, he could've walked down the hall and grabbed Archer by his neck and beat it the hell out of him, where he'd put all of Fetch's money. Less, of course, what the old bastard had already spent drinking and screwing.

Then a thought occurred to Fetch: If Archer was out getting professional pussy, where was Verene? Did his father's confession mean his wife was blameless? Nah. Lerome was right, they were in it together. Which meant thieves had fallen out.

Archer had ripped off Verene, too. The thought of his greedy ex also getting taken cheered Fetch marginally. So did the news that his father was dying — if the old fuck hadn't been lying about that. Which he probably was just to keep Fetch from looking for him.

Karl interrupted Fetch's thoughts, walking into his room — without knocking — wearing his rug and a silly grin. Karl had a newspaper in his hand. He kicked the door shut behind him and sat down on the bed next to Fetch. Which Fetch didn't like at all.

Karl wasn't aware of this invasion of personal space. He seemed to be caught up in a moment of rapture.

"They gave us a name," he said giddily. "We're famous. I got up early to go for a walk and look what I saw in a vending machine."

He showed Fetch the front page of the newspaper. There was the illustration of them robbing Java Joe's again. But, as Karl had said, this time they'd been labeled.

"The No-Place-Is-Safe-Bandits!" Karl squeezed Fetch's forearm just as a shiver of delight ran through him. Fetch felt violated. He pulled his arm free.

"Get the fuck away from me! Get off my bed!"

Karl backed off, dropping the paper, and Fetch could see his eyes flicker like light bulbs on the verge of burning out. Karl couldn't decide which of his personalities to assume: himself or Psycho. Fetch didn't need the madman right now. He got up and grabbed the paper.

"Didn't you notice this?" Fetch stabbed a finger at a subhead pointing out the offer of a $25,000 reward. Karl's look made it clear that, in his mania, he'd overlooked that little detail.

Fetch quickly put on his clothes.

"You think any hooker in this building won't turn us in for that kind of money?" Fetch demanded. The question reached the businessman in Karl, ending his identity crisis. Then Fetch said, "No place is safe? Yeah, for us."

Dan and Erin knocked on the front door of Karl's house;

they'd had Rudy find the address for them. When no one answered, Dan knocked again. Looked in a window. All the lights were out. Didn't look like anyone was home.

Erin said, "Guess we'll have to come back."

Dan tried the doorknob. It turned. Fetch and Karl, loaded up on beer and going out whoring the previous night, hadn't remembered to lock the front door.

"Dan," Erin said, a tone of foreboding in her voice.

"The cops come, I'll do the talking. The way I see it, they'll likely be more forgiving than those lawyers who want my typewriter back."

Dan stepped inside. Mama Erin trembled. Old Erin enjoyed every goosebump on her body. Both halves followed close behind her husband. Dan let her by and closed the door softly.

He called out, "Karl, you home?"

Nobody answered.

Dan looked at Erin and asked quietly, "This place feel empty to you?"

She nodded, eyes wide.

They went farther into the house to see what they could see. Erin held Dan's hand, hard. They searched the first floor and in the living room saw a photo portrait of a man with carefully styled blonde hair. They looked at it and then each other.

"The bald guy?" Erin asked.

They looked again, neither of them sure if it was a likeness of the second robber. Erin had another question, though.

"How're you going to put this into your new book — what we're doing here — without confessing that we've committed a crime?"

Dan was stuck for an answer. "We'll work it out later."

They continued snooping, first upstairs and then, turning on a light, down in the basement. Where they found the collection of Verene's Polaroids that Fetch had left out.

Dispassionately, Erin said, "She's right on the edge."

"Of what?" Dan asked, trying not to stare.

"Porking out. Fat starting to collect at the back of her arms and legs. Sags here and there."

Dan read between the lines and said, "Still looks like nothing but trouble to me."

Erin smiled — until she and Dan heard a door open upstairs. Just as they'd done, a voice called out for Karl. A woman's voice.

Dan and Erin looked at each other, then around the room. There were few places to hide and none of them seemed inviting. But footsteps were now coming down the stairs to the basement.

The woman said, "I thought I saw a light on down here. You here, baby?" Verene stepped into the room, expecting to see Karl, and found Dan and Erin.

It was the first time the two women laid eyes on each other, and it was immediately clear to Verene that she would not be messing with this woman's husband. She was put at a further disadvantage by seeing her Polaroids spread out on the coffee table, knowing these two must have been looking at them. For the first time in many a year, Verene blushed.

Her face stayed red as embarrassment turned to anger. "What the hell are you two doing here? What do you want?"

Dan noticed didn't she didn't threaten to call the cops.

He answered honestly, "I told you before. Fetch stole from me."

"*What?* What'd Fetch steal? And what's that got to do with Karl?"

"Fetch took my typewriter." Dan decided to leave it at that.

"Your typewriter?"

Dan saw Verene's face scrunch up in confusion. Her expression reinforced the notion that she hadn't been the woman who'd called in the ransom demand to Hank.

He answered, "Yeah." On impulse, he added, "I'm offering a $10,000 reward for it."

That got Verene's attention. "What kind of typewriter is it?"

"The one-of-a-kind kind," Erin answered.

The two women glared at each other, cats ready to fight, but Verene looked away first. She turned to Dan and asked, "What makes you think Karl'd know anything about it?"

"We just wanted to let him know. So he could pass the word if Fetch came to see him."

Verene's face closed like a fist.

"Yeah, well, you told me. I'll tell him. You got anything else to say?"

Dan didn't.

Neither did Erin. But before they left she took another glance at the Polaroids.

And smirked at Verene.

After the blonde bitch and her husband left, Verene looked at the pictures. For the first time, she realized her figure was starting to slip. She scooped up the Polaroids, not wanting to leave them for Karl to dwell on.

Before she departed, she scratched out a terse note: *Typewriter worth 10K!*

It'd be okay if Karl collected the reward.

She was going to take him for everything he had.

"Jesus Christ, it's the cops," Fetch muttered.

He and Karl, returning to Karl's house, five minutes after Verene had left, saw a dark blue Ford Crown Victoria pull into Karl's driveway and disappear behind the house.

"You're sure?" Karl asked.

Fetch felt a stabbing pain behind his eyes. What you got working with amateurs.

"Yeah, Karl, I'm sure. Keep on driving."

Karl pulled to the curb, three houses up from his own.

Fetch's eyes bugged out. "What the hell are you doing?" He'd left his gun in Karl's basement, under a sofa cushion, or he would have stuck it in Karl's ear. For his part, Karl was cool as could be. Lerome-like, almost.

"Wouldn't it be a good idea to find out what they want?" Karl asked. "See how much they know."

Fetch had to laugh. "Yeah, Karl, that'd be real good — if we don't have to go to fucking prison to find out."

"Why would they arrest me? It's my house. I'm an honest businessman."

Karl still had his rug on. He might've thought the wig was hot, but his whore had told him he looked sexy in it — Karl never doubting a hooker's compliment — so it'd stayed on his head. He was also wearing his beret, so he wasn't immediately recognizable as the desperado on the front page of the newspaper.

"You think you can pull this off?" Fetch asked.

"Sure. You take a walk and come back in half an hour."

Fetch didn't like it, neither the idea nor Karl telling him to take a walk, but he didn't have a better plan. He got out of the car and headed away from Karl's house, not hurrying but not dawdling, either. He'd give it an hour. Then he'd call Karl from a public phone.

Fetch saw Karl pull into his driveway, blocking the unmarked cop car from leaving. The only thing he liked about the situation as he turned the corner.

Mickey Gruber had pulled the Crown Vic all the way up to the garage's overhead door. The garage had no windows and Tracey found the pedestrian door locked. They were running down all the owners of red Honda VTXs in town.

This was their fourth stop. The first one to prove difficult. The two cops looked at each other, sharing the same thought. Break in now, come back with a search warrant later, if need be. Gruber was happy to let Tracey make the call on that.

Only he didn't have to.

A voice called out, "Something I can do for you guys?"

They turned and saw a man standing next to a small white car near the street end of the driveway. He had the driver's door open and looked as if he might get back in. Take off.

"Guy looks nervous," Gruber whispered.

"Might be a runner," Tracey agreed. Nonetheless, he held up his badge and said, "Police."

The guy didn't run; he slumped against the car. Then he straightened up and laughed. "That's a relief. For a minute, I didn't know if you were burglars."

He closed the car door and walked toward them.

The two cops looked at each other, both irritated that anybody would take them for bad guys, but not about to press it since they had been thinking about making an illegal entry. The guy stopped a few feet away from them.

"So what's going on?" he asked with a smile.

Neither Tracey nor Gruber saw too many guys wearing a beret, especially in summer, but they weren't the fashion police.

"Are you ..." Gruber consulted his list. "Karl Hyacinth?"

Karl said he was.

"And you own a red Honda VTX motorcycle?" Tracey asked.

Candy red, Karl told them.

"Would you mind if we take a look at it, Mr. Hyacinth?"

Karl said not a problem. Right this way. He led them to the pedestrian door, taking his keys out of his pocket. With his back to the cops neither of them saw Psycho make his entrance.

Fetch'd been right after all, Psycho thought. The cops had traced his motorcycle back to him. Now, he'd have to step aside as they entered the garage — out of public view — and find some way to kill them. Fetch'd have to help him dispose of the bodies and the cop car when he got back. Karl opened the door for the detectives and let them enter.

Gruber flipped on the light as he stepped in, but he turned around before Tracey could follow. "Where is it, Mr. Hyacinth?" he asked.

Tracey glanced inside, then he, too, turned to look at Karl.

Psycho — homicidal intent displaced by confusion — asked, "Where's what?"

"Your motorcycle," both cops responded.

"My motorcycle?"

Psycho brushed past them, went into the garage and saw it was empty. His eyes bulged and his jaw dropped. As both cops could plainly see, he was genuinely astonished to find his motorcycle was missing. What they didn't notice was the change of persona. Psycho had bowed out in favor of his meeker self.

"It was ..." Karl began. His voice dropped to a whisper and contained a note of awe, which neither detective assessed accurately. "It was right here the last time I saw it."

Tracey put a hand on Karl's shoulder and turned him around.

"When was that?"

"A couple of days ago, I guess." Then Karl ad-libbed. "Maybe even three or four."

Had it been there when he and Fetch had gone out to see the girls? They'd been so buzzed he hadn't even noticed. He doubted Fetch had, either.

"So you're saying your motorcycle was stolen?" Gruber

asked.

"Well, it's certainly not here, and I don't know where it is," Karl said truthfully.

Karl spent the next hour with the detectives and a uniformed officer answering questions and filling out a stolen vehicle report. He had to move his car to let Tracey and Gruber leave.

He was by himself when Fetch, who'd decided to wait two hours, called.

When Fetch got back to Karl's house, Karl told him, "Verene's been here."

Fetch couldn't believe it. He kept missing the people he wanted to see the most. First, his father. Now, Verene. She didn't have his money any longer — if Archer had taken it — but he'd still like to get his hands on her and ... do something.

"How do you know?" Fetch asked.

Karl showed him Verene's note. Like the one from Fetch's father, it was unsigned.

He looked at Karl and asked, "You're sure this is from Verene?"

"I recognize her handwriting."

Damned if I can, Fetch thought. It occurred to him that Karl knew his ex better than he did. These days, anyway.

Karl interrupted Fetch's musing with a good question.

"What typewriter is worth $10,000?"

"The one Lerome's trying to sell for $100,000," Fetch told him.

"What kind of type—" Karl made the intuitive leap. "He's got the typewriter that was used to write *Time Expires?*"

Fetch nodded, impressed. "He stole the story and the typewriter right after I broke out."

"Damn. That Lerome, he's really something," Karl said

grinning. "You know what else he did?"

Karl told Fetch how Lerome — who else could it have been — had stolen his motorcycle without telling him. So when he went to show the cycle to the cops and it was gone, he was genuinely surprised. No need to try and put on an act and have the cops see through it. Now the police thought he was just another victim of the Java Joe's robbers.

Fetch only nodded, Lerome's cunning being old hat to him. He said, "Sit down, Karl. Let's you and me have a little talk."

The two of them sat on opposite ends of the sofa, Karl above his money, Fetch atop his gun. Fetch thought Karl might feel better taking his wig off, or at least his beret, but he didn't want to get sidetracked.

"Karl," he said, "I've come to have real regrets how Lerome and I have fucked with your life. I was pissed at you before, what with you going to marry Verene. Now, I'm just sorry. I don't know how all this is going to turn out, so I thought I better say it while I have the chance."

Karl didn't say anything, just looked at Fetch and blinked.

"You believe me, don't you?"

Karl nodded.

"Thing is, I don't think we're through fucking with you."

Fetch thought this might provoke an appearance by Psycho, but it seemed to have the opposite effect. Karl sagged with relief, or so it seemed to Fetch Which prompted his next question.

"What was it happened to you, Karl, the night we robbed that beauty parlor? I know you told me some shit about channeling your fear, but it's more than that. Sometimes a change comes over you almost makes me believe in satanic possession."

Karl laughed so hard it made Fetch wonder if he'd

flipped him out again. But then Karl settled down, rubbed tears of mirth from his eyes, and looked more relaxed than Fetch had ever seen him.

"That's just what I was afraid of, Fetch. What I've always been afraid of. Going to hell. I was raised Norwegian Catholic." Karl nodded gravely as if he'd just bared his soul.

Fetch, who'd nominally been raised Roman Catholic, admitted he'd never heard of the Norwegian branch of the faith. Hadn't known Karl was Norwegian, either.

"The immigration man changed our family name," Karl said.

"What was it?"

Karl told him. Sounded just like Hyacinth to Fetch. Then Karl explained about his faith.

"It's a small schismatic sect," Karl told him. "Most Scandinavians are Protestants, of course, but Norwegian Catholics don't think the Reformation hell burns hot enough. Medieval Italy had a much better concept of damnation in their view. Dante's *Inferno,* now there was the way to treat those who strayed from the straight and narrow."

Of course, in later centuries, Karl continued, the Vatican got about as mushy as the Protestants, eating meat on Friday no longer being a mortal sin, and the true believers in Norway had to trod their own stony path. Basically, anything that felt good was sinful and would result in an eternity of demons eating your entrails. As you watched.

"Your parents told you that?" Fetch asked in awe. "Those words?"

Karl nodded.

"And you believed them?"

"I did."

Fetch felt much better. Somebody else had screwed Karl up long before he and Lerome came along.

"I lived by their teachings ...until Verene came along."

"Sure," Fetch said. "It's in the bible. Guy's going along, minding his own business, who struts by and tempts him, has God kick his ass for it?"

"Verene?"

"Eve, Karl, Eve. And women in general."

"You got something against women, Fetch?"

"Hell, no. I love them more than I should."

"Me, too. But see, I thought I was safe. Verene really didn't let me have sex with her. Said I got none until we got married."

"Yeah, but what about other women? The ones before Verene."

"There weren't any."

Fetch gave Karl a dubious look.

"Well, lately I've been trying to hit on this woman who works for me."

"You were a virgin, Karl?"

"Till just the other night with Rhonda."

"So you thought you were safe, until you robbed the beauty parlor?"

"That's when I realized: Even if I waited to get married to Verene to have sex, I was going to enjoy it so much it'd be sinful anyway. There was no hope for me, no escape. I was doomed to burn." Karl shrugged. "That being the case, I thought why not enjoy myself. You know, while I have the chance. But since I haven't had much practice letting myself go, sometimes I get carried away. Maybe the devil's in me already, just like you said."

Fetch sighed. The way people could screw themselves up. Made him wish he could have a beer, but they were out. Denied pleasure, he got back to business.

He asked, "You know if Verene reads much these days?"

"*Cosmo* mostly," Karl replied. "Supermarket tabloids sometimes."

Which meant she likely hadn't read about the reward in

the *Buffalo News,* or seen the drawing of them robbing Java Joe's. Fetch didn't think shaving Karl's head would keep Verene from recognizing Karl. His new hair color wouldn't fool her, either. She'd recognize them as the No-Place-Is-Safe Bandits. She'd call the cops and grab that reward money in a heartbeat. Especially after Archer had ripped her off.

"Of course, she watches a lot of television," Karl added.

"TV, shit!" Fetch moaned. The reward offer had to be on television if it was in the paper.

"What?" Karl asked.

"Verene knows about the reward, Karl. She knows we're the No-Place-Is-Safe Bandits."

"You think?"

"Jesus, you're doubting me again? Was I right about the cops?"

"Yeah, you were. What do you think we should do?"

Fetch was thinking it was time to take his old man's advice and run for Canada.

Karl, as was his way, derailed Fetch's train of thought. "What happened to the Polaroids of Verene?"

Fetch saw Karl was right. They were gone. "You didn't move them?"

Karl shook his head. "And you couldn't have, you weren't here."

"Verene? Why would she leave them, then take them back?"

Wait a minute, Fetch thought, how'd Verene know what the typewriter was worth? And why'd she think it was 10K instead of 100K?

Once more, Karl trampled on Fetch's thought process.

"Who the hell knows what Verene's up to?" he asked. "And why should we care? Listen, there's this wine tasting I know about tomorrow night. Lots of people with lots of money are going to be there. Bet we could grab fifty grand between the cash and the credit card numbers."

Just like that, nothing to it. Karl was on his way to a life of crime. Still, Fetch thought: 50K. Add that to the money he already had. And the 10-100K he'd get for selling the typewriter back to Cameron. Figure in the favorable exchange rate for Canadian dollars. It'd be enough to give him a decent start north of the border.

Maybe he'd scoot all the way out to Vancouver. Nobody'd think to look for him there.

Then Karl added, "Of course, I'd still like to hit that cigar bar I know tonight. That could be pretty rich, too."

Fetch said, "Tell me some more about cigar bars, Karl."

When Dan and Erin got back to the Chateau, Rudy had news for them.

"Mr. Harry Patterson would like you to call," he told Dan, giving him a message slip.

"Do we know a Harry Patterson?" Dan asked Erin, puzzled.

"He's a mail carrier for the United States Postal Service," Rudy added.

Erin laughed, clapped her hands in joy, and gave Rudy a big hug. He tried not to show his pleasure, but couldn't keep the smile off his face. He remembered his proper demeanor only when Erin let him go and he saw Dan grinning at him.

Rudy cleared his throat and concluded, "Mr. Patterson said something about a reward."

"Five thousand dollars," Dan nodded.

He took Erin's arm and they headed for the elevator, Dan thinking, "Figure that one out, Rudy." Erin would have taken pity on him, except she was too excited by the news.

"It worked, Dan, it worked," she said, practically vibrating. She grabbed Dan's arm as they entered the elevator. "The eyes and ears of the USPS have come through for us.

Was that a good idea or what?"

"It was," Dan agreed.

He was happy to see the old Erin back in control, at least for the moment.

Once they entered the suite, Erin got the honor of calling the number Patterson had left. The conversation was brief, ending with Erin getting the mail carrier's address and promising to send him a check right away. FedEx.

When Erin put the phone down, Dan asked, "Fetch?"

Erin shook her head. "Lerome."

"At home?"

"No. The Delaware Park branch of the Buffalo Public Library. And guess what. Harry said he noticed Lerome was reading a magazine story about you."

"We'll get directions from Rudy," Dan said.

They headed back out.

CHAPTER 24

Adriano Trinidad, special agent in charge of the FBI's Buffalo field office, called Gamble Murtree into his office at the Dulski Federal Building. Trini was very solicitous of his former rival, offering him a seat, coffee, and a cigar to be smoked later. The federal building was smoke-free. Gamble took the seat but nothing else.

He looked out the window at Trini's high-rise view of Lake Erie. Buffalo wasn't a glamour assignment in the Bureau, but with the city right on the border with Canada, if a commie mole wanted to help people slip into or out of the country, you couldn't do better.

When Trini inquired about Gamble's health, he said he was fine. Then he added, "Can we cut the shit? You want to tell me what this is all about?"

"I got a call this morning," Trini said. "Dick Tracey's new sidekick, Gruber. You know him?"

Gamble shook his head.

"Doesn't matter. Thing is, Gruber and Tracey've been working these freaky stickups. The beauty parlor and the coffee shop."

Gamble kept a straight face and said, "Don't see any federal responsibility."

"Isn't one, not in that stuff," Trini said.

Guy didn't have a trace of a Cuban accent when he spoke English; sounded like an Iowa newscaster. Just one more thing that made Gamble suspicious about him.

"Anyway, while they're looking, Gruber thinks, 'Is it just a coincidence that Fetch Mcdonald — your old friend — busts out of Camp Alphonse and all of a sudden we got these strange armed robberies going on?'"

Trini paused but Gamble kept quiet.

"So," Trini continued, "Tracey tells him to call us because he remembers somebody over here made a cause of nailing Fetch Mcdonald. Thought that agent might have some insights."

Gamble said, "Me? I'm retired, and the way I remember it, nobody here believed me when I said Mcdonald was the Everyman Robber."

Trini shrugged. "Maybe we were wrong."

"Maybe *you* were wrong," Gamble corrected. "You were the one who ridiculed my theory, got everyone to believe my idea was half-assed. You fucked me over every chance you got. Only reason I came here was to see if you really have the gall to ask me for help."

SAC Trinidad smiled blandly. "I do."

Gamble sat forward in his chair. "I got something to ask you, too. Should've done it a long time ago. You working for Fidel, Trini, or you just like his boxers better than ours?"

Had to hand it to him, Gamble thought. Trini didn't blow his cool. Looked like he wanted to shoot Gamble right there. Only he'd be stuck for a good excuse, so he'd have to wait. Until he found the right time and place.

When Trini finally spoke his voice was filled with contempt. "I thought I'd have to go looking for a retired old shit like you, Murtree. Have to call you long distance, someplace warm. But no, you stayed right here in town. And not long after Mcdonald escapes you showed up right here in this field office. Like maybe you know something." Trini laughed. The prospect of cruel pleasure glittered in his eyes. "You do know something and you don't tell me right now ... well, you know how it goes."

Gamble stood. "I stopped by to visit an old friend the other day, but he isn't here anymore. As for what I know, I don't *know* anything." Gamble walked to Trini's door, stopped, and looked back. "I got my suspicions, of course. But we both know what you think of my theories, Trini."

Gamble grinned and left.

Lerome sat at a table in the Delaware Park branch library, writing on a ruled pad of paper. With Ants' help, he'd outlined the crimes and other story details of *Time Expires*. He'd been right, Terry Phelan hadn't been sending Allie and BooBoo out just to fuck over his old friends.

Ants had summarized for him what happened in the story. What Terry wanted was for his former friends to notice the common denominator of whose places were getting robbed — him. Resentful old Terry. Still stuck working for someone else. Didn't have the family money or connections to get his own business going like they did. Once they put it together, it was only natural they'd point the finger at Terry, have the cops bust his ass.

Which was just what Terry wanted.

Because after Allie and BooBoo pulled their last job, the two young criminals were going to die. Either the cops would kill them as the crime went down or Terry would do it after they got away. Without the armed robbers around to incriminate him, he was going to sue the shit out of all his old friends for defamation of character. That was how Terry planned to get rich.

Cold but very slick, Lerome thought.

Looked like Terry was going to need the money, too, because his boss was about to sell Chicago Psychographics to a big conglomerate. The boss was trying to negotiate for Terry so he could either stay on the job with a promotion or get a golden parachute. But it was uncertain the buyers would go for that, or that Terry's boss, ultimately, would let it screw up a deal that would make him megabucks.

Then there was Fayre. Ants had been right about her. As smart as she was, she caught on to Allie stalking her right away. As tough as she was, too, she had a gun at home. An illegal gun since city law said you couldn't own a pistol in Chicago. Fayre had already hinted to Terry that she wanted his help in doing something about Allie. Terry said he would help, but he couldn't move too soon because he needed Allie to complete his plan.

And BooBoo was finally noticing his girlfriend had a faithless heart and an eye for Terry. There was tension all over the place. But the last goddamn chapter was missing.

So first Lerome had to figure out how Dan Cameron intended the book to end. Then he wanted to see if maybe he couldn't do better. The idea of becoming a storyteller had reached full bloom for Lerome. He was already thinking of the first story he'd write.

Ants was at the circulation desk checking in returned books when a thirty-something blonde wearing a pink polo shirt and khaki shorts walked in and stopped in front of her.

"Hi, I'm new in town," the woman said with a smile. "Can you tell me what kind of identification I'd need to get a library card."

"A driver's license with a local address," Ants replied politely. "State picture ID if you don't drive. Utility bill at a local address ..."

Hearing the two women talk, Lerome glanced up. He'd been aware that someone had just walked past him. The blonde looked over at him, gave him a smile, looked back at Ants. All perfectly innocent. Good looking woman, but not one to stare at. Not that Lerome stared. He went back to his work ... but with less than the complete concentration he'd had before.

The blonde told Ants, "Thanks. I think I'll look around, see what titles you have." She walked off into the stacks, glancing at books, looking around.

Ants put all the books she'd checked in on a trolley for reshelving. She could have left the chore for one of the summer kids, but they were at lunch, so she pushed them over to the table where Lerome sat.

"How's it coming?" she asked.

"The story? What I think's going to happen, Terry's boss will sell him out."

"So Terry'll have to get even with him, too."

Lerome nodded, "Yeah. And that'll be the situation where Allie and BooBoo get theirs."

"So Terry doesn't kill them."

"No. It should look like he's going to get away clean, but then he doesn't."

Ants liked that. "If that's not the way it works out, it should. So then Fayre doesn't kill Allie. What happens with her and Terry?"

"I don't know. But I think Fetch has it right. They don't live happily ever after."

"Yeah, I don't think so, either."

They heard a car start outside. Lerome looked around. "That blonde you were talking to, someone you know?"

Ants shook her head. "Said she was new in town."

Ants joined Lerome in scanning the library. As far as they could tell, they were the only ones there. "Where'd she go?" Lerome asked.

"I don't know."

"She walked past me on her way to you, so she came in the front door."

"Maybe she left by the back."

Lerome got to his feet. "Why would she do that? Enter one way, leave another."

Lerome and Ants headed for the back door, but stopped at a window as they saw the blonde woman driving off in Lerome's stolen SUV.

She saw them, too. Smiled and waved.

Erin pulled into the parking lot of a nearby Tops supermarket on Amherst Street. She parked next to the white rental Chevy in which Dan waited. They'd agreed on the way to the library that if Lerome was interested enough in Dan to read about him, he'd likely have seen a picture of him, too. Would recognize Dan if he walked into the library.

Erin, on the other hand, had been the subject of far less media attention. She could scope things out with less chance of discovery. Dan would wait for her. Come get her if she called. It was a plan, but it made Dan wish Mama Erin was back in charge, not Old Erin. But Mama Erin never would have reclaimed their stolen SUV.

The Camerons got out of their respective vehicles and Erin leaped into Dan's arms.

"God, Dan, it was great! I was so slick. I think the only time I ever had more fun was when we did it against that tree."

"Kinda jazzed, huh?" He looked at the black Toyota Highlander. With New York plates. "It is ours, isn't it?"

Erin leaned back in Dan's arms and held up her ignition key. "Opened the door, turned the engine over."

"Well, that settles that. Kinda like it in black actually."

"Me, too."

"But what made you think it was ours?"

"Lerome was there, the SUV was there, are you kidding me? I was just lucky I had my key with me. You've got to put this in your new book."

275

Dan laughed. "Absolutely."

He kissed his wife. Then he looked over her shoulder. Erin noticed.

"What? You think Lerome's going to chase me?" She shook her head. "Not his style. He's not going to do anything that would draw attention from the cops."

Dan nodded. She was right. Lerome was too subtle for that. Dan let go of Erin with one arm and looked at the interior of the Highlander. Looked good to him.

"It's very clean," Erin said.

"Sure, he didn't want to leave any evidence."

"But I found out something else, anyway." Erin was beaming again.

"What?"

"The woman who made the ransom call."

"You're kidding."

"Unh-uh. She's the librarian. Tall, nice figure, not nearly the Plain Jane she pretends to be. I was peeking around a shelf before I went out to the parking lot and grabbed our car back. She was talking with Lerome. Standing close. Very familiar, intimate body language. And the way they talk to each other, they sound a lot like us."

Dan nodded. "A librarian would know about books, wouldn't have much trouble talking to an agent. Add in her relationship to Lerome ..."

"She's the one. This is the turning point, Dan. We're going to beat those bastards."

"I think you're right. But they might feel the same way: threatened. So we'll have to be careful."

Old Erin said, "They're the ones who should be scared."

Old Dan said, "They probably are. But let's remember one thing."

"What?"

"We write about crimes... these people commit them."

***

At the Delaware Park branch library, Ants pulled a copy of *Indecision Kills* off a shelf. She opened it to the dedication page as Lerome looked on.

For my wife Erin, the love of my life. Thanks for the typewriter, Toots.

Ants looked at Lerome. Who just that minute remembered the picture of the blonde woman he'd seen when he'd picked up the writer's wallet back at that fancy cabin in the woods.

"You think that was her, Cameron's wife?" Ants asked.

"The one and only," Lerome replied.

CHAPTER 25

Fetch and Karl shared Karl's bathroom as they completed their grooming for the cigar bar job. Both of them were wearing conservative business suits from Karl's closet. Karl had helped Fetch pick a tie to go with the suit. Fetch couldn't remember being so dressed up since his Confirmation. Even the rented tux he wore at his wedding wasn't as nice as Karl's suit.

With his hair re-dyed — dark blonde now — Fetch thought he looked sharp. Somewhere there was a good-looking woman who'd smile when she saw him coming. Made him glad he was divorced. He slipped on a pair of clear-lens glasses as a final touch.

Added a scholarly air.

Not that he'd go so far as to wear a bowtie the way Karl was, playing with it now to get it just right. Fetch thought that was something to see: Psycho in a bowtie. Suspenders, too. Karl was also wearing a new wig. Silver gray. He'd bought it that afternoon, also picking up Fetch's hair coloring and a case of St. Pauli Girl while he was out.

Having fixed his bowtie just right, Karl started fluffing up his wig.

"I tell you the salesman said this is the same kind of

hairpiece Burt Reynolds wore in a movie once?" Karl asked.

"You might've mentioned it," Fetch answered. Like thirty-nine times.

But he wasn't going to complain. Karl had gone right along with his idea that they had to change their look for tonight's job. Take everybody by surprise. Give the cops something else to think about. Were these cigar-bar guys the No-Place-Is-Safe Bandits or copycats? Maybe somebody would do a new drawing from their descriptions and help muddy the water.

Of course, if there was some really sharp cop around, he might make a connection with how the Everyman Bank Robber used to vary his appearance. But smart cops were few and far between in Fetch's experience. It was worth the risk.

Karl slipped on his own pair of glasses, not Lerome's shades, which the cops and the public would recognize by now, but a new pair with amber lenses.

He turned to Fetch and asked, "How do I look?"

Fetch flicked a piece of lint off Karl's lapel. "You look good."

Karl turned and grinned at himself in the mirror. "A bad man looking good."

Fetch withheld comment but the conversational opening was filled anyway.

"Glad to see you boys're getting on together," Lerome said from the doorway.

Verene sat in the phone booth at The Marginal Wanker, a mock English pub named in honor of the Prince of Wales. It was the only place she knew that had a public phone that was actually enclosed. In one of those big red boxes like they had in England. Like she heard they had in England. She'd never been. But she planned to go.

Verene still had ambitions. She called the Cameron's suite at the Chateau. Just her luck, she got the blonde bitch.

"You know who this is?" Verene asked brusquely.

"The aging porn star?" Erin replied sweetly. "You find our typewriter?"

"No," Verene snapped. She wished she could do something bad to this woman, spackle her love canal maybe. Only the blonde, damn her, didn't look like she had an ounce of fat on her. Only lean, sleek muscle. She'd probably kick Verene's ass and not break a sweat.

"You still there?" Erin asked.

"Yeah. What'd it be worth to you to get the guy who stole the typewriter?"

"Fetch?"

"That's who took it, isn't it?"

"Yeah. Unless it was Lerome."

Lerome. Verene almost wet herself. What'd this bitch know about Lerome?

"He's not in town," Verene said, more to reassure herself than anything.

"Saw him this morning."

Shit!

"Anyway," Erin continued, "it's ten grand for the guy, whoever took it, but only if he has the typewriter with him."

"Bitch," Verene said.

"Two words," Erin replied. "Consider liposuction."

Verene started cursing, but the connection was broken. Then she continued cursing when some twit came along and wanted to use the phone. Once he was gone, she took a small notebook and a pen out of her purse.

She wrote: 25K reward, Java Joe's and Permanent Fave, 10K reward, blonde bitch and husband. Then she had a thought and got a number from 411.

"Crimestoppers," a voice answered.

"Yeah, can you tell me, is there a reward for the capture of that bankrobber, Fetch Mcdonald? The guy who broke out of Camp Alphonse."

"Hold on a minute." Wasn't ten seconds. "Yes, there is: $15,000. Do you have any information as to his whereabouts?"

"I might in a little while." She hung up.

Fifty grand altogether, the three rewards.

She wrote 50K in her notebook. It wasn't anything like the amount that she'd hoped to have, but it was better than nothing. Enough to go someplace warm. Get something new going.

Didn't seem like a good idea to stick around if Lerome was back. Wouldn't take him long to figure out who'd set up Fetch. Verene looked at the arm she'd used to do her writing. Gave it a little slap. Saw the fat on the back jiggle.

Liposuction ... bitch.

The whore gave Archer Mcdonald's face a little slap.

"You asleep, baby."

Archer groaned but didn't open his eyes.

"You're asleep all right." She thumbed open an eyelid. Looked briefly at the cloudy, bloodshot orb. Let the lid fall. Archer rolled onto his side, grabbed his midsection and curled up into the fetal position. He moaned again. The whore added, "Maybe even dyin'."

The whore slipped out of bed, threw on her clothes, and went straight for Archer's pants.

Archer had thought it prudent to dip his wick somewhere other than his preferred brothel. He didn't want to be there at full giddyup and have Fetch yank him out of the saddle. The boy just might do that as pissed as he had to be at his daddy. So Archer had picked up a girl on the street and repaired to a fleabag hotel.

Hardly the girl of his dreams or the setting for romance, but Archer's hormones most often called for urgency not delicacy. Since Dottie had died, anyway. His equipment was as dependable as ever. Up to a point. The first time had gone off with a bang. Maybe too big a bang. The girl complained about him being rougher than she liked. He wanted a specialist in that kinda shit, she had a friend.

While he was thinking about that possibility, the hooker brought him a drink. He'd bought the bottle so he felt safe about what he was getting. Downed the paper cup of whiskey at a gulp. Wasn't long after that the bed started spinning and he fell down a deep black hole.

The whore who'd slipped him the mickey hoped to find maybe a couple hundred bucks in the old man's wallet, the proceeds of a welfare check or a minor crime, but the roll of bills she pulled out of his pocket made her gasp.

Fifties and hundreds. Right there near the end was one lousy ten-spot. She quickly counted over three thousand dollars. She looked at Archer, worried he might somehow jump up and take all the money back. Unh-uh. That was just silly. The Rohypnol she'd used to spike his booze would have him out for hours. Lotta people called it a date-rape drug. Hookers called it a screw-you drug. Used it on johns they wanted to roll or who gave them trouble.

The mickey wasn't enough, the old man really did look like he might croak. The hooker pulled out the ten and left it next to Archer. That was a good one, her leaving money on a bed.

"Get yourself some medicine," she told him.

Then she wondered what the old man might be dying of. Something that could infect her? Looking at him now, she could hardly believe she'd let the disgusting old fuck stick his thing in her. Bang away at her like he was breaking up pavement or something. He'd probably made her bleed inside. That happened, sure as hell she was going to get sick. Damn!

She went back to the bed and grabbed the ten.

"Fuck you, old man," the whore said, leaving Archer penniless.

As she closed the door, he began to convulse violently.

"Cameron's wife stole your car?" Fetch asked in disbelief.

"The one we stole from her," Lerome replied with a shrug.

He'd borrowed Ants' car for the night. A VW Passat she'd bought legit. It was gunmetal gray, which was her preferred color for cars. Had a black interior, though.

"Still," Fetch said. Like most thieves, he expected that once something had been stolen it should stay stolen. A position he'd been grievously unable to defend heretofore.

"How'd she know to find you at the library?" Karl asked.

"That's the important question," Lerome responded. But he didn't have an answer for that one yet. He'd have to ask Ants to help him with it.

"I think Cameron's been here, too," Fetch said. He told his cousin how they knew Verene had been there; she'd left a note. "But how could Verene know Cameron's typewriter was worth big money if Cameron hadn't told her?"

"Still doesn't mean he was here," Karl argued. "He could've told her somewhere else."

"Could've. But that's not how it feels to me," Fetch said.

Lerome thought about Erin Cameron, smiling and waving at him. Stealing her car back right out from under him.

"Me, either," he said. "It's too bad, though, you didn't get the chance to see Verene, Fetch. Ask her about your money."

Which got Fetch started on missing his old man at the whorehouse, how he thought Archer had taken all of Fetch's money for himself, and waking up to find the note from the bastard in his hand. But he didn't want to dwell on that shit right now. It'd give him a headache.

Instead Fetch asked, "If Cameron knows so much, why haven't the cops grabbed us?"

Lerome told the two of them about Ants' idea: Cameron could be writing a book about all the things that happened since his typewriter got stolen.

"Damn, I'd like to read that story," Karl said with a grin.

"Jesus, Karl, we're living it," Fetch told him.

"Still like to read it," Karl replied like a stubborn little kid.

Fetch threw his hands up.

"There's something else we've got a problem reading," Lerome informed them. He revealed how Ants had discovered the end of *Time Expires* was missing. How that was the way Dan Cameron sold his novels. Got publishers all worked up and made them pay to see the finish.

Fetch was outraged. "That fuck."

"Yeah," Karl agreed, Psycho starting to edge into view.

That didn't seem to bother Lerome. He said, "I haven't figured out how the story gets resolved, but like you said Fetch I don't think it's a happy ending for Allie and BooBoo. In fact, Cameron wrote that Terry's planning to kill them if the cops don't."

"He is?" Karl asked, astounded.

Lerome told them what else he knew.

Fetch came to a decision, "We've got to find out what happens at the end. If Cameron will only pay 10K for his typewriter, we'll live with that. But he's got to give us those missing pages if he wants to get the rest of the story back."

Karl enthusiastically seconded the notion.

Lerome thought maybe Fetch'd make a good editor for him. Tell him what he thought worked and what didn't. Give his plots a push in an interesting direction now and then.

"That's the way you want to play it, we can do that," Lerome said. "Only I think we better wrap everything up pretty fast. This whole thing is coming apart on us."

Fetch knew what Lerome was telling him. Doing any more jobs would be a real risk.

But Fetch and Karl were both ready to go tonight. Dressed for it. And if they got away with the cigar bar, they might as well finish up big with the wine tasting.

"You said Allie and BooBoo got away with those jobs, right?" Fetch asked Lerome.

"Yeah, they did."

"Okay," Fetch said, "then maybe Cameron wants us to get that far, too."

Or maybe I'm going psycho myself, Fetch thought.

He and Karl left, off to rob a cigar bar. Kovac's downtown. Best damn cigar bar in town, if you believed Karl.

Lerome watched them go and thought if he was writing this story, he'd throw in a twist right here.

Glancing at Karl's desk he found one. Verene's note about the typewriter was there. So was the one Archer had left tucked into Fetch's hand. Lerome read them both.

Hell.

With a clue like that, Lerome could have figured out where Archer had hidden Fetch's money even before he started thinking like a writer.

Karl spotted a problem even before he and Fetch entered Kovac's. Just looking through the window he saw it. Grabbed Fetch's arm and pointed it out to him.

"That black guy sitting at the bar, the one who just dipped his cigar into his brandy snifter?"

Fetch had no idea what a brandy snifter was but there was only one black guy in the joint. "What about him?"

"He's packing heat."

"What the hell are you talking about?"

"His suit coat doesn't drape right. Look at the bulge at his right hip."

Fetch saw it but said, "That could be a colostomy bag for all you know." A guy at Camp Alphonse, a crooked financier, had one.

"Looks just like the bulge in your coat," Karl told Fetch.

True enough, Fetch had his gun stuck in the waistband of his pants. Wasn't a bad fit with the gun, Karl's suit being a little roomy for him around the middle.

Fetch said, "You may be right."

Guy could be an undercover cop. Maybe Cameron didn't want them to get as far as Allie and BooBoo. As far as Fetch was concerned, pointing a gun at people was one thing. Shooting a gun — especially at someone who could shoot back — was something else altogether.

He said, "Let's get out of here." But his admonition came too late. To his surprise, he saw Karl — more likely Psycho — was already inside.

Fetch looked on through the window, stupefied. Like he was watching some moronic TV show, the kind you didn't want to leave on but couldn't turn off. That or a car stuck on the railroad tracks with a train approaching.

He observed Karl cross the room and time it just right so the black guy was looking the other way — talking to some other dickhead dipping a cigar in his drink — and slide the gun right off the black guy's hip.

Never thinking that maybe somebody else in there was carrying, lining him up for a shot right now. But Fetch quickly scanned the room and nobody was. Place probably had its quotas: one black guy, one gun.

Karl stepped back from the guy he'd just disarmed and announced the robbery. Fetch heard it all the way outside. Psycho's deep, scary voice.

"All right, motherfuckers, this is a stickup!"

Karl had a gun in each hand now, his own in one, the

black guy's in the other. Fetch had to think the black guy's gun was real. That was a frightening new development. Psycho with a real gun. Luckily, everybody seemed to treat the situation with the proper respect. Half the yuppies in the place had the cigars fall right out of their mouths.

So maybe it'd ... no!

The black guy, clearly pissed about losing his gun, looked like he was getting ready to take a run at Karl. In which case — if Psycho had thought to take the safety off — the black guy would get drilled. Karl might even get away with killing him. He could say I didn't do it, Psycho did. Karl was as crazy these days as Fetch had been when he'd broken out of Camp Alphonse.

Still, Karl shooting the black guy would put Fetch in deep doo-doo. Because as much as Fetch would have like to run off into the night, he didn't see Karl keeping his name out of it. Not if he boogied.

Then there was the fact that Fetch'd had the unfortunate thought that what he was seeing was a train wreck. Took him back to the time he'd pulled Lerome's foot out of those railroad tracks. Karl didn't mean anything to him compared to Lerome. But he'd come to know Karl well enough that he couldn't just leave him behind.

So hoping to prevent the black guy from committing suicide, and having to face a capital murder charge himself, Fetch stepped into Kovac's with his own gun drawn. He cut off a knot of yuppies trying to slip out the door.

Fetch said in a breathy voice filled with menace, "Nobody moves, this'll all work out."

Jesus! He was doing Clint Eastwood. As crazy as Karl now.

A point confirmed by Psycho favoring him with a lunatic grin and saying, "Fucking A."

Lerome brought fresh lillies and a new spade to the

gravesite. Looking at the headstone, he said. "Sorry I haven't been by lately, Aunt Dottie. It's just I'd rather remember you making lemonade for Fetch and me than being out here."

He laid the flowers atop the gravestone.

"I'll tidy up before I go," he told his aunt. "I doubt Archer dug too deep."

Five minutes of spadework proved him right. He pulled a suitcase, a Luis Vuitton knockoff, from the ground. No way the bag was Archer's, Lerome reasoned. Meant the old bankrobber not only stole Verene's half of Fetch's money from her, he'd also taken her luggage. The guy was a real piece of work.

Lerome replaced the dirt and tamped it down. He knelt on one knee, touched the fingertips of his right hand to his lips and ran them across the letters of his aunt's name.

He said, "I'll stop into church tomorrow. Have them say a mass for you."

Twenty-five minutes later, he was back at Ants' place.

"Doesn't look like your kind of suitcase," she told him, spotting the bag.

Lerome unzipped it, flipped it open. Let Ants see how much cash it held.

"Guess I was wrong. How much is there?"

"This is the money Fetch stole. Was almost $500,000, as I recall." He looked at the stacks of cash with a critical eye. "Most of it's still there."

"You caught up with Archer and Verene?"

"No, just found the money."

Ants asked, "So what're you going to do with it?"

"Depends. Fetch doesn't get arrested tonight, I'll give it back to him." Then he added, "Less a finder's fee, of course."

"How much is that?"

"Ten percent. That's fair."

Ants nodded and asked, "If he does get arrested?"

Lerome shrugged. "I guess he'd want me to have it."

Archer was cleaned out. Not only lost his cash, but everything in his stomach and intestines, too. Came out everywhere but his bellybutton. He was a sight. Thrashing around in all that mess. Good thing was, he could move again; he was conscious and functioning.

Whatever that goddamn hooker had poisoned him with, it seriously disagreed with his compromised digestive tract; his body had purged itself but good.

He hobbled naked into the bathroom, sluiced the filth off himself with cold water from a rust-stained showerhead in a tub so filthy sulfuric acid couldn't have cleaned it. He patted himself dry with a gray washcloth, all that was available.

He wasn't surprised to find his money gone. Would have been a miracle if it wasn't. He'd have liked to find that thieving whore who'd robbed him and slit her throat, only he didn't have the slightest memory of what she looked like. But he had a new insight into how mad Fetch must be, what with having had all his money stolen. Verene, too, and for the same reason. He pulled on his clothes, which fortunately he'd removed outside the splatter zone.

Once dressed, he took several deep breaths. Had to make sure his heart and lungs were holding up okay and his gut wasn't going to give him any more trouble for a while. He was going to have to climb that cemetery wall again. It wouldn't be easy, not tonight, after what he'd been through. But that was where he'd hidden the cash, so climb the wall he would.

This time he'd take all the money. Get the hell out of Buffalo. Go someplace warm. See if he could find some whores who could be trusted.

Say goodbye to his Dottie one last time.

***

Gamble Murtree approached Kovac's on foot only to discover that the cigar bar was blocked off by crime-scene tape. Patrolling the perimeter was a local cop. Inside Kovac's, Gamble could see, were more cops and some of his former colleagues from the Bureau. He had arrived too late to capture Fetch Mcdonald.

Couldn't be helped.

Once Trini had called him in, it'd look too much like he'd been holding back on the SAC — obstructing justice — if he went right out that night and grabbed Fetch. Then there was the problem that Trini, himself, after a smoke-free day on the job, liked to head over to Kovac's and light up.

What could Gamble have said if he'd strolled in there, seen Trini, and then had Fetch Mcdonald and friend come in and try to stick up the place? He hadn't known a thing about it? All a big coincidence. And by the way, motherfucker, I'm going to bust these assholes, not you.

Maybe if he'd still been on the job and Trini was retired, but not the other way around.

None of that meant Gamble couldn't be out on a pleasant June night enjoying a stroll downtown — and if he just happened to come across two evildoers attempting a getaway after committing a crime, and if he happened to bring them to justice, well, bully for him.

It'd go to show you couldn't keep a good man down.

Unfortunately, it appeared his timing was off. From the look on the perimeter cop's face, the forces of law and order hadn't been successful in protecting the public. Fetch had come and gone, free to rob another day. What surprised Gamble was why any of his federal brethren were present. Sticking up a cigar bar was a local matter. Where was the draw for the FBI?

And why were a bunch of yuppie types inside standing

around in their drawers?

Gamble strolled up to the Buffalo cop assigned to keep busybodies away from the crime scene and showed his retired agent's ID. He asked, "What the hell happened here?"

The cop told him, "Two guys robbed the place. Took everybody's pants so they wouldn't come charging after them. Hailed a cab and off they went."

"A cab stopped for two armed robbers?" Gamble asked, astounded.

"They were white robbers," the cop said with a tight grin. He was darker than Gamble. "Musta made all the difference."

Gamble laughed. He knew firsthand how skittish cabbies could be about picking up black men. He said, "That or the cab was stolen and the driver was an accomplice. Anybody get the taxi's number?"

The cop shook his head. "Ask me, it was some working stiff doing his job. God knows why he stopped. Those two robbers are smart, or just plain mean, they popped him already."

Not Fetch Mcdonald, Gamble knew. Not unless he'd gone through a big change. He said, "Or they tell the driver they'll find him and kill him if he talks. Then to make him feel better — incriminate him, too — they give him a real big tip. Get out of the cab somewhere safe, walk a little bit, get into their own car, and they're gone. Maybe they even leave all those missing pants for the taxi driver to get rid of, now that he's taken their money."

The cop favored Gamble with a look of admiration.

"You musta been somethin', 'fore you hung 'em up."

Gamble allowed that he had his moments.

"What about my former colleagues? Why're they here?"

"You'd want to ask them." The cop offered to let Gamble cross the tape.

Strictly speaking, the cop shouldn't have done that, so Gamble declined. Didn't want to get the cop in trouble. Didn't want to be officially logged in at the scene, either. Turned out, he didn't have a choice in the matter. Glaring at him from inside Kovac's was Special Agent in Charge Adriano Trinidad. Covering the lower half of Trini's body was nothing more than a pair of micro-briefs in a jungle-cat pattern. One of Trini's clothed underlings must've blocked that sight up till now, Gamble thought.

"You know that asshole?" the Buffalo cop asked Gamble quietly.

"Yeah, but there's no love lost."

"I can see that."

Trini dispatched a brace of his minions in Gamble's direction.

"Looks like he wants to see you," the cop said.

"Lucky me."

Honest, Trini, I was just out for a stroll. Us retired shits, we need our exercise.

"Listen, that guy's been chewing ass ever since we got here." The cop dropped his voice even lower. "One of the robbers stole his piece. Took his gun right off his hip."

There you go, Gamble thought. Stealing federal property was a federal crime. The Bureau would be fully engaged now. For the moment, though, Gamble wanted to kiss Fetch Mcdonald on the lips. Taking Trini's gun away from him. Damn, he wished he'd seen that!

He tried to keep a straight face as he asked, "Really?"

The cop nodded soberly. Then he added, "But I've been thinking: Even armed robbers woulda been scared off, they knew he was wearing his tiger stripes."

So much for straight faces.

Gamble and the cop were both laughing when Trini's men reached them.

**

Archer saw the fresh flowers on his wife's grave and knew the worst had happened.

"Dottie," he wailed, "I was robbed!"

A tide of resentment pulsed through the old crook. If his departed wife'd had any fond remembrance of him, she should have risen ghostly from the earth and torn the thief to shreds. Preserved Archer's retirement fund for him. Where the hell was all that Stephen King stuff when you needed it, anyway?

Archer sank to his knees and began digging in the dirt with his hands, hoping to find the stray fifty or hundred the thief might have dropped. But there was nothing, not a dime. He collapsed onto his left side, holding onto his decaying gut which was aching terribly again.

He looked at his wife's gravestone, mere inches from his head.

"Is this my time, Dottie?" he asked. He cast his eyes heavenward. "I'd consider it a favor if you struck me dead right now. I never thought Fetch'd figure things out this quick, damn him." Looking back at the gravestone, he continued, "But who else'd bring you flowers, Dottie? Not a sorry shit like me, that's for sure."

Archer rolled onto his back and bellowed at the night sky, "Take me now, damnit!"

He closed his eyes and grimaced in mortal pain, as if his demand was being met. Then he cut the loudest, longest fart of his life, the second act of the purge begun in the fleabag hotel room. Which brought a great sense of relief with its passing.

Archer opened his eyes, looked at Dottie's stone once more and said with a chuckle, "Pardon me, sweetheart, musta been something I et."

He scrambled to his feet and patted his stomach, feeling better than he had for some time.

"Appears the Good Lord don't want me yet, Dottie. So I

better catch up with our boy."

In the distance, Archer heard an engine turn over and saw a pair of headlights come on. All his commotion had finally attracted the attention of the groundskeeper or somesuch. The last thing he wanted now was to be arrested.

"Gotta go, Dottie." He scuttled away a few paces and then returned. He took the flowers off his wife's grave. "Sorry, sweetheart, but these'll do me more good than you."

On that count, Archer was sorely mistaken.

"Flowers?" Verene screamed. "Lillies, with dirt on them? Jesus, you get these from a cemetery, or what? Don't answer. It doesn't matter. You take off with all our money, tell me you lost it, and think you can buy me off with flowers?"

She threw them in Archer's face — and kicked him in the stomach. Knocked him right on his ass, left him writhing on her living room floor. The monster in Archer's gut had been roused with a vengeance. But Verene didn't take pity on him. In fact, she tried to stomp him, not having much luck, the way he was rolling around whining and moaning.

"Hold still, damnit!" she yelled.

Even through all his pain, Archer was aware of what she was attempting. Thought this might be his night to die after all.

"Wait, baby, wait," he pleaded. "I know who took the money. We can get it back."

Business before pleasure, Verene abruptly ceased her efforts to crack open Archer's head.

She pushed her hair out of her eyes and demanded, "Who? Who's got it?" She dropped to one knee next to Archer's now stationary head and asked again, "Who?"

Despite everything, Archer was distracted by the fact that Verene was wearing a miniskirt but no panties, giving him an eyeful. She'd shaved. Trimmed her bush into a valentine heart.

Verene recognized the detour Archer's mind had taken and drew back a hand to slap him silly. But surfing a wave of testosterone, the old bankrobber grabbed her, pulled her down on top of him. Verene could feel the bastard was hard already, pressing up against her.

She started to struggle, but Archer held her tight and whispered in her ear, "Fetch has the money. I figure the two of us took it from him once, we can do it again."

Verene stopped struggling, melted against Archer like butter on a griddle. She could always double-cross the old SOB later.

Meantime, all the exercise, she'd gotten a little worked up herself.

And it was reassuring somebody still found her sexy.

Fetch thought he was going to have to shoot Karl after all. He'd come to like the guy up to a point. You couldn't ask for a more cooperative hostage. He was generous to a fault, shared his St. Pauli Girl without complaint. The two of them were each on their fourth bottles of the night down in Karl's basement. But, damnit, Karl was getting uncontrollably nuts.

He was sitting there on the sofa counting their take from the cigar bar for at least the fifth time. Worse than that, he had the FBI agent's ID hanging out of his inside suit coat pocket. He'd taken it along with the guy's wallet. About every ten seconds, he'd flash it at Fetch. Then he'd tried to do Jack Webb — who'd been with the LAPD, for Christ's sake.

"FBI, Mr. Mcdonald. Your robbing days're over. You're coming with me."

After that, he'd giggle and go back to counting the money. If he'd lost count, he'd start over.

Wasn't just any old FBI agent they'd ripped off either. No, it was Adriano Trinidad, special agent in charge. Fucking guy ran the feds in Buffalo. Except for some psychotic sodomites he'd steered clear of in the joint, Fetch didn't have anything against colored guys, but he didn't know what the world was coming to when one — with a Spanish name — was running a big-city FBI office.

What he understood perfectly, though, was that this Trinidad guy was not going to rest until he caught the pricks who stole his gun, his ID, and his money. Made him look like a pussy in front of all his cigar-smoking buddies.

And fucking Karl was trying to make it easy for him.

Refusing to dump either the gun or the ID.

Fetch saw Karl was about to flash the FBI buzzer at him again, and knew he'd kill Karl right there if he did. So he cut him off. He said, "You like that guy's stuff so much, I'm surprised you didn't take those sissy underpants off him."

Karl grinned. Or was it Psycho? It was getting so Fetch couldn't tell anymore.

One of them said, "I was thinking about it. But you know, another guy's underwear. How many times would you have to wash them before you felt right putting them on? Be easier just to buy some of my own."

Fetch sighed. Then he noticed Karl had divided the money into two stacks. Two large stacks. Karl hadn't shared the grand total with him, so he asked, "How much is there?"

"Almost fifteen K apiece. We sell the card numbers, we'll double that."

Despite his misgivings about Karl, Fetch's jaw dropped. Sixty K from a bar heist?

"Those dumb fucks were carrying that much cash?"

"Well, I saw a sign they were auctioning some rare

cigars, but I told you it was that kind of place. Somebody asks how much money you've got on you, you want it to be more than he has."

Concentrating on the money, Fetch started to relax. A comfortable life in Canada was starting to seem closer. More real, eh? All the more so when Karl said, "If you think this was a good take, wait till you see what we get from the crowd at the wine tasting."

Yeah, Fetch thought happily.

Only ... if Karl was loony-tunes tonight, what would he be like tomorrow?

Maybe doing him in right now was the smart way to go. Get him to open that sofa-safe of his, put one in Karl's ear with the FBI man's gun, take all the cash, and burn down the house to destroy the evidence. All he needed to get things moving was a distraction to grab SAC Adriano Trinidad's gun.

Then as if fate had given the nod to his plan, the phone rang and Karl went to answer it. Leaving the FBI gun behind. But before Fetch could go for it, Lerome walked in carry a dirt encrusted Luis Vuitton bag, which he put down in front of Fetch and opened without a word.

Fetch saw so much cash he knew it could mean only one thing. "My money," he said in a whisper.

Lerome nodded. "Your money. I found it while you boys were out." He didn't say where he'd found it, so as not to upset Fetch. "Then I turned on *NewsRadio 55* and heard you and Karl had a successful evening, so I thought I'd bring it over. Now, you can take off in style."

"Yeah," Fetch agreed, his voice still quiet.

He thought things might work out for him after all.

Until Karl said, "Call's for you, Fetch. Your dad's on the phone."

CHAPTER 26

First thing the next morning Hank DeMitri was on the phone to Dan. "You've got to hand over the typewriter," the agent said. "Today."

"Today?"

"Yes, goddamnit. Drive here today, give it to me, I'll give it to the estate's lawyers. If they don't get it by close of business, they'll be in court first thing tomorrow asking for a contempt citation against you. If you don't show up to answer that charge, they'll file a criminal complaint: grand-fucking-larceny."

"They actually use 'fucking' in the charge?" Dan asked. "It's just a typewriter."

Dan was making notes of the conversation with his agent. Erin looked up from where she was busy with her PowerBook. She was visiting the eBay website.

Hank yelled, "It an historic typewriter, a valuable typewriter, but it's no longer your typewriter. Please, please tell me you understand that."

"It was gathering dust till Erin bought it," Dan calmly replied. "They didn't even know it was gone until the stories about me using it to write *Indecision Kills* hit the media."

Hank sighed. "All true, but so what? In this country, a court tells you to do something, you do it."

"Unless you appeal to another court."

"We both know the publisher won't pay for that."

"I might."

"You might?"

"I've got the money. Tell the lawyers for the estate that."

"Tell them you might?"

"Tell them I definitely will if they piss me off."

Erin came over, sat on Dan's lap, kissed his cheek in approval.

"And maybe they like pissing contests," Hank countered, "and go straight to filing the criminal complaint."

"Maybe," Dan conceded. "Fuck 'em if they can't take a joke."

"You want to know what really worries me?" Hank asked.

"What?"

"They'll file the complaint and name me as an accomplice."

Dan said, "Well, sure. You're my agent. It's probably all your fault."

Both Camerons would later agree they heard the sound of Hank tearing his hair out. It was followed closely by the agent screaming, "I don't want to go to jail!"

"Nobody does," Dan replied.

Erin got up to go back to her search of eBay. She didn't like to hear grown men cry. But she said, "Maybe you'd better tell him."

Now it was Dan's turn to sigh. "I didn't pay the ransom, Hank."

"You didn't?"

"You were supposed to be the middleman, remember?"

Hank said he'd forgotten about that.

"Okay," Dan said, "but you're still my accomplice."

"Will you please not say that?"

"All right, but if you don't want to run the appeal bluff at the lawyers, there's only one thing you can do." Dan realized he should have thought of this earlier. Getting the estate lawyers' reaction would be a great addition to his new book.

"What's that?" Hank asked.

"Tell them the truth. Fetch Mcdonald, a fugitive bank robber, stole the typewriter."

"Did you get Hank calmed down?" Erin asked Dan as she drove their recovered SUV.

They'd taken the New York plates off. Rudy had gotten them temporary tags until they could get replacement plates from Illinois. Dan offered to drive, but Erin declined. He wondered if she'd ever let him drive the vehicle again. He might have to get a new car.

"He didn't think the estate's lawyers would take the news well."

"Of course. They'd cry foul. Call him a liar and a thief."

"Pretty much."

"That's not a problem?" Erin wanted to know.

"When I told him a few of the more interesting details we've come up with for *Kidnapping Ben Hecht*, I think he forgot his troubles. He sees selling *Time Expires* and *Kidnapping Ben Hecht* as a package. Seven figures easy. A movie deal for each book, too. By the time we were done I think he was having a religious experience. So he's not going to sweat the small stuff."

"Like going to jail."

"Yeah, like that. He says it could even be a grace note for *Kidnapping Ben Hecht* if I spend a night or two behind bars."

"This from the man who doesn't want to go to jail himself."

Dan grinned. "Maybe I can work out a deal with the judge: Hank, being my agent, has to serve fifteen percent of my sentence."

"The least he could do." Erin stopped for a red light and saw her husband had a look of introspection on his face.

"What are you thinking?" she asked.

"I'm thinking what a great idea you had to dictate the rewrite of *Time Expires*. I think it's going really well."

Erin smiled. "Me, too." She squeezed Dan's hand, took off as the light turned green.

"I'm still pissed off about getting robbed," Dan said, "but I'm ... I'm really happy with us, the way we've pulled together." Dan looked at his wife's clean, strong profile. "I can't wait to see what our baby looks like."

"Don't worry, sweetie," Erin said with a laugh, "you'll be right there for the first look." She glanced over at her husband. "What I've heard, though, is newborns come out all gray and goopy. Have to be swabbed off and warmed up in an incubator before they get cute and cuddly."

"My wife, the romantic." Dan moved on to another subject. "Did you bring in the newspapers this morning? I didn't see them."

"Rudy said the distributor was having problems, running late."

"Oh. So we don't know if—"

"I turned on the radio while you were in the shower."

"And?"

"Fetch struck again. The cigar bar."

They'd agreed to let Gamble cover that target, second-hand smoke not being good for the baby. Dan knew Erin would have told him if Fetch had been captured. They'd be in bed right now, celebrating.

"We'll get him at the wine tasting," Erin said.

She pulled the SUV into the parking lot of the Emerald Club.

According to Rudy, it was the site of the only wine tasting in town for the next two weeks.

Rudy was away from his post — dealing with the tardy newspaper delivery — when Gamble arrived at the Chateau. No big deal. Gamble knew his way around the hotel by now. He took the stairs, telling himself that retired guys really did need their exercise.

When he got to Dan and Erin's suite, the door was open. The housekeeping staff was working their magic within. Made him wonder how much the Camerons were paying for the suite. Whatever it was, moving into a place like this for an indefinite stay was more than he could afford on his pension.

The thought occurred to Gamble that maybe he had some stories from his FBI days that he could collaborate with Dan on. Pick up some of that big-time publishing money.

Gamble knocked on the open door. The two maids working the suite looked up at him. He'd seen them before — one French Canadian, one Mexican — and more important he was a familiar face to them.

Time for a formal introduction, Gamble took out his retired agent's ID and gave the ladies his name. They didn't exactly recoil in fear, but he could almost hear their hearts start to race. Maybe guilty consciences about their immigration status? He did what he could to allay their anxiety. He smiled, suggested they go about their business, said he was waiting for Mr. and Mrs. Cameron. He'd leave when they did if the suite's occupants weren't back by then.

And while the housekeepers were busy in the bedroom and bathroom ... he was free to do a little snooping. Which took all of ten seconds. The salon was immaculate. Wasn't a thing out of place. Nothing to see that shouldn't be seen.

One thing he did find, an amenity of the house, was a safe for the suite. Concealed, if you could call it that, in the closet just off the front door. Which must've been where Dan kept all his materials for his novel and his true-crime book.

Too bad the FBI had never taught him safe-cracking, Gamble thought. If nothing else, he'd have liked to get a hint on how things turned out with Terry Phelan and Fayre Sanderson. Stymied on that front, he sat himself down on the white silk sofa and awaited his hosts' return.

His mind drifted back to last night.

Trini had tried everything he could think of to intimidate Gamble, get him to admit that his presence outside Kovac's was more than a coincidence. Gamble hadn't cracked, but then an interrogator's job was a whole lot harder when he stood there in undies that looked like they belonged on a stick-thin gay man. Not an FBI honcho who went better than 200 pounds.

Gamble thought that glorified jockstrap must've had a death-grip on Trini's johnson. Not the way he'd want to treat his equipment all day. He was a boxer-shorts man.

In the end, there was no way Trini could contradict Gamble's assertion he was only out for a walk. Trini'd made himself look foolish even trying. He'd look a whole lot worse, too, when it was Gamble who finally caught Fetch. It'd be sweet as a mother's kiss, if he could be the one to return Trini's gun to him.

At that moment, the phone rang. Sounded like there had to be three, four of them in the suite, including one on the end table at Gamble's elbow. He knew the housekeepers wouldn't answer, and if it rang long enough the call would be switched to an automated answering system, or maybe in a place like this an actual human being would take the message.

But, Gamble thought, here at last might be a chance to

do a little snooping.

He'd take the message, and if he heard anything interesting ... like Fetch Mcdonald's voice.

Telling him: "Don't say anything. Just listen. Here's how you get your typewriter back."

Verene woke up sore.

She couldn't believe how that dying old man couldn't get enough of her. Or how good that made her feel. She put on a thick white terrycloth robe that was a gift from a businessman who'd bought it at the Swissotel in Chicago. There was a red cross on the breast. Made her feel like an angel of mercy when she wore it.

As she stepped out of the bedroom, Archer still sound asleep, she saw that a small sheet of paper had been slipped under her front door. She regarded it from a distance with some trepidation. The way things were going these days ...

Hell, she kept forgetting that she was tougher than most men, or at least more ruthless. And after the way she and Archer had gone at each other for hours, her sense of animal vitality was back. Somebody tried to fuck with her, she'd eat'em alive.

She crossed the room and picked up the slip of paper. It was from that geek next door, Axel. *We need to talk. You'll like what I have to say.*

Yeah, right. Twerp just wanted to see her goodies again. Maybe even get his hands on her. Fat chance. She crumpled the note and tossed it into her unlit fireplace. She went to the kitchen, got a cup of coffee that was so old she couldn't remember when she made it. Didn't matter. You loaded it up with enough sugar and cream, you couldn't taste the coffee anyway.

She sat at the kitchen table. Resting there was the copy of the *News* that had the drawing of Fetch and Karl robbing the Java Joe's. She'd bought the paper the morning after she'd seen the story on TV. Looking at Fetch, she could remember why she'd first taken up with him, besides the fact he was selling a lot of copiers and making good money at the time. Fetch was cute in a '50s Brylcreem kind of way. Brushed his teeth maybe five times a day, so he had a nice smile. And, Lordy, could he dance!

Karl could dance, too, she thought, switching her gaze to the drawing of her shaved-head fiancé. You wouldn't think it — at least she wouldn't, the way Karl'd let her push him around — but once he got you out on a dance floor, he liked to lead. Took you in his arms, all but swept you off your feet.

She wondered how much Karl had changed, becoming an outlaw. Would she ever be able to control him again? Make him sell his business, his house. Take him for everything he owned. What would happen if he caught her at it? Before, she was sure she could have bluffed, bullied, or fucked her way out of danger. Now ... she might not get away alive.

Instead of that prospect scaring her, it made her hot. She knew how good Fetch and Archer were in bed. But she'd never let Karl have her. That'd been good strategy at the time, but right now it was no comfort to her yearning. She wanted Karl.

There was no escaping it, Verene thought, she had a thing for dancing gunmen. They seemed to like her, too. She took the stack of Polaroid nudies from a pocket in her robe.

Archer had certainly enjoyed them ... but sitting there alone in the bright light of morning, shuffling through the shots, all she could hear in her mind was one mocking word: liposuction.

Verene regretfully admitted, "Bitch has a point."

Then her brow wrinkled. Something was wrong. Besides her widening backside. She looked at the pictures again. Counted them. And realized ...

One shot was missing. It took a minute to figure out which one. Then she had it.

Fetch's favorite fantasy pose.

She'd done the shot for Karl, but she'd bet it was Fetch who'd kept the Polaroid.

Old feelings died hard. Verene smiled.

CHAPTER 27

Karl woke up hung over. He felt like some guy with hairy forearms was banging out the *Anvil Chorus* atop his skull, and his eyes felt like they'd been scoured with Ajax. After a moment he realized he was lying on his basement floor, the indoor-outdoor carpeting rubbing his left cheek raw. In front of him, he saw a long row of St. Pauli Girl bottles lined up like a picket fence.

He remembered Fetch asking him last night why it wasn't a sin for him to drink beer, his religion being so strict and all. He'd said Fetch had to remember he was Norwegian. His people thought that drinking beer was no different than drinking water. Except you got a few cereal grains in the bargain. There was nothing sinful about it.

Sure could give you a headache, though. Maybe that was it. Drinking beer was a self-punishing habit. Pleasure and penance all in one package. Certainly, God would approve.

But no way He'd approve of the thoughts Karl was having about the buxom blonde beer maiden on the St. Pauli Girl label. At that moment, headache or not, Karl was falling in love with her. He knew he couldn't be the first man to feel that way. The brewery hadn't put her there by accident. They knew how to keep guys coming back to their brand. It amazed him more beers didn't have babes on their bottles.

Karl decided what'd be different about him, he'd be the first guy to track down the St. Pauli Girl. Well, the model they'd used for the illustration. He'd spend some of his bad-man money to do it. He'd meet the girl and he'd be dressed all in black leather. His head would be freshly shaved. He'd wear Lerome's sunglasses and he'd be astride a black BMW motorcycle. They'd roar off into the Bavarian Alps and ...

Throw up.

That was another thing about beer. You never knew which way it might exit. Karl lurched to his feet, knocking over several likenesses of his new love, and stumbled into the downstairs water closet. He made it to the commode in time, but put a gash in his chin when it hit the inner rim of the toilet seat.

After he emptied himself, he took a moment at the sink to wipe off his face and stop the bleeding on his chin. That was when he noticed he was wearing both of his wigs, the brown one above the gray one. He yanked both of them off his head. Pulling the well-glued bottom wig free from his scalp smarted seriously.

An occasion, Karl felt, for a full-throated bellow of pain. Which resounded in his throbbing head with such force he had to hold on to the sink to remain upright. Even then it was a near thing. Happily, he knew just what would help him bounce back.

Unhappily, there wasn't a single bottle of beer left. Not even warm. Even the dregs had been drained from the open bottles. Maybe, Karl concluded, there was something sinful about drinking beer after all. He collapsed onto his sofa.

Which was when he finally noticed all the cash sitting on top of the coffee table. He'd counted the cash from the cigar bar so many times that even hung over he knew he was looking at more than that. Laboriously, he sat up and started counting. A millennium or so later, more sober by now, he realized he had in front of him the take from all three jobs: the Permanent Fave, Java Joe's, and Kovac's.

Not just his share, *all of it.* He opened his sofa safe and saw all of his honestly earned money was there, too. Which could only mean Fetch had given him his share of the loot.

Karl got to his feet and called out, "Fetch." When he got no response, he tried again. Then he tried, "Lerome." He sat back down and muttered, "Jesus."

Fetch was gone. Lerome, too. Then he remembered. Lerome had brought a suitcase filled with money for Fetch. With all that cash, Fetch must've decided he didn't need to stick up yuppie gathering places anymore. Karl's heart broke. No more No-Place-Is-Safe Bandits. It was like the Beatles' break-up. Way too soon. With a lot of good work yet to do.

So he was home alone, no longer a hostage.

Just a wanted criminal, that was all. Which made him think with a fright of the FBI man's gun and badge. Where the hell were they? The cash he could always say was his. Who could prove different? But the badge and the gun ...

Were gone. Nowhere to be found in the basement, and he knew Fetch wouldn't have left them anywhere else in the house. He'd taken the incriminating evidence with him when he'd gone. Leaving Karl all the money. Fetch's way of saying thanks. Or sorry. Probably both.

Karl returned to the sofa to stare at the money once more. So there he was. Free to ... do what?

Go back to his old life. Go back to sucking up to the kind of jerks he'd found such joy in robbing. Go back to being the sap who had let Verene twist him around her little finger. He felt like weeping. But not for long. Psycho wouldn't stand for that.

Psycho decided he'd rather die robbing a convenience store than go back to Karl's old life. Only why hit a 7-Eleven when there was a wine tasting tonight? If he could buy a gun somewhere, if he could find a partner.

Verene came down the basement stairs. Archer right behind her. The two of them saw all the money on the table in front of Karl and grinned like a couple of hyenas. Verene tossed an old copy of the *News* on top of all the greenbacks.

The drawings of Karl and Fetch stared up from the front page. Verene said, "Crime pays, huh baby?"

Dan and Erin found Gamble in their suite when they returned, drinking a bottle of kiwi-strawberry Snapple and watching Oprah. He looked up at the new arrivals.

He turned off the TV. "There you are. Got here while the maids were cleaning up. Then Rudy came by with the papers, told me I could stay. Said being a former government employee my fingerprints had to be on file, if something turned up missing. Thought he was funny."

"He told us," Erin said.

Dan added, "Didn't manage to catch Fetch last night, huh?"

"Funny you should mention him," Gamble replied.

"Why?" both Camerons asked.

Erin seated herself at the opposite end of the sofa. Dan took the easy chair.

"Got a phone call about your typewriter while you were out."

"Rudy told you that?" Erin asked.

"Took the call myself. Full service, that's my way," Gamble said innocently.

Normally, newsmen liked to be the snoopers, resented being the snoopees, but Dan figured it was just more material for his book.

"So a woman called about the typewriter?" he asked.

"No woman. Who were we just talking about?"

"Fetch?" Dan and Erin asked in unison again.

"You two're pretty good, the way you do that," Gamble said with a smile. "You must rehearse."

Dan ignored the crack and asked, "How did you know it was him?"

"I attended his allocution hearing, the day he pleaded guilty to the credit union job. I know his voice. It was him."

"What'd he want?" Erin asked.

"He's changing the terms for getting your typewriter back."

"Hold on a minute," Dan said. He got his notebook and caught up with the conversation thus far. "Okay, what's he want now?"

"More money," Erin guessed. "Ten thousand wasn't enough."

Gamble said, "Unh-uh, doesn't want a dime anymore."

"Then what?" Dan wanted to know.

"What he wants is the ending of the story. Wants to know how *Time Expires* turns out."

"He's a fan?" Dan asked, incredulous.

"More than just him. What he said was, 'We want to know how it ends.' Have to admit, I'm fairly curious myself."

Dan shook his head. Caught Erin's eye so she'd play along with what came next.

"What's the problem?" Gamble wanted to know.

"Those pages Mcdonald wants, the last chapter? That's the one part of the story I'm going to need the Remington to write."

Nobody but he and Erin knew that he'd already written the last chapter, that it was the one part of the manuscript that hadn't been stolen. What even Erin didn't know was that Dan thought he probably couldn't use those pages anymore, that they'd be out of synch with all the others he was dictating. He was pretty sure he'd have to dictate the ending, too. But Fetch Mcdonald didn't know that. Neither did Gamble.

Dan said, "I get the typewriter back, then Fetch gets the pages."

"You're making a big mistake," Lerome told Fetch.

After leaving Karl's house, they'd gone back to Fetch's previous hideout, the room Lerome had rented for Fetch in the house on Hennepin Street owned by Mathilde Severin, the old blind woman.

Lerome continued, "I'll buy a car. You take it across the border. I won't report it stolen for a week. You sell it before then. Buy another one. Enjoy your money up in Canada."

Exactly what Fetch had agreed to do earlier, but now he sighed.

"You know the problem with wanting something?" he asked.

"Getting it," Lerome answered.

"I should do exactly what you say. I should do it and be happy."

"Yes, you should."

"But I don't think I would be happy."

Lerome knew what Fetch was thinking and did his best to be patient.

"We've been over this," he said, "but let's do it one last time. Verene stole your money. Archer helped her and he got you to break jail. They did that so you'd get caught, sent back, and they wouldn't have to worry about you coming after them. But once you got your money back, they called Karl's house to see if you were there. So they could come after you."

Lerome took his sunglasses off and looked Fetch in the eye.

"If getting your money back feels lousy, how do you think it'd feel to get Verene back?"

Fetch couldn't face Lerome or the question. He turned away and said, "Shit."

He pulled the Polaroid of Verene out of a pocket, took one last look, and tossed it into a nearby waste basket. Lerome retrieved it and stuck it in his pocket. He wasn't one to leave a clue behind.

He said, "Believe me, Fetch, Verene is a one-way ticket back to the joint."

"Shit," Fetch repeated. He felt almost as bad as the day his mom had died.

"A wine tasting," Gamble said, naming the next scheduled target for Fetch to rob. "After he hits a cigar bar, an upscale coffee shop, and a fancy hair place. All of which follow the pattern of crimes you had Terry Phelan suggest to Allie and BooBoo."

The former fed reflected on that.

"I think Gamble's starting to see the light," Erin told Dan.

Dan nodded, and asked Gamble, "You want a hint?"

"No!" he replied.

"Wants to work it out himself," Dan told his wife.

"All the places Terry has Allie and BooBoo rob, they're all places yuppies would go." Which led Gamble to make the big jump and smile knowingly. "Who're the yuppies Terry knows? The people in the picture he has on the mantel over his fireplace. They own the businesses Terry has Allie and BooBoo robbing."

Gamble thought he had this storytelling thing figured out now. He said, "Terry's using the street kids to do the dirty work to keep suspicion off him."

"Right both times," Erin confirmed.

"And Allie and BooBoo, being colored, they get busted

or killed."

"No happy ending for them," Dan agreed.

"But *why* is Terry having Allie and BooBoo rob these places?" Erin asked Gamble.

The ex-FBI agent looked at a poker-faced Dan. He knew it wouldn't be for the obvious reason, money. In fact, he couldn't see what the reason was, not right now.

"I don't know," he grumbled. "But in the end, I bet, Terry's plan collapses. He winds up broke, goes to jail or ... No, I know, he winds up having to work with his hands like his daddy and brothers."

Dan shook his head. "Unh-uh. He winds up with a lot of money and his career is about to skyrocket."

Gamble frowned. "That stinks."

"Wait," Erin told him.

Gamble didn't wait. "Sure, you're poor, you're black or brown, you're bound to get it in the head. But you're white and got money—"

"That's cynical," Dan told him.

"But realistic," Gamble argued.

Dan assured him, "You'll like my ending. It'll make you smile."

"Just tell me Terry doesn't wind up with Fayre, too."

Dan and Erin didn't say a word. Only looked at Gamble. The two of them.

"You're not going to tell me, are you?" he asked.

"After I get my typewriter back," Dan said. "I'll let you read the final pages."

He could have been nice, told Gamble right then how the story turned out, but it felt right to keep him in suspense. Keep him engaged. For her part, Erin respected the author's prerogative and was a good wife.

Gamble said, "Puts me in the same boat with Fetch Mcdonald. Wanting to know how the story turns out. First time I can sympathize with the guy." The he added, "Okay, let me ask you something. Why do you think Mcdonald changed his ransom demand?"

The former FBI man folded his arms across his chest, smiled, and nodded. Like he had a secret he could hold back, too.

But Dan said, "Well, if he doesn't need the ransom anymore, he must've gotten his own money back. The cash from all those other bank jobs you've always liked him for."

Gamble's arms dropped and his face fell. He hadn't thought Dan would see that as fast as he had. Erin patted Gamble on the shoulder and said, "He can be like that, spoil all your fun."

Then her look of sympathy turned mischievous. "Of course, even Dan can overlook a detail or two. Like, if it's true Fetch has recovered his money, why would he go through with the wine tasting job? Why commit another crime and take a chance of getting caught?"

"He won't," Dan said quickly.

"You sure?" Erin needled.

"No," Dan confessed.

Dan's uncertainty cheered Gamble right up. He said, "If Mcdonald has a brain in his head, and he does have his money, he won't do another job. On the other hand, if he's so caught up in your story — not just reading it, but living it — maybe he can't stop. He doesn't want to know how your story turns out, he's *got* to know."

Then Gamble moved from theory back to nuts and bolts. "But is there even going to be a wine tasting in Buffalo anytime soon?"

"Tonight at the Emerald Club," Dan told him.

"I guess we'll all have be there," Erin said. "Just to see if any of us is right."

Dan nodded.

Gamble said, "I'll be there first thing." No more showing up late for him. He decided if he caught Fetch Mcdonald screw how it looked to Trini. Then he thought to warn Dan and Erin. "This could be dangerous, you know."

"Yeah, it could," Dan agreed. "But if Fetch shows up—"

"You want to see what happens," Gamble concluded. "Because this could be the payoff for the whole story."

"*Kidnapping Ben Hecht*, yeah," Dan said. Being present would be critical to writing a good ending for that. Nothing beats the drama of an eyewitness account.

"So you're writing a story that you're caught up in living," Gamble said.

"Guess so."

"But a smart guy like you, you know there's one more angle to consider."

"What's he mean?" Erin asked.

Dan told his wife, "Gamble's suggesting that in a situation like a robbery it's possible for people to get shot. Fetch, for instance. Gamble might even have to do it himself."

That thought clearly hadn't crossed Erin's mind. But thinking about it she saw that to save himself, or her or Dan, or some other innocent person, Gamble might have to do just that.

"Oh," she said.

"So what Gamble's really getting at is I might want to be there to ask Fetch, in a dying moment, where he's hidden the Remington, as he's unlikely to bring it with him."

"That's it," Gamble agreed. "But do you think he'd tell you?"

"Sure," Dan replied. "If I have to, I'll whisper in his ear how *Time Expires* ends."

"Where's Fetch?" Archer asked Karl.

Karl ignored the old man and looked at Verene.

It wasn't easy for Verene to look back. Karl's head was a mess. Little tufts of orange hair poking up amidst a field of boils. Some of them oozing. The whole thing outlined by a sticky gray stripe. Like he'd glued lint to his skull. Guy was in need of a *serious* makeover.

But she got the feeling those days were over.

"This the geezer you've been screwing when you wouldn't let me have you?" Karl wanted to know.

The picture of innocence, Verene replied, "Baby, there's nobody but you."

She gave the lie her all, but she couldn't keep Archer from rolling his eyes. His head pounding once more, Karl was seriously disgusted with himself.

He said, "Fetch isn't here." Then he remembered: "Lerome told him to go to Canada."

"Lerome!" Archer cried. "That's who robbed Dottie's grave."

Karl and Verene both gave him a look. Archer, chagrined, didn't notice.

"That's it," he said softly, "that money really is gone. Beyond reach. Lerome'd see to that. He's the only one I know who'd play it straight with Fetch."

Archer's despair was Verene's fury.

"And you just let him go, you idiot?" she snarled at Karl. "You let all that money go?"

Karl covered his eyes with a hand. "Jesus, what did I ever see in you?"

Archer thought the moment opportune, with Karl not looking, to inch toward the cash on the table. Without lowering his hand, Karl said, "Try it, old man, and I'll kill you."

Only Karl's voice was suddenly a lot deeper. Archer froze, the better to evaluate the threat. Even Verene looked around to see if somebody new had entered the room. Or someone had been lurking in the shadows. Only there weren't any shadows.

Karl's hand dropped. His eyes opened, and there was Psycho.

"Try me if you want," Psycho told Archer.

The old robber backed up so fast he bumped into Verene. She was just as scared as Archer was, but she'd mainlined greed for so long she couldn't help herself.

"We're still getting married, aren't we, baby?" she asked Karl.

Psycho found that enormously funny. Laughed maniacally.

Verene and Archer backed off in step, the way only practiced dance partners can. Even though she was shaking with fear now, Verene still couldn't let it go. She nodded at the newspaper she'd brought, at the drawings of Karl and Fetch.

"We've got to have some of that money, Karl." She gestured at the cash on the coffee table. "In fact, I think you better give us all of it. So we won't, you know, have to turn you in for the reward."

Psycho got to his feet.

His voice was still ocean-deep, but quiet now, too. "Were you there, Verene? At Java Joe's? Did you actually see anything? You might manage to get me arrested. But I'm a guy with no criminal record. A respected businessman. I'll get bail, and when I do ..."

Both Verene and Archer could imagine this madman slicing and dicing them. They turned to run, but Psycho yelled, "Wait!"

They waited, muscles constricting with tension, awaiting a mortal blow. Which didn't come. When they finally dared to look back, they saw Karl was seated again. The madness was gone from his eyes, most of it anyway.

He asked Archer, "Is it true you robbed banks? Fetch said you did."

Archer nodded cautiously, not knowing what to expect.

Karl asked him, "You up for doing a job tonight?"

***

Fetch looked out the window of his hideaway. As good as his word — as always — Lerome returned in some kind of small blue four-door sedan. Fetch didn't recognize the make. Had to be something that came out while he was locked up. Lerome got out of the car but left the keys in the ignition.

Lerome didn't look up or wave. He'd already embraced Fetch, kissed him on both cheeks, and wished him all the luck he'd never had before. Fetch was the one who waved goodbye.

"Canada, Canada, Canada!" he muttered to himself.

He put the phony Luis Vuitton suitcase holding all his money onto the bed. He went into the room's closet and pulled out a cardboard box he'd noticed on his previous stay there. It was filled with old paperback novels. He looked at them for a moment, their covers tattered and pages yellowed, and wondered if any of them had given a reader the same pleasure he'd gotten from Dan Cameron's story. That rotten sneaky bastard. He dumped the books on the bed, took half the money from the suitcase, and put it into the cardboard box.

He stuck a thick sheaf of bills into a hip pocket, and carried the box and the suitcase out to the blue car. He opened the driver's door, popped the trunk, and put the money into it. He was about to get into the car when he noticed the old woman, his momentary landlady, standing at a first-floor window. Lerome had said she was blind, but she seemed to be looking right at him.

Fetch moved to his left, then to his right. The old lady's eyes didn't follow him, her head didn't move. She wasn't looking out the window, she was only letting the sun warm her face. Then she smiled.

Looked like she was smiling at him, but Fetch knew she wasn't. Old, widowed, and blind, she was just happy to be alive on a sunny day. The realization made him feel both happy and sad. He felt an urge to go back inside and give her some cash.

Give her everything he had if she could tell him how to be that happy. But some things money truly couldn't buy.

He got into the car, which he saw now was a Dodge Neon, and drove off. He took Bailey Avenue to highway 190 heading west. He wanted to see what the little car could do if he had to floor it. He was surprised by its pep. It'd never outrun a police cruiser, but he'd be willing to take risks behind the wheel that most cops wouldn't. Traffic tightened only slightly as he approached downtown. Wasn't too bad for a guy who hadn't driven on an expressway for eight years.

He settled into the number two lane as the road looped northwest along the lakefront, and he saw the sign: *Peace Bridge-Canada.* He actually thought he might do it. Traffic heading for the border seemed light for summer. That was when people liked to go to the beaches and casinos over in Fort Erie. But he must've hit a lull. He could be out of the country in minutes. He was an inconspicuous white guy in a forgettable American car. He'd swear he wasn't bringing any firearms, tobacco, or alcohol into Canada and they'd let him through.

Except he couldn't do it.

He kept going up to the Scajaquada Expressway, took it east, away from Canada, and drove all the way out to Cheektowaga. He got off the highway at exit 52 and pulled into the Walden Galeria Mall. Place looked like it could suck up every dollar he'd ever stolen inside an hour. He went inside and found a newsstand. He picked up a copy of *GQ.*

Maybe Lerome's wish for him to have better luck was coming true. The magazine had a feature on the latest in casual summer wear. There was a picture of beautiful people dressed up to go to a wine tasting. Fetch considered it a sign.

He was making the right choice. That or he was full of shit and couldn't wait to get back to prison.

"*A job?*" Archer asked, astonished. "You're asking me, do I want to pull a job?"

Karl nodded. "Yeah. You got one more in you?"

Archer gave the question serious thought.

"Whaddya have in mind?" He was fearful, but a little excited, too.

Karl said, "I'm going to hit a wine tasting."

"What?" Archer asked, not understanding.

"What?" Verene echoed, similarly clueless.

"It's a party for yuppies," Karl told Archer, pointedly ignoring Verene. "Everybody pretends to know a lot about wine, but mostly they just get gassed and spend a lot of money."

"How much money?" Archer asked dubiously.

"Your share could be 25-30K," Karl told him.

That brightened Archer right up.

Karl didn't mention that he'd have to find Lerome to sell the credit card numbers.

Archer said, "That's as good as a bank. Only it's got to be easier."

Karl grinned and nodded.

"What the fuck?" Archer said. "Count me in."

Feeling left out, Verene shrilled, "Hey, what about me? I want in."

"You would," Karl said coldly. But he looked at her and had a thought. "You think you can look sexy and classy?"

Verene bit back a barbed reply. She nodded.

"Okay, maybe we can use you. But you'll have to haggle with your boyfriend here for part of his share. You aren't getting any of mine."

They're fucking, Karl thought, let them fight over their share of the money.

Karl and Archer started to make plans for that night's holdup. Verene left to work on looking classy.

SAC Adriano Trinidad stormed back to his office after a meeting with the U.S. Attorney for Western New York, Mosely Walters. Walters had told Trini it was time for him to start considering career options. Meaning he'd better update his résumé and check the want ads.

Fuck! Being a black man with a Spanish surname, his position in the Bureau should have been bulletproof. He'd charted his future all the way to the top of the FBI. It'd been easy for him to imagine some not-too-distant future president — Republican or Democrat, didn't matter — introducing him to the whole damn country as the first black Hispanic director of the bureau.

Kill two minority birds with one stone. Milk the political advantage of that come reelection time. Surely, some new president would be smart enough to think of that, and if he wasn't, Trini had people who'd whisper it in his ear. Members of Congress from back home in Florida. Man, that'd been the plan.

Only now it was shot to shit.

Consider your career options. Quit before we fire your ass. What could he do? Say he was a victim of racism? Argue they'd never fire a white guy who got his gun, badge, wallet, and pants stolen off him?

Yeah, right.

If he tried to sue, the bureau would say he couldn't be counted on any longer, given his public humiliation, to inspire his troops to perform effectively. Try debating that, he thought. He'd walked into the office today and everybody had to look away from him so he wouldn't see them laughing at him.

To make sure they covered their backsides, the powers-that-be had Walters give him the word. Another black guy — but an *American* black guy. Would that have tickled the shit out of that cocksucker Gamble Murtree? He'd've died laughing.

Trini didn't believe for a minute it'd been a coincidence, that asshole Murtree showing up at Kovac's. Fucker was probably in on the job. Not that he'd be able to prove it now.

Well, at least he'd be able to get the fuck out of Buffalo before another miserable winter set in. He'd go back to Florida. One of those guys in the House who was supposed to help him become director would get an ambassadorship in South America and Trini would take his seat. His father would see to it. The voters would send him to Washington. He'd wangle a seat on the Judiciary Committee and start planning some serious payback on his old FBI buddies.

Look at my career options, motherfuckers? Guess what I found.

Trini emptied his office safe and loaded the contents into his briefcase. He told his secretary he was taking the rest of the day off and headed for the elevator. As the doors opened, he patted his hip.

He'd been doing that all day. Reassuring himself that his new gun was still in its new holster. The kind with a strap and a snap. Might not make for fast draws like the old one, but sure as hell nobody was taking this gun off of him.

Trini felt like getting drunk. He'd have a few pops at a bar down the block to get started. Then head out tonight to the Emerald Club for the big wine tasting.

In going over what had happened the night before at Kovac's for Dan and Erin, Gamble made sure to detail what happened to SAC Adriano Trinidad. Let Dan put that in his book.

"You don't like this guy, huh Gamble?" Erin asked with a grin.

"Just office politics?" Dan followed up.

Gamble didn't like it that Dan had asked his question with a straight face. Like maybe if Gamble was just dishing dirt to even up a personal grudge, Dan wouldn't bother mentioning Trini's embarrassment in his book.

So Gamble told the Camerons why he suspected Trini could be a commie mole. And how he was in charge of an FBI field office in a city that sat on an international border.

Dan and Erin looked at each other. Gamble's Olympic boxing story seemed a little thin. But maybe you had to be there to get the full feeling of what had happened. And then there was Robert Hanssen, the FBI-agent-turned-traitor who had spied for the commies just to make a buck. Add in all the terrorist assholes running around loose these days and it hardly seemed safe not to check out anybody whose behavior raised an eyebrow.

"You ever look into your suspicion?" Dan asked.

"Snooping on colleagues is frowned on."

"What about his backstory?" Erin asked.

It took Gamble a second to figure out the term. "You mean his biography? He was born right here in the USA. Florida, anyway."

"What about his parents?" Dan asked. "What was their life like in Cuba? Did they have money? If not, how did they get their start in this country? If they started out poor, did they get an honest break, or did they come into some money that would be hard to explain? You're not with the government anymore, so checking it out shouldn't be a problem."

"Unless someone tries to kill Gamble," Erin said.

Dan snorted.

"You don't think Trini's a spy?" Gamble asked.

"It's just not the way I'd write it," Dan said.

"I might," Erin countered.

"Everybody's a critic."

Gamble knew Dan and Erin were just joking with each other, but Dan's idea of looking into Trini's family was taking root in his head. It could be something for him to do — after they caught Fetch Mcdonald tonight.

CHAPTER 28

Verene stepped out of the Permanent Fave a platinum blonde. Her big russet hair was a thing of the past. Her head was now topped by a sleek, shiny helmet the color of a midday desert sun. Her new makeup was every bit as dramatic as her hair. Her old brows had been pruned way back, and what remained had been redone like a color chart, starting with black on the outer tips going all the way to her new hair color on the inside.

The stylist wanted to do a similar treatment of her lashes, but Verene didn't have the patience for that. Just make 'em long, she'd said. The stylist told her where she could buy purple contact lenses to have eyes just like Liz Taylor. Verene had wanted deep red lipstick, but the stylist persuaded her that with her new hair color a soft erotic pink was much better.

Verene hadn't had an appointment when she walked in to the salon, but business was off badly after the visit from the No-Place-Is-Safe Bandits. Her patronage was welcomed gladly. She was treated like a celebrity. Something she could definitely get used to.

Her stylist gave her a whispered account of that deliciously terrifying night, and it was all Verene could do not to brag. Those guys who robbed you? I know them. Hell, I'm one of them. Fortunately for her, she still had the sense not to incriminate herself. She certainly didn't want someone to offer a reward for turning her in.

Even so, she was beginning to see what had come over Karl. How he'd changed. She left a big tip. She slipped on her sunglasses and stepped outside.

The looks she got told her the makeover was worth every cent. She was used to having men stare at her, but not like this. The lechery was so intense it gave her goose bumps.

So why couldn't she get that goddamn word out of her mind? *Liposuction.* It'd be that bitch's fault if she became anorexic. She took a deep breath to get a grip on her emotions. The inhalation lifted her chest. Which made her smile. Liposuction, maybe. Breast reduction, unh-uh. Those beauties were staying just the way they were.

And when she got a new dress and new shoes, she'd knock 'em dead tonight.

Karl would beg her to take him back. Even the new Karl with that spooky voice. Because she was becoming someone new, too. And she'd tell Karl he could kiss her ...

Well, damnit, she would get the liposuction. Then he could kiss her ass. But only if he came across with every cent he had.

If she could get a line on Fetch, maybe she'd make some new Polaroids for him. Verene, right then, refused to concede any man's money was beyond her reach.

She got into her 'Vette to make the drive to the 'burbs. In the old days, you could shop downtown. Close, convenient. Now she had to go all the way across town. A royal pain. But tonight would be worth it.

By the time Fetch had his hair cut and professionally re-colored — dark brown this time with the subtlest of cinnamon highlights — the alterations on his new clothes at Lord & Taylor had been done. Slate blue silk sport coat, peach blush shirt of sea-island cotton, and natural stone linen slacks. Socks the color of old ivory and cordovan tassel loafers. He'd have preferred shoes suitable for running but didn't want to spoil his look.

He donned his new ensemble, added a pair of Ray-Bans with brushed steel frames and topped himself off with a Panama hat with a leather hatband that just about matched his shoes.

Fetch had always considered himself to be a decent-looking guy, but when he saw himself in the mirror now he thought he was gorgeous.

He only wished his mother was still alive to see him. Except, having gone into the family business, maybe it was for the best that she wasn't. The salesman, with whom Fetch had settled his bill, put his old clothes — the things Lerome had bought him at Target — into a store bag and offered them to Fetch.

"Give them to Goodwill," Fetch said charitably.

Treating himself to one last glance in the mirror, he adjusted his hat to a rakish angle and left the store. After paying for his clothes and his haircut, he still had better than twenty-five hundred dollars in his pocket — and time to kill before he went to the wine tasting.

He thought about calling Karl. Get it worked out how they'd handle things tonight. But Fetch had a hard time concentrating because he kept looking at his reflection in store windows. He couldn't believe that was him he was seeing. Damn, he was something.

He didn't really need to get in touch with Karl. He was sure Karl would show up, and the two of them knew each other's moves by now. They were a team. There'd been little bumps in the road at each job, but they overcame them. They knew how to deal with the unexpected.

So what Fetch decided to do was book a nice room at the Four Points Sheraton next door, relax, enjoy a little room service and be ready to go when the time came. That idea firmly in mind, he stepped onto a down escalator — and he saw her coming up to him like an angel.

Platinum hair. Pale face behind dark glasses. Body like what he'd dreamed of for the past eight years. She was looking at him, too, a hint of a smile starting to play at the corners of those pink lips.

The opposing movement of their respective escalators brought them closer. Fetch gallantly touched the brim of his hat, a salute to her beauty. She let her smile grow and gently pressed fingertips to her chest.

They passed each other without a word being said.

Fetch thinking, *So who needs Verene?*

Verene thinking, *The world's full of rich men.*

Karl and Archer were getting dressed. Karl put on his best suit and frowned. It'd cost him over a thousand dollars — this from the days before he'd met Verene — and it was beautifully made. Still fit well. But, damn, it was stodgy.

Dark blue and made for business.

Okay for a job like Kovac's.

Not at all the right thing for sticking up a wine tasting.

He wished he could have gone shopping, picked up something new, but he hadn't had the time. He'd had to break in his new partner, get him to understand their roles: Archer was the straight man; Karl would handle the theatrics.

Then there was the necessity of planning their transportation. He didn't think cabbies would be picking up armed robbers anymore, no matter how nicely they were dressed. Or how well they tipped.

And, then, he and Archer had to buy new guns.

On top of that, Verene wasn't back yet. Karl thought

he'd scared her pretty good, but with Verene you couldn't say for sure she wouldn't go for the reward money. He'd seen the way she'd looked at all his cash. She'd wanted it more than she'd ever wanted him. That would have stung if he'd still cared for her. But right now he really could cut his losses where it came to Verene. Cut her throat if she ratted him out.

Archer, on the other hand, was turning out not to be a bad guy. He'd cleaned up surprisingly well. But like Karl, he had complaints about his apparel.

"These things look like kid's clothes," Archer grumbled.

The old bank robber had tried on the suit Fetch had worn to Kovac's but it proved too big for him. Noticeably big. People'd look at him and know something was wrong. So Karl'd gone for the only alternative available: a navy blazer, white shirt, and gray slacks.

"They are kid's clothes," Karl explained. "My nephew wore them last summer when he worked for me."

"Well, shit," Archer whined.

"Hey, it's just for one night. The money you'll get, you can buy any kind of clothes you want. But tonight you've got to look nice."

"What about my shoes then?"

Archer was wearing his own shoes, black Keds hightops.

"No one'll notice" Karl said. "Who looks at men's shoes?"

Archer shrugged and said once more, "What the fuck?"

Then the old robber had a long overdue insight. Maybe being too casual about things was the reason he'd always gotten caught whenever he pulled a job. What the fuck was hardly the motto for someone who wanted to get away with his crimes.

Of course, he had gotten out of both banks with the money he'd stolen. It was being betrayed later by his partners that had truly been his undoing. A thought that made him look closely at Karl.

"What?" Karl asked, catching the suspicion in Archer's eyes.

"Nothing," the old robber replied.

"Oh, yeah. It's something." Karl figured it out. It made him grin. "You think I'd screw you? That's what's worrying me about Verene right now."

Hearing that, Archer thought, nah, Verene would never betray him. She liked what he did to her too much. The way she wiggled under him, her eyes rolling back in her head, she'd never turn on him. Hell, he was getting worked up just thinking about it. Until Karl interrupted his reverie with practical matters.

"You're sure this friend of yours will have the guns for us?"

Archer nodded. "Donnie's got more guns than the NRA. We give him money, he'll give us whatever we want."

The old man seemed certain about that, but something was still bothering him.

"Look, I'm not going to betray you and—" Karl's voice dropped down into the Psycho zone. "God help you and Verene if you try to betray me."

Archer shook his head quickly. "It's not that."

"Then what?" Karl's voice returned to its normal register, disconcerting Archer further.

Archer gave his new partner-in-crime a look. How did he always wind up doing jobs with crazy men? Still, he explained, "Well, it's just this deal you told me about. How you 'n' Fetch have been following the crimes from some book?"

"Yeah?"

"Anybody who's read it probably knows what you're doin' by now."

"The book hasn't been published yet. We're working from the manuscript."

Karl thought that should reassure Archer, but the old thief had more questions.

"What about the guy who wrote it then? What about him showin' up?"

Karl and Fetch and Lerome had discussed the possibility of Dan Cameron telling the cops, and had discounted it. After the Permanent Fave job, he could have tipped the cops to Java Joe's. After Java Joe's, he could have let them know a cigar bar would be next. He hadn't done that in either case. So Karl wasn't worried about the authorities springing a trap on him tonight.

But they'd never thought about the idea that Cameron himself might show up. To do what? Watch?

Well, he was a writer, so Karl thought that was possible. You considered the matter, the best way for him to write about what happened would be to actually see it. Maybe he'd enjoy comparing how it was done for real to what he'd had Allie and BooBoo do.

Which brought to mind Lerome's idea. Cameron was writing a new book about what was being done with his old book. Meaning, if he was at the wine tasting tonight, what he'd be writing about was ...

Me, Psycho thought.

To Archer, Psycho said, "I hope he is there. We'll give him a show."

Ants stopped by a reading table where the last two library patrons of the day — a gray-haired couple — had their noses in books, clearly having no idea what time it was. "Five minutes," Ants told them politely, "then we have to close."

When she looked up, she saw a nicely dressed man standing at the circulation desk. He was carrying a suitcase. Ants went behind the desk, stopped opposite him, and smiled.

"Sharp," she said, looking him over. "If Lerome hadn't told me you'd be coming, I'd never know who you are." Well, she did recognize the dirty faux-Vuitton suitcase he had with him.

Fetch was checking out Ants, too. Looking past the glasses and the pinned up hair. Saw she was a knockout. Not flashy, but she had a real glow to her. Just the kind of woman who would appeal to Lerome. Made him think he should widen his own horizons. He didn't need Verene or platinum blondes. He was past all that now.

He hoped.

"Real nice meeting you, too," Fetch told Ants.

"I have a couple things for you," she said. "Lerome told me to give them to you."

She put a typewriter on the desk. Glossy black Remington Noiseless Portable. Looked exactly the way Fetch remembered it. She gave him a cardboard box with a copy of Cameron's manuscript in it, too.

Ants continued, "Actually, Lerome hoped you wouldn't come by."

Fetch had called his cousin's cell phone from the Sheraton. Felt he'd owed it to Lerome to let him know what he'd decided.

He and Lerome got to talking about things, one of them being they both wanted to know how *Time Expires* turned out. That was when Lerome told Fetch he'd leave the man's typewriter at the library. If Fetch wasn't going to Canada, he could stop by and pick it up. See what kind of deal he could swing with Cameron for it.

Fetch told Ants, "Lerome wants what's best for me, and I always go a different way." He hefted the suitcase up onto the counter. "Tell Lerome I'd like him to keep this safe for me, okay?"

"Maybe invest what's in it for you?"

Fetch considered. "Only if it's in something he's doing

himself. Then, definitely."

"Okay, I'll tell him," Ants said. She placed the suitcase behind the circulation desk. "One thing, though. Did Lerome tell you I'm looking for my boy?" She glanced over Fetch's shoulder and saw the old couple was about to leave. She told Fetch, "Just a minute. Let me lock up."

Fetch watched Ants share a moment's conversation with the people who were leaving. She laughed, put a hand on the old man's shoulder, then locked the door as soon as they were out. Ants came back on Fetch's side of the circulation desk. She said with a smile, "You meet nice people in libraries."

Fetch could tell more than that was making her happy.

"You found your son, didn't you?" he asked.

She took off her glasses and let down her hair. The way she smiled made Fetch's heart skip a beat. No doubt about it, he'd have to rethink his ideas on women.

"I was going to tell Lerome first, but I don't think he'd mind me telling you."

Fetch agreed that he wouldn't.

"I know where Jimmy is."

"Good for you," Fetch said sincerely.

"Thanks. What I'm getting at, though, is Lerome and I might be on the road a while. If you want to get your suitcase back anytime soon."

"That's okay. I only gave you half of what I have. Just wanted to be sure I didn't lose it all if things go wrong tonight." Then Fetch asked. "You think you could call Dan Cameron for me? Deliver a message."

Ants listened to his request and nodded. She told Fetch, "Good luck."

"You, too."

Fetch had one more question: "Lerome keep a gun around here? I can't find the one I had." They both knew

Lerome had taken Fetch's gun, hoping it would be one more thing to get him to go to Canada.

Ants shook her head.

Then she told Fetch, "But you can have mine."

Gamble wanted to give Dan and Erin a bit of advice before he left their suite at the Chateau to get ready for the evening's ... what?

Gamble said, "You can't call them festivities if there's a felony involved, can you?"

"Excitement," Dan suggested.

"Adventure," Erin offered.

"Well, whatever it is, my advice is sit near the door."

"I got the impression these guys always block the door," Dan said.

"The back door then."

"If that's covered, too?" Erin asked.

"Throw a chair through a window if you have to. What I'm saying, if things get crazy, run. And don't look back."

Erin got up from the sofa, walked over to Gamble, and kissed him on the cheek. "You're such a nice man," she said.

Gamble blushed furiously.

"I've got to go," he said. "Get dressed for tonight." He hurried to the door but stopped when a thought hit him. "What do people wear to these things anyway?"

"Casual," Dan said.

"But elegant," Erin added.

Gamble told them, "Mostly, I've got blue suits. Have to see what I can do."

He left and the Camerons looked at each other. Erin said to her husband, "I take it that was a ploy, telling Gamble you need the typewriter to finish your book."

Dan agreed that it was. Erin came over to Dan, sat on his lap, and kissed him.

"Ploys are good," he told her. "A writer's best friend."

She kissed him again, passionately.

"After his wife, that is," Dan amended.

"Are you worried about tonight?" Erin asked.

"More for you and Petunia than me."

"Petunia?"

"What I thought we'd call our little girl."

Erin laughed. "You better be careful. I might go along with the gag. Like Lerome's mother did."

Dan shrugged. "Then Petunia will have you to blame, won't she?"

This time Dan kissed Erin and they might have been late getting to Emerald Club if the phone hadn't rung. Dan told Erin to ignore it but she picked up.

"Hello ... Oh, hi, Rudy. What? You have? That's great."

The conversation continued with no sign of let up. Dan slid out from under his wife.

"I'm going to take a shower," he told her.

She gave him a distracted wave of acknowledgement.

Dan had shampoo suds in his eyes when Erin came in and told him, "Another call. This one's for you. I'm not sure, but I think it's Lerome's friend, the librarian."

Dan cleared his eyes and asked, "The Remington?"

"She didn't say. But I don't think she's calling about an overdue book."

CHAPTER 29

The Emerald Club was a single-story rectangular structure, slightly deeper than it was wide, of immaculately kept
dark brown brick. The door and window trim were done in
the darker shade of green found on U.S. currency. A small
brass plaque to the right of the doorway proclaimed the
club's name and its status as a private establishment.
Adjacent to the club was its parking lot.

Normally, the entrances to both the club and its parking
area were closely watched. As if something special went on
inside. In fact, it wasn't much more than a nice place to get
a drink. There was a small kitchen in back that wasn't
called on to do more than provide complimentary hors
d'oeuvres. On weekends, there might be a jazz combo with
instructions to keep the volume to a background level.
Occasionally, when higher cultural pretensions were called
for, a string quartet was booked.

The club's biggest draw was that if you obtained a membership it meant you were somebody. On a local scale, anyway.

But tonight was different. The wine tasting was a chari-
table event and the public was welcome. Well, that portion
of the public that could afford to spend hundreds or even
thousands of dollars on a single bottle of wine.

The club's interior was done in gleaming dark wood, tasteful brass accents, flattering indirect lighting, and bar stools with deep green leather seat cushions. Dan and Erin were among the first to arrive. Taking Gamble's advice, they sat at a table just inside the front door and next to a window where they could watch everyone come and go.

The waitresses were all pretty young women who represented the vintners whose wares were being hawked that night. A saucy sheila from Melbourne got Dan to go for a chenin blanc from Down Under. Erin stuck with a sparkling water from Saratoga Springs.

No wine for expectant moms, she said.

Once they'd been served, Dan told Erin in a quiet voice, "Seems inconsistent, worrying a sip or two of wine might hurt the baby but not sweating the armed robbery we expect to happen."

"That's why we're sitting near the door, remember? In case we have to run for it."

"Still," Dan said.

"Gamble's in the back room talking to the club's manager right now."

"Still," Dan repeated.

Erin shrugged. "Okay, let's leave — both of us — if you want to be consistent."

Clearly, that wasn't what Dan had in mind. He hadn't even liked it when Erin had persuaded him not to bring his notepad. Told him it would look dorky. Obvious, too. He'd remember anything important that happened. But in order to do that he had to be present.

"You know what this is?" Erin asked, sensing Dan's discontent.

"What?"

"This is the B-movie scene where the hero tells his sweetie to stay behind while he risks getting his wienie shot off. You really think I'm the kind to stay behind?"

"No." Except for a few times lately, he thought.

"Would you want me to be that kind?"

"No." It would be easier, but not as much fun. "Don't want my wienie shot off, either."

"There you go." Erin knocked back a gulp of her sparkling water.

Dan sighed, thinking no blessing went unmixed.

Erin put her glass down and took his hand.

"Petunia and I will be just fine." Dan thought Erin was about to dole out further words of comfort but she broke into a devilish grin and whispered, "Don't be obvious about it but take a peek out the window. Look who's here."

Dan flicked his eyes to his right and saw a platinum blonde in sunglasses. She was wearing a slinky black dress that displayed an acre of cleavage.

"You could chip ice with those heels she's wearing," Erin said.

It never occurred to Dan to look at the woman's shoes. He whispered to his wife, "You know her?"

"Wait," she said.

The blonde stepped into the club, drawing every male eye in the place. Even a casual glance to her left would have let her take in the Camerons. But she didn't look their way. She made eye contact with a silver-haired guy with a dark tan sitting at the bar. He was wearing a vanilla linen suit and a pale salmon T-shirt that did nothing to hide his potbelly. As a distraction to his physical flaws, he flashed a gold Rolex — his coat sleeves being rolled up — and a diamond ring. The effect was predictable.

The blonde headed for the jewelry display like it was a homing beacon.

"You figure it out yet?" Erin asked quietly.

Dan shook his head.

"Look at her ass," she instructed her husband.

He gave Erin a look, but did as he was told.

It escaped him, who that ass belonged to.

"Okay, imagine her naked," Erin exhorted.

Dan gave his wife a serious look. He'd heard about pregnant women going nuts, but hadn't known it could happen so early. She patted his hand and told him to look.

The blonde had reached the silver-haired guy by now. She stood in profile to Dan.

He looked ... he imagined ... he grinned. Turning back to Erin, he whispered, "Liposuction."

She squeezed his hand and nodded. "Watch. I thought I saw her spot us from outside. But she didn't let on. She fixed on that sugar-daddy. Went straight for him. I bet she doesn't look over this way, not once."

"She's avoiding us? Why?"

"One guess."

Dan got it. But didn't know if he agreed. "She's in on the heist?"

"I know that's not what you wrote, but she knows Fetch, she knows Karl, and she's here. All a big coincidence? Unh-uh. I think the bad guys are improvising."

So maybe he agreed now.

He looked back at the bar. Verene was seated next to the silver-haired guy. She had a hand on his leg. He had the hand with the ring and the watch on hers. They were smiling at each other, the beginning of a beautiful friendship.

"That was fast," Dan told Erin.

"He probably imagined her naked, too. Didn't mind the extra on her hips."

The Camerons grinned at each other.

"How'd you know it was her?" Dan asked.

"I look at faces, not boobs."

"You look at feet, though."

"Yes, I do." She laughed like a kid. "All this, tonight, it's too good to miss."

"Critical to *Kidnapping Ben Hecht*," Dan replied.

"But just in case somebody starts shooting, Dan?"

"Yeah?"

"You'll throw yourself in front of Petunia and me."

"Sure, that's what dads do." He glanced at the doorway. "Maybe I'll even have to."

Erin didn't look, just whispered, "Fetch?"

"Rudy," Dan said. "But where Rudy goes, can Fetch be far behind?"

Fetch stepped into the lobby of the Chateau. He was carrying Dan Cameron's typewriter and manuscript; Ants had put them into a shopping bag from Kaufman's for him. In his finery, Fetch thought he fit right in with the elegant surroundings.

Better yet, he didn't see any cops or hotel dicks eyeing him.

Maybe what he should do, he thought, was book himself a room. Right across the hall from Cameron and his wife. Come back here after the job. Enjoy a night in the lap of luxury. Call his neighbors in the morning, invite them over for breakfast. Fetch could ask Cameron did he plan to mention Fetch's name in the acknowledgments for his new book.

Fetch strolled over to the check-in counter. A good-looking redhead was working there. She looked up from whatever she'd been doing on her computer and gave him a smile. A real smile, not the kind her job required. A nametag on her blouse read Cordelia.

"Pretty name," Fetch said.

"Thank you, sir. Would you like a room tonight?"

Just what he'd been thinking. Add Cordelia to his plan, it'd be a night to remember. But if he went ahead and acted on the idea now, he knew he'd be getting ahead of himself. Asking for trouble. Something was bound to go wrong with the wine tasting job.

Thing to do was take tonight one step at a time. Pull off the job. If that went right, then come back and see what else might go his way.

"Not right now," Fetch said. "My name's T. McGee." The alias was Ants' suggestion. He'd thought of using Remington, the name on the typewriter. "One of your guests, Daniel Cameron, might've left something for me."

Fetch put the shopping bag on the counter while Cordelia went to check.

The way Fetch figured it, he'd given Cameron more than an hour to write the ending of his book; shouldn't have taken him any longer than that. How hard could it be? You had a story in your head, you wrote it down. Wasn't exactly a ball-buster like plumbing or wiring. Hell, selling copiers.

So now all Cameron had to do was hand over the pages — and not call the cops on him — and he'd get his precious typewriter back. Fetch had to get rid of the damn thing anyway. Having the typewriter found in his possession would tie him to the theft of Cameron's SUV. He certainly didn't need that. So he was shedding as much evidence of his criminal activity as he could.

Cameron had been warned that if he tried to have Fetch arrested in the lobby there would be terrible consequences. Unnamed but awful. Let the writer's imagination fill in the blanks.

As it was, Ants'd said the guy had been a little surprised to hear from her at his hotel. But once Cameron's wife had stolen back the SUV, Lerome and Ants had thought it'd be a good thing to know where the writer was staying.

If it'd been in a private home, they'd have been out of luck. But assuming he was in a hotel, they'd tried the best place in town first. Bingo.

Cordelia returned and handed him a number ten envelope addressed to *T. McGee*.

It was way too small to hold the rest of the story. Unless the ending was really shitty.

Fetch asked Cordelia to excuse him a minute. He left the shopping bag on the counter and took the envelope over to an easy chair where he could read in private whatever Cameron had left for him. It didn't take long.

On one sheet of paper, Cameron told him he had to have the typewriter to finish the story. Couldn't do it without the Remington. What kind of bullshit was that? You were a writer, you wrote. Didn't matter what you used. What Cameron promised was, if Fetch left the typewriter, Cameron would send a copy of the final pages wherever Fetch wanted.

Guy pissed Fetch off. Made him feel like a salesman again — someone who could be bargained with — not a thief. Definitely not the guy who was in charge. Right then Fetch understood why Karl felt the way he did, not wanting to go back to his insurance business.

Fucking Cameron had also put his name down as Fetch, not T. McGee. Like you couldn't put one over on him. But what could Fetch do? He got up and walked back to Cordelia at the counter.

"You have a pen I might borrow?" he asked politely.

She gave him the one she'd had in her hand, had been using right that minute. Their fingers touched briefly and that took some of the anger out of him. Paid to be cool.

He'd never be as cool as Lerome, but it was something to aim for.

He scrawled two words on the bottom of Cameron's note: *You better.* He folded the sheet of paper and was about to stick it back in the envelope he'd ripped open when Cordelia offered him a new one. He said thanks and made sure the flap was tightly sealed.

Not that Cordelia would snoop but you didn't know who else might come along.

He put the envelope into the shopping bag. "Would you please give all this to Mr. Cameron?" he asked.

She took the bag and said, "My pleasure."

She put the bag behind the counter and when she straightened up, Fetch asked her, "You read that first book Mr. Cameron wrote?"

She took a hardcover copy of *Indecision Kills* from beneath the counter. "I'm reading it right now. I mean, when I have free time."

Fetch saw there was a picture of Cameron on the back. Much better shot than on his driver's license.

"Is it a good book?" he asked.

"I like it a lot, even though I have the feeling the ending's going to be sad," Cordelia told him. "I hope I can get Mr. Cameron to sign it before he checks out."

"That going to be soon?"

"Well, my boss heard from his wife that it might be only another day or two."

"They're not here right now, are they?"

Fetch thought maybe Cordelia could call their room, get Cameron to come down to the lobby, have him tell Fetch the ending. Argue with the guy if he didn't like it.

Cordelia shook her head, an adorable frown on her face. "I'm sorry, they're out."

"Yeah?"

"I heard they went to the wine tasting at the Emerald Club."

Should've known, Fetch thought.

"I wish I could be there, at the wine tasting," she said.

He told Cordelia, "I'd like to take you, too. But it looks like we both have to work tonight."

Verene was enjoying the company of silver-haired Stanley Sumner. He'd told her he owned eight car dealerships around the state. She told him she owned a classic

Corvette Stingray. Stan said he'd really like to see it. Verene told him she'd show him hers if he showed her his. They both laughed and Stan ordered champagne.

Then Stan grew serious and told Verene he had a problem.

"What's that?" she asked with concern. The hand she'd been working up the inside of his thigh now caressed his cheek. She hoped to hell it wasn't that he couldn't get Old Woody up.

"It's not exactly a matter of life and death," he said. He took her hand and put it back on his leg. "It's just that I'm trying to decide which of my vacation homes I should go to this year."

"How many do you have?" Verene asked innocently. She was hoping for eight, one for each dealership.

But Stan said, "Two. One in Portugal, one in Bora Bora." Stan said his choice would likely depend on who his traveling companion would be.

Verene had no trouble reading between the lines on that one. She knew Portugal was in Europe, but she couldn't remember if it was part of Spain or an island off the coast. Bora Bora definitely sounded like an island, but maybe it was one of those back-to-nature places like they had on *Survivor* or something. None of that eating rats stuff for her.

She said, "Well, Stanley, I can't speak for anyone else, but I can never get enough of Europe." She was going to shit if Portugal turned out to be someplace else and she'd just blown the whole thing. But Stan beamed and she knew she'd guessed right.

"Then Portugal it is." His face lapsed into a look of puzzlement. "But who will I take with me?"

"Gee, I don't know ... but I did buy a new thong bikini just today." She hadn't but she could get one in no time.

Only Stan told her, "The beach behind my house is topless, and part of it is clothing optional entirely."

He could see most of her boobs already, but he was curious about another matter.

"What's your real hair color?"

"Look at my eyebrows, Stanley."

He did, and noticed for the first time they spanned the spectrum from dark to light.

"My natural color's in there somewhere, but only a very special man will ever get to see."

She had him hooked, boated, and gaffed with that line. She was on her way to Portugal She could've kicked herself that she hadn't started playing in this league a long time ago. Why the hell had she wasted her energy on small-timers like Karl?

Before she could begin planning her adventure with her new sucker, another guy came over to make it a threesome. This guy was black. Verene didn't have anything against black guys, but this one didn't look to be in Stanley's class financially. And he was already half-in-the-bag. Verene never believed in letting herself get picked up by a drunk.

Only she could see that Stanley was already acting defensive, possessive. It would make him feel that much better if he thought he'd won her in a stiff competition. Maybe she'd even get him to think he rescued her from this new guy. Then the money would really flow.

Verene felt like she'd just found the back door to heaven.

"Look, Mr. Murtree, I'm skeptical. Very skeptical."

Gamble was having a hard time with Casper Shabouh, a manicured, oily-haired, black-eyed SOB who was trying too hard to look like a young Omar Shariff. Casper was the Emerald Club's general manager, and Gamble couldn't persuade him that an armed robbery was about to occur on his premises.

"Where have you been, man?" Gamble asked him.

"Don't you read the newspaper?"

"Not for some time. I've been hiking in the Canadian Rockies."

"Then you don't know. Two guys have been sticking up yuppie places all over town. Just this past week."

Casper's smile oozed condescension. "In that case, we're perfectly safe. The Emerald Club is for those who've arrived, not for those who are still striving."

"Only tonight you're open to the public, remember?"

"Even so, the club's reputation is well known. It's somewhat ... socially intimidating. Our aura keeps out the less desirable elements."

Fucking foreign-born snob, Gamble thought. First Trini, now this guy. Well, Trini'd been born here, but what the hell did that matter if he was a commie spy? Who was letting all these damn people into the country anyway?

"Look," Gamble said, "how about a couple unmarked cars from the Buffalo PD in your parking lot — just in case?"

That sounded entirely reasonable to Gamble, but Casper —Casper!— didn't think so. It wasn't in keeping with the club's image.

This pretty boy's family — Iranian, Gamble was pretty sure — must've gotten out of the old country with some big money before the ayatollahs started kicking ass. They came here and ... it all clicked for Gamble.

"You fell into this job, didn't you? Your daddy or your uncle or somebody gave it to you."

Casper flushed. "I have an MBA from Columbia."

Gamble laughed. "I'm talking armed robbers here. They teach you how to deal with that in grad school? You going to scare them off with your résumé?"

Casper stood up behind his desk. The look on his face was fierce. "I'm also the master of four martial arts."

Gamble sighed and got to his feet, too "Yeah? Well, let's

347

hope one of them is marksmanship." Leaving, he added, "At least you put me in the mood to have a drink."

The former fed left the club manager's office grimly accepting that he'd have to do all the heavy lifting tonight. Four martial arts, shit. That fool Iranian didn't even notice —

Trini sitting right there at the bar. The only reason the commie Cuban didn't spot Gamble, he had his eyes all over some bleach blonde with most of her goodies hanging out. Gamble started to move out of the hallway from Casper's back office when the blonde took her sunglasses off. She began nibbling one of the stems, giving Trini and a slick old white dude sitting next to her something oral to think about.

Right then, Gamble recognized the woman. Bleached hair or not, she was Verene Digby, Fetch Mcdonald's exwife. After following her the past few days, he had that foxy little face sharp in his memory.

Now, if she was here ...

Gamble looked at the front door.

CHAPTER 30

Dick Tracey picked up his squad room phone on the first ring. While he was listening to the caller, he glanced over at his young partner, Mickey Gruber, and gave him a look of suspicion. Gruber was at his desk scanning the Events page of the *Buffalo News*. Tracey wasn't sure if the kid was planning his weekend or on to something. Just of late, Gruber seemed to notice a lot of things that Tracey missed. Made the older detective fearful that he'd lost a step. Left him slow to criticize, too. So he wouldn't have to eat his words.

Which'd be an admission the game was leaving him behind. But he'd just come up with something good. He told the caller thanks and hung up. Now, he could afford the pleasure of being Socratic with young Gruber.

"You think we got anything at all on these asshole armed robbers?" he asked.

Gruber looked like he had an idea and was going to tell Tracey all about it. But Tracey didn't want to hear it. Not right then. Maybe never. He wanted Gruber to play along.

He cut off his junior partner by asking, "I mean, all the people we talked to, you think maybe we actually conversed with one of the bad guys?"

Gruber tabled his idea, and gave Tracey's question serious thought. He was sharp enough to do that and come back to his own point later. After a quick review of the case, he said, "No. I don't think we did. Do you?"

"Well, who, if anybody, sticks out in your mind? Of the people we talked to?"

"The guy whose motorcycle was stolen." Gruber flipped through his notebook. "Karl Hyacinth." He snapped the notebook shut. "He was the only one who didn't know where his red Honda VTX was on the night of the Java Joe's job."

Tracey saw that Gruber didn't have to refer to his notes to remember the color, make, and model of the motorcycle used in that particular crime. Made him envious. Maybe he ought to forget the Viagra and try some of that ginkgo biloba stuff.

Gruber continued, "But Hyacinth was honest-to-God shocked his bike was gone. No way was he acting. Somebody stole his machine."

"Yeah, but why his and not somebody else's?"

Gruber shrugged. "I don't know."

"I didn't either, but it was the one thing we had to go on. The only solid clue from that kid ... what was his name?"

"Elroy Sundquist," Gruber supplied without checking his notes.

Fucking show-off, Tracey thought.

"Yeah, Elroy. He knew what kind of cycle it was. And Hyacinth had one, only it got stolen. How convenient. That ate at me. So I checked Hyacinth out."

"He doesn't have a criminal record," Gruber said. "I checked that. The local chamber of commerce even named him businessman of the year in '98."

"Glad to see you did your homework, Mickey. But you shoulda looked a little harder."

"Meaning?"

"Meaning, Hyacinth's gonna get married this coming Saturday." Tracey let it hang there, so Gruber had to pick it up.

"Yeah?"

"He's marrying one Verene Digby. Fetch Mcdonald's ex-wife."

"Sonofabitch," Gruber said.

"Of course, that could be a big coincidence," Tracey said with a broad smile.

"Yeah, sure." Gruber bowed graciously to the master. "Nice going, partner."

"It gets better, and you helped on this one. That call, it was from the boyfriend of the owner of the Permanent Fave. She's still got the shakes too bad to talk with the likes of you and me, but at my request her boyfriend asked her had she ever heard of our friend Karl. Like maybe did he invite her to his upcoming wedding?"

"She knows him?" Gruber asked hopefully.

Tracey nodded. "But not so they get dressed up and go to each other's parties. She said Karl once tried to sell her business insurance, only she went with somebody else."

Gruber grinned. "Karl was getting even with her, and that's how the robber knew what went on in the ladies room at the salon."

Tracey got to his feet and slipped on his suit coat.

"Let's you and me pay a visit to Mr. Hyacinth."

"Yeah, let's," Gruber agreed, following the senior detective out of the squad room.

He thought about telling Tracey the idea he'd just had. How there was this wine tasting tonight at the Emerald Club. Seemed to him it'd be just the kind of yuppie gathering the No-Place-Is-Safe Bandits would hit. Only Tracey's lead had facts behind it, not just a hunch.

Besides, even if the Emerald Club did get hit, they'd be waiting for Karl when he got home.

***

Erin was checking out the growing crowd at the Emerald Club, paying special attention to their clothes and accessories. She loved Dan's writing, but thought he could be a little more descriptive about the things his characters wore. Paying attention to details like that would help the reader to picture the story more easily — and Erin's research would help make the Camerons' evening out a legitimate business expense.

She was distracted from her work when she felt Dan grip her forearm, hard.

"Sonofabitch," he whispered, "I think this is it."

Erin turned her head to look at the club's front door. Two men had just walked in. One, Erin was sure, was wearing a wig. And the other was Archer Mcdonald.

"I think you're right," Erin told Dan. She nodded in the direction of the old bank robber's sneaker-clad feet. "Archer's wearing his felony fliers."

Casper Shabouh emerged from his office, seething. Never before had anyone had the insolence to question the legitimacy of his position. In Iran, under the shah, such an insult to a Shabouh would have cost the offender his tongue. Possibly his head.

Unfortunately, punitive amputation was not legal in the United States, though some conservative Americans of Casper's acquaintance thought the idea had merit. Even so, he could still throw the black bastard out of his wine tasting. He might leave himself open for a civil rights suit by doing so, but —

He'd never seen such a magnificently carnal woman in his life. Blonde like nothing in nature. The breasts, though, were as real as they were plump. The black dress she wore was of the type a woman put on only so a man could tear it off. The stiletto pumps — Casper was one of those rare men who noticed a woman's shoes — those she could leave on.

She was certainly not a candidate for marriage, or even membership in the Emerald Club. But starting tonight he would feast on her for as long as he could stand to debase himself. Then he would send her away, holding on to the memory of her with both delight and horror until the moment he died.

She seemed to be with two men, Stanley Sumner and Adriano Trinidad, both club members. But Casper was sure he could vanquish both of them. He was as wealthy as Stanley and as virile as Adriano — and far more handsome than either of them.

Casper started to cross the room to claim his prize when he saw two men enter the club. Two men who clearly didn't belong there, even on a night when his door was open to the public. He felt a sudden chill as he remembered the warning he'd received only moments ago.

Then, as if watching a nightmare come true, the larger newcomer, smiling like a madman, opened his mouth and said ...

"Good evening, ladies and gentlemen," Psycho said to the hundred-plus people in the club, "this is a stickup!" With that, Psycho pulled a .44 Magnum from under his coat.

When he and Archer had gone to buy their weapons earlier that night, Donnie — the illegal gun-dealer or 2nd Amendment patriot, take your pick — had told him this was exactly the kind of handgun Clint Eastwood had used in all his Dirty Harry movies. Psycho had thought, hell, if it was good enough for a movie madman, it was good enough for him.

Donnie warned him the huge weapon had quite a kick, but Psycho held it at arm's length and drilled a photo of

Charlton Heston. Got the sucker right between the eyes. Donnie'd had the framed portrait hanging on a wall above a sign that said: *That's My President!*

Kick? What kick? Gun shot straight and true.

Donnie got a bit upset, though.

"You sonofabitch, that picture was autographed!"

Psycho gave him a look and said, "Chuck would appreciate the irony."

Donnie didn't, and he was armed, too.

But Psycho had his weapon in hand, and looking at him the gun-dealer harbored no doubt he'd use it. At that point, a highly nervous Archer intervened, told Donnie he could always get Mr. Heston to sign another picture for him, and they'd throw in an extra hundred for his trouble.

Only mildly appeased, the gun-dealer sold his troublesome customers the .44, a Smith & Wesson .38 Snubbie for Archer, and a two-shot English derringer for Verene.

But he told Psycho, "Those are the only weapons you'll ever buy from me."

"That's real un-American of you, Donnie," Psycho replied.

Donnie didn't have an answer for that, so they left. But as they drove away, Archer asked, "What the hell was that all about, shooting the guy's picture?"

"Just getting my game-face on," Psycho told him.

Now the crowd at the Emerald Club got to see Pyscho's game-face. And his .44 Magnum. And Archer taking a large black plastic bag out from under his blazer.

Nobody moved an inch. They'd reached the same assessment of Psycho's volatility that Donnie the gun-dealer had.

Psycho continued, "Now, if all you nice people will be kind enough to drop your purses and wallets into the bag my friend will be bringing around ... why I won't have to shoot you."

Psycho giggled. Like shooting someone was the funniest idea in the world. It was so creepy even Archer turned around and gave him a look. Wondering what the hell he'd gotten himself into this time.

At their corner table, almost in the madman's shadow, Dan scanned the room and whispered to Erin, "Where's Fetch?"

Across the room, also searching the crowd, Gamble muttered to himself, "Where's Fetch?"

Trini slowly reached for his hip and quietly unsnapped his holster — and Verene noticed.

Casper Shabouh, master of four martial arts, started inching back down the hallway toward his office.

"Oh, one little thing I almost forgot," Psycho announced. He gave it a beat to make sure he had everyone's attention. "In case anyone's feeling foolish or, you know, brave, I have a few friends in the crowd. You work a room this big, you have to staff up."

People started looking around nervously.

Especially Gamble and Trini.

"My friends don't have their guns out now — but they will if anybody gets stupid."

With that, Psycho delivered another chilling giggle.

Dan and Erin's eyes went to Verene.

"You think she could hide a gun under that dress?" Dan whispered.

"Only if it's intrauterine." Then Erin gave her husband a nudge. "I think I know where Fetch is."

Dan looked at his wife and saw her cock her head at the window. Standing outside was a guy who looked like he'd just walked off a fashion shoot. He peered at what was going on over the top of his lowered sunglasses. His mouth hung open like he couldn't believe what he was seeing.

"Must make you feel bad when they start your armed robbery without you," Erin murmured.

Dan wished he could write that line down. He'd have to remember it ...if they lived that long.

Ants was waiting in her VW Passat when Lerome came out of the Queen City Pawn Brokerage with the genuine Ben Hecht/Dan Cameron Remington Noiseless Portable in Glossy Black. He hadn't wanted to have the machine found in his possession, but now that he and Ants were leaving town, and Fetch had taken the duplicate machine — with the original's serial number — to give to Cameron in return for the final pages of his manuscript, it was time to pick up the typewriter. Lerome was sure he'd write great stories with it.

He put it in the trunk of Ants' car, behind their luggage, and got in on the passenger side. The engine was running but Ants didn't drive off. She saw that Lerome had something to say.

He asked, "You know how much Fetch left me?"

"Half of what he had," Ants told him. "That's what he told me."

"Yeah. Close to a quarter-mill."

"Not enough to go to prison for, believe me."

Lerome nodded. "No money's worth that. And we do have to go get your boy."

"And you want to become a writer."

"That, too."

"But you're worried about Fetch. You think you got him into all this."

"I did," Lerome said.

Ants felt some responsibility, too. Giving Fetch her gun.

Lerome asked, "What would you think if we parked down the block from the Emerald Club? For a couple of minutes, no more. Just in case."

What could she say? Lerome had wholeheartedly agreed to drive most of the way across the country with her to kidnap her son from her former in-laws.

She said, "Okay. For a couple of minutes. No more."

"Where'd he go?" Erin asked quietly.

"Who?" Dan replied.

"Fetch."

Dan looked outside. The well-dressed man was gone. Dan had been paying attention to Archer, who was drawing near with the collection bag from the Church of the Big Gun. Now, Erin noticed the old robber approaching, people giving him their wallets and purses without a word of demurral. Or even a dirty look. The mad giggler had everybody scared.

Escaping with life and limb seemed to be a deal everybody could live with.

Only problem Dan could see, the plastic garbage bag Archer was toting was already getting full, didn't look like there'd be enough room in there for everybody's belongings.

"How much money do you have?" Erin asked.

"Hundred, hundred-and-fifty. In there."

"Is that enough? Not to piss them off."

"It'll have to do."

"Next time we're likely to get robbed, let's bring more."

The Camerons looked at the window, the one they'd been advised to break through if worse came to worse. Then they looked back at Archer.

He saw them, too. Recognized them. Veered away, surprisingly, with a look of embarrassment. Maybe remembering Dan and Erin had once caught him in his undies.

Now, he was headed in Trini's direction.

Fetch found his way to the rear entrance of the Emerald Club. No fucking way was he going through that front door. He had thought he'd give Karl a hand with the job, but Karl had obviously switched to full-lunatic mode and brought Fetch's old man along to help.

Verene, too.

Fetch had remembered the gorgeous blonde from the Galleria that afternoon, and now that she had her sunglasses off he recognized her. His lying, cheating, thieving ex-wife. And right next to Verene — Jesus! — there was that black FBI guy they'd pantsed at Kovac's.

Then not three feet away from where he'd been standing, he saw the writer, Cameron, and a woman who had to be his wife, the way they were whispering into each other's ears. Fetch thought if he'd walked through the front door the whole place would have exploded.

Especially with Psycho holding that artillery piece in his hand. So why had he gone around back? Why not just run like hell?

Finally get his ass across the border.

Especially since he didn't know how long this whole horror show had been going on. For all he knew, time had expired. Cops could be on their way right now.

There was only one explanation he could think of, why he didn't simply disappear. He'd gotten hooked on the story. Not just the one they'd been reading, but the one they were living. Exactly what he'd told Karl. Only he hadn't realized how fucking obsessive he'd become.

He couldn't walk away now without finding out how it all ended. Without making it end the way he wanted.

Turned out, he was every bit as crazy as Psycho.

Which was an epiphany that brought him a sudden sense of peace. And if he was lucky a way out of this whole mess.

Fetch tried the back door and found it unlocked. A sign, possibly, that his luck was changing for the better. He eased inside and silently closed the door behind him. He was in a corridor, looked like the way supplies got brought in. A busy night like this, someone hadn't wanted to bother unlocking the door every time somebody needed to get inside.

Ahead on the right a door was open and the lights were on. Fetch heard a click and then a heavy metallic thunk come from the room. He took out the gun Ants had given him, a Glock, and being who he was, he left the safety on. He inched forward and peeked around the doorway.

He saw a Middle-Eastern-looking guy down on one knee pull open the door of a large floor safe. Inside the safe were mounds of cash and maybe half-a-dozen gold bars. There was also a gun — an old Luger or something — the guy was reaching for.

Fetch stepped silently into the room.

Verene saw Archer coming her way, but she didn't look directly at him. She wasn't going to let anyone see her make eye contact with the old bank robber. Wasn't going to leave one damn clue she knew the sonofabitch.

Her new plan included Stanley Sumner not Archer Mcdonald. Not crazy Karl Hyacinth, either. Definitely not going to jail. But she started to feel confined as the two men she'd met that evening leaned in on her.

As the sense of competition she'd fostered between Stanley and Adriano had built, they'd begun crowding her. Getting all the physical contact they'd dared. Seeing who could be bolder without crossing the line that would get one of them smacked. But now the nature of the contact was changing dramatically.

Stanley was clinging to her arm like a frightened kid hanging on to his mom. Adriano on her other hip, damnit, he was getting hard! And he was the one she was sure had a gun. Verene felt sure he was going to shoot Archer — which was perfectly okay with her — and then cream his drawers.

She'd be halfway home then. Unless crazy Karl got pissed at her for not plugging Adriano before Adriano shot Archer. Karl wasn't likely to forget he'd given her the two-shot derringer. It was currently tucked into a garter high on the inside of her left thigh. In case of emergency, she was supposed to use it to deadly effect.

But that was before Verene had decided to change teams in the middle of the game without telling anybody. She wasn't about to let her new golden opportunity slip away. If Archer and Karl had to be sacrificed to that reality, well, that was just too bad.

Thinking fast, Verene came up with a bright idea.

Gamble's eyes darted all around, trying to spot the gunmen's covert accomplices. He didn't see anyone whose hands weren't in plain sight: holding a wine glass, a wallet, or empty. He thought maybe his best play would be to grab the old guy making the collections and —

Hey! The old guy was Fetch Mcdonald's father. Gamble recognized Archer now, and it gave him a moment of dizziness. Could the elder Mcdonald have been the Everyman Bank Robber all along? The fucker had done two jolts for bank robbery. Had Gamble been off-base about Fetch? Had the son discovered what the father had been doing, tried to imitate him, and gotten caught his first time out? The very thought made Gamble woozy.

Then he remembered that Archer was still serving his second sentence when Everyman first struck. That put the former fed back on an even keel. But his plan to grab the old man and use him as a shield evaporated as he saw Archer was closing in on none other than fucking Trini.

Gamble couldn't believe that Cuban cocksucker's luck. But then — what the hell? Fetch Mcdonald's ex-wife, sitting right there next to Trini, opened her legs.

Gave the whole place a show.

***

Fetch put his Glock behind Casper Shabouh's right ear and told him, "Put the gun down and don't twitch a hair on that pretty mustache of yours."

Casper released his grip on the Luger, but despite Fetch's warning, an involuntary shudder ran through the club manager.

"You piss or shit, you'll hate yourself in the morning," Fetch warned.

Casper brought himself under control. Many things could be denied, he knew, but not soiling oneself. The man with the gun was perfectly correct about that.

Still, his voice quavered as he asked, "Wh ...what do you want?"

"How about this?" Fetch asked. "You keep your life and the gold, I'll take the cash."

Casper started to reply, but Fetch creased his skull with the Glock.

"That was a rhetorical question," he told the recumbent Casper. Just like Terry Phelan had told Allie and BooBoo.

Showed how reading could improve your mind, he thought.

Ants drove past the Emerald Club a mile or two per hour under the speed limit. Traffic was unusually light even for a weeknight, and she and Lerome apparently were the only two passersby, vehicular or otherwise, who noticed Karl standing in the open doorway. All they could see was his back, but both felt it was safe to assume they were witnessing a robbery-in-progress.

Ants glanced back at the road and then at Lerome. She didn't say a word.

Lerome said, "Have to be crazy to get mixed up in that."

Then out of the corner of his eye, he noticed the Camerons' SUV — ever so briefly his — in the Emerald

Club's parking lot. It was parked in the first slot next to the street. He still had the key. In fact, Jessi had made a duplicate for him, and a valet key, too. Well past the Camerons' vehicle, parked at the far end of the lot, was the Neon he'd obtained for Fetch.

He told Ants, "Pull over a second."

She complied without objection.

Lerome said, "Drive two blocks, make a right, and park. If I'm not there in ten minutes, take the money Fetch left for me and go."

Ants gave Lerome such a fierce look it made him think that's what her husband saw right before she ran him over.

"You better be there," she said. "I want you, not the money. I'll burn the damn money."

Lerome gave her a smile and a kiss.

"Okay, I'll be there."

"In ten minutes."

He got out of the VW moving quickly, knowing he had to marry this woman.

"What is that woman doing?" Erin demanded, looking at Verene.

"It's called flashing beav—" Then Dan noticed something more important.

"Look!" Erin said, no longer whispering. "Look what she's reaching for!"

"Never mind that now," Dan countered. "Look who's heading our way."

Pscyho was coming to see why Archer had skipped past the Camerons.

Gamble, like Erin, saw what Verene was reaching for. Years of training took over and he reflexively yelled, "Gun!"

He scrambled to grab his own weapon, thinking, *Damn,*

the ex-wife is in on the job.

Before he could get a bead on her, the sugar-daddy in the white suit next to her sagged a bit, just enough to bring him into Gamble's line of fire and shield her.

Holding a large satchel, Fetch appeared in the rear hallway entrance to the main room — and saw Verene shoot his father.

Hearing Gamble's cry of "Gun," Trini went for his own weapon. He'd been thinking for the past few minutes — however the hell long the robbery had been going on — these guys looked real familiar. If he hadn't been drinking steadily the past six hours or so, he was sure he could have placed them. The *maricón* by the door with the big pistola, anyway.

Didn't matter who they were, really. The last thing he could afford was to get robbed two nights in a row. Hey! That's who that dick-licker was! Maybe not the old man, but the other one was the sumbitch who robbed him last night!

Plug him an' his buddy right now, Trini'd leave the bureau on a high note. Be a big hero when he ran for Congress. Gunning down armed robbers, they ate that shit up in Florida.

Only problem was, the blondie he'd been groping all night had faster reflexes. She grabbed this little gun she musta hid up her bush, an' pop goes *el viejo*. All the while, he's still trying to get his weapon clear of its fucking stiff new holster.

Goddamnit, he had to hurry or this *puta* would plug both the bad guys, and he'd look like a worse fool than ever.

Trini finally yanked his gun out of his holster but in his impaired state he somehow managed to get the strap caught inside the trigger guard. He pulled hard to dislodge the fucking thing and his weapon discharged.

Not into one of the bad guys.

SAC Adriano Trinidad shot himself in the foot.

Verene heard Trini's shot and thought it was somebody shooting at her. Karl, she thought. But then she saw that goddamn black FBI guy, Gamble, who'd been following her had a gun pointed her way. Well, she had one round left to fire herself.

She tried to shrug Stanley off. The fool was falling all over her. She'd make him pay for his cowardice and clumsiness later.She managed to push him upright and aimed at the FBI man.

Shooting a fed was no small matter but in a situation like this confusion reigned. She saw a guy pointing a gun at her, she fired at him. Self-defense pure and simple. Who could say different?

Psycho saw Verene point her gun at a black guy. A different black guy. Not the bigshot FBI guy they'd robbed last night who'd just shot himself. That fucking guy couldn't win for losing. Maybe this second black guy — who did have a gun in his hand — was also a lawman. So Verene was doing the right thing throwing lead his way.

But why the hell had Verene shot Archer? So she wouldn't have to split her take? Jesus, he was glad she was no longer his fiancée.

Right now, though, the other black guy with the gun was the problem.

Psycho pointed his gun the black guy's way.

Dan saw the madman draw a bead on Gamble, and Verene was also pointing her weapon at the former fed. Without giving a thought to what he was doing, Dan got out of his chair and picked it up.

Erin was also on her feet, tugging her husband in the opposite direction. Then something outside got her attention.

"Hey!" she yelled. She let go of Dan and ran for the door, calling over her shoulder, "Come on, Dan. Petunia and I need you!"

Dan didn't follow, but Erin started a stampede of panicky oenophiles.

Gamble saw he was about to be caught in a crossfire and dived for cover. Fate reminded him that such feats were best left to stuntmen and others who'd yet to see their sixtieth birthday. His shoulder caught the edge of a table and his gun went flying from his hand.

Fetch watched in amazement as the black guy hit the floor and suddenly he was in the line of fire from both Psycho and Verene. In his darkest, most penitent nightmare, he'd never thought his career in crime would end like this. Gunned down by his ex-wife and an insurance salesman he'd turned into a homicidal maniac.

He did the only thing he could think of.

He raised the satchel he was carrying and ducked behind it.

A split-second before Verene fired, Stanley Sumner's heart gave out. He fell against Verene once more. His arms instinctively grasped for support and he took her down with him. Her gun went off, struck the fallen Trini's weapon, and ricocheted neatly into the satchel that shielded Fetch. The small-caliber round didn't penetrate the contents of the case but the impact knocked Fetch back a step, sending his Panama hat flying.

It was still in the air as Karl's .44 Magnum boomed and turned the hat into a cloudburst of straw that rained on

Fetch's head.

Wide-eyed that he was still alive, Fetch saw Psycho start his way.

Recognizing Fetch, Psycho stopped and said, "I wondered if you were going to show up."

Fetch did more than show up. He quickly crossed to Karl and pushed him aside. Standing behind the maniacal robber, chair drawn back to deliver a smashing blow, was Dan Cameron. Fetch put the barrel of the Glock to the bridge of the writer's nose.

Dan wisely let the chair fall and meekly raised his hands. But now Psycho had a grasp of the situation.

"Was that guy gonna smack me one?" he asked.

"Looked like it." Fetch replied.

Psycho raised his .44, and Dan's knees began to wobble.

"You don't want to do that," Fetch told Karl.

"Why not?" There was bloodlust in Psycho's eyes.

"Because this is Dan Cameron. Kill him and we'll never find out how his story ends."

Turned out Psycho was as star-struck as a teenage girl. Because in his normal voice, Karl asked, "That's him? It's really Dan Cameron? Mr. Cameron, I *love* your book."

"Thank you," Dan croaked from a dry throat, still not sure if his number was up.

Fetch made Dan right the chair he'd been carrying and sit on it. He got the impression that Dan recognized the Glock's safety was on, but with Psycho/Karl hovering in the background the writer wasn't about to blurt it out the way that snotty kid had.

Fetch told Dan, "Stick to writing before you get hurt. I want those pages. I better get them, too. You understand?"

Dan nodded, profoundly glad to be alive and aware he had a promise to keep.

"Okay, then," Fetch said, and he added, "By the way,

your typewriter's at your hotel."

Karl wanted an autograph, but Fetch grabbed him and said, "Come on, it's time to go."

They left, neither of them looking back at Archer or Verene.

Gamble finally found his gun, but his right arm was tingling so bad he couldn't pick it up much less shoot it, and he'd never been any good shooting lefty. He watched as Fetch Mcdonald got away from him. Again.

He looked around and saw both Trini and Archer Mcdonald lying on the floor bleeding. Trini looked like he'd gone into shock. Archer still held the bag of loot in one hand and had his other hand clasped over the wound in his stomach. Gamble had always heard that the only thing worse than being gutshot was being nutshot, but he thought Archer looked almost peaceful.

Verene was leaning over the sugar-daddy in the white suit. Looked like she was giving him CPR. With tongue.

Dan Cameron sat on a chair looking dazed. For a moment, that terrified Gamble. But when he didn't see Erin lying in a pool of blood, he heaved a sigh of relief. The writer, himself, hadn't seemed to suffer any injuries. Things had just gotten a little too close to the bone for him. Maybe he'd have nightmares to deal with. Probably put that in his book, too.

Otherwise, the place was empty. Made Gamble wonder where that fucker Casper Shabouh had gotten to — and if he'd even bothered calling the cops.

Gamble decided he'd better do it just to be safe. He picked up his gun with his left hand, got to his feet and found a phone behind the bar. He punched in 911.

Wondered what the response time would be.

On the sidewalk outside, Karl told Fetch he wanted to go

back into the club.

"We left the money behind, Fetch. We do that, what kind of robbers are we?"

Fetch looked over Karl's shoulder and saw Dan Cameron's wife, standing next to her SUV, the one Lerome had stolen and she'd stolen back. It was parked at the curb and the engine was running. Cameron's wife had her hands in the air, like she was patiently waiting for someone to please come over and rob her.

Fetch picked up on the cue. He reached into his coat pocket and pulled out the keys to the Dodge Neon he'd driven to the club. He gave them to Karl and pointed out the car to him.

"Take it," he told Karl. "There's over two hundred thousand dollars in the trunk. If it makes you feel better, it's all stolen money. I want you to have it. I also want you to stop pulling jobs. If you're dumb enough to keep on ... I can't help you."

Fetch took the .44 out of Karl's hand.

"This is it?" Karl asked regretfully. "We're really done, you and me?"

Fetch nodded, then said, "Lerome keeps telling me to go to Canada. You might think about that yourself."

Receiving advice that had come from Lerome firmed Karl right up.

"You know, I think I will. Right after I pick someone up."

For a dreadful moment, Fetch thought he was going back inside for Verene. But Karl jogged to the Neon at the end of the now empty lot. Fetch turned to the writer's wife.

He walked up to her and asked, "You really want me to point a gun at you?"

"It'd look better," Erin said, "since you're going to steal my car."

"Why're you doing this?" He declined to aim either the Glock or the .44 at her.

"I saw your cousin. He was stealing my car again. When I went to stop him, he said you might need it. Your car, where it was parked in the lot, might get stuck in the crowd."

Just then Karl zipped by, honking a farewell as he turned onto the street and sped away.

"Guess it wasn't necessary," Erin added.

"Lerome likes to be careful."

"He didn't threaten me or anything when I went to stop him."

"No, he wouldn't."

"He said you'd make sure Dan and I got the typewriter back."

"I already told your husband, it's at your hotel."

"Good."

"I also told him I want those final pages."

"You'll get them."

Fetch got into the car, stuck the guns under the front seat, threw the satchel he'd taken from Casper's office into the back. He was more than a little surprised the cops hadn't shown up by now. He had one more thing to clear up with the writer's wife, though. He lowered the passenger side window so they could talk.

"What's your name?" he asked.

"Erin."

"Your husband's a lucky man."

She beamed and said, "I'm lucky to have Dan, too."

"I know why you're doing this, Erin."

"Doing what?"

"Letting me have your car. This is the ending you want to see."

Erin grinned. "Everyone wants to be the writer."

Fetch nodded and told her, "Could be I've got an ending of my own." He drove off. In the rear-view mirror, he saw Erin drop one hand and wave to him with the other. He waved back, but he didn't know if she could see it. In the distance, he finally heard the wail of police sirens, a lot of them, but they seemed to be moving in the other direction.

Made him think maybe his luck finally was changing for the better.

CHAPTER 31

The Remington Noiseless Portable in Glossy Black was sent to Hank DeMitri the next day. He carried it by hand to the Hecht estate's lawyers. They inspected it carefully for damage or defect, and matched the machine's serial number against the one on the estate's inventory list. Satisfied that they had reclaimed the estate's property, they returned the typewriter to storage. All threatened legal actions were dropped.

The Saturday following the robbery at the Emerald Club all 246 guests of the Digby-Hyacinth wedding showed up at St. Norberta's Norwegian Catholic Church. They were joined by Detectives Tracey and Gruber. Father Alfroth Andersson stood in front of the congregation with altar boys Balki Bryntensen and Hafgrim Johansson. The only people yet to arrive were the bride and the groom. After waiting for the two principals twenty minutes past the appointed hour, the crowd started to grow restless. Especially the two cops. Father Andersson frowned fiercely, and the altar boys muttered that they were going to be stiffed out of their traditional nuptial mass tip.

At that point, Karl's office manager, Judith (Don't Call

Me Judy) McGuire, stood up in the front row pew and pulled her boyfriend, Leo Malloy, to his feet. The two of them marched up to the altar for a confab with Father Andersson. She stated the obvious to the irate cleric.

"Father, what we have here is a rare case where both the bride and groom have sought to leave the other at the altar, with the net effect that we've all been stood up."

"Yes, and after I wrote a sermon especially for this couple." Karl had shown the priest a snapshot of Verene and he'd known immediately Karl would have to be instructed how to avoid the sin of lust. Even with one's own wife. Especially with this wife. He told Judith, "Perhaps it's all for the best. We'll all simply have to go home."

The priest started to turn away, but Judith grabbed his sleeve. "Father, you wrote a sermon, but I wrote a check for this shindig. You've been paid."

"Yes, but—"

"You can marry Leo and Me. We're both Catholics. Come to that, why don't you marry any couple here who wants to get hitched? And renew the vows of the married people."

Balki and Hafgrim loved that idea. The tips would be enormous. But Father Andersson was reluctant — it was all very irregular — until Judith played her trump card.

"Father, the reception's been paid for, too. You don't marry somebody, all that food, all that beer, what'll happen to it? Waste's a sin, isn't it, Father?"

Good Norwegian Catholic that he was, Father Andersson had to agree.

Fourteen couples were married that day; twenty-three more renewed their vows. The reception was the best anyone could remember. Only Dick Tracey and Mickey Gruber were disappointed because Karl never showed.

It took Dan two weeks of intense work to finish dictating *Time Expires* to Erin. He didn't need to do that, of course. Fetch had returned a copy of the manuscript Lerome had stolen. Only when Dan reread it, compared it to what he'd done working with his wife, he found nuances in the dictated copy that the original lacked.

Besides that, he and Erin had developed the habit of showering together after every dictation session. Sometimes they'd make love under the spray, other times they got into bed. Wherever they began their amorous activities, each session ended with Dan pressing an ear to Erin's abdomen and listening for a fetal heartbeat.

They agreed Petunia was a silly name for a child, especially if they had a boy, but neither of them was in a hurry to come up with anything else.

On the day they finished the manuscript, Rudy brought up a printer and two reams of paper. They printed out two copies. Rudy took one copy to Kinko's and under his personal supervision had ten more copies run off. One was a gift to him. Dan inscribed the title page.

Erin did, too.

Exhausted from their efforts, the Camerons celebrated the completion of the novel with a room-service dinner, a split of champagne for Dan, and a bottle of sparkling water for Erin. All compliments of the house. But as they retired for the night, Erin sensed something was wrong.

"What is it, Dan?" she asked.

"I was just wondering if we can do another novel this way. With *Time Expires*, I'd already written the story. Had it in my head. But starting from scratch ... that seems kind of scary. And what about after Petunia's born? She's going to take up most of your time. How will you be able to care for her and take dictation from me?"

"Daddies change diapers nowadays, you know. We'll share the load, no pun intended, on both jobs. What you ought to worry about, you'll want to spend so much time with our baby, you won't have any left to write."

"You have an excellent point there."

Dan kissed Erin goodnight.

After his eyes closed and his breathing turned rhythmic, Erin told her sleeping husband, "Just you wait, Danny boy. I've got more surprises for you."

Stanley Sumner's heart was restarted by paramedics who arrived at the Emerald Club after a protracted wait. But it failed again on the way to the hospital and all efforts to revive the auto dealer proved futile.

Verene had followed the ambulance to the hospital in her Corvette and demanded that she be allowed to perform oral sex on the patient. She claimed the way she gave head was guaranteed to get any man's heart racing. Her novel approach to CPR was disallowed as not being in compliance with the hospital's malpractice insurance.

Escorted from the emergency room, she sat in her car and sobbed for over an hour. There would be no trip to Portugal for her. No chance to marry Stanley. No hope that any court would ever compensate her for one bar conversation and a little grab-ass.

Worse, she'd lost all of Fetch's money, she'd lost Karl, she didn't even have Archer to screw her silly anymore. Thinking of Archer, she wondered if he'd survived, and if he'd rat her out. That she'd been in on the robbery. She didn't think so. She'd given him more hot pussy than an old shit like him had any right to expect. There was bound to be a price to pay.

She thought briefly about trying to play the reward angle on both Fetch and Karl. But Karl had been right. She couldn't prove anything. Karl could do awful things to her if she caused him trouble. Even if Karl didn't hack her to pieces, he could rat her out for being in on the Emerald Club job.

No, the way things had worked out, she was shit out of luck. For the moment, that was. Because there was a never-ending supply of men with testosterone counts higher than their IQs. With that hopeful thought in mind, she started her car.

When she got home, she found her dweebie teenage neighbor, Axel Dengler, ensconced in a sleeping bag lying across her front door. After she booted him awake, he gave her a check for $50,000 and a business proposition.

Axel told her the money was her share, thus far, from his live Webcast and re-casts of *Bedroom Peeper*. He said he wanted to shoot her naked and writhing in every room in her house and let the whole world watch — for an appropriate pay-per-view fee.

For her participation — and, damn, she looked hot as a blonde — Axel offered Verene twenty per cent of the action.

Verene quickly took Axel inside and told him she'd cut his heart out with a can opener if the check was a phony. When he convinced her it was real, she made a man out of him. She soon did the same with Axel's partner, Petey, and in a very short time controlled two teenage boys' hearts and minds, and owned eighty percent of VAP Adult Entertainment Productions.

Within a year, Verene was an Internet sex star, making more money than she'd ever dreamed possible.

Karl moved to Miami — after he took Rhonda the dancing hooker for a month-long stay in Canada. It was the most blissful time Karl had ever had. He was thinking of proposing marriage to Rhonda when he woke up one morning and found a note from her. She was sorry to inform him, but she'd met a sergeant in the Royal Canadian Air Force. He didn't dance quite as well as Karl, but he was willing to learn, and he looked so much like her dear old daddy it liked to break her heart — except it made her real happy instead. She pleaded with Karl to understand. She'd always love him, too. Only from afar.

Since Rhonda easily could have taken the $170,000 dollars left over from the money Fetch had given him — but hadn't — Karl thought who was he to begrudge Rhonda her happiness.

Karl went home where he found two business cards from policemen stuck in his door. The two cops who'd come to see him about his motorcycle. The same note was scribbled on each card: *Call me.* He threw both of them in the trash.

He sold his house and his business, the latter to the newlywed Judith who'd been running the place flawlessly in his absence. He cashed in to the tune of $1.5 million. On top of that, he had what was left of the money Fetch had given him, the take from the Permanent Fave, Java Joe's and Kovac's robberies, and his own personal reserve from his sofa-safe.

Arriving in Miami, he bought a 40-foot motor-sailer and christened it *A Likely Story.* He invested his money conservatively, lived nicely, and was soon bored silly. Psycho kept nibbling at the edge of his consciousness, insisting he do something interesting. Something illegal.

Which was in direct conflict with Fetch's advice to avoid a further life of crime.

As a compromise, Karl started reviewing novels of other people's crimes — mysteries — for his marina's giveaway newspaper. His pieces were well received and one of his readers turned out to be an editor for the *Miami Herald.* He told Karl he was quite impressed with his astute analysis of where most crime novelists went wrong, and Karl's seemingly expert knowledge of how crimes really got done. He asked Karl to start reviewing for his paper.

Karl had found his niche.

The following summer he reviewed Daniel Cameron's new bestseller, *Time Expires.* He still loved it, but he panned it. To cover his ass. Critics always had their own agendas.

Adriano Trinidad was given a disability retirement from the FBI for his efforts to stop the armed robbery at the Emerald Club. It was politically far wiser for the bureau to pension Trini off than to fire him. Trini even received a commendation for bravery, even though only one of the robbers was apprehended, and that one had been shot by a female civilian — against whom no gun charges were pressed so as not to muddy Trini's separation from the bureau. So Trini went home to Florida, a hero, where his father immediately began the political machinations that would send his son to Washington as a member of congress.

Seeing Trini fall into a pile of shit and come out smelling like a rose was more than Gamble Murtree could bear. He followed his nemesis to the Sunshine State intent on whispering the truth about why Trini walked with a limp to whatever Democrat ran against the sonofabitch. The word was already out as to what Trini's future plans would be.

Only, on his drive down to Miami, he met Etta Mae Jenkins in a diner in Cocoa Beach. Place was called Teddy's just like back in Buffalo. Etta Mae was the owner. She'd lost her husband, the diner's namesake and cook, the year before, and her dishwasher quit on her while Gamble was eating the breakfast she'd both cooked for him and brought to his table.

What Gamble liked — besides how fine Etta Mae looked for a mature widow woman — was she didn't plead with the dishwasher to stay, didn't wail to Gamble he'd likely be the last customer her place would ever have. She just firmed her chin, sat down at the breakfast counter and started to look at the want ads in a newspaper somebody had left behind. She was going to take care of herself.

Gamble quietly finished his breakfast, which, truth be told, was far from the best cooking he'd ever had. He took his dishes out to the kitchen and started washing them. When he was done with those, he washed the other dirty plates and cups he found there.

Etta Mae, who'd come to see what he was doing, told him, "I can't pay you, either."

She didn't have to. Gamble, the lifelong thrifty bachelor, bought into the business. He called Nick Mylonas at the Teddy's up in Buffalo and told him he needed a first rate short-order cook and a waitress who was as pretty as Adara right away. His new employees boarded a plane from Greece the next day. Teddy's in Cocoa Beach soon prospered and Gamble and Etta Mae were married six months later.

Etta Mae loved to read, and she especially enjoyed reading aloud to Gamble. The former fed forgot all about foiling Trini's plans. A commie mole who shot himself in the foot wouldn't be much of a threat anyway.

He didn't have to worry about Fetch Mcdonald, either. Fetch was back in custody. Story had made *USA Today*.

Fetch had decided that his best bet was to get locked up again. But not sent back to prison. Not even minimum security. No, he had to convince everyone that he'd gone crazy. Insanity was why he'd broken out of Camp Alphonse with only three weeks left on his sentence.

He thought it shouldn't be too hard to sell that idea because he'd already firmly convinced himself that he had been nuts to do that. He'd had that thought a few times after he'd escaped, but that day he'd gone to rob the Emerald Club the realization finally hit him. He could use insanity as a legal defense for his actions. But he had to play it so he'd be confined in a mental hospital.

So he hid his haul from Casper's office — where nobody but him would ever find it. He had the new color stripped from his hair and had it redone in his natural shade. Then he started living outdoors, in parks and on public golf courses. He wore only underwear. Which tore the shit out of his feet. Cut and gouged the rest of his body, too. Trying to subsist on mulberries he picked from trees, he dropped enough weight that his ribs stuck out. Drinking rain water gave him the trots.

Two weeks along, fearful he might die if he kept at it much longer, he provoked two cops into arresting him by peeing on a rose bed in LaSalle Park on the Lake Erie shoreline. Just south of the Peace Bridge to Canada.

When the cops questioned him, he only babbled in response. His eyes wandered in random directions. He had trouble walking — a genuine result of malnutrition.

They took him to the prison ward of the Erie County Medical Center — and put him in a bed next to his father. The two of them were the only patients there.

The doctors had taken Verene's bullet out of Archer's gut and closed him right back up. He would never come to trial for his role in the Emerald Club robbery. Would never be sent back to prison. The hospital bed where he lay was his last way station in life. The medical consensus was that nobody had ever seen intestinal cancer so advanced. Even beginning a criminal prosecution of Archer would be a complete waste of time and money.

Archer's imminent demise also robbed the Erie County D.A.'s office of any leverage in persuading him to identify his confederates in the Emerald Club robbery.

Archer didn't blow Fetch's act, either, when his son was brought in. Archer never gave up a criminal accomplice, even though three of them had betrayed him. He waited until the ward was dark at night and then he began to whisper to his son.

Told him how sorry he'd been for everything. Right from the start. Not realizing that he really hadn't been good enough for Fetch's mother. How he'd failed her time after time. How he hadn't been there for Fetch. And then he'd stolen Fetch's wife when Fetch got locked up.

"My money, too," Fetch added.

"Yeah, your money, too."

"And set me up to break jail, get caught, and go back for a helluva long time."

Archer sighed. "Can we just say I'll never be Father of the Year and leave it at that?" Then he asked, "What pissed you off more, losing Verene or losing your money?"

Fetch shook his head. "I honestly don't know. They were wrapped up together. Both part of the same dream."

The next morning, they identified Fetch. Several cops came and tried to get him to talk sense. Or at least English. Fetch declined to cooperate.

Archer rebuked the lawmen. "Leave my poor boy alone. Can't you see he's gone crazy? Musta suffered more than the likes a you would ever know."

Fetch had a hard time staying in character, listening to his father not only defend him, but seem to understand him as well. The cops weren't impressed. They told Archer shut the fuck up. Nobody wanted to hear from him. A piece of shit con about to croak from cancer.

It was all Fetch could do not to lash out. But a voice in his head warned that would be just what these cops wanted. Didn't mean he couldn't shit his sheets, though. His bowels were still loose, and the mess and smell got rid of everyone with a badge. But that afternoon, Warden Parker from Camp Alphonse stopped in to look him over.

The warden only shrugged. "I said he'd have to be crazy to break out like he did."

They weren't done trying to smoke him out. They rolled out the biggest gun they had the week after he'd been confined there. An orderly came by and dropped a manila envelope on the tray where they put his food.

Orderly told him, "You got mail. From somebody name of Daniel Cameron."

The pages. The ending of *Time Expires*. Cameron had come through for him. Only now they were using it against him. It was all he could do not to rip open that envelope and read those pages. If he did, though, it was all over. There was no question in his mind somebody was watching him. They might even be videotaping. So he just kept on playing his game, the frustration nearly driving him crazy. Crazier.

When night came, the lights didn't go down the way they usually did. Fetch thought maybe the cops needed it brighter to accommodate their camera. He didn't know how long he could last, those pages sitting there, tempting him with every passing second.

He began to cry soundlessly. He couldn't pull off this plan, either. Sooner or later, he was going to give in and read those pages. He was fucking hopeless.

Then he heard the sound of paper tearing. His old man was opening the envelope. Had to be. That could be the only expla—

His father began to read aloud. He wasn't fluent. Had trouble with anything more than simple words. But he sounded out the big ones a syllable at a time. Fetch lay back, closed his eyes, and listened to Archer's voice.

Allie and BooBoo sat in the back of the caterer's van, looking at all the tall buildings rising up around them as they headed south on Lake Shore Drive. The two of them had lived in the city their entire lives, but they'd never seen it the way they were seeing it now. Rushing along between the great dark mass of the lake and brilliantly lit forest of skyscrapers, it was easy to be overwhelmed by both the power of nature and the audacity of man's ambitions.

BooBoo whispered to Allie. "This is where you 'n' me shoulda been livin' all along. In one a those big places. Maybe at the top a the biggest fucker they got down here." BooBoo smiled and spoke directly into Allie's ear. "After tonight we be able to afford it, too."

Allie shook her head. "Boo, I just wanna go home. I'm tellin' you this is all gonna be a—"

"Damn, would you look at that?" BooBoo said loud enough for everyone to hear.

He was staring at Buckingham Fountain, shooting jets of water high into the night sky, each of them illuminated by a colored light. Several others in the catering crew looked back at BooBoo and Allie, grinning at their lack of sophistication.

"Shut up, fool," Allie told BooBoo under her breath. "You got everybody watchin' us."

BooBoo calmed down but only for a minute. Then he gave Allie a nudge and nodded his head to the left: McCormick Place, their destination. Home of the Chicago Auto Show, and the special sneak preview dinner for 200 of the fattest cats in town.

BooBoo told Allie softly, "They say you stood that place on end, it'd be higher than Sears Tower."

Allie's eyes widened. Even driving by the huge exposition hall at 45 miles per hour, it took a good minute to get from one end to the other. And we're gonna do a hold up in a place that big, Allie wondered, just BooBoo 'n' me? I gotta stop this shit before we both get killed.

"Good thinkin', girlie," Archer said as he turned a page.

That's when it hit Allie. That motherfucker Terry Phelan had set them up. He wanted them to get killed. He knew all along there was no way two people could pull off this job. Allie had felt something was wrong as soon as she and BooBoo had gotten hired on by the caterer. It was too easy. They'd needed a way to get into this fancy dinner. Terry'd told them how, and just like that — snap your fingers — you're in. Man, nothin' was that easy unless the fix was in.

But here they were pulled up to some service entrance, everybody getting out, BooBoo about to join the crowd until Allie grabbed him back.

"They're waitin' for us," Allie said as soon as they were alone.

"Then we best not keep 'em waitin'," BooBoo told her with a grin.

"Don't you get it, man? We been set up."

BooBoo's grin disappeared. He leaned in close to Allie. "Now who'd wanna do that? Your boyfriend Terry?"

Allie didn't say a word.

"You think I don't know?" BooBoo said. "I been askin' myself if you fucked him already. I don't think so. But I know it's what you want. Too bad he's got that rich bitch a his. Maybe you'd do better she wasn't around."

Allie's face burned with shame.

"I don't care if we been set up," BooBoo said. "I'm gonna pull this motherfucker off anyway. You don't wanna help, fuck you, too."

BooBoo got out of the caterer's truck. A moment later, Allie followed.

Oh, man, Fetch thought. Time's already expired on these two. He glanced over at his father, saw he felt the same way, shaking his head at poor Allie and BooBoo.

The two doomed kids entered the building and Archer fell silent. He was taking too long for it to be just an unfamiliar word that had stopped him. Fetch opened an eye and took a peek. The old man had a worried look on his face. His eyes were racing down one page of the story, going on to the next, and the one after that

Fetch wanted to ask, "Dad, what the fuck're you doing?" Then as Archer got to the last page, Fetch heard footsteps, coming fast.

"Hey, you old shitbird, what the hell do you think you're doing?" A guard. Fetch closed his eye.

"You think you can open somebody else's mail? That's a fucking federal crime. You weren't on death's doorstep, we'd let those cocksuckers have you, too."

"Yeah?" asked Archer, a man no longer frightened of anything. "That means you're gonna let me stay here? You're gonna be my cocksucker?"

Fetch pulled a muscle in his belly not laughing. The guard cursed Archer some more and left, taking Dan Cameron's story with him. Before Archer could read him the ending.

But five minutes later, Archer said quietly, "Okay, boy, listen. This is what happened, the best I could make out."

Fetch reopened an eye to look at his father.

"That BooBoo got kilt all right, tryin' to do the job. The cops was waitin' just like that Allie thought. She got out because she didn't try 'n' help her boyfriend. Didn't even bring her gun with. The cops had no way to hold her.

"So she goes home, gets the gun she shoulda had at the job an' goes to kill Terry. He's with that Fayre woman — kinda like that name, Fayre. Anyway, Allie busts in on them, Terry jumps in front of Fayre to take the bullet. Allie says that's fine, she's gonna kill them both. Only Fayre's got her own gun. She shoves Terry outta the way 'n' plugs Allie.

"Too bad. I kinda liked that young gal's grit and smarts. So there's Fayre with a dead body on her floor and she wants to know just why Allie hated Terry so much she had to kill him. But Terry's not talking. Instead, he says Fayre has to keep his name outta it when Fayre calls the cops.

Fayre thinks, okay, the guy at least tried to save my life; I'll do him that favor. But they're done as lovers. She doesn't need any more shit like that. She sells her building and is gone.

"Terry's boss sells his company and Terry gets his boss's old job. Makes a shitload a money and gets a fancy office. His neighborhood gets took over by rich people so the money he put into his building doubles or triples or some shit like that. Everything's hunky-dory ... except there are some people who got pushed outta the neighborhood who're pissed off.

"Two in particular, who're just about to leave, decide what they'll do before they go is rob as many of the new rich people as they can in one night. Even things out a little bit. Now, Fayre had a good idea somethin' like this was comin' because she'd been talking to the old neighbors and knew they were sore about what was happenin' to them.

"Only she figured if Terry's got secrets he ain't sharin', then fuck him, she won't share hers either. So right at the end, there's Terry all fat and happy, and he's going out that night to some fancy bookstore or somewhere.

"Except the two armed robbers're out there, too, this guy and his girlfriend, kinda like Allie and BooBoo come back to life. They see Terry up ahead a them 'n' the girl turns to her boyfriend with a smile and says, '*Let's start with him.*'

"And that's all she wrote," Archer concluded.

Damn, that was good, Fetch thought. Satisfying. There's Terry thinking he's got the world by the ass, but not so fast, my man. Maybe the armed robbery'll get out of control.

You had to use your imagination to decide.

It was pretty good, too, the way Archer saw those robbers at the end echoing Allie and BooBoo. People kept surprising Fetch the way they could see beneath the surface of the story. His dad, Karl ...Karl? Damn, Fetch was glad he didn't learn about the hold up at the auto show. Weren't any in Buffalo, but that lunatic Karl would have had Fetch and himself on the first plane out to a place that did.

Pretty damn nice of his old man, though, to quick read ahead, before the guard grabbed the pages, so he could tell Fetch how the story ended.

Fetch fell asleep that night with a smile on his face. When he woke up, his father was gone. He knew without asking — he couldn't ask — that Archer had died. He'd helped his son keep his cover by reading him a bedtime story and then he'd died. The fucking mess the two of them had made of being father and son their whole miserable lives, Archer had finally put it right at the end.

All Fetch could do was cry soundlessly once more. And resolve that wherever they buried his father, he would have him dug up and laid to rest next to his Dottie. Just as he'd asked Fetch to do.

Observation and treatment of Fetch's mental state would continue for another eighteen months. As ever, Fetch was a model guest of the state. Then the New York Department of Corrections decided it would require he spend no more time with them.

It was concluded that Fetch Mcdonald had indeed been insane, and therefore not responsible for his actions, when he'd escaped from Camp Alphonse. Having morphed from a con to a mental patient, he didn't even have to check in with a parole officer.

Fetch was a free man. He found the money he stole from the Emerald Club right where he'd left it.

Lerome and Ants found her son, Jimmy, near Glasgow, Montana. The boy had been living with his paternal grandparents in a cabin on a ranch owned by some people named Crumley. There hadn't been the least bit of trouble taking Jimmy from the old folks.

Mainly because they'd picked the kid up on the highway, his thumb out to hitch a ride. He was running away from home. When he found out Ants was his mother, he almost jumped out of the car. Grandma and Grandpa had told him many a horror story about his homicidal mom.

Only the kid had taken an instant liking to Lerome. Thought he was cool. If Lerome was going to be around, it might be safe to stay. He decided he'd definitely stay when Lerome told him to look what was in the suitcase there in the backseat with him.

Money. More than Jimmy had ever seen in his life. Three hours after they'd picked him up, he fell asleep using the suitcase as his pillow. Lerome and Ants were heading west, thought they might give California a try. People leaving Buffalo tended to go someplace warm.

"Give the kid a chance," Lerome told Ants as he steered the car south onto US 15. "He'll get to know you. Won't be long until he's crazy about you."

Ants replied, "Yeah, maybe ... after he sees you like me." She let a few miles roll by in silence, then asked, "Is this the way you'd write it?"

"What?" Lerome asked. "We find your kid running away and he likes me more than you?"

Ants nodded.

Lerome smiled. "I hope I can get that good someday."

"You will," she assured him, smiling now, too. "Thing is, you'll need a pen-name. What with your stolen typewriter and all."

"Yeah? Got any ideas?"

"Maybe make it a play on your real name. An inside joke."

"What do you mean?"

"Well, let's see. Lerome D'Arnole. What could you do with that?" Ants thought for another mile or two. "You drop the apostrophe, change the letters around, you could be ... Elmore Leonard."

Lerome said, "Cool."

One of the things Dan had to do to complete *Kidnapping Ben Hecht* was find out what took the cops so long to get to the Emerald Club. Reviewing the matter, he, Erin, and Gamble all agreed that the robbery had to have taken at least fifteen minutes. Certainly somebody who'd fled the club must have called 911 to report the crime. So where the hell had the cops been?

Finding the answer turned out to be ridiculously easy. The headline of the following day's *Buffalo News* explained the reason in a banner headline: *Sabres Win Stanley Cup, Riot Ensues.*

The hometown hockey team, after years of being a doormat, had won the NHL championship on the same night the Emerald Club was robbed. They'd beaten the hated Detroit Red Wings, long the league powerhouse, in the seventh game. In overtime. The local populace mocked Detroit with its own cephalopod tradition. They threw octopuses on the ice.

Several Detroit players took exception to this, cursing the fans and making rude gestures. Whereupon those ticket holders with octopi left to hurl fired them at the Detroit bench. Players climbed into the stands, the crowd rushed the players, the handful of Detroit partisans on hand leaped to the defense of their own kind and the melee was on.

There were no deaths but injuries numbered in the hundreds, and every on-duty patrol cop on the Buffalo PD was called to the scene.

Fortunate timing for the robbers at the Emerald Club.

Great bit for Dan to use in his true-crime book, too.

Time Expires brought a $2 million advance; *Kidnapping Ben Hecht* fetched $3 million.

The two books were released simultaneously. Dan and

Erin went to New York City for the publication party. Having delivered herself of little Mary Frances Cameron — named in honor of Dan's late mother, but always Petunia in her parents' hearts — Erin celebrated with champagne. After the festivities were over and the Camerons had retired to their hotel suite for the night, and spent thirty minutes just watching their little angel sleep, Erin informed Dan that she had a surprise for him. Two, actually.

They sat in the suite's salon, the lights of the city spread out before them.

"The Remington?" Erin asked softly.

Losing the typewriter was still a sensitive subject to Dan. He had an idea for a new novel but was dragging his feet about starting.

"Yeah?" he responded.

Erin took a deep breath. "I found out that Ben Hecht didn't use it to write *Notorious.*"

"What?" Dan asked, staring at his wife. "You're making that up. Trying to make me feel better."

Erin shook her head. "I did some research. Found the answer right in the good old *Chicago Tribune.* March 31, 2002 edition. We missed it because that was when we were living at Uncle Les's cabin, but you can check. The story's titled, "Sorting Out Ben Hecht." It says he used a typewriter when he was a reporter, but when he wrote screenplays ... he used pencils."

Dan slumped back against the sofa.

"Pencils?" he asked, incredulously.

"If it's in the *Trib* ..."

"It must be true," said the paper's former employee. "Story is, he wore down 75-100 pencils a week."

Dan smiled weakly, "So that typewriter wasn't magic after all."

Erin responded by handing Dan a small gift-wrapped box. He eyed it suspiciously.

"What is it?" he asked.

"Open it up."

Dan knew he had no choice but to comply. He saw an old-fashioned but very nice ball-point pen. He looked at Erin and asked, "Whose is it?"

"Yours."

"Yeah, now, but whose was it?"

"It belonged to James Jones."

Dan laughed. His wife was simply incorrigible.

"I suppose he wrote *From Here to Eternity* with it?"

"No," Erin answered. "Just the margin notes."

"Anybody going to want it back?"

Erin smiled. "Unh-uh. I had a private investigator check that out."

Dan took the pen out of the box. Clicked it. But no nib appeared.

"Well, no wonder nobody wants it back. It's broken."

"Not broken. Only needs a refill."

Erin produced an everyday refill for the pen. She took the pen from Dan, inserted the refill, and gave the pen back.

"You're the ink, sweetie. The words you write are all your own. Just like with the Remington."

Dan nodded. He stared into Erin's eyes. Just when he thought he loved her as much as he possibly could, she found a way to make him love her more.

"I'll use the pen the way Mr. Jones did. Make notes with it. But the new novel, that's me and you. We'll go the tried-and-true dictation route."

"Great," Erin said, "but when are we going to start?"

Dan looked at his watch.

"We've got an hour till Petunia's two o'clock feeding. How about now?"

About the Author

JOSEPH FLYNN is a Chicagoan, born and raised, currently living in central Illinois with his wife and daughter. Distance has allowed him to become a recovering Chicago sports nut. Other hometown affections persist. So if you find yourself at Pizzeria Uno, 29 E. Ohio Street, send pizza. Plain cheese. (Due's and Gino's East are good, too.) Mr. Flynn is the author of *The Concrete Inquisition, Digger, The Next President,* and *Hot Type*.